THE MAKING OF
MRS. HALE

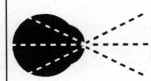

This Large Print Book carries the
Seal of Approval of N.A.V.H.

THE MAKING OF MRS. HALE

CAROLYN MILLER

THORNDIKE PRESS
A part of Gale, a Cengage Company

LIBRARY OF CONGRESS CIP DATA ON FILE.
CATALOGUING IN PUBLICATION FOR THIS BOOK
IS AVAILABLE FROM THE LIBRARY OF CONGRESS

ISBN-13: 978-1-4328-6957-1 (hardcover alk. paper)

Published in 2020 by arrangement with Kregel Publications, a division of Kregel, Inc.

Printed in Mexico
Print Number: 01   Print Year: 2020

For Michael & Maria
brother & sister-in-love

Loved by God

Winthrop Family Tree

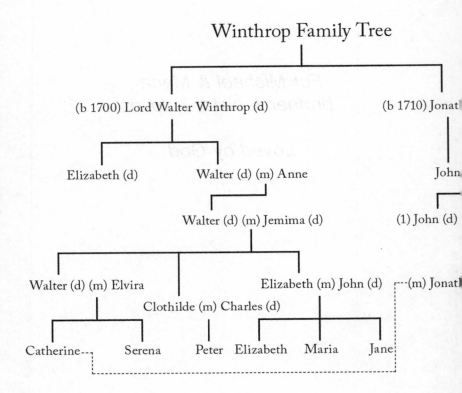

(b 1700) Lord Walter Winthrop (d)

(b 1710) Jonat[

Elizabeth (d)   Walter (d) (m) Anne

John

Walter (d) (m) Jemima (d)

(1) John (d)

Walter (d) (m) Elvira   Elizabeth (m) John (d) ┌---(m) Jonat[

Clothilde (m) Charles (d)

Catherine---┐   Serena   Peter   Elizabeth   Maria   Jane

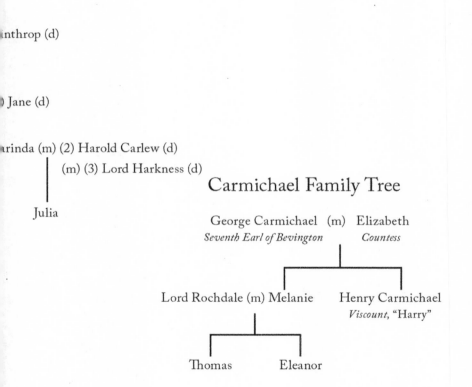

nthrop (d)

Jane (d)

rinda (m) (2) Harold Carlew (d)
       (m) (3) Lord Harkness (d)

Julia

Carmichael Family Tree

George Carmichael (m) Elizabeth
Seventh Earl of Bevington   *Countess*

Lord Rochdale (m) Melanie   Henry Carmichael
                            Viscount, "Harry"

Thomas   Eleanor

CHAPTER ONE

Cavendish Square, London
October 1818
Julia Hale lifted a weary hand and rapped on the yellow painted door. *Please let him be in. Please!* Whom she murmured to she did not know. The last person to pay her any heed had only wanted payment, and when she could not offer what he wanted, he'd sought payment of a vastly different kind. Which was why she now stood here. Hoping, begging, desperate for a miracle.

To no avail.

As the door remained closed, the now familiar ball of hopelessness swelled within, pushing against her chest, pushing against her thin veneer of self-control. She should have known it was too much to ask for help from a God she scarcely believed in, who would turn His back on her now even if her faith were as deep as Jon's. Stifling fears, she tugged at the blankets and peered at her tiny bundle. She *had* to do something. Perhaps God would respond to the innocent, even if He turned His back on the guilty. And this was her last hope; every other avenue had closed. All that remained were the paupers' homes, and she'd heard what those places were like. Nothing on this earth would induce her to leave a child in such a place.

Arms aching, feeling heavier than lead, she rapped again. *Please answer. Please!* She had seen the lights last night. Someone *was* home, even if it were just the servants kept to mind the house while the Earl of Bevington attended his estates in Derbyshire. Why wouldn't they answer?

Another fit of coughing wracked her body, sending fire through her lungs and up her throat. She placed a hand on the iron balustrade as lightheadedness swept through her again. But she'd had no opportunity to rest, and no money for medicine even if she could. When the spots cleared from her vision she peeked at the face asleep in the blankets. Thank God the babe had not caught her illness. Not yet.

She bent down to place the bundle back in the willow basket, tucked the blankets around to protect from the damp morning air. "I'm sorry," she whispered, her voice

10

scratchy and raw. "I cannot help you any-more."

Blissful ignorance was the only response, one she was growing more accustomed to as the days dragged on. How long had it been since she'd been deemed worthy of anything more than a scrap of attention? Three months? Six months? More?

She bent to press a kiss on the downy head before rapping a final time on the wooden doors. Still no answer.

With a final desperate glance at the basket, she stumbled down the marble steps, grasping the balustrade for balance. God forgive her, but she had no choice.

Guilt pressed heavily on her heart. She tugged the dark hood closer, hiding the dirty, stringy locks of fair hair of which she had once been so vain. Not that anyone would recognize her now. That girl had existed in another world, one that now often seemed more fairy story than real.

She stumbled over a broken cobblestone, refusing to look behind. That way lay regret. But she *had* tried, had hoped to somehow see this wasted life redeemed, at least in part, through her actions today. Though what lay ahead of her now she could scarcely imagine. Was she now considered a fallen woman? Or had she been regarded as such

11

since her flight from Bath all those months ago? A blur of tears filled her vision. Foolish, *foolish* girl . . .

A street sweeper glanced at her, his lip curled in derision. She did not blame him. She looked exactly what she was: pitiful.

Somehow, she stumbled on. God help her — what *would* she do now? Where could she go? Who could save —

"Miss? Can I help you?"

A well-bred voice, a youthful voice. Julia peered over her shoulder, blinked. Shook her head as if she could clear the blurriness. The lady — if lady she was, dressed in a most odd ensemble — seemed to own a poise Julia had never known, yet appeared younger even than Julia.

"You came to Lord Carmichael's house?"

The lady knew Lord Carmichael? Was she a maid? Julia swallowed. "Yes."

"I am the viscountess."

Julia blinked again. No.

"Please, is there some way we can help you?"

She moistened her lips before managing to rasp, "He's married?"

"Yes." The lady smiled, glowing with internal satisfaction, tinged with something almost like surprise, as if she couldn't believe her good fortune.

12

Envy tugged within. Oh, how well Julia remembered those days.

"We've been away," Lady Carmichael continued, "and only returned two days ago."

Julia nodded, surprise filling her as the viscountess drew closer and offered a hand, helping her to her feet. What an unusual bride Henry had chosen.

Conscious she was being watched carefully, she stuttered, "I-I s-saw the lights last night and knew someone must be in. Nobody is in Berkeley Square, or Portman. I don't know . . . Mama . . . Jon."

Where *were* they? Mama almost never left town, and Jon's business interests made his staying in London something of a necessity. Surely he hadn't been serious about retiring to that dreary corner of Gloucestershire?

Her arm was gently clasped, and she was led back to Bevington House, away from the prying eyes of the street sweeper. Now she noticed her benefactress had bare feet, undressed hair. What an odd woman! Was she serious about being Henry's bride? Oh, if only she could remember —

"You left your basket — oh, it's empty."

Julia gasped. "No! Oh, no!" What could she do? She had failed! Who could have taken — ? Guilt misted her senses, and she stepped back, desperately searching for the culprit. But she had passed no one! Oh, where could he be?

"There you are!"

She swiveled back to the now opened door, stifled another gasp. Lord Henry Carmichael, dressed in a quilted dressing gown, held a white bundle and a bemused expression. His white teeth flashed as he smiled at the lady dressed equally *dishabille*. "Serena, can you tell me why we have a baby on our front step?"

"A baby?"

Serena? A memory flashed. A black-clad, cool-eyed schoolgirl. Henry — her Henry — had married *her*? The lady drew closer, her expression now even more alive with interest, alert with piercing intent.

She swallowed, heart thudding, as the viscountess's breath caught, her expression clearing into comprehension.

"Julia?"

Spain

Major Thomas Hale shifted, the perpetual ache from the hatch of welts on his back easing a mite as the pressure released. He drew in a breath and opened his eyes. The nightmare remained.

A dark, dank cell with barred window. A

14

sloshing sound. A screech of laughter. Babble in a foreign tongue. He glanced at the other occupants. Grimy and unkempt as he, no doubt wishing they had never agreed to be ensnared by fortune's fickle fancy, and thus be caught in this dire situation for — how many months now? He peered at the wall, counted the strokes denoting the days as if he didn't already know, as if — by some miracle — he might have miscalculated, and this episode not be near as severe as he knew it to be. Five months. Five months!

Pain rippled through his chest. He'd been absent for almost half a year. A mission that should have taken a quarter of that time had been thwarted by lies and loose lips. A rumble of indignation churned within. How could the Crown abandon them, leaving them to rot? He peered across at young Desmond, whose right foot held all the signs of gangrene, the black decay creeping a little farther each day up his leg. How much longer did the lad have? Weeks? Days?

A creeping sound, like the slither of rats, slid through the room. He swallowed the bile. Muttered a curse. Wished for a boot to throw at the perpetrator. Settled for a barked utterance, not dissimilar to that which he used to bark at men a lifetime ago

15

when his majority meant something.

The creature scuttled away. The room lapsed into silence. Desmond's half-crazed moanings had ceased. Benson wouldn't speak. Smith and Harrow, the two men with whom he'd communicated the most, had retreated into despondency. Fairley had been taken away two days ago. Thomas shivered. He dared not think on his fate.

How could a simple desire for gold have led them to utter misery? It was not as though they had engaged in anything illegal. The Crown itself had endorsed such activity. And it wasn't as if he'd been motivated by greed. He swallowed regrets, focused on the truth that he'd *had* to do something; his prize money was near all spent trying to establish themselves respectably enough so she did not feel a whit of deprivation. His fingers clenched. If only he'd planned things better, if he had not listened, had not succumbed —

"*Señor.*"

Thomas blinked, refocusing, his gaze cutting through the dimness to the creature at the door.

She smiled. "I *weesh* you would not reject me." She tipped forward, her soiled garments doing little to constrain her buxom figure. "Just a *leetle* talk, eh?"

16

He swallowed. Magdalena might be just another ploy used by the guard to get them to admit to their supposed crimes, but she was certainly the least unattractive one.

"You were not so cold last time, *señor*," she continued provocatively, in that lilting, wheedling voice.

Guilt speared him. He closed his eyes. *Forgive me,* he cried within, turning away from temptation. God forgive him, but he'd stupidly thought he could learn something, possibly even learn a means of escape.

He'd learned something, all right. Learned that even the comeliest wench in Spain could be responsible for guilt every bit as lethal as that inflicted by thoughts of his wife.

His wife. *Oh God,* his wife. As the instrument of torture sauntered away with a lewd comment and a ribald laugh, his thoughts clattered. What was she doing now? How could she have borne so much time apart? Had she given up on him? Probably. Wretchedness echoed within. Still, she at least had options. She could always return to her family, even if he would stake his life that they'd take care never to receive him, should he ever return to the land of the living. He hoped, regardless of what happened, that his Jewel would not forsake him completely.

"H-Hale?"

A whimpering sound drew his attention to the prone figure nearby. "Desmond?"

The boy gasped, before emitting a series of piercing shrieks. "Get it off! Get it off! It's eating me!"

Thomas stumbled from the pallet, hurrying to the boy's side. A large rodent was indeed nibbling at the boy's foot. He grasped the furry pelt and slammed it at the wall where it spattered with a sickening, satisfying thud.

The boy's eyes turned to him, his teeth chattering. "I c-cannot do this anymore. Please, *please* make this stop."

His heart wrenched at the hopelessness he saw in the boy's eyes, hopelessness reflected in his heart. "I wish I could. But we have told them all we know."

A tremor ran up the boy's frame. "They will never believe us." He groaned, the low sound soon changing to an ear-splitting shriek.

"Desmond, calm yourself." If the lad weren't injured he'd slap him.

"I want to die! I want to die! I want to —"

"You there!" A heavily accented voice growled from the door. "Shut up!"

18

"I want to die! I want to die! I want to die!"

Thomas shook him fiercely. "Desmond, you must be quiet, else they will —"

A heavy boot knocked his feet from under him, and he crashed to the floor, his jaw cracking on the refuse-smeared stones. He tried to push to his feet, but a musket butt smashed against his temple, felling him once more.

Panic reared within as the guards dragged Desmond to the door. "Leave him! He's just a boy! He knows nothing —"

The business end of the musket poked at his face. *"Cállate!"*

He pushed to his knees, begging them in English, in Spanish, in French, but Desmond — his high-pitched cries continuing — was dragged from view.

Head throbbing, Thomas staggered to his feet, the taste of blood trickling into his mouth. He stood at the bars and shouted for mercy, but he could barely hear his own voice over Desmond's shrieks.

There was a shot.

Desmond's cries ceased.

And the now familiar soul-numbing despair crashed over him as he sank to his knees.

CHAPTER TWO

Julia shifted restlessly in the darkness, her movements jerky, her breath tight in her chest. The man leered at her, his lips drawing back in a grin that arrowed fear deep within. Why had she thought this a good idea? She lowered her gaze and moved past him, hurrying to the stairs where the woman had said her room was. Step after creaking step. The corridor was dim, the flickering light from the candle she held revealing a ceiling draped with cobwebs, like something she imagined from *The Castle of Otranto.* Her heart hammered, and she clutched her precious bundle closer to her chest. A whimper rose from within, and she forced herself to shush aloud, the sound an explosion in the unnatural quiet. She counted the doors: one, two, three, until she reached hers. Carefully shifting her bundle between her chin and shoulder, she moved the candle to her left hand, then grasped the door handle and moved inside the room.

"Wotcha want 'ere?" A voice growled. A figure sat up in the bed.

She had the wrong room!

Muttering an apology, she hastened outside, turning swiftly into the *real* fourth room on the right, and quietly closed the door. How she hoped the man didn't think her a woman of easy virtue and follow her here! How she wished she could lock the door for protection.

She carefully laid her burden on the sagging bed before shifting a spindly chair, the only other piece of furniture in the room, to the door. Her small trunk containing her meager possessions had been placed just within the door; she moved this atop the seat. At least she would hear any intruder, even if the flimsy chair would not hold them at bay for very long.

Weariness escaped in a silent sigh as she eased down next to the tiny child, her shoulders slumped in defeat. How her body craved rest. She could sleep for a week. But responsibility still nagged. She quickly undressed him. Sure enough he had soiled himself, and would doubtless soon awaken if he were not cleaned and dressed appropriately. And she could not permit the rash on his little body to worsen. She pushed to her feet and examined the pitcher of water dubiously. It might not be fresh but it would have to do. Another trudge to the trunk and she pulled out the last of the linens, eyes filling as she wished for the hundredth time to have brought more. The exchange of soiled linen for clean woke the babe, startling him into weak cries. Poor baby. She nestled him to her chest, the hungry mewling tugging at her.

"I'm sorry I cannot help you," she whispered. Giving him what he craved was impossible.

When her arms felt like they must surely snap, the babe's cries faded to exhausted whimpers, then silence, and she carefully wrapped him once more and placed him in the bed.

How she wished to sleep, too, but that rash would never heal if she did not wash the linen. She eyed the worn rag beside the enamel bowl, evidently left there for cleaning purposes, and quickly washed her face, feeling momentarily fresher as the past two days' grime lifted from her skin. No wonder the people downstairs had looked at her askance.

After cleaning the soiled linen as best she could, she draped it in front of the fire, stirring the coals into something that might actually dry the cloth and take away the room's chill, a chill that puffed her breath into tiny white clouds. From downstairs came a shout followed by raucous laughter. An eerie whistle blew around the window frames, like the sound of moaning spirits. Would she be safe? Shaking her head at her ridiculous thoughts, she pulled back the covers carefully, laid the child down, and slid between the too-thin sheets. She pulled the covers up to her chin, careful not to cover the baby, then blew out the candle and closed her eyes.

Darkness drew heavy around her, within her, pressing against her, tugging her to sleep —

A sound came, like the scurry of tiny feet. She shuddered. *Please God, let there be no mice tonight.* There was a trip, the tread of heavy feet in the corridor. Her heart thundered. She could hear a drunken murmuring, something she had heard many times before, something she knew would lead to bad things, things no gently bred young lady should ever have to know about. She closed her eyes again and prayed the drunk would stay away. *God, protect me . . .*

A faint noise intruded. A swish of curtains being dragged apart. Light seeping in. Someone scuttling about —

"Who's there?" Julia sat up in a hurry, blinking as the light startled her to alertness. "Oh!"

A maid dressed in dark blue with a white apron and mobcap curtsied. "Begging your pardon, miss. Lady Carmichael sent me to see how you be."

Lady Carmichael? Julia put a hand to her head. Who — ? Where — ? Had that been a dream, or was she living in one now?

"They have been quite worried about you, sleeping as long as you have and all."

"How long . . . ?" she rasped.

The maid handed her a glass of water. "Nigh on two days, miss."

"Two days?"

The maid nodded. "Her ladyship was getting quite worried."

Julia swallowed the water, reveling in the sweet freshness slipping down her throat. Oh, she could drink gallons, her sudden thirst unable to be quenched.

The maid placed the empty glass on the small table beside the bed then gestured to the door. "Shall I arrange for some food to be sent up?"

"I'm not —" Her stomach grumbled, making a liar of her. "Yes, please."

"Very good, miss." The maid curtsied and disappeared, gone before Julia could correct the misnomer.

Julia pushed herself higher in the bed, glancing around the room. The bedchamber was painted a soft green, trimmed with cream. Silk curtains gracefully framed a window she judged overlooked the mews, their fabric an exact match for that trimming the bed's canopy and covers. She fingered the lace detailing the pillowcase. No small amount of money had been spent on making this room as beautiful and comfortable as possible. She peeked under the covers. Gone was the tattered rag of a gown she had spent too many days and nights in. Vague memories swam of a hot bath, a meal. But why could she not remember this Lady Carmichael person? A memory tugged, but was smothered under a foggy wave of tiredness as she yawned again.

The door opened mid-yawn, admitting the maid followed by —

"It's you!"

"Dear Julia. Finally, you rejoin the land of the living." The elegantly dressed blonde woman smiled. "I had wondered if you remembered meeting me. We only met a couple of times, as I recall."

"I — of . . . of course," Julia stammered. Though the cool-eyed young lady of her vague memories bore little resemblance to the elegant society matron standing before her now.

"It was over eighteen months ago, so I would not blame you if you had forgotten. And of course, I was just a schoolgirl then, and being married to Lord Carmichael was really the furthest thing from my mind." She sank to the velvet-covered chair. "I am pleased to see you awake. We were beginning to worry about you, seeing as you slept so long."

The door opened again, admitting another maid carrying a tray of food that was soon carefully deposited before Julia on the bed. Toasted bread, strawberry jam, butter, eggs, and most pleasing to see, a steaming pot of tea. The maid poured the tea before withdrawing to the corner. Julia eyed the food, her mouth salivating. Her stomach growled insistently. But manners recalled from long ago refused her to eat.

Lady Carmichael gestured to the plate. "Please do not refrain on my account. You need all the nourishment you can get, it would seem."

Julia glanced at her, then, upon receiving a nod of reassurance, began eating. After a few minutes, her insides spasmed, and she fought to hide a wince. It had been so long since she had eaten heartily, no wonder her body protested.

"Now, Anna is here to help you choose something to wear." Lady Carmichael gestured to the maid, who offered another curtsy. "I'm afraid we had to burn the gown you wore on arrival, and we were not precisely sure of your measurements. But never fear, we shall have a *modiste* arrive and you shall be dressed appropriately soon enough. In the meantime, I have some of my own gowns available for your use, though I rather fear they shall swim on you a little."

Julia forced herself to swallow another bite of eggs. "Thank you, Lady Carmichael."

"Oh, it is no trouble. And, please, call me Serena, just as I hope you don't mind if I call you Julia. We are related by marriage, after all." Because Serena's sister had married Julia's half brother, Jon. At her nod, her hostess continued. "I cannot tell you how relieved we are to see you awake. I suppose I should not be so surprised, as the doctor said it was probably just exhaustion."

A doctor had seen her? Julia shivered. What else had happened while she had been unconscious, reliving the nightmares of her journey? She dropped her gaze, focused her attention on carefully slicing the toasted bread into triangles.

"No doubt you will be relieved to know the doctor has pronounced your baby healthy."

A corner of toast caught in her throat. "He's not —"

"Such a handsome young man," murmured Anna, coming forward to pour Julia another glass of water, which she accepted with murmured thanks.

"Yes, he is, and quite well-behaved. It appears he didn't seem to miss his mother *too* much," Serena said, her smile almost wistful before dimming a little. "He is a charming boy. It seems he's managed to keep the staff quite entertained these past days."

"Such a pet, with that lovely red hair," the maid offered.

"Yes." Her hostess gave Julia a long appraisal. "I'm sure that must have proved something of a surprise."

Two pairs of eyes gazed at her expectantly. What could she say but the truth? Or at least a version of veracity. "It was a surprise," she finally admitted.

Serena nodded, before rising. "Well, I shall leave you to the rest of your meal. Please don't hesitate to ask Anna for anything." Her smile warmed again. "We are so *very* pleased to see you."

"H-have you spoken to Jonathan yet?"

She shook her head. "I'm afraid he and Catherine are in Paris at the moment."

So that was why the London town house was vacant.

"You did know they had married?"

"Yes." The newspapers had reported her brother's marriage even hundreds of miles away.

"Henry has sent a letter, though. He expects it to reach them in the next week or so."

Julia nodded. "And Mama?"

"Lady Harkness accompanied them. Apparently she needed to see the fashions again, although we suspect it was more to keep an eye on little Elizabeth." Something akin to envy flashed across her features before her expression cooled. "Her grandchild."

She blinked. "Jon is a father?"

"And Catherine is a mother." Again, that flash in the blue eyes. "Now, I must leave you. Please excuse me." Serena offered a smile that looked somewhat forced before exiting the room.

Leaving Julia reeling. She was an aunt? What else had happened in the time she'd been away?

"Now, miss." Anna held out two gowns, one pale pink, one light blue. "Which would you prefer?"

"I . . ." It had been so long since she'd seen such pretty gowns, since she had even had a choice, her mind felt numbed by indecision. "I cannot choose. Which would you recommend?"

"Well, the pink is a very pretty color, and is nice and warm — it's quite cool outside, you see. And the blue would help bring out your eyes, so . . . shall we say the blue?"

Julia nodded.

"I think you will look very fine, miss. Besides, I cannot imagine you would wish to go outside today, seeing as it's so cold and windy out, and — if I might say — you still have something of a nasty cough."

Julia glanced out the window, the view eliciting another shiver, as if she still braved the cold and windy elements herself. Thank goodness someone had been here at the town house. She did not know how she would have survived the elements had they been away, too. And as for poor, sweet Charles . . .

Her heart wrenched. "Where is Charlie?"

The maid's eyes lit. "Oh, is that the name of your son? Never mind, miss, the house-keeper is taking good care of him."

"I . . . I would like to see him, if I may."

She cringed. What was she doing, request-

30

ing permission from a servant? Exactly how far had she fallen from the girl she once had been?

The maid smiled. "Well, of course you can, miss. Just as soon as you're dressed. Now, are you quite finished with your meal?"

Julia pushed away the remnants of her breakfast, slightly horrified to discover that she seemed to have dragged her bread crusts through the trail of egg yolk on the plate. Had she been *that* hungry?

The maid picked up the tray, bobbed a careful curtsy and exited, leaving Julia with a moment's peace. She sank into the feather-stuffed pillows, stretching in another unladylike action as she luxuriated in her surrounds, and the thought of being cared for. How long had it been since she had been pampered in this way, since she'd been the object of someone's attention? How long since she hadn't had to fight and claw and do whatever was necessary to protect herself? She could not remember.

The door opened and the maid returned. The next half hour passed in a delightful dream as she was once again provided with hot — hot! — water for bathing, and the daintiest of undergarments — "Lady Carmichael apologizes if the sizing isn't quite

31

right" — and the delightful gown offered before.

"Now, miss, let's get you dressed. Yes, slip your arms in here, and like so. Oh, that's such a pretty color for you. Now, I shall do the buttons for you if you like. And shall I do your hair? Yes? Wonderful. Now just sit here, and let me take care of you."

But even as these moments reminded her of who she once had been, the sense of things being right did not truly resound until little Charles was back in her arms. He blinked sleepy eyes then appeared to look at her with a wondering expression, as if unsure who the pretty lady in the pretty dress was.

"Hello, my little man. Yes, it is me under all this finery." She rubbed a hand over his copper curls. "Don't we make a pretty picture, you and I?"

She snuggled him close to her breast, cradling his soft curls with her hand. Sorrow twisted within. Poor wee mite. Had anyone ever mourned at that mound of earth in the Scottish churchyard? She blinked away the burn at the back of her eyes.

Anna finished her duties and moved to the door. "His lordship and her ladyship await you in the drawing room."

Julia nodded, even as she felt the ease dissipate, the words pricking at the bubble of security. It would not do to imagine all would be well, that she could simply slip into her former life, that there would be no further judgment or consequences for her sins. Sure, and she held a consequence in her arms even now! How would they cope if she told the whole truth? At least it was only Henry and his wife, two people who would be far less likely to winkle the truth in its entirety from her than Jon or her mother may. *Their* disappointment she would prefer to put off for as long as possible.

Julia pulled Charles close and whispered, "We will have to make the best of things and pretend."

He gave a gurgle which she took as affirmation. Holding the boy as her shield, she rose to follow the maid who waited in the hallway, while her thoughts flew frantically, alternately collecting then rejecting partial, hurtful truths as she wondered what would be most believed, and what would evoke their sympathy — and not their rage.

CHAPTER THREE

A creak came from the doorway. Thomas cracked open an eye, the despair so heavy on his chest tightening as he heard a footfall, the faintest jingling of keys.

"*Señor?*" The whispered guttural sound made it hard to distinguish whose voice it was. Their jailer's? The jailer's daughter? Another soldier?

He stayed motionless, his eyes searching the blackness. Perhaps if he said nothing they might assume he was asleep. He could not imagine they could see in the dark any better than he, not if they were forced to eat the same slops that Thomas and his cellmates had been surviving on for months.

He glanced to where he approximated the window must be. No trace of dawn lit the sky behind the bars. What did the person at the door want? Wisdom suggested he do nothing, say nothing. Chances were it was another trap.

"Señor?"

The daughter. Her lilt at the end sounded almost desperate. Well, he would most definitely maintain the pretense of sleep; he'd been stung by her before.

The sound of her breathing filled the room, then he heard a shuffle, a cooling whisk in the air, as if she'd gone. He lay where he was a moment longer, in case she decided to return. When no further sound came, he got up, checked the cell, then moved closer to the door. It was ajar.

His pulse tripped. This had to be a trap. Had to be. Surely she wouldn't leave it open for him? But if he left, and by some miracle it was the route to freedom, then how could he leave his fellow Englishmen behind?

He glanced back at the dozing figures, even now tossing unquietly in their sleep. Would Smith have strength enough to attempt escape? Perhaps it was best to see how far he could go, then return if it truly was a miracle provided by an unclean Spanish angel, and not the trap arranged by a fiend from hell.

Thomas eased open the door, and peered through the murk. Nobody. Nothing. Nothing discernible anyway. But did it matter? Well he understood Desmond's despair. His own misery writhed within, a living mess, like maggots infested his soul. Something *had* to change. His men were going mad. He must attempt escape again, for their sakes as well as his, or die trying.

With one hand stretched before him and the other to the rock-hewn walls, he followed the passage, carefully placing each foot, working to avoid the slightest noise that might alert his captors. After what felt an age, he reached an iron-barred door. A dragging of fingers over cold metal bars and he discovered the lock. With no key.

"*Señor.*"

He startled.

"I hoped you come."

The faintest light skimmed her features, the bold dark eyes, the brazen mouth, the curves so sensuous, at once appealing and repellent. Remembrance tugged of another woman, her features fair and pure. He shook his head, clearing the memories, focusing on the woman before him, not the one who would doubtless hold him in disfavor, if she cared to remember him at all. "What are you doing?"

Her teeth glinted in the darkness, then with a twist of her hand, she unlocked the door. Dragged it open. "You want to escape?"

"I don't understand," he whispered. "Why

are you doing this?"

She shrugged in that way peculiar to those of Spain. "I feels sorry for you."

He snorted. "You could have felt sorry for me months ago."

"Months ago, they not going to kill you next day."

His heartbeat intensified. "They're going to kill me?"

"Kill all of you," she said, with another dismissive gesture. "Not that I care too much about the rest of your silly countrymen, but you" — she traced a finger down his shirt — "you, I do care for."

Thomas swallowed the revulsion. "Why kill us now?"

"I hear you cost too much food."

He almost laughed. Their rations were meager to say the least, a mere fraction of what he'd had to exist on in his most trying days in wartime India. "I need to get the others."

Her fingers pinched his shirt. "Let them die. You must live." She placed a hand on her stomach. "For you know why?"

Dear God, no. He pushed her against the wall. "Tell me you are not pregnant," he whispered close to her ear.

"You wish for me to lie?"

Bitterness filled his mouth. He would

never forgive himself. If, by some miracle, he did return to Julia, he could never look her in the eyes again. And if she ever found out . . . he might as well be dead. "How can I know it's mine?"

She made a pretense of looking hurt, but he'd seen the way she acted, looking for whatever attention she could get, wherever she could get it. "You cannot know it isn't."

He groaned, the sound louder than he wanted. "I wish I had never met you."

"But you did, and you made the most of it." Her smile grew seductive. "We had a good time, did we not, *señor*?"

He shook his head. "I need to get the others."

She pouted. "But I do not want them to leave. I only help you."

"It's all of us, or none."

"But you are my child's papa! They are nothing to me."

He ignored her, moving rapidly along the corridor back to the cell. If he did die, maybe that would solve all his mistakes. Remorse panged. If only it would not leave poor Julia forever wondering what had happened to him. Surely she must have given up on him by now.

He bent to shake his cell mates awake. "Get up," he whispered. He shook Benson harder. "They're going to kill us."

"Leave me alone," the man mumbled, rolling onto his other side. "I want to die."

"No, you don't." Thomas gritted his teeth as Benson ignored him, and then turned his attention to his other comrades. "Get up," he whispered urgently to the young red-headed lieutenant. "We can escape."

Harrow opened his eyes. "Is this a dream?"

"It's no dream," Thomas assured him. "We can leave right now."

"You've said that before."

So he had. There'd been lashes and reduced rations for weeks following the previous escape attempt. "We must escape, else we shall surely perish."

Mumbling a protest, Harrow stumbled to the door. Thomas clutched Benson by his arm, pulling, dragging him out into the passageway before returning for Smith, whom he hauled back to the exit. He had to hurry. Any second now the guards would be up. When he returned, there was no sign of Magdalena. And the door was closed, locked.

"What are you doing?"

"Have you brought us here to die?"

Heart sinking, Thomas shook the iron bars but they refused to give. Then he noticed the key, inserted in the outside of the lock as if an angel had placed it there. Letting Smith slide ignominiously to the floor, he reached his arm through the iron bars and managed to grasp it, for once thankful for their pitiful rations that made his arm half the diameter he once could boast.

He heard the key catch as it twisted, then move no farther. "No."

Daylight seeped beyond. Somewhere outside a rooster crowed, as if warning their captors. Their need to escape magnified. He jerked the key, working to unlock the door. "Just open!" A curse fell from his mouth, followed by a prayer borne of desperation. "Dear God, have mercy!"

Behind them, he could hear the sounds of waking, the tromp of feet upstairs. He wriggled at the lock again. This time there was a plink as the catches loosed their grip and the door opened with a hissing screech. "Come on!"

The passageway continued a short distance before another — thankfully unlocked — door led to early dawn and outside. The dusty courtyard was dim, barren save for a few scratching chickens and the crowing rooster. Half dragging Smith, they made their way to a low stone wall beside a scraggly pine. It provided limited protection from observation, but gave them precious seconds to regroup, for Thomas to reiterate the plan he'd imagined a hundred times but never dared dream might actually come to pass.

A shout came from inside. Benson swore. "The guards!"

Smith sagged, his bristled face paling.

"We must get to the harbor," Thomas urged. "Come on."

Pulling Smith's arms over their shoulders, he and Harrow half carried, half tugged Smith past a series of stone buildings, down towards where the tang of sea carried on the chilly breeze. Thank God his memory had not failed him, that the months of incarceration had not made him forget his bearings completely. Thank God the early hour meant few were stirring. He did not think the town's inhabitants would prove sympathetic to English runaways.

"Señor!"

His gaze jerked to the left. The jailer's daughter, Magdalena, gestured inside a barnlike building.

From behind, Benson uttered a mild oath. "Is that — ?"

"Yes." Thomas turned to follow her, but Benson grabbed his free arm, and he lost his hold on Smith, who slipped from Harrow's grasp and collapsed on the ground

41

with a thud.

"I don't trust her," Benson muttered.

The sound of shouts and running feet spurred Thomas to action. He plucked Smith from the ground and pushed past Benson to the door. "I don't think we have a choice."

Apparently the others agreed, as they followed him inside the dim room.

"*Señor!* I thought you would never come!" She eyed the others and made a dismissive sound, before pointing to Smith. "That one too sick. He never make it."

"We should leave him," Benson agreed.

"No," Thomas said. "He's coming with us."

Benson eyed him askance. "It's a trap. It has to be."

"If it's a trap, I don't care," said Harrow. "I'd rather die fighting to escape than give up in there." He jerked a thumb back in the direction of the prison.

"But why is she helping us?" Benson's eyes narrowed. "I don't understand."

Magdalena placed a hand on her belly. "It's the babe —"

"We don't have time for questions," Thomas interrupted. Heaven prevent them from knowing. Although he suspected his nocturnal visit had not gone unnoticed. *God forgive me!* Guilt twisted his insides. "Benson, you're welcome to make your own way to England or we can trust Magdalena here. Seeing as she unlocked the cell door, I'd rather take my chances with her."

Harrow eyed Thomas but said nothing, only gave a nod. Smith could say nothing; he seemed barely conscious. Thomas turned from the hesitation filling Benson's pock-marked face toward the jailer's daughter. Her eyes were big with fear.

"The soldiers will be looking for you. Here." She thrust a hessian sack at Thomas. He pulled out a collection of old clothes. They were enough to replace the tattered garments of one man.

"What good is this?" Benson swore. "So, you'll be all right, but the rest of us —"

He ceased talking as the tramp of feet came nearer. Magdalena hurried to relock the door as they scrambled behind large crates. The door rattled, Thomas's heart pounded, even as he flung clothes at Benson, Harrow, and Smith: a rough cotton shirt, a pair of nankeen trousers, a dark blue coat. Each could wear but one piece. Would it be enough to allay suspicion? For himself he removed the bloodstained tatters of his shirt for the remaining piece — a tunic miles too big for him, but at least it did not shout the owner was an escapee from prison.

Magdalena drew near, and in a broken whisper murmured of a beach, a fishing boat, a town closer to the port of Aviles. "Now go."

"Gracias."

Tears filled her eyes, and she leaned in as if to kiss him. He turned at the last moment, seeing Benson's look of disgust, the disapprobation of Harrow, as her lips met his bearded cheek.

He could not argue with them. His actions were as shameful as they plainly believed. Only now it seemed his actions were the ones responsible for their being free. Or almost free, at least.

Actions that meant perhaps, one day, should the gods smile upon them, he might be free to see his beloved Julia again. If she ever deigned to see him.

CHAPTER FOUR

"And that is what happened."

Two pairs of eyes stared at her, one pair hazel-green, one blue, Lord Carmichael's now shaded — predictably — by anger. "You mean to say he abandoned you?"

Her eyes filled, as they did every time she thought on him. Which was why she tried not to think on him any more than was absolutely necessary. She glanced down, working to check her emotions as the couple continued to converse in hushed tones.

"Henry, please. You are distressing her."

"Serena, we need to know the truth," he murmured. "How else can we help if we don't know all the essentials?"

Julia swallowed, lifting her head to encounter their concern. She pushed her lips up. "I appreciate your consideration, but really, there is nothing more to say. All I know is that one day he left in the morning and didn't return. I do not know why. If I

45

did perhaps I wouldn't be here. But there seems to be only two possibilities." And either one was anathema to her.

Serena's eyes shifted to the infant in Julia's arms. "And he left you with a little baby."

God forgive her. "It is true that I would not have Charles were it not for my husband," she said in a low voice, not meeting their eyes. For if she had not gone north she would not have met —

"I imagine he gets his wonderful hair from your mother," Serena said, interrupting Julia's inner self-justification. She gave an unsettling, piercing look at the babe, before her face resumed its usual coolness.

Henry turned to his wife with a small smile. "I don't believe that can be quite right, my love. I'm sure young Charles did not inherit his hair color from Lady Harkness. I imagine she was far away when *that* particular event occurred."

Julia's lips twitched despite herself. Her brother's best friend's sense of the absurd had always managed to soothe her own inclination to worry. A glance at Serena suggested she found it likewise, the aloof features warming with a flash of amusement, before tranquility returned.

"Please forgive my husband, Julia. His

propensity for levity can outweigh his sense of what is appropriate."

Julia managed an uneven smile. "I can scarcely be considered a judge of propriety."

"None of us follow society's expectations all the time, that is true." Serena exchanged another private look with her husband.

Uncertainty twisted within. Did Serena mean that in opening their house to Julia that they had flouted social conventions? Did she regret it? "I hope you know how very sorry I am for imposing upon you. I truly do not wish to be a burden —"

"Nonsense."

"Henry is right," Serena said. "You cannot know how relieved we all are to see you."

"We are so glad to have you here, safe at last." Henry's look of good humor faded as his eyes sparked. "I cannot think of that blackguard —"

"Henry," his wife said reprovingly, taking his hand once more.

"My love." He lifted her hand to his lips, exchanging a look with her that made Julia glance elsewhere, her heart writhing in remembrance of when Thomas had done so with her. Back when she thought he loved her. Back before she realized he never had . . .

A cleared throat drew her attention back

47

to Lord Carmichael. "Forgive me, Julia. It seems I must submit to my wife's superior judgment on such matters."

"But of course." Julia glanced at Serena, heartened by the return of the smile now tweaking her lips. Whatever it was that had bothered her seemed to have gone. "A husband should always bow to a wife of superior understanding, should he not?"

"A wise man would," she murmured.

Henry grinned at Julia. "My wife is most fortunate to have married a man of great discernment."

"And such a modest man, too," Serena said, to his crack of laughter.

Had she simply imagined that earlier moment of strain? It would not be the first time she had misread a relationship. Julia bit her lip, remembering occasions when she had tried to hide marital disharmony behind a façade of good cheer. Why had she never recognized the cracks between them before they splintered into fissures so wide her husband thought his only option was to leave?

"Please know you are welcome for your own sake as well as Jon's," Serena continued, her look giving a greater measure of reassurance that Julia's presence was not wholly unwanted.

"That's right," Henry said with a nod. "I cannot imagine the old man ever forgiving me should we not insist on you staying until their return."

A small smile crept onto her face as she remembered times of banter between her brother and his friend, younger by one day. "I would not wish to be the cause of any dissension."

"I'm glad you can appreciate my predicament. You must know, Julia, that I live in daily fear of incurring your brother's wrath, so I beg you will not think it necessary to depart until his return."

Her smile grew tremulous, as she recognized the kindness behind his teasing banter.

"You have been greatly missed," Serena said softly.

The words forced her head down again. That her brother and mother would be glad to see her again she did not question. But whether that translated to forgiveness . . .

"They will be extremely happy to see you," Serena said, thus forging a fresh ball of emotion in her chest.

"I hope so," Julia managed to whisper. "I fear I have disappointed them so much."

"They will be very relieved," Henry agreed. "So please, do not worry."

She chewed the inside of her bottom lip. Telling someone to not worry was as futile as telling a baby to not cry. Over the past year, worry had become her normal companion; she did not know how to live with peace. Even now, surrounded by luxury, surrounded by assurance and kindness, tension snarled her chest. For so long she had needed to survive by relying on her own wits, her own efforts, that to be blithely told not to worry felt irresponsible, almost like being told to give up. She could not do it. She *would* not do it, not until everything was settled, finally. And how could that ever happen while her husband remained missing?

The Bay of Biscay
Four days later
The ship tipped and swayed, the roar of water, of tossing seas, filling his ears. A barrel dislodged, slamming into his shoulder with such force he had to bite back a curse. Thomas had never imagined his death at sea, had not realized just how rough the passage could be. Neither had he realized just how long the trip could take. Or just how sick Harrow and Smith would be.

Another lurching wave sent his stomach spiraling to the floor. One good thing about their escape: the lack of food meant there was less risk of casting up their accounts and soiling their flimsy disguises. Although how much longer they could go without food . . .

Rubbing at his throbbing shoulder, he forced himself to refocus on the grumbling men beside him, their position in the ship's hold deep enough to escape detection. So far.

As if noticing Thomas's renewed attention, Benson fixed him with a piercing eye. "I still don't understand why we must do this."

Thomas said nothing; he'd explained enough times as it was.

"You said we were going to England!"

"And now we must go by way of France." Benson's near nonstop complaining grated away at whatever patience he could lay claim to. Some days he wished the man had chosen to fix his own course home. "Beggars cannot be choosers, especially when they are stowing away."

"But, but —"

"Oh, stubble it, Benson," Harrow snapped. "D'you want everyone to hear you?"

Thomas nodded to Harrow, his heart paining with pity. Well he understood the desire to go home; Harrow had a wife and two children to return to. They were probably as desperate to see him as he was to see them. What would that be like? Did Julia long to see him as he did her? Hope flickered. Sputtered. Probably not.

The scent of brine filled his nostrils. He drew up his knees, splayed his hands across his legs, seeking to give poor Smith a little more room. Poor cove. Some days he'd questioned whether it would have been best for the lad to be left behind; certainly, sailing under such conditions had not helped his health any. He shook his head. None of their escapades had.

After fleeing the garrison town, they had found the beach with its waiting fishing vessel and just managed to evade capture from the indignant owner and his sons, only recently returned after their night of industry. Thankful for the breeze, and for Benson's prior boating experience in Dorset, they had somehow managed to find the port that Magdalena had spoken of. Hiding for a few days until he heard of a cargo-laden merchant ship heading to France, they had survived on a few scraps of fish, the wisdom of which he questioned as soon as Harrow started clutching his middle and retching. Turned out there was a good reason why that fish was discarded. He shook his head again. Would he ever stop making mistakes?

Another barrel rolled across the deck, slamming into the side with a mighty crack. His neck prickled. That had been close. Beside him, Smith mumbled prayers for divine protection. How ridiculous it seemed for a major to be stuck like a rat in a trap, stuck aboard a floating disaster. He would ask God to protect them but he feared he'd used up all his prayers. Besides, it was unlikely God would want to answer his prayers anyway. After all — an echo from long ago whispered — didn't God hate sinners? He wasn't good enough for God to pay attention to. Truth be told, he'd never been good enough, not even in his most triumphant moment of victory in India. Perhaps if he was like Jonathan Carlew then God might deign to listen, but Thomas knew his past was filled with too much sin.

A parade of his misdemeanors passed through his mind. The times he'd skirted round the truth. The women. The lies he'd lived, the men he'd killed. His majority hadn't been paid for; he'd earned it the hard way, laboring long days under an Indian sun. It was a miracle Jon Carlew had ever considered him much of a friend; they were as unlike in character as chalk from cheese.

Not that he had repaid Carlew much in the way of friendship, running off as he had with his sister . . .

Julia.

His heart panged anew, his feelings tipping as surely as the movement of ocean beneath them. Was her hair as fair as he remembered? Were her eyes as blue? Did she still hold secrets in her eyes, in her skin? How he wished he remembered her scent. He stifled a groan. Torturous dreams. Torturous memories. It could not do any good to linger on these. She would be sure to cast him aside, as she must think he had done with her.

But thoughts of her would not submerge; she was like a lifeline, calling him home. To what, exactly, he did not dare think on. Their future would be so uncertain, but it always had been. He grimaced, forced the guilt down. He would see her, perhaps not as soon as he wished, but he *would* see her. One of these days. *Please God,* he dared pray. Soon.

CHAPTER FIVE

"Now, hold still."

Julia did as requested. While cradling the little boy in her arms, she eyed Serena as the smell of linseed oil filled the room.

The past fortnight had gained a new routine of mornings spent playing with Charles and deciding what to wear, and afternoons visiting Hyde Park and doing her best to avoid the visitors that occasionally called at Bevington House. Julia was pleased to find that Serena and Henry did not entertain overly, that Serena seemed to prefer to spend her time painting in the room at the back of the house designated as her studio. That was, when she was not playing with little Charles herself. He had filled out so quickly, growing plumper, more lively, more willing to interact with those around him, his cheeks pushing wide in pink delight whenever he drew attention. Such animation contrasted mightily with the lethargy of the previous two months, as if distress had masked his personality before, his now-happy nature wrenching renewed tenderness from within.

Serena had even requested to paint him, and while Julia had her doubts about his ability to hold still, she had agreed to pose for a painting which Serena was working on most afternoons. When she wasn't playing with little Charles, that is.

Julia wondered about the light that crept into Serena's face whenever she saw the little boy. Did she wish for a child of her own? There was obviously a great deal of affection between Serena and Henry, she saw the loving glances, the loving touches, actions that fueled envy and regret, and made her wonder why her own husband had not demonstrated his regard in such a way. Perhaps he had, and she couldn't remember anymore. Such things seemed an eternity ago.

Her thoughts churned on as she contemplated her own failure of a marriage. Had it been doomed from the start? Thomas had seemed so affectionate when they were in Bath, his words so sweet, his attention proving a tender balm at a time when she felt besieged by her family's opposition and unwillingness to believe she had a mind of her own and could be trusted with her own choices. Of course, now she wondered just how wise had been that decision to run away to Gretna Green with the man who had proved to offer little beyond sweet sayings.

She shook her head. Wallowing in the past would not help. She had to look to the future — including facing Mama and Jon when they returned, as their recent letter promised. Or was it threatened?

"Julia, I'm afraid you simply must keep still if I'm to have any hope of finishing this picture this year." Serena's eyes shaded with a look of concern. "Or is Charles proving a little heavy?"

"He's not heavy," she lied, hefting him back into position.

A raised brow suggested the artist's mistrust, so she sought to change the topic, asking again about Jon and Catherine's child. It still seemed so impossible to believe she was an aunt.

Serena answered in a noncommittal way that made Julia wonder.

"Are you looking forward to having your own children?"

Serena paled, her movements at the easel stilling. "I . . ." She visibly swallowed. "If God so blesses us, then yes. Very much so."

Julia waited, uncertainty knotting her stomach. Such a personal question should never be asked. No wonder the experts in deportment had always washed their hands of her. "Forgive me. I should not —"

"No, I suppose I should learn to deal with such questions." Serena gave a wry-looking smile, and raised her brows. "I believe every new bride must face enquiries of that nature. Is that not so?"

Julia forced herself to nod, remembering once again that Serena and Henry were married but a few months ago. How different their experience would prove to hers. Here, in society's eye, news of an upcoming birth would be welcomed nearly as warmly as the excitement surrounding the birth of a royal baby; Henry and Serena's child — if a boy — would be heir to one of England's great families and estates. As for her own situation back in Scotland, nobody had known their newlywed status; fear of being discovered had led them to present themselves as married for several years, amidst other falsehoods.

Conscious that Serena was looking at her as if in anticipation of further response, she murmured, "I believe that is often the case."

Serena gave her a shrewd glance before eyeing little Charles with that intensity that prickled alarm within. What if she were to guess? How would she explain herself? Would they understand why her lie was necessary? She lowered her gaze in case the truth be dragged out by those too-discerning blue eyes.

There was silence for a while, so long that Julia believed the subject had been closed. Then Serena said, "I . . . I do not know if it is possible."

"I beg your pardon?"

"I . . . have a condition that makes conception . . . challenging."

A knot loosed inside, chased by a rush of compassion. Perhaps that explained why she gazed with such avidity at little Charles. "But you have only been married for a few months, have you not? It is early days still."

Serena offered a twisted smile. "That may be true, but it doesn't stop me wishing I could give Henry his heir, that the unknown was not quite so . . . unknown."

Julia nodded. How well she understood. The unknown filled her future and her past. The future seemed so vast, so overwhelmingly weighty with its questions, with decisions to be made, with her options — well, did she truly have any? And as for the past . . .

The past few months had been filled with

wondering, the helpmeet of worry. The quest for answers had taken her through parts of Edinburgh she hadn't known existed, all the while her thoughts churning "he might be here, he might be there, just one more attempt to find him." Thinking she had glimpsed him. Chasing a man down the street only to discover him a stranger. Believing she heard his voice. Her heart battling between hope and despair, hope the tiny white-frothed crest of all-too-harsh waves that pummeled reality into her soul.

He had gone. He had abandoned her. He did not love her anymore, if indeed he ever had.

The now-familiar sting burned in her soul. Was thinking herself abandoned better than thinking him dead? That was a trail she had also pursued, one her pride shouted *had* to be the truth. If he was dead, she would be freed to regain something of a future. Mother and Jon would be far better pleased by that outcome. Was Thomas dead?

She blinked against the burn, swallowed the tightness in her throat, lifted her chin to approximate the position Serena had chosen for her pose. The unknown of her future must be faced, regardless. And at least here in London it seemed she would no longer have to face it on her own.

The door opened and Henry walked into the room, greeting his wife with a kiss, Julia with a smile, and Charles with a tickle.

"How goes your painting, my love?"

Serena murmured something of her dissatisfaction with the rendering of light.

"I see," he said, frowning slightly as he studied the progress she had made. His gaze lifted to Julia. "I'm afraid I had no notion you would prove such an obstreperous subject to paint."

"I beg your pardon?"

He smiled. "My wife can take a likeness in an instant, but it seems your picture is one she must labor over."

"Do you not remember the pains I took with your picture?" Serena asked her husband.

"Of course I do," he said, eyes now fixed on his wife. "They remain some of my favorite memories." They exchanged a look of tender affection, an action that again fueled envy, but also strange gladness for her brother's friend.

Julia watched him surreptitiously. How different he seemed to what she remembered. The jokester friend of her brother was still there, but he possessed a new maturity now, a gravity no doubt forced upon him by the circumstances of his father's ill-health, as Serena had explained, and perhaps by his marriage. Like her mother, Julia had always enjoyed Henry's polished manners, manners that some might consider flirtatious. He was good company, his good humor still quite at the fore even as he discussed the news of politics. He could make her smile, could obviously make his wife smile, and when he was in that good humor, she enjoyed their company immensely.

As the couple murmured together, regrets nibbled her soul. Had she failed in not discerning her husband's character before agreeing to wed? Wise people might say yes. Wiser people had tried to warn her, but had she listened? Certainly, Catherine, Jon's wife, had tried to help her see the consequences of such an action. Perhaps she should have heeded the gentle remonstrance. Catherine had proved to be one of the few people Julia had been able to trust back in Bath. She could not but be grateful that her good-hearted brother had at long last found a woman who loved him in the way he deserved.

Her spirits dipped, her lips twisted. Perhaps in marrying Thomas Hale she had married a man whom she deserved.

"Julia?" Serena's face held a tinge of

worry. "Are you quite well?"

"Just reminiscing," Julia said, offering a smile to assure. It was always best to turn attention away from herself, to turn a question back onto the enquirer, to ensure people did not get too close to the truth. She knew she would have to admit everything soon, but this bubble of near peace was one she was loath to lose. Besides, there had been so much to catch up on, things that had happened to her friends, to her family, even to the Royal family, that sharing all her secrets seemed a little . . . unnecessary. One day she would fully share her heart. Just not yet.

"Now, Miss Julia," said Henry. "Are you ready to pay attention?"

"I beg your pardon?"

"And so you should," he said, a twinkle in his eye. "I fear you have been ignoring my extremely engaging remarks."

"They cannot have been so engaging, my love, if Julia is not engaged," murmured Serena, who had once more picked up her paintbrush, and was eyeing Julia with a frown of concentration.

"Ah, what can I do but to agree with my wife? She is so eminently sensible; do you not agree?"

"You are blessed with a wife as sensible

63

and as creative as she is beautiful."

"Now *that* is a sensible thing to say," said Serena, the corners of her mouth lifting with amusement.

Henry laughed, the sound jerking awake the babe in her arms. His brown eyes widened, and he glanced between them as if unsure whether to laugh or cry.

"There is nothing to worry about, my little love," said Serena, swooping forward to draw him away. "You are quite well here."

Julia caught the worry shading Henry's eyes. Was he starting to wonder whether his wife was growing too attached to the little boy? For herself, she was in two minds. Staying here, being cared for in this way, had relieved her of much pressure. She scarcely need make a decision except for what to wear, and even then Anna was more than happy to oblige. But perhaps she should not stay much longer if doing so proved injurious to Serena's state of emotions.

After a moment's further cooing, Serena returned little Charles to Julia, and resumed her stance behind the easel. But still the worry gnawed, as Julia's thoughts flicked to that earlier conversation. It must be so extremely hard to wish to have a child but be told such a thing was unlikely. Was their presence here a hindrance? Was staying here wise, after all? But if she left, where would she go? Perhaps it was best to hold off making any decisions until Jon and her mother returned. They would certainly not be backward in offering their opinions.

"There you go again" — Henry's eyes creased as he glanced at Julia — "off to dreamland."

"Forgive me. I . . . I was just wondering when we might expect to see Jon again."

"Soon, very soon," Henry assured. "Jon's letter suggested by the end of this week. He seems extremely eager to see you."

Unspoken was the degree of Julia's eagerness to see him.

"It will be good to see them," she allowed, forcing her smile not to waver. Though what she would say when she finally did see them she still did not know. Rehearsing her explanations — her apologies — each night did not seem to help, only caused a tightness in her shoulders and a cramping in her stomach. Would they listen? Would they blame her? Or would they blame everything on the man they surely now despised — the man she had run away with to be his bride?

She swallowed bile. And how could she cope with their platitudes, their "I-told-you-so"? How could she brazen out her humiliation so it was not quite so . . . humiliating?

Henry cleared his throat. "Miss Julia?"

Her attention snapped to his. "Oh, forgive me. I was woolgathering."

"You know, I cannot quite picture you as a gatherer of wool. My experience of woolgatherers is that they tend to be rather less genteel-looking, though kindly, honest folk, of course." He slid a look at his wife, who was manipulating the brush in deft movements. "We shall soon have opportunity to judge more precisely if I have misrepresented the woolgatherers we know."

"I beg your pardon?"

"What Henry is trying to say in his ever-elliptical way," said Serena, looking up from the canvas, "is that we shall have to go north to Derbyshire before too many more weeks pass."

"Oh." Julia bit back the protest. Tried to look understanding, and not like the thought of their departure filled her with misgiving. How could she withstand her mother and brother without the support of the Carmichaels?

"Never fear, my dear," Henry said. "I'm sure Jon will have returned by then." He offered a smile that possessed less than its usual brightness. "It appears from today's correspondence that circumstances draw me

66

north to resume my responsibilities, among which are those sheep, whose wool the estate farmers like to gather. I would prefer to be there by Martinmas."

"Of course." Her spirits sank. How nice it would have been to have the support of a friend while she had to undergo the barrage of questions her mother and brother would no doubt throw at her. She forced a smile to her lips. "I'm sure your family will be very glad to see you."

"It has been a little while, so perhaps they will." His chuckle held no rancor. "One person they will all be glad to see is my wife — that was part of the reason I married her, you see. Their decided preference for Serena gave me hope that attaching her to myself might one day mean they overlook their decided non-preference for me."

Serena's swift glance at the ceiling suggested this was more of her husband's nonsense.

Henry continued, "But whether the same can be said about her seeing them I rather suspect will depend on whether this painting is finished before we need to depart."

"A circumstance that may only occur if you cease from visiting every moment of the day," Serena said, with a return to her most serene-like countenance. "Now go."

He sighed heavily, glancing at Julia. "See with what a Gorgon I must live?"

"Your trials are heavy," Julia said, shooting a quick glance at Serena, who seemed to be ignoring their byplay, save for the slight lifting of the corner of her mouth.

"I am so pleased that *someone* in the room understands. Now, I must go before my fair Gorgon turns me to stone." He made a theatrical bow, then quit the room, but not before Julia saw him exchange another tender smile with his wife.

"He loves you very much," Julia said, not without another wisp of envy.

"He is a good man," Serena agreed, before meeting Julia's gaze in that long, clear look she had. "Please do not fear that we shall depart before matters are fixed to a certainty with you."

"A certainty?" Julia gave a spurt of laughter edged with bitterness. "I do not believe anything as certain these days."

Serena eyed her for a moment longer, then placed the brush down and moved closer, putting out her hands for little Charles again, whose little pout bent into something approximating a smile. Relieved of her burden, Julia sank onto a nearby chair.

Serena looked at her seriously. "Forgive me for asking what may seem an impertinent question, but do you want things to be resolved with your husband?"

"Of course!"

Her hostess studied her, one eyebrow aloft.

"But he might be dead."

"I can understand that might be easier to accept."

Instead of knowing he rejected her? Of course it was. She gritted her teeth, forced the corners of her mouth to remain pinned in place as those blue eyes studied her for another long moment.

"If he is alive, and he returned, would you be pleased to accept him into your life again?"

"*If* he returned." Serena's gaze bored past Julia's insouciance. "Well, yes, of course I would."

The appraisal continued, then Serena gave a slow nod. "I would find it hard to trust again, but I believe that is what God wants us to try to do."

God? What did He have to do with her marriage?

Serena continued, "And what about beyond that? Would you wish to resume life in society again?"

"I do not know. I might wish it, but it does not mean society would accept me again.

Not that I care terribly much for what others may think."

"It is good you think so now . . ."

"But?"

"I'm afraid that while you have been shielded from the gossips so far, I have no doubt that when your family returns, so too will the gossip."

Because Julia's mother had never courted anonymity.

Serena gave a faint smile. "I am sorry to have to speak on such matters, but I know to my detriment just how scorching such words can be, which is why I much prefer to be far from here if at all possible."

"You think it best I leave London?"

"I think it best you talk with Jon and Catherine when they return. Perhaps there is someplace where you might be able to regain your place in society without the critics watching your every move."

Hope flickered. Perhaps she *could* reestablish herself as a widow in a village where she was unknown. She and Thomas had previously managed to assume new identities in a social scene far from their norm; she knew what would need to be done. For a moment, a glorious vista unfurled before her: a cottage of her own; a child she would raise; a place where she would be respected, not condemned; and perhaps, one day, even a new husband — one she would be very sure was safe, and would lead her to security, not into fears.

The remembrance of her reality dissolved the dream, dissolved her hopes. So many questions clamored for attention: her husband's whereabouts — if in fact he *was* alive, her family's reaction, her future, society. How would she survive the next few weeks?

"I do not wish to alarm you, but I feel it best you are prepared."

"Thank you." Julia forced a smile.

"I hope you know we will be praying for you."

Heat edged her eyes, and she forced back the tears at the younger girl's kindness.

Perhaps God would pay attention to sweet Serena and kind Henry, even if He had no time for her.

As for the rest of it? She lifted her chin. Her mother and her brother would require tact to help them see her point of view; Serena and Henry might have to help them see things from her perspective. And society? Maybe one day she might be accepted in society again. Maybe one day she might even care.

CHAPTER SIX

Dover

"Well, hello there." A buxom woman with eyes as empty as her smile sidled up to him. The Golden Anchor was not his usual port of call, but when a man was desperate for the readies he would do anything, even cross the threshold of a public hostelry that shouted its antecedents as a place of ill-repute. He'd be willing to bet his life that this place once was home to not a few smugglers, and he would stake his health that descendants of those same smugglers still lurked within its walls today. At least, that's what he was hoping for.

"A man like you looks like he needs to relax," she continued, tracing a finger down his shirtfront.

He forced himself not to flinch, nodding instead, before allowing himself to be gently drawn inside. He had no intention for the type of relaxing she seemed to have in mind, but he would certainly relax once he had coin in his pocket again. And the only way to do that was to hope the luck that had brought them safely back to English shores would continue to hold.

Within five minutes he had a drink. Within ten he was reasonably sure he had been sized up as something of a flat, an easy mark. No doubt the ill-matched Spanish clothes he now wore had engendered such belief, his prison-tattered trousers and coat exchanged for the slightly cleaner garments worn by Harrow and Smith. Or perhaps it was the poor accent he'd adopted, or the certain look of vacuity he'd assumed which had won him more gold than it ought over the years, from White's in London to the gambling hells of the Subcontinent.

Within fifteen minutes, by pretending to be in his altitudes, drinking a little too deep, he had given the impression that the Spaniard could not hold his liquor. This seemed to convince the decidedly smoky tavern inhabitants that he was ripe for the plucking, as, after giving their game a suitably interested look, they invited him to join their card game.

Within the hour, he had given an altogether different impression as the sharp memory he liked to hide behind droopy eyelids had helped him to win more than enough to finance the onward journey, for both himself and the three men shivering in a laneway outside.

"*Señors, gracias* for the game but I must go," he mumbled, depositing his winnings into the coat pocket; he hoped it had no holes. He pushed back his chair, rising.

The man seated opposite — a cursed ivory turner if ever he met one — seemed to want to gnash his teeth, offering a very peculiar smile instead. "Please, don't be so quick to leave. The night be young —"

"But I be not." Some days, like now, he felt older than the hills. If only he could sleep. But first to find his —

"Siddown." A hand clamped on his shoulder.

Thomas flinched. Forced himself to relax. Ran a surreptitious eye around the room, noting the way many of the tavern inhabitants leaned forward as if expecting a fracas to commence. Well, he wouldn't want to disappoint . . .

He slumped, as if to resume his seat. As soon as he felt the hand on his shoulder relax he used the extra momentum to elbow his captor in the groin before smashing his clenched fist into the bulbous nose. He caught the look of shock on the faces around him — yes, it was dirty fighting, but effective — and knew he had but a moment before they joined their compatriot in routing the supposed Spaniard. He leapt to his feet and spun around, tipping over a chair in his haste to reach the door.

Yelled obscenities filled the room as a surge of men followed him. But only so many could meet him in the narrow hallway, and the skills of years of boxing soon came to the fore, as one man after another soon followed their friend to the filthy floor.

But even as he felt the adrenaline surging, he knew his strength to be rather less than par, and prepared to make his escape. A bear of a man pushed past a table, sending it crashing to the ground. "Oy!"

"*Sí?*" Before the man had a chance to touch him, he kicked out at the man's knee — another dirty trick, but there was no honor among men like these — heard the loud huff of surprised indignation, and finished him off with a fist to the jaw. The man staggered backwards. So much for thinking his fighting days were behind him.

Without waiting to see if the bruiser joined the upended table, Thomas fled into the frigid night air, working to ignore the throbbing pain in his hand, the burn in his lungs as he hastened to the point of rendezvous. God forbid the men not be there . . .

A twist of a lane, a back alleyway more, and he had joined Benson, Smith, and Harrow, motioning them for silence even as he struggled to quiet his breathing as the sounds of pounding footsteps filled the street.

He jerked his head towards the door opposite, another tavern. After a hasty exchange of coats and a general dusting down of their apparel to release the worst of the fight-acquired dirt, they followed him into the dim interior, eyes wide, mouth closed. He nodded to the innkeeper, ordered a round of ales with the precious coins, and settled into the darkest corner of the room.

"What happened?" Harrow asked in an undervoice.

"I have the funds, which I shall give you when we don't have a dozen pairs of eyes watching."

Harrow nodded. Benson grunted. Smith's face wore a look as vacant as Thomas had tried to assume. His heart twisted with compassion. Poor lad.

"It appears the men took exception to someone like me winning at their expense, so I had to rely on other methods of persuasion." He held up a fist. "Here's hoping they feel no need to visit every tavern in Dover to search for poor Pedro."

"Pedro?"

"*Sí.*" He smiled.

It wouldn't hurt for them to know he could hold his own in a brawl. And provided they could leave without further assault — poor Smith would never last a fight — then they should be free to carry on with their plans to finally, *finally* return to their loved ones. Whatever the men's feelings about such things, they should not complain too much. He had just won their passage back to their respective homes.

The door burst open and in surged a group of men. Thomas forced himself to appear relaxed as he searched the room for potential exits. He dipped two fingers in his beer and smoothed his hair, encouraging the others to straighten to the stance of the soldiers they had once been. A couple of twists of the sad strip of linen that had once served as his cravat and he hoped he appeared more like a man who once had counted a viscount as his friend.

A loud voice came from near the taproom. "I'm looking for a Spaniard. Any newcomers in here?"

"The only strangers be that group in the corner."

Heart sinking, wishing he'd had time to

scrape the fuzz from his face and further disguise himself from the role he'd played earlier, Thomas turned to the others. "Seems we shall need to brazen things out. Follow my lead."

By now the men were approaching their table, their eyes hard, tight with suspicion. "Smith, sit up," he muttered.

"Sir! Your hand."

Spying the hatch of bloodied grazes Harrow referred to, Thomas tucked his right hand from view, and wrapped his less fight-affected left fingers around the pewter tankard as the men loomed above their table, chests puffed out like bantam cockerels.

"Oy, I rec'nise that jacket!" One of the men blustered. "Oy, you!"

"Ignore them," Thomas hissed, before taking a deliberate sip of beer.

"Oy! I be speaking to you. Look at me." The man said, nudging Smith, who turned to look up at them with a creased brow.

"I beg your pardon?" he said in his soft voice.

Thomas held his breath, glad the fool had chosen the mildest of them to make his accusation, and not chosen Benson to vent his spleen. Who knew what that hothead might say.

"That's not 'im," one of the others said, among a chorus of disapprobation.

"Excuse me," Thomas said in a stern voice that had never failed to win him respect on the Subcontinent. "I do believe you owe my friend an explanation for your rough behavior."

"And who be you?" the man said, eyeing him narrowly.

"I be Major Thomas Hale, of the Nineteenth Regiment of His Majesty's Army." He eyed the man with a straight look, surprised at the tinge of honor he felt at finally speaking the truth.

The man sneered. "Sure, and I be the King of England."

"Really? You surprise me. I did not think such an exalted personage favored these types of places."

The other man swore, then said in a low voice Thomas supposed he was not meant to overhear, "He *looks* like the one they called the Spaniard."

Thomas flicked a warning look at Benson, whose hands had clenched at the words, and forced his shoulders back in the manner opposite of the vacant creature whose pose he had earlier assumed. "I beg your pardon, I must have misunderstood. Do you dare have the temerity to accuse me of not being who I say I am?"

"Well, you surely don't look like any major I've ever seen."

"And precisely how many majors of His Majesty's Army have you had opportunity to meet?" He raised an eyebrow in the manner of his former friend Carmichael, an effective means to dampen pretensions.

"Well, I, er . . ."

"My good man, although it pains me to stoop to even acknowledge such levels of derogatory accusation, I can supply you with the direction of more than a dozen men who can vouch that I have most certainly served His Majesty in this way. Or would you prefer the recommendation of an earl?" Carmichael *would* be an earl one day. Although whether he still deigned to stand as Thomas's friend . . .

"I . . . er . . ."

"Have you paper and ink? My friends and I have just recently crossed over from France, and our trunks were mysteriously waylaid" — all true, although the trunks had disappeared somewhere during their imprisonment in Spain — "and we are forced to wait until such means are afforded us for their return. But I am more than willing to oblige those of you who have the nerve to doubt my veracity." He turned to his men seated at the table. "I must be in a good mood, for I do not normally appreciate being thought a liar."

They murmured their agreement, with louder references to "major."

He glanced at his accusers, whose air of suspicion seemed now clouded with confusion, then pushed to his feet and said in a carrying voice, "I say, barman, this ale is the finest we've had in a good long while. We need another round. I assure you, the Frenchies have nothing to compare."

There was a general murmur of agreement, and he could feel the subtle shift in the atmosphere of the tavern's clientele veering to his side, especially when the barman placed their tankards before them and Thomas paid him with more of their hard-won coin. "Do you know how many months it is since we've enjoyed such superior beverages? I'm sure you cannot. Shall you tell them, Captain Harrow?" he continued, elevating his friend a rank.

"Six."

"Six months?"

"Yes, nigh on half a year." Thomas said. "Do you know what it does to an Englishman's soul to be deprived of quality libations for so lengthy a time? Why, it sends him almost mad." He eyed his main accuser's attire with an upraised brow. "Tell me, have you also risked life and limb to serve His Majesty and know what it is to forgo such pleasure?"

"Well, I . . . no."

"Really? You astound me."

The man muttered to his companion, "He don't *sound* like no Spaniard I ever heard."

"A Spaniard?" Thomas arched his brows. "Don't tell me you were seeking a Hibernian? What did he look like?"

"Well, not unlike you, but a bit coarser, seemed like something of a loose fish."

"I am gratified that you can observe the difference," he said, not without irony.

Harrow coughed, forcing Thomas to eye him sternly, before he returned his attention to the men who remained before them. "You must forgive the good captain here. I'm afraid he must have picked up a little something on the journey over." He leaned forward. "I'm hopeful it's nothing *too* infectious."

The men took a step back, eyeing them all with one more glance before finally trudging from the room.

"Hold," he cautioned his friends, Benson in particular seemed ready to leap up and run away. "We cannot afford to draw suspicion upon ourselves by instantly fleeing."

"Do you think it wise to give your own name?" Harrow asked.

"I cannot be sure, but perhaps the ring of truth might well be what persuaded them to finally leave."

"That or your attempt to sound like a gentleman," Benson muttered.

How to explain he used to talk like that most of the time? That he used to dine in superior circles and had counted numerous men of rank and fortune among his friends? He might have shared much about his life in recent months in attempts to stave off madness, but certain more personal factors like this were hard to explain. So he did not.

"Talking fancy like that made 'em go away," Smith said.

"Exactly so," said "Captain" Harrow, with a narrow-eyed look at Benson.

Thomas could feel the level of amity decreasing with every passing minute. Smith uttered another of those lung-rattling coughs that dug further resolve for Thomas to return him home as soon as possible. God forbid Smith get this close but no farther. His family had to see him, even if it be for one last time. No, they needed to leave, but before they could do so, he still had some important things to do. He waited until watching eyes had grown bored and turned away before drawing the rhino from his pocket. He counted out the coins, preserving a slightly larger portion for himself, and handed the three men their shares. "That should do you for a passage to London," he said.

"Why'd you have to buy more grog? We would've had more if you hadn't spent it," grumbled Benson.

"Acknowledging another's superior qualities tends to have a disarming effect," Thomas said. "You might have noticed the general mood grew decidedly warmer toward us when the men could see we appreciated such ale."

"But it wasn't even that good," Benson griped, eyeing Thomas's pile of coins. "Anyway, why do you get to have more?"

"Because I'm the one who took the risk by gambling. And I'm the one who saved your necks back in Spain. And I am the one who has the farthest to travel, home to Edinburgh if you must know." He looked at the pittance of coin in his hands. "I don't even know if this is enough for me to get halfway there, but that's better than nothing. And at least it's enough for a hot meal."

They all rose, Thomas again loudly proclaiming the merits of the establishment. Once outside, it was determined wisest to separate and arrange their passage to their various locales: London, Leicestershire, and Scotland.

"Thank you, sir," said Smith. "I would've been dead many times over by now were it not for you."

Thomas clasped the outstretched hand in a careful grip. "You and I shall travel northwards together. I'll see you to Leicester, don't you worry."

The lad repeated his obligation, the pale face twisting concern within. Smith would be lucky to make it home alive, but Thomas would do his best to ensure he did.

"Well, I too am right thankful," said Harrow. The redhead shook hands firmly. "If there's anything I can do for you, you need only shout."

Thomas nodded, eyeing the other man, whose sullen expression had not wavered despite the other men's expressed gratitude. "Godspeed, Benson. I trust your family will be pleased to see you return."

"Even if it's only six months late."

"That was not my fault," Thomas said. "Besides, it cannot be helped now."

Harrow eyed Benson as one might a loathsome insect. "Anyone would think you held Hale responsible! What kind of worm-meal of a man are you?"

Benson's lips pulled back, his pock-marked, freckled face flushing as his hand clenched.

"Let's have none of that now," Thomas cautioned. "We don't want to draw further attention to ourselves. Godspeed, Harrow."

"Thank you, sir." Harrow smiled. "I trust your wife will be pleased to see you, sir."

"I trust that, too," he said, with an attempt at a grin.

"And I trust that your wife will never find out how you got us out of jail," Benson said, sneering.

Thomas's neck prickled, his good humor melting faster than summer snow.

Harrow's brow creased, his look anxious as he glanced between them. "What's that supposed to mean, Benson?"

"Just that your high and mighty savior did the low and dirty deed with the Spanish whore in that jail."

Thomas stared at him, the coldness sweeping over him giving way to a fury clamoring loudly within his chest. "You do not know of what you speak," he said in a low voice.

"Really? Don't think we didn't see you, or notice how she lusted after you, filthy cow that she was." Benson laughed, a sound with more than a note of hysteria in it.

His fingers clenched. There'd already been

too much fighting tonight, but he'd be hanged —

"Pay no attention to him, sir," urged Harrow. "He's always been a mite unhinged."

"Wouldn't it be funny if you got that Spanish cow pregnant?" Benson gave another wild shriek. " 'Twould be even funnier if your wife found out!"

Crack!

Benson crumpled to the ground, a smear of blood trickling from his mouth to his fair hair.

Thomas massaged his hand, looked sideways at an open-mouthed Harrow, who closed his jaw with a snap. Remorse stole through him. "I shouldn't —"

Harrow shook his red head. "He deserved it, useless cur. How dare he treat you so, complaining like he's done, 'specially after all you did for us? And as for threatening you . . ." He shook his head again. "He had it coming."

Smith murmured agreement.

Thomas shook his head. "I could not listen to him anymore. I could not bear for Julia to hear such things."

"Well, she won't be hearing such things from us two, believe you me," said Harrow. "Now, probably best we move him."

Thomas watched as the short, squat Harrow, supported feebly by Smith, dragged Benson's slim frame to the darkest part of the alley, back behind a row of large crates. "I shouldn't have . . ." He shook his head again.

"Never mind now. I'll keep an eye on him, sir. We'll both be going back to London anyway. Whereas you and Smith 'ere need to catch that coach north to Scotland. I'll be saying goodbye now, sir. Smith." Harrow offered them both his hand.

"Goodbye."

"If ever you need assistance, you know who to call on."

"I will. Thank you, Harrow."

Thomas gave him a nod and, together with Smith, exited the alley, staying in the shadows until he drew close to a far more reputable-looking establishment. He quickly secured passage for himself and Smith on a northbound carriage that left early the following day.

He glanced at Smith. The poor lad looked hardly fit to stay on his feet. Biting back a sigh, he bespoke a room for Smith and two hot meals to be served as soon as possible. When Smith protested, Thomas merely shook his head and ignored his inner qualms. So what if he no longer had enough to pay for his trip to Edinburgh? At least if Smith got some rest he might return home alive.

Besides, Julia would not know his return had been delayed an extra day or so. His note of explanation written so long ago had mentioned the possibility of an absence of weeks, not months. His heart pounded. He just hoped she still missed him and was looking forward to his return, like he dreamed about returning to her, seeing her smile, holding her in his arms, remembering the warmth of her, the scent of her, the taste . . .

He forced his thoughts away. Delectable as they might be, they would only lead to frustration.

Instead, he forced his thoughts to how he could attain more funds before the coach left on the morrow.

CHAPTER SEVEN

Through the drawing room windows Julia could see the small park centering the bleak square, the heavy skies and wintry wind tossing the branches and a few dead leaves. Today seemed a day made for misery. Hourly she lived in dreaded anticipation of seeing her relatives, of hearing their accusations, their censure. Her lips twisted. And the worst of it was that she could not pass the responsibility for such censure to anyone else.

Shivers rippled through her, and she moved from the windows to the crackling warmth of the fireplace. What would she say when she saw them? What should she say? For in all fairness she could not heap *all* the blame onto her runaway husband, although she had a very strong suspicion that nothing she could say would assuage their wrath towards him.

The past nights had been filled with

turmoil as she'd awaken when the watch-
men called the early hours, wondering what
to say, what her future held, until fatigue
dragged her back to restless slumber. She
knew she did not look her best; her eyes
were heavy rimmed, her face pale, and
anxiety had erupted on her skin. At least
with regular and extremely satisfying meals
she looked less like the scarecrow she must
have seemed upon her arrival. But still, her
appearance was so far removed from the
carefree girl she once had been — the girl
her mother would remember — that it was
sure to give comment. But she *was* so very
different, carefree no longer. Could never
be carefree again, despite the prayers for
peace Serena said she prayed.

Julia caressed Charles's auburn curls as
he lay asleep, safely tucked in a cradle
before the fire. Her heart swelled with
tenderness toward him, with gratitude. She
had changed so much, and much credit for
changing her from the selfish, vain girl she
had once been, to someone who cared
about deeper things now, belonged to him.
If Charles had not arrived in her life when
he had, she might well have lost all hope, all
sense of reason. His life entwined in hers
was truly a blessing.

She blinked back tears, forcing herself to

control her breathing and focus on the child's tranquil brow. He slept so peacefully, blissfully at rest. Thank God those initial days of exhausted confusion and countless tears had passed, and he knew now how to slumber. How she envied him. What would it be like to relax, to truly relax? What must it be like to know such innocence, to know no fear, to have every need attended instantly simply by the emitting of a cry? How wonderful it would be to slip back into those days of being cosseted and cared for. But how futile to think on such things, as her responsibilities would not, could not, allow them anymore.

Her eyes closed, the broken night's slumber making her long to sink into sleep also. The sound of her heartbeat, her slowing breathing, filled her ears.

The stillness dissipated as the clatter of wheels on cobblestones drew her eyelids open. Her pulse picked up in pace, and she strained . . .

A door opened. There came the faint sound of voices, low-pitched, high-pitched, the shutting of doors, the whinny as horses were driven away. Her pulse grew more frantic. Oh, when would —

"Julia."

"Oh!"

Two people Julia had never seen before entered the room behind Serena. Serena gave her a tiny helpless-looking shrug before saying, "Forgive me for intruding. A former school friend of mine has called, and I thought I might introduce you. Caroline, this is Mrs. Julia Hale. Julia, this is Lord Aynsley's daughter, Miss Caroline Hatherleigh."

The young lady eyed Julia avidly, rather like a squirrel might eye a particularly tasty nut, but all she said was, "Pleased to meet you," as they exchanged curtsies.

The young gentleman standing beside her — sandy-haired, with an open, genial countenance — held a similar look of interest in his eye, almost like he had heard of Julia by reputation, a thought that made her stiffen and draw her shoulders back. His smile, however, possessed a warmth reflected in his eyes that was far more engaging.

"And this is Mr. Amherst, Lord and Lady Aynsley's neighbor from Somerset."

"How do you do?" He bowed, his look of interest melding into something that almost looked like appreciation, a look that disconcerted her as much as it seemed to dismay the young lady he accompanied.

Miss Hatherleigh glanced at Julia before returning her attention to Serena. "You must forgive me, but when I learned you were in town I could not pass up the opportunity to see you again. It has been so many months since Miss Haverstock's, and I cannot but wish we had stayed in closer contact this past year." She chattered about some of the *on-dit* of town before saying, "Oh, it is good to see you again, Serena."

Serena's face had adopted the coolness Julia was fast learning masked her true feelings as she murmured something of her pleasure. Clearly, the wish for renewed acquaintanceship was not equally shared.

As the conversation between the ladies continued, Julia became increasingly aware that Mr. Amherst's attention was fixed on her. He smiled again upon her notice, and drew nearer. "It would seem that our presence is somewhat superfluous."

Well, his was. She, at least, had been invited to be here. She forced a polite smile to cover her inner acerbity. "What brings you to London, sir?"

"Miss Hatherleigh. Although, really, that makes it sound as though she drove me, when in fact it was quite the other way around. Not that I drove her, *per se,* because really, that would be considered quite untoward. I know her mama would have to have a fit of the vapors if she thought I was doing such a thing."

Julia blinked. What a rattlepate the man was!

He smiled. "Did you know, Mrs. Hale, you have the loveliest blue eyes I have ever seen?"

She took a startled step back. "I beg your pardon?"

"Your eyes. They are quite a lovely shade of blue."

"Oh! Well, er, thank you."

"I hope you don't mind me saying so," he continued in his lowered voice, with a conspiratorial glance at the other visitor. "I'm sure Caro would not mind me saying so, she is a good sort after all, and I do think it only proper to give a compliment when one can. This practice of paying homage to one after one's death I find quite absurd. Surely the dead person would have preferred to know of such praise when they were still alive, would you not agree?"

"Er, yes."

"That is why I felt you should know that you have very pretty eyes." His smile took on a greater warmth.

The moment stretched, her thoughts unable to form cohesion. It had been so long since she had been the object of any form of gallantry, she barely knew what to do.

Which was in itself strange, especially when she had once been so deft at deflecting the interest of any young men who did not capture her fancy. Really, this young man with his disconcerting rapid-paced rabbit-trail-like comments was most peculiar. But he did possess a sweet smile.

"And may I be so bold as to return your question?" he continued.

Question? Had she asked a question?

"Are you from London or visiting?"

She licked her suddenly dry lips. "I . . . I grew up in London, and have recently returned. To see family. Lady Harkness is my mother. She . . . and my brother, Lord Winthrop, they are arriving soon."

"Ah! I gather our timing has not been particularly judicious. Forgive us for taking up your time, but" — he leaned closer, a twinkle in his eye — "I cannot be unhappy that chance has led us to not be strangers."

Whether it was his cheeky comments, or the engaging nature of his smile, or the sparkle in his eyes, she could not help but smile back at him, conscious of a little ripple of pleasure such open admiration had evoked. Perhaps she was not as sadly hag-like as she'd imagined.

He bowed, then turned to his companion. "Caro, I believe it is time for us to depart.

Thank you, Lady Carmichael, for the chance to meet you and your lovely friend."

Serena inclined her head, in a gesture befitting a duchess, and murmured something of her pleasure at the unexpected visit, but made no mention of hopes for a return call.

When they had left, Serena turned to Julia with a small sigh. "I am so sorry to have interrupted your afternoon in that way. Had I known that Caro would insist on staying so long I should never have invited her in. But she is one of those people who are forever pushing their way into other people's affairs, but in a way it becomes increasingly difficult to know how to extricate oneself from their determined interest."

Julia managed a chuckle. "I think you managed very well. One look from your queenly stare . . ."

Serena's lips twitched. "That is what Henry says also." The amusement slid from her face as her forehead puckered. "I do hope Caroline's friend wasn't being overly forward. I believe I heard something about blue eyes?"

To her chagrin, Julia felt heat sweep her cheeks. "Just a bit of nonsense."

"Hmm. He seemed quite taken with you."

"He seems quite unusual." She hurried

on to avert the speculation in Serena's eyes, "Is he betrothed to Miss Hatherleigh?"

"I do not believe so. Why?"

Oh dear. More unfounded speculation. "I just wondered, that is all. It seems most unusual for a gentleman to escort a young lady on a morning call when they are unrelated."

"Yes, I suppose it is." Serena eyed her carefully. "He is aware that you are married?"

"He addressed me as such," Julia said. "I cannot think he misunderstood."

"Well, I should not worry anymore — wait. Is that the sound of a carriage? Excuse me."

Serena exited, leaving Julia standing alone, her nerves from half an hour ago reigniting their harried patter. Was *this* to be the visit she had equally dreaded and longed for?

She glanced at the sleeping baby — unnoticed by their previous guests. What would Mother say? What would Jon?

"Julia!"

She looked up at the figure framed in the doorway, her heart dropping. "Mother."

"Oh, my darling girl!" Mother's red-gold hair flashed under the afternoon light as she rushed towards Julia. "Oh, it *is* true! We came as soon as we heard."

Seconds later Julia was smothered in a hug, clasped to her mother's breast like she herself sometimes held Charlie. As if she could never let go. As if, if she held on long enough, tight enough, somehow, she might be able to protect them from life's harsh realities.

It took a moment, then Julia realized that her mother, her beautiful, vibrant, ever-assured mother, was weeping. She had never seen her mother weep before. Her heart wrenched. Her throat cinched. What a bad daughter she had been.

"Mama," she finally managed to murmur against the bright hair, "I'm so very sorry."

"Oh, my darling daughter," Mother said, "how I wish you had trusted me."

Julia silently agreed. If only she had trusted her mother, how much heartache might have been avoided. Her eyes filled, and she closed them tight to hold back the tears that begged to fall. Shame gnawed hard at the edges of self-control. If only she had not run away; if only she had not placed her trust in a scoundrel rather than those who truly cared about her. If only . . .

It took another moment before Julia realized that someone else had entered the room. She peeked up from her mother's embrace to see two someones: her brother and Catherine. Jon's face lit with gladness, then he drew close and clasped them in his arms.

"Julia." His deep voice rumbled in her ear. "I'm overjoyed to see you are safe."

This time she could not hold back the tears; they leaked out, trickling past her nose. She knew her mother's affection was real, but especially since her father's death, she had known her brother's concern stemmed from a weighty groundswell of love that held her best interests at heart. *His* disappointment in her seemed all the harder to bear.

"You'll never know how much I have regretted everything," he said in a raspy voice.

A giant knot of emotion clogged her throat. "It was never your fault."

His chin grazed the top of her head as he shook his head. "I will always blame myself. If only I'd never introduced you to Hale."

She kept her protest behind her teeth. How could she admit that it was her impetuous behavior and desire to have things her own way that had led her to this? She couldn't.

Her mother eased back, allowing Jon to move in for a closer hug, where she could breathe his scent, and allow his warm strength to permeate her being. There was something so safe and comforting about receiving a hug from a tall man, the sign of affection something she'd craved since —

No, she could not think on him, *would* not think on him. He would be as dead to her.

"I missed you, little sister," Jon continued in that deep low rumble. "Please forgive me for not listening to you."

"Only if you forgive me."

"You were forgiven long ago." He eased back, gave her a small smile, and handed her his pocket handkerchief. As she mopped her cheeks he said, "Now, can I introduce you to my wife?"

A chuckle broke through her tension. "I think we've been introduced. Hello, Catherine."

"Hello, Julia," said Catherine. "It's wonderful to see you again."

She drew near for a hug, and again Julia was wrapped in security, reminded once more why she had confided in her nearly two years ago in Bath. She had the sense that in Catherine she had found a true friend, someone whose gentle demeanor masked a strong spirit, someone she knew capable of standing up to Jon's domineering manner. Julia had seen her demonstrate such spirit before.

"And this is our little girl," Jon continued. "Elizabeth, come meet your Aunt Julia."

A tiny blonde girl who looked to be about five months of age was brought forward, held in the arms of a servant.

"She is a dainty thing," Julia said, marveling at the sweet expression on the child's face.

"And who is this?" Catherine asked, eyeing Charles, still blissfully asleep in the cradle.

"Julia, tell me this is not —" Mother's voice hitched.

Julia fought a wince as she bent over, swept him from the cradle. Ah, the moment of truth, or at least partial truth. What should she say? She swallowed. "This is Charles."

"So sweet!" Mother stroked his downy curls, such maternal softness Julia could not recall ever seeing before. "Oh, look Catherine, he has my hair color!"

Catherine murmured words of concurrence, twisting guilt deep in Julia's heart. She had to say something. She opened her mouth to speak when her mother met Julia's gaze, tears glistening in her eyes. "I cannot believe you had a child and I did not know."

"Mother," Julia began, "I'm sorry, but —"

"I cannot believe that man did this to you, to all of us!"

Further explanations died on her tongue at her mother's passionate outburst. Now *that* was more like the mother she recalled. "Mother, I'm sorry." Regrets roared. Would the apologies never stop? Would that be her role now, the forever sorry child?

She hugged Charles close, a shield against further censure, censure sure to pour forth once they learned the truth about his parentage. Perhaps it was best to admit all, especially with her mother gazing at him with that unfamiliar softness in her eyes. "Mother, I should tell you —"

"I'm sure there will be many things we can learn over the next few days and weeks," Jon said, eyeing Julia in a way that stilled her words.

Perhaps he was right. Waiting a few days might relieve the shock of too much revelation too soon.

Jon wrapped an arm around Mother's shoulders. "Today is not a day for recriminations, but for celebration. That which was lost has been found again."

"The prodigal daughter has returned," Julia said, forcing her lips upwards.

The sound of a cleared throat drew their attention to the door, where Henry and Serena surveyed the room with something that looked like satisfaction. "Forgive the interruption, but I'm of the understanding that reunions with prodigals deserve fatted calves." Henry glanced around the room. "I trust you all know that you must dine here tonight? My wife insists, and I, being a man ever under her thumb, find I must bow to her decree."

"Thank you, Carmichael," Jon said. "We appreciate the offer."

"I'm sure you do, old man."

Her brother exchanged smirks with his best friend, leading her traitorous heart to wonder about the missing member of their trio. He seemed so very absent right now.

"You shall barely be able to get rid of us while Julia stays here," Mother said. "I cannot believe she has finally returned."

"You are sure you feel well enough?" Catherine asked in a low voice, studying Julia, concern edging her eyes. "You seem so much thinner than I recall. I would not have you feel obliged to entertain if you are not well. You truly don't mind us visiting today?"

"Of course!" Julia said, pushing her lips up in a gaiety she did not feel.

How on earth would she avoid giving her family the answers they were looking for without telling all the truth? She would just need to tread as carefully as she had once done across the ballroom. Although she suspected maintaining this charade might prove more challenging than she had anticipated, more challenging than any dance step.

What would happen if she stumbled? She glanced at Charles, resolve firming once more. For his sake, for hers, she could not, *would* not, fall.

CHAPTER EIGHT

Edinburgh

The anticipation fizzing within bubbled higher with each step he took along the narrow cobblestoned streets, just as it had each mile the carriage had traveled northwards. The journey had seemed too long, with too many obstacles, but now here, it would only be a time before he was finally reunited with his bride.

Would she understand? He hoped so. Not all of the delays were of his making, though some were. After seeing poor Smith reunited with his overjoyed family, Thomas had yielded to their offers of hospitality, and allowed himself the luxury of a hot meal, a warm bath, and a restful night's sleep. The following morning he'd been surprised with a gift of clothes, "a small token for what the major has done for our boy." Thomas had been touched, had recognized the immense practicality of such a gift, and had neither the heart nor the income to return the slightly worn items to their owners. He would make restitution, as soon as he returned home and was restored to the garments in his wardrobe, and endeavor to replace the borrowed items on a return journey one day.

That stop was a small candlelight's worth of hope in an otherwise bleak stretch of days. Finding a conveyance north was expensive, taking nearly the last of his gold. As it was he could only afford the cheapest seat. For too many long hours he had shivered atop the stagecoach, fighting the cold, fighting the corners, the only thing buoying his spirits the thought that he would finally see Julia again. Would she wish to see him? What if she did not?

But . . . no. He must continue to deliberately place his fears to one side, chase them from his mind. He would not permit negativities today; today was a day to rejoice. His legs held a spring, as though he could skip on the cobblestones like a child. Today he would finally see his wife again!

He turned the corner, huddling into his borrowed greatcoat to avoid the sudden rush of a sub-Arctic wind, the sights of the streetscape growing familiar once again. He grinned, his strides eating up the half mile to home. It was not long now, and he would see her once more. Would have a bath, would exchange these garments for something in his old wardrobe, would finally see, would finally kiss, would finally hold his lovely wife in the way he'd dreamed for so many lonely months.

Fair Julia, beautiful Julia, who had taken a chance on him and his dreams, casting aside her family in favor of their love. Once upon a time he'd never thought to be the kind of man to want to settle down, to contain his passions for one woman, but she had managed the feat. He'd always known her to be attractive, but as his best friend's — former best friend's — sister, she had always been forbidden. Besides, there had been too many other, older, experienced ladies, more than happy to catch his eye and play the game and fall into his bed. He'd been content enough until he realized Julia's interest in him was deeper than mere flirtation, deeper than her desire simply to annoy her overprotective brother; that she actually seemed to admire him.

God knew why. He'd never been accounted as particularly handsome amongst his acquaintances; he held no title like Carmichael did, nor an estate that drew women like bees. Granted, he'd had some money, but as Julia had her own he did not think such things mattered terribly to her. Well, they hadn't then. He fought the pang, fought to stay positive on this most propitious day. Whatever his faults she *had* seen something in himself that he could not. Regardless, Julia's admiration had only made him wish to be a better man, to continue to earn her approbation, while her smiles had drawn a tenderness from within that he'd long thought he had lost.

He swapped his small bundle to the other hand and stretched out cramped fingers as he smiled over that last thought. After the trials of past months, he had not realized just how soft he had become. But the hardness on which he'd once prided himself in India was something that he could not take pride in any longer. He liked himself more when he was with her.

For even after their blacksmith ceremony at Gretna Green, and once they'd settled into life as husband and wife in Edinburgh, Julia had continued to act like she cared. Despite the roughness, despite the cold, despite the times of hasty removal from one place to another, she continued to see him with something akin to stars in her eyes. God willing, she might still.

His feet were beginning to ache as he

rounded the corner to the stretch of terraced houses forever shadowed by Edinburgh's castellated hill. In this section of Edinburgh it was rare to find a house possessed by one household; instead, many of the houses had been divided into flats, each floor or part thereof let to different families. And while the accommodation was a thousand times improved from his more recent experiences, he could trace the grime and soot stain in the stones, could smell the acrid stench and hear the sour sounds that denoted a life a thousand times removed from the elegancies Julia had once enjoyed.

Another pang struck. He didn't deserve her; he hadn't treated her as he ought. Dear God, he'd even forced her to suffer under the yoke of another man's name. Granted it had been to avoid detection, and they had both enjoyed the silly connection to his real surname, but the knowledge he'd found such things a necessity still swirled shame inside. If only he had done things differently. She was much too good for him, her quality such that he'd always tried to prove himself worthy.

Worthy? That might be a stretch too far. But at least he would ensure things would change. It had been a mistake to trust his future to others; he saw that now. After missing her so much, he knew he could not afford to chase gold if it meant her love for him might grow cold. He'd taken her for granted, not realizing how much he loved her until he realized how much she uncomplainingly endured the life so different from the one to which she had been born. She possessed a far greater resilience than her dainty appearance suggested.

He tromped up the steps to their dingy flat — another thing he'd change as soon as he could afford to — and rapped on the door. Anticipation curled within as he imagined her surprise; hopefully her look of delight.

The door opened. "Hello, my —" His words faltered at the sight of the bedraggled woman there, mousy brown hair and wrinkled face. Had Julia employed this lady to be some sort of housekeeper? A spark of irritation flared. Hadn't he warned her countless times not to waste money on unnecessary household arrangements?

"Yer what?" she said suspiciously.

He offered a small bow. "Forgive me, madam." It wouldn't do to offend the hired help. "I was wondering if Mrs. Rayne be home."

He suddenly grinned. What was he doing waiting in the hall? This was his home. Well, if Julia was acting the grand lady and refused to answer the door, then he'd simply just go find her. "Excuse me." He pushed past the woman.

"Oy!" The woman protested, slapping him on the arm in a manner most unservantlike. "What d'ye think ye be doing?"

"Finding my wife," he said, frowning as he glanced around the meager room. It was furnished not unlike he remembered, but missing so many pieces it begged him to reconsider whether this flat was in fact his. He glanced out the window; no, the glimpse of brooding castle remained as it had in his memories. What was he thinking? Of *course* he was in the right place.

"Get out! Get out, I say!"

"Madam, I know we have never met, and that it has been some months since I was in residence, but I assure you I am Mrs. Rayne's husband."

"I don't care who ye are, or whose husband ye say ye be, get out of my house!"

"Your house?"

"Oy, what's this?" A burly man appeared from where Thomas knew the bedchamber to be. "Who in Hades are you?"

Thomas straightened his spine. "That same question might be asked of you, sir."

"Sir?" The man sniggered, but his eyes

112

grew hard. "You heard the missus, get out."

"But this is *my* house."

"Not for the past fortnight, it ain't."

"What?"

"Ye heard 'im," the woman said. "It's ours."

"But . . . those are my pictures on the wall."

"You 'spect us to believe you?"

"Yes. Yes, I do, because it's the truth. Look." He strode to the mantelpiece, where a small sketch of an Indian scene rested. "This was given to me in recognition of services performed in Calcutta by General Whitby."

"I don't care if it was given you by King George, it ain't yours anymore."

"But it is." He put steel into his voice. "I will have you charged with theft."

"And I'll have *you* charged with trespass and making false claims!"

He clenched his fingers, feeling his choler rise. How the blazes dared these people carry on so? And where the blazes was — ?

"Mr. Rayne."

He turned toward the voice at the door. A wisp of a woman stood there. What was her name? "Becky?"

She nodded. "Are you looking for Julia?"

"Yes. Where is she?"

She shook her head, beckoning him away from the curious ears. She led him across the landing to her own small flat.

"Julia is not here anymore," she said.

"I don't understand."

She shrugged. "She left."

"What?"

"She thought you were dead."

No. She couldn't think that. Hadn't he written a note of explanation? Admittedly he was several months later than what he'd mentioned, but still . . . She couldn't think he was dead!

At the tense, sad look on Becky's face, his indignation faded, dwindling into a sickened understanding, a queasiness hovering low in his gut. Perhaps he should have insisted on seeing her before he left, but how was he to know the job that was supposed to take a few weeks would end up stealing five months of his life in prison?

Still, regrets wouldn't take him there more quickly; he'd simply ascertain her new abode and speak to her then. Although he didn't quite understand why she would leave so many of his prized possessions behind . . .

He pushed a smile past the shard of doubt. "Well, obviously I am *not* dead. So, if you would be so good as to give me her

114

direction?"

"I'm sorry, sir, but I cannot."

His gaze hardened. "Becky, I have spent several long days traveling and I'm in no mind to be put off. Please tell me at once where my wife is."

"Sir, I wish I could, truly I do, but she left no forwarding address."

The alarm bells ringing in his soul grew louder. "Do you mean to tell me she has disappeared?"

She considered him, her own gaze narrowing. "I don't know, sir. I knew she was struggling for a long time, and didn't have enough coin —"

"Struggling? No, I left enough for her if she were careful." His chest tightened. "Unless she spent it on silly fripperies."

"She barely had enough to eat!" Becky said, eyes now hard with disdain. "How could you leave her for months on end with no word?"

"But I *did* leave word. Admittedly, I was absent far longer than I'd anticipated, but I definitely left word, and money." He frowned. "You mean she did not receive it?"

Her sharp expression softened a mite. "I don't think she could have. She was doing her best to sell what she could, but the paintings and pretty clothes could only fetch so much."

He swallowed. "She was selling her clothes?"

"She must have been, for the ones she was wearing near the end were not much better than mine, that's for certain. And you know she always loved wearing her pretty things."

Yes, he did. Guilt pounced. He *should* have spoken to her, should have said something at least. He moved to the window to stare at the bleak rows of dingy houses. "I believed I had left her well provided for."

"Well, you didn't." He turned to face the faded woman who straightened as she eyed him. "You left her with nowt."

His fingers clenched. "I will not stand here trying to defend myself to you. Just tell me this: where is my wife? You two were always friends —"

"Like I said, I don't know where she is." She shook her head again. "All I know is that she came, said goodbye, said that she had to leave to find her family. She seemed so lost." Her pale eyes stared at him accusingly.

Her family. In London. Or possibly Gloucestershire. The ones who would likely wish to see him hung. He muttered a curse under his breath. How in blazes was he to afford a southward journey? Just when he had spent the last of his coin on arriving here. Seemed like it would be back to the tables for him. "And these two?" He jerked a thumb behind him.

"They be friends of Mr. Henderson. You remember Mr. Henderson who was always coming by about rents?"

He gave an impatient nod. Yes, because the gouty landlord used to do that even when their rents were on time, then spend the time ogling Julia if she happened to be nearby. He recognized a man who appreciated a pretty face. "What of him?"

She shrugged, a helpless gesture. "I overheard him and Julia exchange some bitter words. Seemed she couldn't pay, but didn't want anyone to know she had no coin."

The old Carlew pride. He swallowed the first retort. Swallowed the second one, too. Worked to moderate his tone of voice. "And you think she has returned to England."

She nodded. "She only took what she could fit in a small trunk. Sold as much as she could." She gave a long sigh. "Aye, it was all such a terrible time. You remember poor Meggie from downstairs? She got desperate sick about the same time, had just received news her husband had died, poor lass. And her, but newly delivered of a bairn! Oh well, she didn't have to grieve him long."

He fought impatience. He neither remembered nor particularly cared about such things. "I see." He drew in a deep breath that felt tugged from his toes. "I'm afraid I shall have to have a word with Henderson."

She nodded. "He should be downstairs."

He uttered curt thanks and hurried down the narrow stairs. After he spoke to Henderson, he'd be sure to revisit his old flat and regain the treasure Julia had obviously thought worthless. Then he'd pay a visit to someone else. Someone who had a lot of explaining to do.

CHAPTER NINE

"He is a scoundrel, an utter scoundrel!"

"A blackguard, with no sense of honor."

"I'm sorry, Julia, but that man was always something of a loose screw."

Julia gritted her teeth, as the now-familiar invective she had feared swirled around the drawing room, and into her heart, stifling her confidence, smothering her future. Really? It had taken only hours for sweet reunion to descend to this?

"I want him tried and prosecuted," Mother snapped. "I cannot believe that scoundrel abandoned you in this way!"

"Mother, we don't know that he did," Julia said wearily.

"That's right. For all we know he might be dead."

"Jonathan!" cried Catherine. "You cannot say such things."

"I cannot deny such things either." Jon glanced at Julia. "And I suspect Julia has thought the same."

She jerked her head away, sorrow stealing across her heart, refusing her to meet anyone's gaze. Why she felt like crying she did not know. He was not worth her tears. Unless he really was dead.

"What would you prefer?" Jon continued. "That Hale be dead or have abandoned her?"

"You know, it really would be easier if he were dead," Mother mused. "Then Julia could be a widow, and we could almost pretend none of this ever happened."

"I am sitting right here, you know," Julia murmured, her desire to cry dying as she worked to stem the frustration heaving against her chest. Really? Why must her brother always assume this superiority and treat her like a little child? She was a woman now, a mother, a wife. Surely she should be treated with more respect than this! "I would prefer not to speak about him," she said in a louder voice.

"I'm afraid we must do so," Jon continued. "We must find out what has happened. Surely you want to know the truth?"

But did she? Did she really want to know that he had abandoned her? Would she really want to know if he was dead? Perhaps it *was* best to pretend the past two years had been some kind of nightmare. Now that she was back with her family, life could resume as it had before she'd run away to Gretna Green. Back when she'd been the pretty, spoiled daughter of Lady Harkness, back when she felt like she had the world at her feet.

The tiny boy in her arms yawned, reminding her both of the late hour, and that amid the pain of recent months there had been glimpses of joy. Surely, if nothing else, rescuing Charles from a life more destitute than hers had been something of a blessing. For her, as well as him.

"No," said Jon. "We *must* find Hale, and when we do, he shall be forced to explain his actions."

"I find it hard to believe your enquiry agents could not find him," Mother said.

"I shall renew my conversations with them, I assure you. Edinburgh is not so very far away."

Jon's gaze searched hers, forcing her to admit to another truth. They *were* trying to help her, after all. "Perhaps . . ."

"Yes?"

He frowned, an action almost enough to make her waver, but she drew in a breath and forced herself to continue. "Perhaps if you do so, you should ensure they search for a man called Rayne."

"Rayne? I don't understand."

"It . . . it was the name he used when we traveled north." The name she'd happily owned when she did not want to be found, either. "He rented our different lodgings under that name."

"He did not even have the decency to use his own name?" Mother muttered something decidedly unladylike.

"You say different lodgings?" Jon's frown seemed permanently etched between his brows. "How many did you stay in?"

She thought back, remembering the surprised delight of their first town house, in one of the most modern buildings in New Town, and how happy they had been there, until it became evident her husband had not the talent of managing money that her brother possessed. They'd been forced to abandon the pretty house with its views over the park and find something less substantial, and rather less clean, complete with a reduction in servants. She had tried not to complain, had tried to improve the place with what pretty fripperies she could afford from the housekeeping money given her. But even as she'd tried to be careful, she'd noticed the way his face would tighten when he asked about such things. He didn't seem to understand just how hard it was to be forced to do without.

Of course, she had not realized just how much she would do without until they moved to their final lodgings. She shuddered. The only good thing about those dingy, smelly flats were the friends she had made. Her eyes pricked, and she hugged poor Charlie closer.

"Julia?" Catherine's eyes were soft with compassion.

She forced trembling lips into what she hoped resembled a smile. "I was just remembering."

"Your time away must have been very hard."

Julia nodded, ducking her head, even though she saw no censure in the mild brown eyes. Still, she could hear the unspoken condemnation: by running away to Gretna Green Julia had certainly made her bed. And now had come the inevitable challenge of assuring herself she really had enjoyed lying in it . . .

After a few moments, she became aware that Henry was speaking.

". . . don't believe it follows necessarily that he has abandoned you, or indeed that he is dead. Really there could be countless other explanations for why he did not reappear. What if he has a brain injury and cannot remember who he is or where he is from? He could even be trapped somewhere."

"What? Like imprisoned in a castle in some Gothic novel?" Jon scoffed.

"No," Henry said quietly. "But perhaps he has an illness like my father and cannot remember who he is anymore."

Their faces shadowed. Here was something else she had missed, some secret sorrow that she would have known once upon a time, but now had to guess. His father was that unwell?

"I'm sorry, Henry," she said.

Serena, silent until now, moved beside her husband, and placed a hand on his arm. "The earl has not been well for some time now. It might only be a matter of months."

Julia's heart panged. Poor Henry.

"I feel it only fair to say that we must head north as soon as we are able." Henry gave Jon a small smile. "Terribly sorry, old man."

Jon shook his head. "You have responsibilities that cannot wait. We understand."

Julia peeked at her brother. Would Henry and Serena's departure mean she would need to stay with him instead?

"You will, of course, send our regards to your parents, Henry," said Mother. "I would

124

like to see them, and perhaps inquire on the progress of my little mining venture, but things being what they are . . ." She fluttered her hands in a helpless gesture and glanced at Julia.

"Of course. I'm afraid I will need to postpone such talk until matters are more . . . resolved." Henry's face shadowed.

Compassion stirred her heart again. Like when his father died.

The tea tray was brought in, and conversation veered to other concerns, until Julia wondered if they would ever return to the topic that had held her prisoner in her chair for so long. Charlie made the mewling noise that denoted his hunger. Fortunately, she no longer needed to resort to the watered milk of those first weeks when she'd tried to feed him, nor the thin gruel that had been all she could manage on their journey south. She glanced at little Elizabeth, whose healthful appearance bespoke what money and settled family life could obtain. She would certainly never lack for anything . . .

"We digress," Mother said firmly. "It should be a matter of the utmost importance that Hale be found and brought to justice. I will *not* let him escape the consequences of what he has done to my daughter."

Julia lowered her head, but the protest

would not remain quiet. "I went willingly. Really, he cannot be held to account for my choices."

"But you were so young!" Mother said. "He took advantage of you. You did not know what you were doing."

"I knew exactly what I was doing," Julia confessed, peeking up. "I know it wasn't right, I knew it then, but I thought I loved him."

"And now?"

Five pairs of eyes stared at her.

She shrugged helplessly. It was so hard to know anything now. So much of what she once thought true had turned out to be a lie. And if by some miracle Thomas returned, she scarcely knew what she would say. Would those feelings of passionate love return? Would she ever be able to trust him again? What would he say when he met Charles? The unknown held an oppression that seemed to encumber the very atmosphere, fears that weighed heavily on her soul.

If he were brought before the courts, what was the penalty for running away with a minor? Would he be sent to Newgate? How would he survive prison?

"Poor dear sweet Julia," Mother said, drawing her into her arms again. "Do not worry. If that man should return, we will protect you."

But did she want protection? Did she want to meekly return to the family fold? Now she had tasted freedom, did she really want to return to being the dutiful daughter, the unexceptionable sister, back to her old life? Even now she could feel the stifling nature of their affection, could feel the pull to succumb to their will. Was following so tamely the best thing after all? Serena's words stirred through her consciousness. If only she could have a cottage of her own, the chance to start afresh, without the frayed and tangled cords of kinship that flayed against her heart.

Besides, somewhere, deep below, she still felt a faint throb of affection for him. She *had* loved Thomas Hale, even with all his faults, had once believed he could nearly hang the stars. His bravery, his kindness, his efforts to please her, those were traits she needed to remember, too, even though they seemed quite drowned out by more recent actions. Did she still love him? Perhaps. Could such love be rekindled? Possibly. It was hard to know what might happen if he did return. Would she offer him her lips, her arms — perhaps more? Her face burned. Trying to sort through these shifting emotions was exhausting, and so confusing. She was not sure of anything anymore.

"I think some of these questions are best left for another day," Henry said. "I know we want to solve everything immediately, but I think tiredness leads to ill-judged decisions." He gave a wry smile. "Speaking from personal experience."

"I believe you are right," Catherine said. "And if you have need to return to Derbyshire, I think it best for us to release you so you can begin your preparations to leave."

"Soon enough," Henry said. "We have no desire to rush people."

"Nor have we any desire to impede your departure."

"Ah, but mine are not the only wishes to consider."

They turned to her. Julia's cheeks heated. "I would not wish to be the cause of your delay."

"I'm afraid it is not just your company that would be missed."

Another look heavy with meaning passed between Catherine and her brother-in-law, and Julia saw how they turned to look at Serena, who was holding little Charles.

Their conversation continued in low tones, the focus shifting away from Julia.

She exhaled. There would be many questions to face over the next few days and weeks, not least of all the matter of where she would live. The familiar churn of worries began. After such a long, long day of tumultuous reunion, sleep would take a long time to arrive tonight.

Thomas walked into the tavern — one that brought back not a few memories of several he'd visited on his journey north. And a place he'd need to visit again if he was ever to find enough coin to return to England's capital and — please God — find his missing wife. That is, unless he could find the man who might hold the keys to everything.

He glanced around the room, spying a few familiar faces, but not, unfortunately, the man he was looking for.

"Och, and would ye look what just dragged in!" His gaze settled on the genial-faced Munro tending the taps, a man with whom he had enjoyed many a conversation prior to his mission to Spain.

"Munro." He made his way to the bar and ordered a dram of Scotland's finest. After all the disappointments of the past twenty-four hours, he was more than due a tot or two. He downed a fingerful, felt the heat slide satisfactorily down his gullet to warm his belly.

"How are ye, ye wee bittie Englishman? Where have ye been a'hiding? I've not seen yer ugly mug in here for well on six months. Ye almost had me wonderin' if ye got religion!"

Thomas snorted. Religion? What good would such a fool thing do him? "Ye be a funny, funny man, Munro."

"Aye, that be true," he said complacently. "Now, despite ye drinkin' that whiskey like ye hadn't had a drink in years, ye have the look of a man on a mission about ye. Is there something we can help ye with?"

"I'm looking for Joseph McKinley."

"McKinley, McKinley." The man stroked his chin. "Can't say I've seen him recently. But I have heard he's been getting around town a bit lately. Swimming in lard he be, said he came into a windfall or some such nonsense. Trying to make a name for himself." He nodded slowly. "I've seen him down at the Black Harp a few times."

Thomas raised a brow. "They let you out of here sometimes?"

"Aye, and I be needin' to. The clientele ain't what it used to be." Munro eyed Thomas's attire with a grin. "They be lettin' all the riffraff in."

"Thank goodness for that," Thomas said,

offering his own grin and farewell. Information about McKinley's whereabouts was worth the price of a drink.

Two streets away he stood outside the Black Harp, an establishment of definite superiority to the one he'd just visited. A quick scan of the room brought a measure of relief. Finally.

He strode to the corner table, where a mustachioed man — dressed almost as well as Thomas had on his good days — was holding court with several gentlemen whose avid interest suggested they were his inferiors. He did not hesitate to interrupt. "McKinley."

"Hale!" The swarthy-faced man's eyes opened wide. "Well, this is a fine surprise."

"Is it?" He eyed the other men. "Excuse us. We have a matter of urgent business to attend."

There were vague murmurs of complaint, but after quick glances at McKinley, whose nod granted permission, they exited.

McKinley leaned back in his seat. "Not the most elegant of interruptions, my friend."

"I have no time for elegancies these days."

"No need to tell the world. Your raiment shouts the fact," McKinley murmured, examining Thomas's attire with disfavor.

131

Thomas stifled his impatience. His former colleague had always held the aspirations of a dandy. "Tell me, where is she?"

"Where is who? My dear man, this interview has all the appearance of an attack! Come, let me buy you a drink, and celebrate your return." Ignoring Thomas's protests, he snapped his fingers, and ordered a bottle of whiskey. "Y'know, we all thought you were dead."

"Really?" Thomas watched the man's face for the faintest trace of guilt. "Why would you think that?"

He shrugged. "Word gets around. You know how it is."

No, Thomas didn't. But he sensed McKinley would not be forthcoming should he press the matter. "Well, I am very much alive."

"Thank the good Lord above." McKinley raised a glass of amber liquid to the ceiling. "Glad to know you're back among the living." He took a large swig.

"I was never among the dead."

"No? That's not what I heard."

"I beg your pardon?"

McKinley took another swig; his nose was growing red. "On the day I went and visited your poor little wife and gave her your note and money —"

132

"What? You say you gave it to her?"

"Of course I did. What do you take me for?" McKinley eyed him curiously.

Thomas pressed his lips together. Who to believe? The testimony of Becky, who had never approved of him — more than once he'd overheard the poor widow's remarks about his rascally ways — or that of his closest friend in Scotland, the former military major whose acquaintanceship in India had been such that Thomas believed him the only man who could be trusted with the truth, and with securing his wife's future.

But if McKinley was right, why *had* things been left behind? Henderson — weasel though he be — had been quite plain about matters. Julia had not paid rent for nigh on two months, and he'd been as patient as he could, "but a man's got to eat, and when she couldn't cough up the brass for the third month I had to let yer rooms go to someone who would."

How could he reconcile these conflicting views? Unless his first instinct was right, and Julia had overspent as she used to. But would that account for her selling her clothes like Becky said? Unless — his stomach lurched — Julia had parted with such things to leave all traces of *him* and their ill-conceived marriage behind.

He wrapped his hands around the glass, stared into the amber liquid.

"Hale? Forgive me, but you do not look at all the thing. Have you eaten?"

"Eaten?" He shook his head. "I cannot remember when I last ate."

Another snap of his old friend's fingers brought a servant and a request for food. This gesture drew the attention of another man, who, after a quick look at Thomas, claimed McKinley's attention for a few minutes.

Around him the noise seemed to intensify, to infect Thomas's ears with chaos. He felt himself sway, although perhaps that was the effect of alcohol on an empty stomach.

How could he know what was right and true? Whom could he trust? How he longed for the days when his friends were such that he knew their word was as sound as their principles. Before he'd been the one to betray their trust by running off with the sister of his best friend.

Dear God . . .

He shoved his head in his hands, willing the food to arrive so he could eat and escape the madhouse of confliction. But when the food came, his stomach protested the greasy stew and black pudding, contented only with a taste of tattie and some bread.

"She really is a pretty thing, your little wife," McKinley said. "Now, there be no need to look at me like that, 'tis merely the truth I acknowledge, that's all. But I'll confess she did not look best pleased when informed her husband was going away with scarcely a word of notice."

"The notice was in the letter you were supposed to hand over."

"I tell you I did! You dinnae believe me? Well, and this be a fine way to treat your fellow officer. And after all we went through in Poona, too."

"I'd rather not think on India right now. I'm more concerned about the whereabouts of my wife."

"You mean you don't know where she is?"

"If I did I wouldn't be here talking to you."

"Well, that puts a different light on things." McKinley leaned back in his chair, a strange smile on his face. "I'm certainly very sorry to hear that."

"So, you're saying you definitely gave her the money?"

"I'm saying that, yes."

"And she definitely received my note?"

"Of course." McKinley looked at him with something like pity in his eyes. "I'm sorry, Hale. This must be very hard for you to accept."

135

What, that his wife had left him? That he now had to track her to England's capital? He shook his head, still feeling a measure of strange reluctance to believe such a thing of Julia. Had she indeed left him, or was it easier to believe that his friend could look him in the eye and lie so blatantly? He pushed away the plate, unwilling to be indebted to the other man for a second longer.

"Like I said, my friend, I'm very sorry for you. You seem to have had a rough time of things."

Thomas gave a bark of laughter. "You don't know the half of it."

"Please, enlighten me."

But something about the widened eyes, the pity he could see lurking there, made Thomas reluctant to share all his suffering. In fact, for a moment, it seemed as if a look of satisfaction had crept onto McKinley's rather toad-like face. But why would his old comrade be glad about Thomas's present suffering? They had served together, had been brothers-in-arms. He'd always counted him a friend. *Could* his old friend be lying?

"And when you spoke with her she said nothing of her plans?"

"No. I'm so sorry." McKinley offered a

sympathetic smile. "You plan to find her then?"

"Of course."

"I, er, hesitate to ask concerning what might be considered something of a delicate matter, but have you enough in the way of funds to ensure your safe arrival?"

"Naturally," he lied.

McKinley eyed him askance, but said nothing.

Thomas pushed back his chair, muttered something of his obligation and turned away before he said something he would forever regret. But before he could flee, the shorter man was clasping him in an awkward half embrace, patting his back.

"It has been good to see you. For old times' sake."

Thomas forced a smile. "And you. Thank you for all that you've done."

"It was nothing." McKinley offered a bow and a smile, and then his attention was quickly reclaimed by his former associates.

Thomas escaped the room, escaped the weight of obligation and unease, though they hurried his steps as he ventured onto the street. He closed his eyes, drinking in the frigid air, before setting his mind to the onerous task that lay ahead.

This interview had left him with only one

choice: he was going to have to track down his wife and get the truth at last. He should've known that she would never be content with him. He should never have allowed himself to trust her, to trust that what they had would last. He should never have believed her lies when she said that she loved him.

It was time to learn the truth, one way or the other.

Chapter Ten

"Julia, I really think it is time for us to release dear Henry and Serena from any sense of obligation so they can return north. It has been very kind of them to have you stay, but I believe it is time to return to your family."

I know, she wanted to say, but refrained. Where would she go? She knew her mother meant for her to return to live at the town house in Portman Square, but something within bucked at the thought of being swallowed up into her mother's desires once more. It was almost like Mother had forgotten what happened these past months, had forgotten that Julia was a married woman, and someone who might have a mind of her own and independent wishes to fulfill. Even if she lacked the means to fulfill them.

But yesterday had convinced her all the more of the ever-deepening bond between little Charles and Serena. It seemed Henry and Catherine were also aware of Serena's growing fixation with the child, which no doubt accounted for their shared desire to see Henry and Serena return north. And while Julia was reluctant to inflict pain upon someone who had helped so much, it probably was best that she leave, and probably best she stayed at Mother's, at least for the short while.

She had wondered at the way Catherine moved, if perhaps her brother was to become a father again. Nothing had been said, but from the secret glances they exchanged with each other she wondered if something might be said soon. And she was sure if something like that was the case, the last thing they needed was a troubled Julia in their midst, especially one with a child who last night seemed to have forgotten how to sleep, and had taken to waking at all hours.

No, the sooner she and Charles left the better.

The news was broached that evening. Henry's look of relief was quickly replaced by his usual affability. Serena's face looked rather less than serene, but she, too, managed to assume a social mask. Catherine's response, however, was the most unexpected.

"Forgive me, Lady Harkness, but I wonder about the wisdom of such a plan. You are very sociable, and your house is often filled with guests. Julia may need some more time before she is introduced back into society, if indeed she would wish to go into society at all."

"And why would she not?" Mother asked. "She is my daughter after all."

"Mother," Jon said in his deep voice, "I think Catherine is right."

"Of course you do," was the grumbled response.

"It is not as if we can pretend the last year and a half did not happen," her brother continued. "People will know what occurred, and there will be questions, awkward questions. I think we need a little more time before Julia has to face such things."

Julia eyed the table. Did they not realize she was sitting here? That she might have an opinion of her own? Why did everybody treat her as if she were irresponsible?

"It is such a shame that we announced in the newspapers that Julia had lately married and moved to Scotland. If we hadn't, we could have pretended that the last year or so hadn't transpired, and have the marriage annulled."

"But *I* can't pretend it didn't happen," Julia said loudly. "Nor do I want to. I loved him. Sometimes I think I still do."

An awkward silence fell, finally broken by her mother's sigh. "How you can after all he did —"

"And what's more" — Julia lifted her chin obstinately — "if we pretended the last year had not taken place, then what would that mean about poor Charles?"

Somebody exhaled. Jon frowned. Catherine chewed her lip.

Her mother shrugged. "We could say you are looking after him for a friend."

Julia gasped. Had Mother suspected? Fortunately, the other occupants of the room suspected a different reason for her response.

"Lady Harkness, you cannot ask a mother to give up her child," Catherine said.

"It would be unconscionable," murmured Serena.

"I'm sure I do not want to appear hard-hearted," said Mother, doing her best to look penitent. "I'm just trying to think of Julia's best. And with no sign of that scoundrel, one can only assume he is dead. Which is quite the best outcome, I believe."

A burn began at the back of Julia's eyes. She wanted to believe the best, that Thomas was out there looking for her, wanting to

142

return. But perhaps thinking he was dead *was* the best option. At least it would mean she could bury any semblance of hope, and somehow find in her heart a way to move forward.

"Yes, I think it quite the best thing," Mother continued. "I shall have my solicitors look into whether that man can be declared dead —"

"Forgive me, Lady Harkness, I hate to bring such matters of law into consideration," Henry said. "But does not the law of Scotland hold that Julia is still married? Forgive me, but I fail to understand how assuming Hale is dead is going to help Julia. He may be dead, but until we are certain, we cannot allow Julia to be thought a widow, for what should happen if he suddenly returns?"

Jon rubbed the back of his neck. "I will need to look into this."

"I believe Julia would be far better off returning to Gloucestershire or even farther afield until she can return to society and not be subject to vicious lies and rumors," Henry said.

"I agree," said Catherine, turning to look at Jon. "Jon, perhaps Julia can come and stay with us."

"Oh, but —"

"Mother, I know you wish to help, but Carmichael raises some valid points. We do not want to court unnecessary speculation if we can avoid it." Jon turned to her. "Julia, where do you want to live?"

Oh, so they were finally going to ask her? "Thank you for asking my opinion."

"Now don't get in a miff. We're only trying to help you."

"By managing me?"

"I forgot you don't like to be managed," Jon said, a sardonic glint in his eye.

"Do *you* appreciate the interference of others in your affairs?" she asked him, putting up her brows.

"Nobody does," said Catherine softly.

"And you forget, Julia, that these matters don't just affect you. They reflect on the rest of us as well."

She drew in a deep breath, forced her fingers not to clench. "Then perhaps it would be best if I moved someplace far away where my reputation will have no impact on yours." Hope lit her heart. "I could be satisfied with a little cottage —"

"You?"

"What is the point in asking me if you don't want to know my feelings on this matter?"

"How would you afford it?"

144

"Perhaps if my dowry was released —"

"I utterly *refuse* to let that man have a penny of your settlements."

"But, Mother —"

"No. Your removal far away cannot be countenanced. You cannot know what it is like to think your only daughter lost to you."

Guilt massed again, heavy on her chest, forcing her to aim for a more conciliatory tone. "I am no longer a child —"

"We know that," Mother interrupted. "We simply care about you, and want to ensure you are safe."

How could she fight against such concern? Was she so ungrateful? But she could see her future narrowing to only her mother's and brother's interests. "I know you care, but sometimes it seems like you have forgotten that I *am* married —" Their faces blurred. Frustration lashed her chest. Tears would not help her claims of maturity.

Catherine rose and gave her a hug. "I'm so sorry, Julia. Nobody wants to make things more difficult for you. If only we knew where Hale was, then so much would be clearer. But know that you are very welcome to come and live with us, should you wish," she added in a whisper.

"Thank you," Julia murmured. She glanced at her mother whose face had tightened with checked anger.

"Don't look at me like that, my girl. Don't expect me to rejoice in the fact that my daughter wishes to live far away from me."

"Mama —"

"And do not *ever* think I will welcome that man into my home. I would sooner see him hang."

Her chest constricted. Catherine's arms tightened. How could Mother be so cruel?

"What would you like to do?" Catherine murmured near her ear.

What she would *like* to do would be to flee to a cottage by the sea, and live freely with little Charles, and not succumb to any pressure of familial obligation. But such a thing seemed impossible. At least for now.

After a moment to regain her composure, Julia said to the room, "I suppose I shall stay with Mother for the moment" — the words tasted like gall — "at least until circumstances become clearer." Or until circumstances made it impossible for her to live with her parent.

Amid her mother's and brother's vocal approbation, she whispered to her sister-in-law, "But if your offer remains open, then perhaps I will come for an extended visit. We could get to know little Elizabeth better."

Catherine's eyes lit. "It would be wonderful for the little cousins to become friends."

Guilt knotted her heart. One day she was going to have to explain the truth, but not on a day of such drama. She glanced at Mother, whose unyielding look had eased into something approaching taut cordiality. Julia forced a smile. Perhaps staying with Mother would be best, at least for the moment. Besides, she couldn't really see her husband returning to find her anytime soon.

Thomas's teeth chattered as he clung precariously to his seat atop the stagecoach roof. He hoped to high heaven he need never travel in such misery again. But the knowledge that he must escape the wretchedness of Scotland and get to London as quickly as he could had led him to once again find what methods he could afford. And he could afford so little, even with the money he'd won in a midnight gambling session, and the mysterious ten pounds he'd found in his greatcoat pocket, a surprising gesture he suspected to be of McKinley's doing. He had too much pride — or was it too little? — to return to see if his army friend had truly slipped it inside his pocket during their last exchange.

No, he'd needed to leave as quickly — and

as cheaply — as he could manage. He *had* to find her, had to make her understand that he had tried, that he had not abandoned her, no matter what others might say. He had tried to be a good husband. Well, he had *wanted* to be. He just wasn't a good husband. Indeed, his actions in recent months had proved he wasn't any kind of husband at all. For what kind of man abandoned his wife for the lure of gold?

He glanced out across the fields where sheep grazed on lonely moors. He watched a distant shepherd, crook in hand, steer the sheep towards his goal. Never harsh, only gentle. Simply present, not hundreds of miles away. Regrets soared. A shepherd's role was what he should have assumed, someone guarding his precious lamb, protecting her from the storms of life, guiding her to shelter. His actions were more that of leaving his prize sheep to the mercy of wild dogs, hoping that when he returned after six months that the sheep would remain as healthy and well as when he left it. What kind of man was he? A failure of a husband. A failure as a man.

"Miserable, is it not?" muttered the passenger perched alongside him.

"Indeed." Thomas agreed with his fellow traveler, a young clerk named Sidden, whose

148

frail frame seemed scarce strong enough to last the miles to the next posting house.

Little wonder he complained. The journey had been punctuated by delays as the carriage had been forced by treacherous mud to slow several times. Steep ascents had more than once necessitated the removal of all passengers and the employment of all able-bodied men in pushing it uphill, activity that had contributed to barked orders, shortened tempers, and mud-bespattered clothes.

Today had proved particularly challenging, as their early rousing from flea-ridden beds was followed by a chorus of complaint about the tepid tea and watery stew offered by the innkeeper eager to hurry them from his premises. As they'd waited in the stable yards, a portly gentleman fussed about losing a piece of gold in the straw-strewn floor, something Thomas was fairly sure he'd seen one of the ostlers surreptitiously bend to collect. Later, the same portly gentleman had eyed his fellow inside passengers warily before making a loud observation that the small boy traveling next to him looked as though he had measles-like spots. That observation was met with black looks and strident disapprobation from the boy's mother, and their continued sounds of disharmony escaped the window as the miles rolled on. Thomas's lips twisted. Perhaps there were some advantages to being an outside passenger, after all. Be they few.

Shivers rippled down his spine, and he hunched deeper into the greatcoat, rubbing his gloved hands against his sleeves. He'd heard of men who died of frostbite, some who literally froze to their perch, others who grew so numb that they could hold on no longer and tumbled a great height to the ground — and a broken neck.

But for a man with scarcely a sixpence to scratch with, this was the fastest, cheapest way, a route that — God willing — should see him in London in a few days, and in Julia's arms shortly thereafter. He clenched his teeth to stop their clatter, and forced his attention back to those thoughts that fueled his purpose.

His first port of call: Henry Carmichael's town house. He dare not presume to visit Jon Carlew straightaway; far better to find out from someone other than Julia's brother where she might be. Besides, he had no doubt Jon would refuse to see him, let alone give him any clues as to her whereabouts. Carmichael, on the other hand, might understand; he'd never been quite so exacting in his dealings with people. He'd seemed to understand a man could have flaws — did have flaws. Unlike Jon, whose rigid principles had always made him a little harsher in his judgments, a little less sympathetic towards those he thought lacked moral fiber.

Thomas's mind flicked back to the last time they had spoken. Two years ago, when he had visited the new Baron Winthrop at his newly inherited Winthrop Manor. Thomas had murmured something about desiring to marry, and Jon had laughed at him. Laughed at him!

"You?" How well he remembered the contempt curling Jon's lip. "I cannot conceive why you would wonder at a man's hesitation in wanting to recommend someone in his care to your protection."

The attitude, so reminiscent of his father's, had stung. Then when he'd questioned Thomas's sense of honor . . .

The old indignation surged. He'd vowed in that moment to prove his friend wrong. Wooing Julia had not been revenge; he had enjoyed her company, her spark of mischief one he could well understand. He knew too well what rigid strictures did to a young person's soul, how it made them want to escape the confines of their life and discover what lay beyond what they'd always known. In Julia, overprotected, shielded Julia, it had not taken long to recognize the same sense of adventure he possessed, that spirit that had led him to join the army as soon as he was sixteen, then taken him to India when others sought glory on European battlefields. He'd had a wonderful time there, something he'd once imagined might even appeal to the woman he loved. But when he'd mentioned it to her she'd merely laughed, and said it seemed an impossible dream.

Well, perhaps it must always be so, a glimmer of hope from his past, something he could look back on to remind himself he'd once been braver than the man whose face he saw in the looking glass. But regrets also lived in the past. Too much time dwelling there and he would be tying himself in knots, wondering, despairing. Far better to focus on the future, on what could be done, on what yet needed to be done.

The coach rattled over a bridge, the ridged surface sending a fresh ache down his spine, new chills along his skin. Beside him, Siddens groaned, his teeth starting to chatter. Thomas forced his mind to keep thinking, planning; anything to distract from the cold that threatened to steal his breath. He had

152

high hopes for Carmichael, but if the viscount refused to help him then perhaps he would dare to see Jon. It wasn't as if Jon could send him to prison; he and Julia were legally married after all. At least in the eyes of the powers that be in Scotland. And surely Jon should know where his sister was. He might even be pleased, perhaps, that Thomas had sought his help. He liked to be considered in that role.

And if Jon refused to assist, then he could perhaps go to Portman Square and face the tigress in her den. He was sure Lady Harkness would *love* to see him. Or shoot him. Or see him strung up with a noose.

His breath escaped in a long white stream of air. Though his conscience stabbed that he needed to go and explain the situation to Julia's mother, his heart still withered at the thought of facing Lady Harkness. Had he once thought himself courageous? A different man had faced a raging elephant in India — a moment Jon had said was the worst of his life. Thomas had not flinched then. He'd known his duty and done what was needed. But though he knew his duty now, he knew equally Lady Harkness would not help him. If Julia had sought refuge at her mother's house, Lady Harkness would be far more likely to spit in his face than tell him where her daughter was, sure to protect Julia like a tigress protects her cubs. Without mercy, without favor. Without a shred of compassion.

And the worst thing was, Thomas couldn't really blame her.

He blew cool air onto his freezing hands, willing them to warm. He could not afford frostbite, could not afford his concentration to slip and he tumble unceremoniously to the ground.

No. Carmichael simply *had* to help him.

Thomas had to find where his wife was. His heart, his soul — the very marrow of his bones — begged to know whether he had any chance.

Another bridge, this over an icy stream far below, made their high perch seem very high indeed. The coach suddenly dipped. Siddens gave a shriek. Thomas turned as the clerk, thrown from his seat by the rough passage, propelled over the side. He leapt across and grabbed the back of the man's coat. "I've got you!"

"Don't let me fall!"

"I won't," he gritted out. God help him; if the lad fell he'd tumble near twenty feet straight over the edge of the bridge, quite likely to his death, by the looks of that rushing water, which was even now swallowing the younger man's hat.

Left hand grasping the carriage roof edge, right arm feeling near wrenched from its socket, he slowly hauled the dangling man up. "Stop . . . moving," he muttered between grunts of exertion.

Siddens's cries alerted the coachman, who made a loud clucking kind of noise before demanding that Thomas not release his passenger. "Else there be a deuce of a dust up wiv me bosses!"

Finally Siddens was able to catch the luggage compartment slung between the back wheels, and dropped unceremoniously in the basket, the truly poor man's perch for such trips. Although Siddens could scarcely claim poverty; instead, he should be thanking God Thomas had grabbed him in time.

Within the minute of being assured his passengers were safe, the driver slapped the reins and the carriage was once more moving. Thomas brushed aside the clerk's fumbling thanks and ignored the small boy's comment about heroic acts. The portly gentleman moaned about yet further delays before demanding, "What *is* that infernal odor?"

Thomas rubbed at his shoulder, working to release the pain. Thank God he'd been here when he had, that he'd had opportunity to save Siddens's life.

But seeing Julia, being with her once again . . .

That would be one thing for which he could truly thank God.

If God ever deigned to listen to such a sinner.

CHAPTER ELEVEN

Portman Square, London

Julia glanced around the bedchamber, drawing off her gloves, as the footmen bustled in carrying the trunks. She glanced at her mother, whose air of complacency seemed tinged with faint self-satisfaction ever since she had won at yesterday's polite fencing for the privilege to host Julia. "I cannot believe you managed to pack everything up so quickly."

"Of course, darling, I want you here with me. And it wasn't as if you had very many things, anyway. Indeed, it seems little Charles has as many items as you. I confess I am a little surprised."

Julia forced a smile. She *could* have said that Serena had ensured all of Julia's and Charlie's former garments were burned, declaring them not fit for the grubbiest of street urchins, and that apart from a few small trifles she'd managed to bring from

Edinburgh, everything else she now possessed was due to Henry's generosity and Serena's good taste. But she sensed her mother's appreciation for their kindness was growing thin, that she wished the obligation to come to an end, so she said nothing.

They had made their farewells earlier that day, Henry's urbane good manners ensuring Julia felt as though they had no wish to be parted from their company, even though she knew just what a disruption to their household she and little Charles had been. But his smooth manners were not quick enough to hide the flash of concern at his wife's long cuddle with Charles before she reluctantly returned him to Julia's waiting arms. No, it had been necessary to leave, to allow them to return north to his ailing father. It was necessary to leave the bubble of content and somehow negotiate this new life that would be hers.

She moved to the window, stared out at the stark park centering the square, a patch of dingy grass, trees, and shrubs surrounded by black spikes to protect it from intruders. On the opposite side stood the neoclassical Montagu House; nearby, the elegant residence of the Countess of Home. Grand establishments for the wealthy and titled. How ironic that she who had thought such things at an end lived here now.

It was strange to be back in Mother's house. Jon had always complained that the house was too sterile, too cold, but Julia had not minded its newness. And having lived in the grubby flat in Edinburgh, she could even better appreciate the cool classical lines that made this town house so sought after. It would be so much easier to clean, too. A smile pushed past her lips. Yet another way she had changed these past months, for she would never have once considered ease of cleaning to be a benefit in a house.

"What are you smiling about, my dear?" her mother asked, an indulgent expression on her face. "Are you glad to be back?"

What could she say but yes?

"It is so wonderful to have you home," Mother said with an affectionate hug. "I have missed you so."

Again, the only correct response was that she had missed her, too.

And perhaps she had. It *was* nice to feel important in Mother's eyes again, to feel her care and concern. Serena's efforts at clothing her appropriately had been put in the shade by Mother's plans to ensure Julie was dressed in the latest fashions. Where exactly Julia was expected to go to wear such fashions was another matter. She had no desire to attend social functions, she certainly would not attend the theatre, or any balls. Catherine had been correct: Julia had no wish to go places to be stared at, to have people whisper about her. The whirl of gaiety Mother seemed to thrive on, the scandal in which she so often had figured, held no charm. Not for anything would Julia leave her child to peer wistfully from upper windows at the glittering guests arriving for one of Mother's soirees, to grow up listening to laughter pealing through the small hours, wondering why her mother never laughed like that with her. Julia only wished for a quiet domesticity, something like that she imagined might exist in Catherine's house, or in a cottage by the sea, a place with peace within four walls, a child, and her husband.

Her husband. Her eyes burned, her throat clogged. The ache grew in her heart.

Three days later
"Now, Julia, I hope you will take some time to rest. It simply will not do for you to carry on this way, tending to that little boy's every cry as though we don't have a capable staff and a highly qualified nurse."

Julia bit her tongue, as she'd been forced

160

to do a dozen times since removing to Mother's house. Yes, she knew she needed sleep, she *craved* sleep — longed for it with every ounce of her being — but her inner restlessness would not allow it. Whether it was simply induced by tiredness or whether she writhed against the resumption of the old roles of Mother Superior and her inferior daughter, she couldn't help but feel edgy, like she wanted to cry, or scream, or shake something, or do something wild and extremely irresponsible. All she knew was that she seemed to be holding onto a veneer of social polish by the outermost edge of her teeth.

It had only taken a day of Mother's self-imposed exile from the whirl of engagements with friends and mantua-makers before she recollected how boring she found maternal duties. A smile twisted Julia's lips. Of course, she should have remembered just how tiresome Mother had found the banalities of raising her own children. Or maybe it was just Julia's upbringing she had thought best left to other people. Mother had always liked Jonathan more.

"Julia? Why are you looking like that?"

"I'm sorry, like what?"

"Perhaps you should come with me. It might do you some good to get out into the fresh air. Perhaps a carriage ride to Hyde Park —"

"No." Be looked at by gossips? She would sink.

"Really, Julia, you are not looking at all well. I cannot think you would want to be cooped up in here, hovering about as if waiting for that child to cry. That is what we have Crabbit for."

How to explain the worry that made her desperate to attend him, to ensure he would be well? "Mother, I have no inclination for anything of a social nature. I will try to rest, I promise."

"Well, I hope so."

At just that moment the sound of crying started up again. Julia caught the look of exasperation flitting across Mother's features, the way she glanced at Julia as if expecting her to run to the child's aid. Julia forced her feet to remain still.

"Please, my dearest daughter, let Crabbit do her job. If you become exhausted then things will be all the harder for everyone."

"I will go upstairs now," she promised.

"To rest?"

"Yes." She summoned up a smile, forced it to not waver. "I appreciate your solicitude for me, Mother."

"Hmm." Her mother eyed her with that

shrewd look that suggested she'd seen past the façade to Julia's frustration, but was not going to speak about it anymore. "Well, if you do find yourself resting, I'll ensure you are not disturbed, not even for dinner if you wish."

"I would appreciate that, thank you."

Mother drew near and, with a small, sad smile, caressed her cheek. "I just want you to be happy, my dear, and I know when we're overtired how difficult a thing that can be."

Her solicitude made the oh-so-ready tears spring to Julia's eyes. To her surprise, and relief, Mother said nothing further, only kissed her brow, then sent her upstairs, proclaiming to the servants that under no circumstances was Miss Julia to be disturbed, and any visitors were to be denied entry.

Julia dragged her feet up to the landing, turning to lift a hand as her mother called her farewell before the front door was closed behind her.

Perhaps her heart was too quick to find fault with her mother, for she was tired. *So* tired. A desperate chuckle broke past her weariness. She might writhe against being treated like a child and being sent to bed, but it appeared sometimes such things were indeed necessary.

Charles's crying, which had abated, suddenly roared back to life. She gritted her teeth, wondering why his cries could slice through her skin like no other sound. No wonder Mother was so keen to escape the little boy. The poor pet was not a happy lad these days.

She hesitated at her bedchamber door. She should sleep . . . but what if he was crying because he didn't like the new nurse Mother had employed? Mother had misliked the nursemaid Serena had employed, saying she had a sly look about her, and wouldn't trust *that* woman in her house if her life depended on it. Well, maybe Mother's life did not, but Charles's life certainly did. She turned her unsteady steps to the nursery on the second floor.

"Hello, Crabbit."

"Good afternoon, miss."

Julia didn't bother to correct the appellation, even though during the darkest hours of night she wondered just what the servants thought of her. A jade? A fallen woman? Another way she had changed — caring what servants might think. Stifling the insecurities, she moved to where the nurse held the little boy in her arms.

"Sorry, miss," Crabbit murmured. "It

always takes a while for the child to recognize a new set of arms."

"Of course." His crying soothed a fraction as she smoothed a hand over his gingery curls, and joined her voice to the nurse's implores to hush. "Come, little man, it's time to get to sleep."

He hiccupped, then drew in a shaky breath, as if uncertain whether to scream or settle.

"Ah, the sweet lad knows his mother's voice."

Julia forced a smile, remorse writhing within. No, he would never know his mother's voice again.

Charles squirmed a little longer, and she dropped her hand, stepped away. Perhaps Mother was right and she should let the nursemaid do her job. "Shh, it's time for sleep."

Yet his anxious red face still twisted guilt inside. Had she done badly traveling an immense distance with such a young babe? So many times she'd begged for a little milk for him, but too often had to make do with water or thin gruel. Had the deprivation harmed him? Numbers of people on her journey had proved kind, and had even gone out of their way to assist when they saw Charles's tender age. But she was one of countless poor travelers, far too many of whom held the emaciated look of numerous cares and inadequate sustenance.

The questions had been alleviated somewhat by the doctor's visit yesterday, assuring Julia that little Charles was growing healthy and strong, and the crying bouts were nothing to be worried about. His words reassured somewhat, but she would feel easier if the little boy slept.

He stirred, opening his dark eyes in that unblinking gaze she found mesmerizing, before screwing his face up and beginning another bout of hearty tears, a saw-like sound that penetrated between heart and skin.

"There, there," Crabbit said. "Let's have none of that, my lad. Your pretty mother needs her sleep, too." She offered Julia a look of supreme capability mixed with complacent superiority. "Now don't worry, miss. I'll stay here with him and you can go have a rest."

"Are you sure?"

"I'm sure little Charles isn't the only one in desperate need of sleep."

Julia offered a weary smile. "Very well."

But when she removed to her bedchamber, rest would not come. Not with the curtains pulled tight, not with a pillow over her eyes, not even when she exchanged her morning gown for nightwear and slipped under the covers, begging her body to respond to nighttime cues. She still felt that restlessness, that anxious unease. Perhaps reading would dull her senses and allow her sleep.

She threw off the covers, slipped on a robe, and moved downstairs — mercifully absent of either baby cries or servants — to the bookshelves that anchored a corner of the drawing room. After a moment of looking at the titles she picked up a copy of *Pope's Sermons,* checked the prose. Yes, that should suit. With the book tucked in her arm, she exited the room and moved to the staircase.

A knock came at the door. God forbid whoever it was saw her in such a state of *dishabille*! She hurried up the stairs to the landing, glancing down to where a footman was opening the door.

And heard a voice. A masculine, deep voice. A familiar voice. The book slid from her grasp as her heart began a rapid tattoo. No.

"I'm sorry, sir, but Miss Julia is not at home."

The standard reply to unexpected visitors. But *this* visitor . . .

Her mouth had dried. She swallowed. Swallowed again. "Thank you, William," she finally managed to call, grasping the hand-rail, ignoring the footman's look of surprise as she descended the stairs unsteadily. "I am home."

Like she was in a trance, she slowly walked towards the vestibule, her gaze fixed on the face she'd wondered if she'd ever see again. "Thank you, William, you may go."

She vaguely heard the sound of his retreat, her gaze refusing to leave the familiar features, at once so well-known and yet so different, his cheeks carved sharper, his coffee-colored eyes holding something that looked like suffering. "Thomas."

"Hello, Jewel."

His eyes, dark, intense, searched her hungrily, like he couldn't get enough. Her breath caught. Her heart's pounding intensified. The unsteadiness begged release. "What . . . what are you doing here?"

His lips twisted with that wryness she remembered. "Looking for you."

A rushing sound filled her ears. Dizziness consumed her, like she might faint. He stepped forward and — just as her knees buckled — caught her.

Then she was in his arms, smelling his musky scent, feeling the bristles of his chin, hearing his murmured endearments. She was dimly aware of being carried through the empty hall to the drawing room, the door closing, being carefully laid on the couch. She closed her eyes. This wasn't real. Was it? Or was she reliving their honeymoon, a few nights in a little place called Kirkcudbright, a Scottish hamlet on the coast near the Solway Firth. Those nights learning to love, learning to be loved, learning what it was to be husband and wife in every sense. She *had* to be dreaming. It must be her exhaustion —

"Oh, my darling, how I've missed you!" he murmured, his lips grazing her brow.

Her eyelids flew open. It *was* real. He *was* here, alive, his eyes feasting on her, like he had never wanted to be parted. She reached out a hand, touched the roughness of his chin, felt his exhalation on her skin. "I thought you were dead."

He gave another of those expressive grimaces. "Nearly."

"I waited, and waited . . ." Her eyes filled with tears.

"I'm so sorry." His lips were on her forehead, on her cheeks, before hesitating above her own. There was a moment when their breath mingled, their gazes intertwined, the longing she knew she could see echoed in his, then their lips met in a kiss at once familiar and yet new.

Something like a deep internal sigh released.

He wrapped his arms around her, a cocoon of affection and assurance. Her senses tingled at remembered nearness, her earlier anxious exhaustion now replaced with wild elation. Heart singing, she wrapped her arms around his neck, and gave herself up to that kiss, returning his fervency with passion of her own. In this moment, she had no need for explanations; it was enough that he was alive, he was here, and he still loved her.

"Darling Julia, we should not stay here," he finally murmured, his voice thick with ardor. "Your mother —"

"Is not here," she whispered against his cheek.

"But the servants . . ."

Could come in at any moment, would see the daughter of the house engaged in *most* unladylike conduct, thus confirming their worst suspicions. She drew in a sharp breath, pushed him away, pushed herself into an upright position. "Come upstairs."

"What? I cannot — your mother . . . the servants —"

She laughed softly. "My mother *and* the

servants believe me to be resting."

"But the footman —"

"Will say nothing. He didn't see you come inside, did he?"

"I don't believe so."

She pushed to her feet, saw how his gaze trailed her attire, his look of surprise melding into renewed desire. She gathered his face in her hands, pressed her lips to his, and murmured, "I've missed you."

His pupils dilated, he finally nodded, and she tugged him from the room, across the room, up the stairs, to her bedchamber, and closed the door, heart exultant such a journey was accomplished without witness.

She leaned against the oak door, saw him glance around the dim room, notice the rumpled state of her bed, the way his attention returned to her, how he eyed her like a thirsty man might eye a long glass of fresh water. Yet still he hesitated, like he dared not move without her say so. So she smiled, and locked the door, and moved toward him.

His eyes darkened further, yet he remained unmoving. "What do you want from me?"

Just this.

And she arched up and pressed her lips against his.

She felt the moment of surprise, then the

171

surrender, as his arms encircled her, and crushed her to himself, like he never wanted to let go. His kiss grew deeper, drugging her with its intensity, as his body against hers rekindled fire deep within.

She dragged her lips away, desperate for breath, only to hear him whisper, "I love you."

The past months' mysteries did not matter; he was here, with her, in this moment made for love. The rest did not signify. Not Charles. Not her mother. Not Jon. Nothing.

"I love you, too."

Then his lips found hers again, his arms — so strong, bunching with muscle — gathered her close, his kiss holding her, assuring her, adoring her, promising his future with her, until her freshly awoken senses reminded her whirling thoughts that the best thing they could do was to relax, and not worry about a thing.

CHAPTER TWELVE

Thomas blinked, his eyes taking a moment to adjust to the dimness, the unfamiliarity of the room. The scent of something sweet teased his senses, begging him to inhale more. Gradually the corners of his mind sharpened, his senses roused, his thinking cleared, his reason for being where he was filling his chest with exultation and something deeper, something like profound relief.

The bed dipped as he shifted to his side, Julia's bare back before him, the fragile, slender curve of her spine bringing a smile to his face. He traced a finger down her perfect skin, marveling at the texture, glad she did not stir. Her skin had always fascinated him, so fair, so smooth, so unblemished, so unlike his own. The differences in their skin seemed almost representative of something deeper: she was soft and pure and lovely; he was hardened, darkened by an Indian sun, scored by life experiences he only wanted to forget. His heart panged; he strove to ignore it. There'd be time enough for explanations, on both their sides. He leaned close and breathed in her scent, that fragrance that reminded him of perfume, like the vanilla-scented orchids huddling in the garden his mother used to grow back in Norfolk.

Memories rose; he pushed them away. Moved instead to brush the lightest of kisses on her shoulder, to savor once more that sweet aroma. "I love you," he whispered.

Her cheeks rounded, as though she smiled in her sleep. Was he a fool to think his words brought happiness to his wife? Perhaps. But he cared not. His body, relaxed for the first time in what felt like years, begged him to sleep, too, but watching his wife sleep had always been one of his favorite things. He liked to see the look of contentment on her face, knowing he was responsible.

He peered closer through the dawn light seeping past the curtains, saw her lips were indeed curved as he'd hoped, so eased back against the pillows, satisfaction filling his chest. A smile tugged at the corners of his mouth as he stared up at the intricate plasterwork gracing the ceiling. How wonderful, how astounding, that things should have worked out so smoothly. He had scarcely expected such a thing, when, after finally arriving earlier than expected in London, and stealing a few moments at a cheap inn to bathe and assume an appearance more respectable, he had arrived late morning at Carmichael's London town house only to find it closed up and absent of servants. His spirits had dropped; he'd need to see Jon, somehow explain his absence in the hope of forgiveness and Julia's direction. But when he had called there, the servant answering the door had informed him that Lord and Lady Winthrop were out for the day. His hopes plummeting further, he hadn't left a name, had thought of nothing more than proceeding to Julia's mother's house as quickly as he could and throwing himself at her feet in the hopes of finding a smidge of mercy.

Then when the servant had said she, too, was absent, before denying Julia's presence as well, his heart had felt like it might crack under the weight of despair, only to miraculously be restored by the heaven-sent sight of his wife walking towards him, her eyes wide with the wonder he too felt deep within his soul. For a few moments, she had seemed to waver, but then her earnest response, her deeply satisfying response, had left him in no doubt as to how she might feel.

She loved him. She had forgiven him. He wanted nothing more.

He tugged the covers higher, closed his eyes and floated to sleep.

A sound, like that of rattling keys, woke him. His ears pricked, his body tensed, heart hammering. Where — ? The soft bed reassured. He exhaled. Julia's mother's house. The murmur of voices wafted through the door. It had been a miracle they'd been undisturbed for so long.

"Julia."

She slumbered on, her need for rest suggesting she'd slept as little as he had in recent times. "Sweetheart," he murmured. "Sweetheart, wake up."

"No," she mumbled. "This has been such a lovely dream. Don't want to wake . . ."

He smiled, leaning close to press a kiss against her bare shoulder. "Much as I wish we could stay here forever, I think someone might be outside."

"What?" Her eyes widened and she sat up, the blanching of her face suggesting she heard the sound of people outside, too. "Oh, no!"

A knock came at the door, followed by a

voice, a voice he knew only too well. "Julia? Julia, are you in there?"

Fear slid onto her face. "Mother," she whispered.

"Julia? Is someone else in there with you? I can hear voices."

Amusement flashed across Julia's face before fleeing again, replaced by that look of fear. "What should I say?"

"You could tell her most people who hear voices are sent to Bedlam."

She made a muffled sound, as if choking back laughter, before worry filled her eyes once more. The gentle knocking quickly intensified in both force and volume.

"Julia? Open this door at once!"

She shot him a glance, and he gestured for her to say something. She sighed, then called out, "Mother?"

"Julia? Oh, my dear girl! We were dreadfully concerned that something had happened."

He bit back a laugh. Something most definitely had.

She threw him a mock glare and cleared her throat before saying, "I'm sorry you were worried. I seem to have slept rather long."

"I should think you have. But you must have needed such a thing."

He couldn't help it. He laughed.

Julia's mouth sagged, her blue eyes as wide as saucers.

The dreadful silence outside the door was replaced by louder murmurs, then a renewed knocking. "Julia! Who is in there with you? Open this door at once."

Thomas slid from the bed, dragging on his clothes with as much speed as possible. He for one was not going to be discovered in the buff by his mother-in-law. "Get dressed," he hissed at Julia, who seemed frozen by indecision.

"Julia, I demand you open this door."

His wife turned to him, hands raised in an attitude of helplessness. "What do I do?"

"Do you want your mother to see you dressed like that?" He gestured to the sheet.

"Oh, my goodness!"

She slipped from the bed, forcing him to pause in his attempts to tie his neckcloth to admire her form. She picked up her nightgown from the floor and pulled it on.

"Julia?"

The sound of keys fitting into the lock spurred her to hasten to untwist the lock, and almost tumble out the door. "Yes, Mother, what is it?"

Thomas held his breath, indecision staying his steps. Should he make his presence

178

known, or would it be best for Julia if he stayed where he was, half-hidden by a large wardrobe?

He edged forward half a step then paused. Lady Harkness pushed past Julia into the room. She took a look at the rumpled bed linen, uttered an inarticulate cry, and glanced around the room, until finally, her eyes fixed on him. "No!"

Thomas drew himself up, trying desperately to remember he'd once led hundreds of troops into battle, had once faced a charging elephant. But all of that paled in comparison to the woman bearing down upon him now.

"How dare you?" She lifted a pointing finger. "How *dare* you come into my house!"

He eyed her advance, working to keep his voice level as he said in a low voice, "How dare you try and keep her from me?"

"Me?" Green eyes blazing, she lifted a hand and struck him across the cheek.

A flash of pain spread across his face. His anger surged, but he clenched his jaw, refusing to show any reaction. That way weakness lay.

"How dare you speak so? Not when you are the" — she spat an obscenity — "who stole my precious daughter away, convincing her with your lies —"

He watched her warily, ready to dodge should she try to strike again, wishing Julia — and the rest of the household staff — could not hear the woman's diatribe. When it seemed she had finally run out of breath, he simply said, "I am sorry for the manner in which we wed, but cannot be sorry for loving your daughter. She is —"

Smack!

"Mama!"

He blinked, gritting his teeth as fierce fire swept through his other cheek, due only in part from the woman's hand. Well, he hadn't seen that one coming. "Would it make you feel better, madam, to treat me like one of Jackson's boxing bags?"

"Yes, it would!" she snarled, reached up, her hands like talons, ripping into his face.

"Mother, stop!" screamed Julia. "Stop it, both of you!"

He grabbed his mother-in-law's wrists and held them loosely but securely, glaring at her with the look that had flailed many a subordinate in India. "You must stop such unseemly behavior," he said in a low voice. "You're embarrassing yourself in front of your staff and upsetting my wife."

"Julia is *my* daughter," she panted. "*My* daughter, not your wife."

"Your daughter *and* my wife."

She jerked her wrists from his grip and rushed to Julia's side, holding her tightly. "I will not let you take her again. You cannot take her. You cannot!"

"Madam, I have no desire to bring further estrangement between you and Julia, but Julia herself must speak about what she desires."

"You admit then that you brought division between us!"

"A division caused by the separation of miles, but" — he softened his voice — "I believe the estrangement existed long before I was on the scene."

"How dare you?" she said, her eyes rekindling with resentment. "I hate you! I will never forgive you for what you have done."

"As I said, madam, I am sorry for having caused you grief, but I cannot apologize for my feelings about Julia. I love her."

"Love her?" she sneered. "That's a fine way to speak when you abandoned her for half a year!"

Julia, whose horrified face kept glancing between them, grew even paler. "Mother, that is something between Thomas and me."

"Oh, no, it is not. His actions have affected us all! He is therefore obliged to explain to us all."

Julia turned to him, her face white, her expression pleading. "Thomas?"

He drew near, secured her hands in his. "And so I shall, but not like this." He glanced to the open door, to the servants who suddenly scuttled away, no doubt to pretend to do something while still keeping their ears peeled for further sounds of discord.

His attention returned to Lady Harkness. "I am quite willing to explain my actions over the past months, but my wife is owed the respect of hearing such things first. I would appreciate the opportunity to do so privately."

"I've no doubt you would, and no doubt that you'd twist the truth to suit your own purposes!"

"I would tell her all —"

"You will only manipulate her and lie!"

His eyes narrowed. "I am a man of my word."

"You are a conniver and a sneak! How else would you convince her to . . ." Her words faltered, her gesture to the rumpled bed revealing just what she thought he'd done.

He glanced at Julia, his lips tweaking in a half smile he hoped reassured. No, he wouldn't expose just who had led whom to *that*.

Smoothing his face to neutrality, he offered Lady Harkness a bow. "I shall return in two hours, when Julia is dressed and ready, and shall speak with her then. Then, if she is willing, I shall endeavor to explain things to you and your son." He gave a tight smile. "I'm sure you'll be able to summon him here in that time."

"What if he's not in London?"

"Oh, I know he is." He flicked at his sleeve. "His servants told me just yesterday."

He offered her another bow before stepping forward to swiftly kiss his wife. Heard the hiss of disapprobation. Endeavored to reassure Julia with a press of his lips to the back of her hand. "I will return, I promise."

"In two hours?"

"Yes."

And with a warm smile for his wife and none for her mother, he executed a final bow and made his exit.

CHAPTER THIRTEEN

"Julia, you have no idea how ashamed I am of your conduct right now!"

Her mother's usual implacability seemed gone forever, the reddened cheeks and angry glint in her eyes suggesting that sparks might erupt any moment. Oh, she had some idea.

"How you could think of speaking to him — let alone anything else! Oh, I'm so ashamed I barely know where to begin!"

"Mother, he *is* my husband —"

"Is he? Is he really? How can we be sure of anything that man says? It may be well and good for some to say that such marriages in Scotland are legal but *I* am not convinced. Such barbaric practices —"

"Hardly barbaric, Mother," Julia murmured, her mother heedless, her diatribe persisting.

Perhaps the method of transport to Gretna Green had been a little unorthodox, the flight by carriage from Bath to Bristol, the sailing ship to Liverpool, before the mad dash — "like a greased flash of lightning" the postboy had said — to the border.

But the ceremony itself had been proper enough, albeit not in a church but in a whitewashed sitting room in a country inn, before a clerical-looking gentleman, and a collection of tavern keepers, postboys, and peddlers, who appeared to have more curiosity than wit. Instead of a prayer book there was a simple request if they were willing to marry, to which they agreed, then a plain gold ring was placed on her finger. They were asked to fill in a paper, headed by the Royal Arms of the United Kingdom, with the names of the parties joined together in holy matrimony, and the witnesses thereof. A simple declaration that they were man and wife, a handshake and a kiss, and that was it.

There had been no coercion; she had been willing. Thomas had paid the blacksmith-parson twenty pounds. They had had champagne, then a meal, before being escorted to a perfectly adequate bedchamber, where she had truly become a wife. Heat filled her cheeks.

"Yes, I should think you would look like that!"

Julia lowered her eyes to hide her conflicted amusement.

"For I do not trust him, not for a second!" There was a pause in the tirade, and Julia forced herself to look upwards to encounter her mother's raised brow. "Well? Nothing else to say for yourself?"

"Nothing that you would wish to hear," she murmured.

Her mother's eyes flashed, and she opened her mouth to speak but seemed to think better of it, as she closed her lips, turned on her heel, and walked past the gaping servants and away.

Julia closed her eyes, her emotions tipping up and down, lurching through her midsection not unlike the nausea incited by her runaway voyage from Bristol to Liverpool. What a mad four-and-twenty hours the last day had proved! And what a wonderful day it had proved also. Who would have thought such a thing might occur? Her eyes opened as a smile crept onto her face. Thomas had been everything she remembered: gentle yet strong, handsome yet humble, his passion tempered by humor. Granted, his hair was a little longer than she remembered, and he seemed thinner and wearier than she recalled. She frowned. From the way they both had slept so long, it seemed his exhaustion matched hers.

"Excuse me, miss."

Her reflections were interrupted by Crabbit's voice from the door, assuring her that Master Charles had slept well and was even now playing happily. Her report was followed by the entry of the maid wishing to know if she might be helped into her gown. She acquiesced, nodded for another maid to clean and tidy the bedchamber, all the while silent, waiting for them to leave, while her mind spun with the possibilities of what he might say.

That he loved her, she now knew. That she still loved him, she realized, too. For as soon as the shock of his appearance had faded, she knew that under the confusion and the arrows of resentment her love had never really died. But that didn't stop the questions. What could have kept him away for so long? And how could they make their marriage work? Where would they live? Was there income for a flat? What would he do? What would he say? What would Jon say?

She had no doubt that Mother was at this moment sending a servant to Jon's, nor that she would insist on having him here to hear Thomas's explanation, Mother reasoning his words might yet be edited for the ears of someone not his wife. Julia chewed the inside of her bottom lip. Thomas would not manipulate the truth, would he? He could be trusted.

Couldn't he?

The zephyr of doubt floated through her heart, stirring the trust rekindled in his arms.

"Will that be all, miss?"

Was that contempt in the chambermaid's eyes? Julia lifted her chin and nodded. Oh, why had Mother not thought to hide the family troubles from the servants by shutting the door and lowering her voice?

She sighed, smoothed her skirts, and moved downstairs, past the wide-eyed footmen, past the watching maids, and entered the drawing room. She chose the sofa where he had carried her, striving for dignity, while the tumult in her breast, the memories of his kiss, held sway. Oh, that he could take her home, wherever home might be now. A pang struck. Had it been wrong for her to leave Edinburgh without word? He had found her, to be sure, but perhaps explanations might prove necessary on both sides. Regardless, he would be here soon, the doorbell would sound, and the next stage of her life would begin.

Please God . . . she dared pray. *Please let everything be sorted out at last.*

The doorbell rang. She leapt to her feet, then resumed her seat again. It would not do to look too eager, even if she could not wait to feel his arms around her again, to feel his lips pressing on hers, his hands —

She blushed, ears straining to discern the words the low voice was saying out there. She was pretty sure she heard a "Julia" and a "Charles," but the rest was too faint. She forced herself to remain seated as the door opened and in walked —

"Jon!" Her heart, her shoulders slumped.

"I'm here to protect you," he said, his mouth tilting as if in semblance of a smile. But his features didn't light, his eyes hard and flinty.

"You mean protect me from myself." She phrased it as a statement, not a question, and was unsurprised at his nod.

"Catherine did not wish me to come, she thinks it best you and Hale speak alone —"

"That was good of her," she managed, in a tone that did not sound too sarcastic.

He lifted an eyebrow. "And I was half-inclined to agree with her —"

"Jon!"

He ignored their mother, his eyes fixed on Julia. "But your attitude reminded me of all the reasons why I should be here. I do not trust Hale not to induce you to actions you

189

will further regret."

She tossed her head. "I don't regret *any* of my actions with him."

"Not even those from this morning?" said her mother. "My dear, I cannot understand why you would agree to such a thing!"

"And why shouldn't I sleep with my husband?" Julia flared. "We are married! We love each other —"

"What I don't understand is what he was doing here in the first place. Did you have some secret assignation?"

"Jonathan!"

"I just wish the servants did not know," Mother moaned. "It is bad enough for our friends to speculate about my daughter, but for the servants to gossip —"

"They wouldn't have known if you hadn't insisted on coming into my room," she muttered.

"Have you lost all respect for your family?" Jon said.

"I believed you to be ill!"

"Mother, you told me to sleep as long as I needed."

"But not with another person in your bed!"

Heat filled her chest, and she clenched her fingers into fists. What could she say to make them understand? She exhaled, forced

190

herself to calm, to look them levelly in the eye. "I love him."

Her mother protested, and her brother said in his deep voice, "He is not someone you should waste another second of your life on."

She shook her head, resuming her earlier dignified posture. "When he returns, I hope you will do him the courtesy of listening."

"When he returns," her mother jeered. "You cannot count on that man to keep his word."

"He will prove you wrong," Julia said, tossing her head.

"Well, if he's to do that he'd better get here soon. It's almost at time."

Julia waited, working hard to ignore their muttered censure, working to calm the tumult in her breast. Thomas would come; he would! And they would leave this place, leave London, go and live in a sweet cottage somewhere in the country with little Charles and be so happy —

Charles.

Her heart wrenched. She would need to tell Thomas about Charles. She would need to tell him the *truth* about little Charles. Her teeth caught her bottom lip. Yes, further explanations were indeed most necessary on both their parts.

The nearer the clock's hands drew to the hour appointed for his arrival, the greater the tumult within her breast. She had to force herself to remain still, to not look anxious, even as the expressions of doubt continued from her mother and brother.

Please God, let Thomas come, and let his explanation be all that can be acceptable. Not that she believed her mother and brother would consider very much to be acceptable. But perhaps something he would say might cause them to bend to his favor.

The clock struck two, and she had to force herself to breathe, her ears alert for every sound. Surely he would come. Surely. He had to!

The minute hand passed a full rotation, and she could not look. Well, if he was a minute late, that would be perfectly understandable. Perhaps his pocket-watch was in error.

Four more minutes passed before her mother turned to her triumphantly and said, "He's late."

"He's on his way," Julia murmured.

"He's not. He's taken his pleasure and now he's off doing goodness knows what —"

"How can you say such things, Jon? He was your friend!"

"*Was* being the operative word."

"Surely you could see his good qualities, otherwise you would not have befriended him."

"He misrepresented himself."

"Oh, and you've never done such a thing?"

His cheeks reddened, but his gaze remained fixed and hard. "I like to think my character is one that can be considered trustworthy."

"One can trust you to cast off your friends, that is certainly true."

His eyes narrowed. "What do you mean by that?"

She lifted a shoulder. "Simply that I cannot think it such a Christian attitude to cast off your friends just because they don't agree with you."

"And I don't think it a very Christian attitude to stand by and condone the actions of a rake with my foolish sister," he said in a level voice.

Heat rushed through her chest. Well, there was no point continuing this. She tilted her chin and resumed her attitude of detachment as she waited for the knock that would signal Thomas's arrival.

But such a pose was hard to maintain when the clock struck the quarter hour, and her mother's expressed doubts began gnawing away at her self-control. Thomas was on his way. He had to be. He wouldn't let her down.

"I told you he would not come," her mother said, a tight smile on her face. "You must face facts, my dear. Your husband is, as Jon says, a rake, who only seeks his own interest. You would be far better to forget him —"

"He must be delayed!" Julia said, in a voice far louder and less controlled than she intended. "I am certain he will arrive at any moment."

But behind the bravado, her certainty was beginning to falter, fueled as it was by her brother's and mother's oft-expressed recriminations. She forced herself to avoid their eyes, to avoid their looks of pity, as she remained seated.

Even as the clock showed half past two.

Even as the clock struck three.

Even as her mother and brother cast her pitying looks before exiting.

Even as the shadows lengthened through the room.

Even as she sat in a darkness as heavy as the one filling her heart, her heart that was breaking. He had not come. Was she such a fool to believe — to hope — he loved her?

Perhaps her family was right, and she was

wrong, and Thomas could never be trusted to keep his word.

Perhaps this marriage which she so valiantly tried to believe worth fighting for was nothing more than a fool's paradise, one to which she had too eagerly succumbed.

Perhaps their relationship was as Jon described, with Thomas as a snake who charmed a mouse with its hypnotic eyes. She was the mouse, the mouse that had been mesmerized, seduced, devoured, before the snake moved on to further prey.

Her heart wrenched, her eyes filled, she bent her head, and in the darkness, she wept.

"Ah. Major Hale. It has been some time since we've met."

"Certainly has," Thomas gritted out. "Perhaps, sir, you were not aware that we were captured within a week of our arrival."

Colonel Fallbright, his former commanding officer in Poona and in more recent times, elevated to serve in the Foreign Office in a division known for its covert operations, eyed him with a look not wholly pleasant in his rather protuberant blue eyes. "I sense a degree of frustration, Hale."

"You could say that, sir, seeing as we were held in that prison for nearly six months."

"These things happen. They are the risks one assumes in such a role."

"I understand that, sir, but —"

But it seemed as though his commanding officer had no interest in anything but the sound of his own voice, frustrating Thomas's attempts to explain why he was here, instead of being with Julia to offer far more important explanations.

Not ten minutes after leaving Portman Square he'd been accosted by a former fellow soldier, whose startled exclamation had made him pause, turn, and hold out his hand.

"Captain Wheeler."

"Major Hale." They shook hands. "This is a surprise. Word was that you were dead."

"And yet here I am." Why did so many of his former colleagues think such things? It was enough to make a man mistrustful. "Tell me, is the old battle-axe still in charge?"

"Do you mean Colonel Fallbright?" Wheeler said stiffly.

"I think you know I do," Thomas said, eyeing his friend. Why did the man seem so standoffish? He never used to be.

"Well, yes, he is."

"Good. I need a word with him. Do you still act as his secretary?"

196

"Why, yes, but I'm afraid he's a very busy man —"

"Then he'll understand I have need to speak with him urgently, as I am a very busy man also."

"You?"

"Yes. I have but very recently returned to London, and my wife awaits my return —"

"Oh, well, then you should go to her."

Thomas gritted his teeth at the man's patronizing attitude. He would return but not before he received his dues. If he could return with the finances owed him, then surely Julia and her mother would be far more open to receive him. And if that necessitated a short delay while he did so, well, Julia would understand. He hoped. "And so I will, but I wish to clarify some matters with the colonel first."

"I'm afraid you will need an appointment."

"Consider this me making one."

"Yes, but I'm afraid he won't be able to see anyone today."

"Nonsense. He will see me. Surely he wishes to know how the mission went."

"Well —" Wheeler coughed. "I'm afraid the thinking around Whitehall is that the mission failed when you did not return as promised."

"As promised?" Irritation prickled against his chest. "Tell me, is he in his office today?"

"I . . . I cannot say."

"His own secretary does not know? Seems it more a case of *will* not say," Thomas said, his misgivings growing. "Very well. I shall go see him myself now."

"Oh, but sir —"

Thomas shook his head and strode off in the direction of Whitehall, unsurprised by Wheeler's shouts behind him. A hackney rolled past a minute later and he spied Wheeler's profile. His suspicions rose all the more. Why was Wheeler so insistent he not speak with the colonel? Mistrust stirred his feet to a faster walk through the cross streets, and then a run.

By the time he arrived at the building that housed the Secretary of State for War and the Colonies, he was hauling in great breaths, doing his best to approximate the appearance of a gentleman, though he suspected his efforts were in vain. He strode through the front doors, ignored the porter's request to halt, and hurried up the marble stairs to the offices of those involved in England's activities overseas. He ignored the muffled oaths as he passed men he'd considered more like friends than mere acquaintances, and opened the door to the colonel's chamber.

Wheeler's desk was empty, the muffled voices from the room beyond giving little doubt as to where the secretary was.

"I say, sir —"

Thomas shrugged off a restraining hand, clasped the door handle, and plunged into the room, the urgent conversation coming to a startled stop.

After the preliminary expressions of mutual pleasure at renewed acquaintance were exchanged, Wheeler was dismissed, the door was closed, and Thomas was finally face-to-face with the man who had orchestrated the fateful mission. Fallbright's sonorous explanation finally wound to a close, with the reiteration of his earlier comment. "Those are the risks when one assumes such a role. Besides which, you were ably compensated."

"I'm afraid not, sir, which is why I am here." Instead of being where he'd prefer, with his wife. As Fallbright began another lengthy exposition on the honor of serving one's country and the King, and how demands for recompense were anathema to those of true honor, Thomas's frustration mounted.

"That may be so, sir, but I have not seen a penny of what I am owed, and I must press for reimbursement for both myself and those men I served with."

"Well, I can understand your desire —"

"Forgive me, but I don't think you really can, sir. I repeat, I have seen nothing of what I was promised, and I'm afraid the need for money is becoming increasingly urgent each day."

"I am sorry you have not managed your finances more appropriately, Hale —"

Thomas ground his teeth.

"But my hands are tied. I'm afraid the promise of reward was entirely dependent on the success of the mission, and as you have yet to deliver any information of value, then I cannot distribute funds. I'm sure you can understand."

"What I understand, sir, is that you sent myself and five others to Spain on a mission that seemed doomed for failure from the outset! There was nothing to indicate insurgency as you suggested, rather a feeling of relief that the war was over. We encountered none of the conditions you said we would, but rather the opposite. Indeed," he eyed the older man narrowly, "it seemed almost a fool's errand, with nothing to suppose such a place could warrant any interest from the British government at all."

Colonel Fallbright sat back in his chair, his expression inscrutable. "What are you saying, Hale?"

"I am saying, sir, that it appears that we were sent on a mission of no worth and no substance."

"Are you accusing me of something?" Fallbright said softly.

Thomas opened his mouth to speak, then closed it. Something suggested he tread very carefully, if he ever wanted to see a penny for the past half year of hard labor. *Help me say this right.* He took a deep breath, forced his tone to sound conciliatory. "Sir, I simply wish to know when my men and I can expect to see some form of compensation."

"And as I said earlier, that money was entirely dependent on receiving news that was satisfactory. And as that has not been delivered, and definitely not within the time frame allocated, then I'm afraid there is nothing more that can be said on the matter."

Thomas blinked, rekindled anger pushing against the cage of his ribs. "Are you saying my men will not receive a penny?"

"I'm afraid so."

He breathed out a long, uneven breath. *Dear God, have mercy.* "You are aware, are you not, that two of the men died in prison, and their families have been left destitute?"

"An unfortunate consequence."

201

"Not unfortunate. Tragic!"

"There is no need to take that tone with me, Hale. I will do what I can —"

"Will you? I rather feel that you would prefer me to have died than to have returned."

The colonel was a second too late in his protestation.

Thomas stared at him, uncertainty filling his chest. Why would his former commanding officer wish him dead? He stepped back, and said in a quieter voice, "I do not understand, sir, why you will not help me in this matter. It seems that you would prefer to ignore this, rather than wish to aid someone who only sought your good when we served in India."

Something — annoyance? regret? — flickered across his commanding officer's face before he said slowly, "Of course I am grateful for your help in Poona, Hale, but we cannot live under obligation for the rest of our lives."

His words weaseled into Thomas's efforts at mollification. If he returned with no money, what would Julia say? What would her mother say? "I'm not asking for a favor based on obligation," he managed, before desperation drove him further, "simply asking for what I and my men are due according to your word!"

The words rang through the chamber. Thomas noted with dismay that the colonel's face closed up, his features blanking to impassivity. Frustration lashed him. Why was the man so reluctant to assist him?

"Wheeler!"

The door opened behind Thomas. "Yes, sir?"

"Escort the major out."

"Sir, please," Thomas tried one more time. What did it matter if he appeared to beg? "The men are relying on this —"

"I've given you my answer, Hale. Good-bye."

His arm was grasped; Thomas shook it off. "Sir, if you do not, then I shall be forced to take matters to a higher authority. I will speak with Lord Bathurst."

"I rather doubt the Secretary of State will have time for you."

"Then I will speak with Undersecretary Goulburn."

Fallbright smiled. "As you wish. But you will not get far. Do you really think anyone will listen to a man like you, a known gambler and rake, when they will hear the truth from me?"

"The truth?" His fists clenched, he took a step closer to the pompous little man. "You

203

have said nothing but lies!"

A hand was clamped over his mouth, and he was yanked off his feet, his arms pinioned behind by another man. Thomas wrested his shoulder free, jerked his head away to shout. Seconds later a vicious blow splintered fire across his forehead, felling him to the floor. His head met the corner of a brass fireplace fender in a fresh burst of pain followed by merciful blackness.

Chapter Fourteen

He had not come.

He did not love her.

He was a liar, a bamboozler. He had used her — used her body — then abandoned her.

Again.

The enormity of his duplicity ballooned again within her chest, the heated pain threatening to crack her ribs. She closed her eyes against the trickling moisture, and drew in a breath. Released it. Drew in another breath. Caught the scent of Charlie's freshly washed hair. Forced her clutch on him to loosen a fraction, though she kept him close to her heart. His presence was solid comfort at a time when all else seemed unclear.

It was the knowledge that she had blithely allowed herself to be betrayed yet again that almost caused the greater sting. How could she be gulled once more? Her brother and mother had been proved right; her tears last night wretched acknowledgment of the fact.

The despair she had felt yesterday had this morning given way to something even more painful: the realization that she could no longer rely on her ability to sense right from wrong. Was her judgment so very poor? Had it always been this way? Mother seemed to think so, her endless complaints about the man who had stolen her only daughter's virtue gradually boring into Julia's ability to reason, her memories of why she had done what she had done.

Round and round the accusations circled, the only bright spot being the moment when little Charlie had been brought to her, and for a few precious minutes she could pretend that the past hours had been but an awful dream.

She closed her eyes, felt his tiny fingers brush her cheek. Her heart ached. Oh, that she could experience this sacred place of tenderness forever. Oh, that she could open her eyes and pretend this nightmare done. Was her mother right in desiring Julia's marriage to be annulled? What would have happened if she had never met Thomas, and fallen under his spell?

Her thoughts traced back to the first time she had seen him. Jon, newly returned from India, had brought his two friends with him to the house in Portman Square. Lord Carmichael had instantly impressed both her mother and herself with his title and smooth mix of polished manners and flattering attention.

But it was upon being introduced to Jon's other friend that she'd felt a tug, almost like a profound sense of recognition. Major Thomas Hale might not have the viscount's easy manner, nor the features most young ladies found attractive, but he possessed a certain something in his dark brown eyes that made her thrill whenever he gazed in her direction. She rather suspected those eyes had seen far more of the world than Jon had — his family, when questioned by Mother, was indeed less well connected and financed than hers. Those eyes had held a magnetic quality, one which made her quite unable to look away. And when he spoke — not with the flattering charm of Lord Carmichael, but with a wryness almost tinged with pain — something within her leapt to hear more, and all the poise she'd learned at Miss Ingham's Seminary for Young Ladies seemed to drain away, and she could only meet his enigmatic sayings with soft giggles and mild confusion. She must have seemed so very naïve to him. Was that why he had pursued her, made her fall in love with him?

Were Mother and Jon right, that Thomas only wanted her for the fortune she would inherit when she came of age?

At the sound of a knock at the door her eyes snapped open. Was he here now? Oh, all might be forgiven if he appeared, begged her forgiveness for his delay, and explained his absence these past months . . .

A sound of muffled voices at the door, then it was closed with a rather large bang. Had Mother refused him entry? Indignation filled her, forcing her to rise, being careful not to wake the sleeping child at her breast, as she peered through lace curtains to the street.

A peddler.

Her sigh woke poor Charlie, who stirred, his look of confusion swiftly followed by puckered lips which could only mean it was time for his next feed. His crying soon returned Crabbit to the parlor, and Julia was not at all sorry to relinquish her charge to the nurse. Not if it meant she could return to her contemplations from before, to consider what she would say or do if — or when — Thomas returned.

What would happen if Mother's threats to annul the marriage took on legal ramifications? Would Thomas really be sent to prison? She had heard of other men prosecuted for luring young ladies to a runaway marriage — some had even been hung for such an offense!

No — she shook her head — she might not understand all his reasons for abandoning her, but she could never wish such a fate for him.

"Ah, here you are," her mother said, entering the room. "How are you today?"

Julia eyed her dispassionately. Did her mother wish her to pretend all was well? She could not lie, so she said nothing.

"I do hope this resentment will not continue forever, my dear. Such childishness has carried on long enough."

Furious words burned within. She bit them back, to not give credence to her mother's accusation, and willed her face to neutrality.

Her mother's expression softened a mite. "I know this has been very hard for you, my dear, and I'm sure you feel a little confused at times. But I do hope you know Jon and I only want what is best for you."

"I know that, Mama," she said, her heart softening at the gratified look in her mother's eye. "But what if what is best for me is to be married to Thomas?"

That pleased look vanished. "You cannot be serious. He has proved his lack of honor one too many times, my girl. You did not seriously think he would return?"

"He is my *husband,*" she pleaded.

"But barely," her mother sniffed.

The door opened and Jon entered the room, greeting Mother with a kiss on the cheek and Julia with a bow that seemed a little strained. She forced a smile. She did not want to create further estrangement between her brother and herself, not after finally being reunited after these past two years apart.

"Good morning, Poppet."

His use of the old endearment suggested he felt the same, and stirred further feelings of conciliation. "Hello, Jon."

"Still no word?"

"Nothing," Mother confirmed.

His look spoke volumes of his resignation; his words confirming it all the more. "You know I am not surprised. I am sorry, Julia, but I cannot like what he is doing to you. You would be far better off to forget him, and we shall endeavor to purchase a divorce —"

"No, Jon. Marriage vows are sacred! Surely you must believe so."

A startled look crossed his features, as if he'd not previously contemplated her marriage in such terms. Hope rose. If only he could be brought to realize —

"Did you even make vows?" Mother questioned, a frown marring her brow. "I did not think a marriage would be considered sacred when not made within a church." Her frown plunged deeper. "You had no minister, did you? Not even a Scottish one?"

"No," she said in a small voice.

"Then I can hardly think God would be paying attention —"

"Mother."

Jon's deep voice brought their mother to a halt. She closed her mouth and looked at Jon with a puzzled air. "Yes?"

"I find I cannot subscribe to the notion that a marriage officiated outside of a church is anything less than valid in the eyes of the law. And it is the legality of the marriage that is in question here, not whether it is approved by God or not."

"Don't you think God would want me to honor my husband?" Julia demanded.

"I cannot think God would want you to honor vows made with a man who has proved himself to be a rake, if that is what you are asking."

There were footfalls, and the opened door widened, admitting another visitor.

"Oh!" Julia's gasp echoed that of her mother. Thomas's face was lined with bruises, as if he had been in a scuffle and left for dead. Yet here he was. At last.

Her heart pounded fiercely — finally, he was here! — but Thomas's grave expression was reserved for Jon.

"Good day, Lord Winthrop." A muscle ticked in and out of his jaw. Clearly, he had heard the words his once-best friend had uttered. Clearly, he was angry. Clearly, he was saddened. "I am sorry to hear the proverbial eavesdropper's lot is mine."

His gaze swept the room, including Mother in his small bow, before giving Julia a swift, strained smile. "I am glad to see you, my dear."

Julia forced a wobbly smile. Somehow standing there, before two members of the peerage, he seemed far more noble, his dignity high. This despite Mother's scratches that glowed red amid the bruising darkening his cheek. He looked quiet, but not chastened; humble, but not shamed.

"Excuse me, madam, but I believe I requested an interview with Julia initially."

Mother sniffed. "I do not recall you requesting an interview at all! Your high-handedness merely assumed one would be granted you!"

He simply directed a steady gaze toward her.

"And did you not say you would return in two hours? This is certainly not two hours, sir. And look at the state of you! Well, what have you got to say for yourself?"

"As I said previously, madam, I wish to speak with my wife, where such matters will be explained."

"And you may do so now, we shall not stop you," Mother said, settling in her chair with an air that suggested she would not be easily moved.

"Lady Harkness, forgive me, but I wish to speak privately with my wife," he replied, with a slight smile directed at Julia. "I have the right to speak with her."

"And I have wish to speak with you," Julia finally said, in a voice loud enough and firm enough that she hoped would brook no opposition. "You may go, Jonathan. I do not need to speak with you. This is a private matter between my husband and myself."

"But —"

"You may leave also, Mother. No, I am not a child, nor do I need a chaperone. If I require assistance I shall call for you, but at present I do not, so I beg for you to leave us alone."

"Julia, you are my daughter, and I simply —"

"Will have to leave me to conduct my

interview with my husband as I see fit! Or do you wish to never see me again?"

Her mother blanched, Jon's eyes narrowed, but neither of them said anything more. Under Jon's escort, Mother left the room and the door shut behind them.

Julia exhaled and met Thomas with a smile tinged by relief. "Stubbornness seems to run in my family."

"It does, indeed," he said, moving forward to clasp her in a hug. "Oh, my dear. I trust they haven't turned you away from me completely."

"No," she murmured, her cheek pressed against his woolen coat. "But they tried."

Oh, how they had tried. Pointing out argument after argument for why she should avoid him, feeding on her doubts and insecurities, recalling all his faults and failures. Yesterday. Last night. This morning. And though she had felt herself waver, still something deep within begged her to give him one more chance.

"I'm so sorry I did not return yesterday when I said I would. I imagine the past few hours haven't been so very pleasant for you." His arms loosened and he drew her to sit beside him on the sofa. "I should never have left you, but I figured you might need some time to . . . recover."

"I don't know if I'll ever 'recover' after such exertions. Nor that I want to."

He chuckled, and her heart eased a little. Perhaps there was a chance this might work out. She swallowed, offered up a silent prayer, and touched his bruised face. "What happened?"

He shook his head. "Oh, my dearest, if only I could be sure . . ."

"Sure of what? What is it you wanted to say?"

"Besides this?" His lips settled on hers, quickly becoming insistent.

She broke the kiss with a gasp. "Oh!" she drew in a shaky breath. "No, be serious. You cannot expect me to think that was all you wished to say."

"Perhaps it is all I *wish* to say," he said, the lurking twinkle in his eyes fading, "but you are right. It is not all that I need to say."

Something fluttered in her stomach. "What do you *need* to say?"

He moistened his bottom lip, the action one she remembered he would do whenever he felt nervous. "I need to tell you about the past six months."

CHAPTER FIFTEEN

As he explained, Thomas watched his wife, careful not to betray his anxiety, not to give her suspicion that what he spoke was not the entire truth. For he could not admit to his sordid encounter with Magdalena. He would never admit to such a thing. He was determined never even to think on her again. She might as well be buried like his mother, she had so passed into his past.

"You were engaged as a spy?" Her eyes were wide, blue as an Indian sky.

"I could not speak of it before."

"But now you can?"

He swallowed. He could not admit to the entirety of this recent encounter, either. Not after his unfortunate run-in with Fallbright. "I cannot tell you the all, I'm afraid."

"Do you not trust me?" Her lips pushed into a pout.

He had suspected she'd react emotionally.

He hedged with, "I have no wish to distress you."

"It is perhaps a little late for that." She gave a bitter sounding laugh.

Fear arrowed through him. *Please let Julia forgive me.* "I'm so sorry."

"These past months have not been pleasant."

Was it true what Becky had said? *Dear God, let it not be so.* He possessed himself of her hands. "My darling, forgive me. It was never my intention to cause you a second of concern."

She studied him for a long moment, before finally nodding. "I knew it must be so. I could not believe it when he said you wished to leave."

"What? When who said?"

"Oh, some man, he said he was a friend of yours. Apparently you had given him a message to pass on to me."

"Was his name McKinley? A squat man, with a frog-like face?"

"Yes! That's him."

"He did not give you my letter?"

"You wrote a letter?"

"Of course I did. You could not think I went away without telling you something of my intent."

"Well" — she glanced down, her lashes

feathering her cheeks — "I did not *want* to believe it . . ."

He could hear the "but." He winced inside. "I wrote you a letter, Jewel. I gave it to McKinley along with an amount of money to give to you, knowing it might be a while until I could return —"

"You left a letter and money?" Her eyes searched his. "I never got either."

His fingers clenched. How could such an innocent face lie? So, McKinley *had* lied all along. He swallowed the growl wishing to erupt from his throat. "He lied to me."

"You saw him?"

He jerked a nod. "He said he saw you and gave you the money and the letter, but that you did not seem pleased."

She gasped. "He said that? Well, he lied! He gave me nothing. And as for being pleased, how could I be when I did not know where you were? When I cried every day wondering what had happened, half starving myself while I tried to sell every scrap we possessed — even my gowns — in order to pay the rent. Everything I kept was either too worthless or too precious to sell."

Just as Becky had said.

"I'm sorry for ever trusting him." He pulled her close so she could not see his frown as his thoughts tumbled over each

218

other. How could his friend have betrayed him like that? What kind of gull did McKinley take him for? Surely he must have expected Thomas would find out the truth one day, then return for revenge another? What kind of game was the man playing at? And what game was Fallbright playing at? Why was he surrounded by evil men?

"Thomas?" Julia pulled back. "What is it? You're trembling."

"Forgive me." He willed his smile to look genuine. "Is that better?"

She shook her head slowly. "There is more you are not telling me."

He strove not to shrink from the too-perceptive blue eyes. There was so much he needed to hide, not least was the attack last night. "Darling, please trust me."

She studied him for a long moment before nodding. He opened his arms and she snuggled close, causing his breath to catch. If only he could be sure she would remain safe.

He stroked her hair, drawing in a deep breath of the sweet scent she used. The scent eased a smidge of his concern before the worries crowded in again. Why had Fallbright deceived him? Why had he been attacked so?

When he awoke early this morning in a

dim backstreet alley — his conscience panged, much like he'd left Benson — it had taken some moments before his throbbing head had permitted him to move, much less given him the capacity for rational thought. He'd been dumped like a piece of refuse! But why had Wheeler done so?

He would return to demand answers, but he sensed he'd only be met with more prevarication, and that Julia had waited for his explanations long enough. So, after tidying himself as best he could, he had returned to Portman Square, where his first attempt to enter the house had been met with swift refusal and a door closed with a bang, like he was a common hawker. His second attempt to visit had met with more success. The butler had somehow recognized him beneath his veneer of grimy injury and allowed him admittance. But so many explanations — from so many different people — still remained. Why hadn't McKinley given Julia the money like he'd promised? He would have to return to Scotland to find out. He tried to stifle a groan; realized he had been unsuccessful when Julia shifted in his arms and glanced at him with a questioning look.

"What is it?"

"I just realized I shall have to return to

Edinburgh to find out why McKinley lied to me."

"Oh, but not yet." She nestled close again. "Don't leave me, not when we've just found each other again."

He pressed a kiss to her brow in reply.

But still the swirling anger refused to dissipate, only hardening instead. He'd given McKinley fifty pounds, fifty pounds Julia had well needed. How much had she needed that? And he'd spent it on — what? New coats and whiskey? He muttered a curse under his breath.

"Darling?" Julia looked up at him worriedly. "Please don't let that man bother you anymore. I don't want to think about him, about any of that time." She shuddered. "I cannot bear to think what your life must have been like in that horrid, filthy prison."

He'd painted his words earlier carefully, giving enough truth to gain her sympathy, but not so much as to incur her wrath.

She snuggled against him, eliciting a curl of heat within. "I'm just so glad you're back here, back home and safe."

"Julia," he gently removed her from his side, before continuing slowly, "you do know this is not our home."

"Well, it *is* mine. Or at least my mother's."

"But *not* mine." His lips twisted wryly.

221

"Your mother has made that very clear."

She shrugged. "So, we'll live somewhere else. I don't mind. I don't need such fancy dresses." As if to emphasize her point she pinched her silken skirts. They slid back with the soft hush he recognized as expensive.

"Julia, darling, we need to think about more than just clothes. There are things like food, and rent."

"Well, we need not eat much. And we can grow things. I can always learn to be a farmer's wife. I daresay I'd enjoy picking vegetables and collecting eggs."

He drew in a sigh. Did she not realize this was not a game? "Darling, I know that sounds easy, but I'm afraid it won't pay for other expenses."

"Like what?"

"Like rent."

"But I'd be content to live in a cottage. Surely we could afford that."

How he wished he could give her the answer she craved. But he could say nothing.

Her brow furrowed, and he was conscious of having pricked the idyllic bubble she'd been forming within. "Have you *no* money?"

Not anymore. "Not much," he prevaricated.

"Well, I have my dowry," she said, sitting up, her smile reappearing, sunshine after night. "I'm sure Mother will not mind —"

"I am equally sure she will. As will your brother." He continued gently, "The release of such funds was dependent on their approval of your marriage."

"That is ridiculous!"

"That is the way things are."

"But it's not fair!" Her eyes snapped. "Do they think I'm nothing but a piece of chattel?"

Again, he could say nothing, for in the eyes of the law, she was.

"What are we going to do?"

He could offer only a strained smile. *God, help me.* Where had the self-made man gone, the one who had left his fractured family in order to slowly work his way up through the ranks of the armed forces, eventually exulting in the reception of their commendation and society's smiles?

The door opened and Julia's mother and brother reentered the room, their hard gazes suggesting recent battles were not nearly done. The dim throb in his head thudded louder.

"So, what have you got to say for yourself?"

He tried not to take offense, willed his voice not to sound defensive, as he briefly explained something of the past few days and months.

"You expect us to believe you?" Lady Harkness snapped.

"I only offer the truth."

"Hmph!"

Thomas dared glance at his former friend, whose frown had deepened with every line of his explanation. Jon met his gaze with a long assessing look. Thomas waited, his chest thumping loudly with the hope Jon would somehow believe him, as his sister had. If he only had an ally, someone who might help him extricate himself from this giant knot of mischief and mischance, then perhaps he might feel his way forward to something approximating the future he'd once envisaged with Julia.

"Mother," Jon finally said. "I wish to speak with Hale in the study."

He gave Thomas a look that almost bordered on a challenge, which he accepted with the slightest of nods. Something eased within his chest. He squeezed Julia's hand. Perhaps there was a chance, after all.

Ignoring his mother's protests, Jon gestured for Thomas to follow him across the hall to a paneled room that was far more masculine than any chamber he'd visited prior. Thomas knew Lady Harkness's husband had died a number of years ago, but it seemed strange to see a room decorated in such somber tones, according to a taste unlike the rest of the house's décor.

Jon took the chair behind the desk, gestured Thomas to the seat opposite. Still that clear look appraised him, inducing a shiver of apprehension lest he not be believed. But if that were the case, surely he would have been turned out on his ear, and not invited to converse inside?

Jon cleared his throat. "I cannot like any of this. I do not like how you have treated my sister. I do not like your abandoning her. And I certainly can't help but think you ran off with her as some revenge against me."

"You? My marrying Julia was not about you."

"No?" Jon leaned forward. "You would have run off to Gretna Green even if she hadn't been my sister?"

"I wouldn't have needed to," Thomas said quietly.

Jon blinked.

Thomas pressed his advantage. "I understand you thought me less than suitable for your sister; I imagine you'd feel that way about any man who offered for her. But just because I was only an army officer, and do not possess the wealth or lineage you do does not make me less able to love her."

"Except you abandoned her. That is not love. A husband is supposed to protect his wife, not let her nearly starve!"

Thomas sucked in a breath. "She nearly starved?"

"You did not see Julia when she first returned, but Carmichael did. He and Serena took her in — thank God they were here in London — Julia was nearly skin and bone!"

No wonder Jon viewed Thomas as less than a cur. He swallowed. "I thought I had made provision." He explained about McKinley, absurdly grateful he could speak his piece without interruption.

"So why did McKinley lie?"

"I don't know. I wish I did, but . . ." He shook his head, studying his near-threadbare trousers, yet another thing he would need to attend to, if he was ever to find his way to finances again. Was it any wonder Julia's family held him in contempt, dressed as he was like a near savage? Despair roiled within. "I cannot believe I ever trusted the man."

"Indeed."

The word was said with no trace of sarcasm, permitting Thomas to raise his gaze to meet the puzzled frown of Julia's brother.

"And your bruises?" He gestured to Thomas's face. "How did you say they came about?"

Thomas briefly explained, relief sifting through his apprehension as Jon's head tilted, his expression grave.

"I cannot understand why you would be treated so."

"Neither can I." He swallowed. "I know I am not what you wished as Julia's husband, but please believe I would never willingly cause your sister pain."

Perhaps he said the wrong thing, for the blue-gray eyes studying him narrowed fractionally, before a wry laugh escaped. "I suppose I cannot hate a man my sister professes to love."

A tiny flame of hope lit his heart. "Carlew" — the old name slipped out — "I'm so sorry for this bad blood that has arisen between us. I wish you could believe my love for Julia is genuine, and that I could prove myself worthy in some way —"

"Perhaps you can."

Surprise stole across his heart. "Anything. Tell me what I can do."

There was another long moment as Jon eyed him, before finally nodding. "What are your plans for her? Do you intend to return to Edinburgh?"

"I only intend to return to interrogate McKinley. Beyond that, I have no wish to live there again."

"Where will you live?"

"I —" The words drew his past back to mind, when a similar question had been posed by a very different man. His stomach twisted; he forced himself to say, "I have some connections in Norfolk, and will endeavor to provide a home for Julia there."

Julia's brother raised a brow. "Endeavor, or will?"

"I will," he said firmly. Whether his father liked it or not. He couldn't refuse to admit him now, could he? Not with such a pretty wife in tow.

"And will there be room for Charles?"

"Charles?"

Jon's other brow rose. "You mean Julia hasn't told you?"

"Apparently she has not."

He muttered something under his breath before pushing back his chair and excusing himself to find Julia. "I think this is something you should hear from her, not from me."

Thomas forced himself not to pace, not to fidget, though his impatience begged to escape his fingers with nervous twitches and the like. Who was this Charles person? When Julia entered the room, her cheeks aglow, her hands outstretched, it was all he could do not to clasp her to his chest, she looked so lovely.

"Julia," Jon said, eyes fixed on Thomas. "You need to tell your husband about Charles."

Thomas sent her a look of enquiry, which she met with a gasp, a blush, and a downward glance at her now-clasped hands. "Oh, my goodness!"

Jon sent Thomas a look that could only be described as sardonic before he settled back into his seat as though he was a spectator at a boxing match.

Thomas turned his attention to his wife. "Julia, who is Charles?"

"I'm so sorry. I should have told you sooner, but with everything else it completely slipped my mind." She smiled, placed a finger on her lips, and with a soft, "Wait here," slipped from the room.

The dull pain in his head sharpened. He knuckled his forehead, wishing to keep the headache at bay. He needed to think clearly, not have his thoughts shrouded in pain.

What was he to do? What were they to do? Was it truly fair of him to ask her to leave this life of comfort, or should he somehow beg her to stay while he sought his fortune? Although look at where that had got him last time . . .

The door opened, and Julia walked in, holding a bundle of blankets, followed by her mother, whose sour expression could not contrast more severely with Julia's sunny countenance. "Look who I found!"

She dipped her bundle forward, and he saw tiny red curls, tiny perfect features, the features of a little baby sucking his thumb — a boy if the color of blanket was any clue. "Who is this?"

"Your son," Lady Harkness said, with narrowed eyes.

"My son?" He touched the tiny fingers, something of awe forming within. Never had he imagined how such words would make him feel. He was a father? Dear God he would do better than his own father had done. He glanced up at Julia. "We have a child?"

Her sunny features shadowed. "This is Charles."

Hurt cramped, mingling with an emotion far darker. How could she name their son — *that* name — without asking him?

230

But wait . . . He frowned, doing the mathematical calculations. This baby had to be at least three months old. Julia had not been expecting when he was last home. Had she? The sliver of doubt crept in. Or had she kept such news hidden because the child was not his own? He looked at her sharply.

Her cheeks had paled. "I will tell you later," she whispered.

"You should tell me now," he said in a low voice. "Who is this?"

She gave him a look that could only be regarded as pleading, and he forced himself to relax, to not question. It was obvious she wished to speak with him outside of her mother's hearing. "He is very . . ." What was he supposed to say? His experience with small children was naught. "Very sweet."

Julia sighed with what he imagined was relief. Her mother drew close, caressed the small boy's crop of gingery curls, before her green eyes — cat's eyes, he'd always thought — pierced him.

"I cannot like anything you have done, but I will admit that your son has something of beauty about him."

His lips twitched despite himself. Was that because she believed the red hair an inheritance of her own making?

231

"What?" She peered at him. "I demand to know what is so amusing."

He'd rather die than expose Julia's charade to her. "Forgive me, madam. I am just so pleased to learn that at last you believe me responsible for something that has met with your approval."

"Believe you responsible?" Her brow lowered with suspicion. "Do you not claim Charles as your son?"

Her daughter may not have inherited her mother's hair color, but nobody need doubt where Julia got her sharp wits from.

"How dare you?"

Lady Harkness's slap across his cheek did not splinter him inside as much as the look of horror Julia gave him. She shook her head, her eyes filling with tears. "Mother, please don't!"

Jon's staying hand on his mother's wrist forced her returning hand to still.

Julia hugged the child to her breast and looked down, but not before he saw the glisten of tears. His heart wrenched further. He was supposed to be bringing her peace, not further pain.

Jon whispered something to his mother, after which she sniffed and left the room, the door closing with an emphatic thump. "I apologize," Jon said with a sigh. "She is not quite herself these days."

Guilt gnawed anew. No guesses why that might be.

Thomas glanced at his wife. She was biting her lip. "Julia?"

She shook her head. "I should have told you. I'm so sorry."

"Whose child *is* this?"

Behind him he heard Jon's gasp. He kept his eyes on his wife. Surely she had not betrayed him?

She finally lifted a tear-stained face to him. "Do . . . do you remember poor Meggie from the flat below us?"

Meggie? When had he heard that name recently? He strained his memory. Came up empty. "Barely."

"She was sick, so sick, and her husband had but recently died." Water-filled blue eyes turned to him. "Before she died she *begged* me to bring little Charles up as my — our — son. I couldn't leave him there, not in that godforsaken place." She shuddered.

Her eyes owned truth, silencing the whisper of doubt within, even as he stared at her in something akin to horror. "But surely this Meggie" — why could he not remember her? — "or her husband must have had family who could have taken in a young relative. I cannot believe this would be regarded as quite legal."

She uttered a broken laugh, and fire flashed in her eyes. "*Now* you want to talk about what is lawful? I never thought to see the day."

Thomas fought the swell of anger at her sneered aspersions. He could not refute such a comment. For too long he had skirted certain niceties of the law, in an attempt to achieve results more expeditiously. He glanced at Jon, but his frowning attention was firmly riveted on his sister.

"Julia," Jon warned from his corner. "Hale is correct. Unless there is some written proof, I'm afraid the law might consider that you have kidnapped the child."

"Kidnapped?" She clutched the tiny child closer to her chest. "I only did what I could to help."

Thomas drew a step nearer to her. "I am sure you did, but I cannot think —"

She shook her head, taking a pace back, as if she feared he might snatch the child from her grasp. "Do you know how hard it was to bring him here? He was but four weeks old, crying for his mama, and always so hungry for food which I could not provide." She made a noise like a sob and took another step back. "I won't let you take him. I'm the only mother he knows now, and it would be too cruel to pluck him away and leave him stranded in some orphanage or home for the indigent."

"Nobody is suggesting we do that," he tried to reassure. "It's just that we cannot keep pretending he is our child when he is not."

"Why not?" she demanded.

"Because . . ." Sometimes the subtleties of morality were a mystery to him. "Because it is wrong."

"I cannot think it so, when he is being protected and nurtured, and in a situation far better than any of Meggie's relatives could offer."

Yes, but whether Thomas himself could afford to offer such a degree of comfort . . . He shook his head. He could not.

Julia's bottom lip trembled, and he caught a glimpse of the pretty child she had been, the one disappointed when her will was thwarted, the one who had known herself to be in the wrong but determined to fight for every inch she could maintain. Her spirit was one of the things he loved about her so.

As if sensing her agitation, little Charles, until that moment blissfully asleep, opened his eyes, and stared at Thomas, his gaze every bit as dark as Thomas's own. The little boy blinked, then screwed up his face in a howl of protest.

Julia's efforts to shush him became increasingly frantic, her pats on the boy's back seemingly more forceful than soothing. Thomas drew near, and once again she stepped back. "I won't let you take him! I won't let you —"

He reached out and grasped the boy, saying with a firm voice, "Charles, stop that now."

The baby startled, glancing up at him as if to question who this stranger was who dared raise his voice to him. For a moment, the dark eyes seemed to penetrate his, eliciting a tender tug deep within. Before commencing to cry all the harder.

"I don't think we will solve this . . . dilemma this afternoon," Jon said. "Perhaps when we are all not so tired we might be able to find a solution."

"There *is* no solution," Julia said, "except that little Charles lives with me."

This was said with a raised chin that Thomas knew from past experience never boded well for her opponent. However, the lack of sleep from last night, combined with the ache now thumping behind his eyes, brooked no further opposition. "Julia, I only want what is best for you, for us, for our marriage. Please believe me."

Her glare softened, her shoulders slumping as if the battle had drained her, and she made no protest when the door opened and a middle-aged slouch-shouldered woman walked in and plucked the child from his arms, murmuring something about getting Master Charles back to bed upstairs, all the while shooting him a most interested gaze.

Jon released an audible breath when the door closed behind her, before saying wearily, "Now I suppose we must give attention to what happens next."

Thomas felt his every fiber stand to attention. What would happen next? God help him, he barely knew.

CHAPTER SIXTEEN

Ten days later
Julia lifted her eyes from the silent dinner table. Tonight's dining companion: her mother, whose arctic glare since Thomas's arrival last week, punctuated by snapped remarks and icy directives, left Julia in no doubt as to her feelings on the matters that had arisen since that fateful afternoon.

For herself, Julia could hardly understand such matters, either. One moment, Jon had been vehement in his disdain for Thomas; the next, he had invited him to stay at his house in Berkeley Square, as though they had never been separated by such things as, oh, Thomas running away to Gretna Green with her!

She lowered her gaze as resentment rankled inside. Yes, she might be behaving like a child, but it was not fair. Why had Thomas been invited to stay with Jon, when she was still stuck here with Mother's icy disdain?

Especially when Julia had been the one first invited to spend time with Jon and Catherine at their London residence. Granted, Thomas had stayed only long enough to recuperate before heading north to Scotland yet again, but still . . . It did not seem fair.

When Mother had learned of Jon's intention she had said some very hard words, but Jon had simply replied that he could not in good conscience leave his injured brother-in-law to fend for himself, not when he had family and friends with the means to support him. Thomas had protested, murmured something about going to an inn, but Jon insisted, even in the teeth of Mother's very vocal opposition. Since then, the house had been very quiet, as if Mother had used up all her words in anger and had nothing left.

Julia forced herself to swallow a piece of venison. The taste, the texture, made her stomach lurch. Her husband continued to evoke mixed feelings. Apart from resentment that he could leave and she had to stay, there was the residue of confusion induced by that afternoon's — upon reflection, somewhat embarrassing — outburst in the study. She still could not quite rationalize her panic concerning Thomas's questions about Charles. Only that it seemed so

239

wrong to have the one constant of the recent months suddenly ripped away, as if his destiny held no more consequence than hers did. Little Charles was an innocent and, as such, should be protected from life's cares and turmoil for as long as possible.

"Well?"

Julia glanced up to meet her mother's eyes. "I beg your pardon, Mother. Did you say something?"

Her mother sniffed. "I suppose you are thinking on that fool husband of yours."

Well, at least Mother now acknowledged him as her husband. She bit back a wry smile. As per usual, Jon only had to say something was so, and Mother would eventually follow, albeit with bad grace. "I am . . . hopeful he will return soon."

"Don't expect me to ever welcome him with open arms."

"I have no expectation of the sort."

"Hmph."

That sounded like tacit acceptance at least, a thought Julia hugged to herself.

"And I do not want to talk about him. He is *persona non grata* to me. I hope you understand."

"Yes, Mother." Yet for a person she found unworthy of consideration, Mother seemed to be doing a great deal of talking about

240

him. She kept that thought behind her teeth also.

"The only reason I shall not press for legal action against him is for the sake of that dear sweet boy. I would not wish to have it on my conscience that I was responsible for sending his father to the gallows, even though that is where he belongs."

Guilt chased the earlier amusement away. Jon had counseled Thomas and Julia not to reveal Charlie's true parentage just yet, not until Thomas had time to further investigate Meggie's wider family.

Another reason her feelings remained ambivalent. How could she know that Thomas would prove trustworthy in his search? Doubt whispered that he would seek answers to benefit himself. And if he did find Charles's family, how could she give up her one source of comfort these past months? At least by taking care of him, she had felt she was taking positive steps to her future, and not feeling like she was being dragged along by the whims and notions of everyone else.

Julia forced herself to cut another piece of venison, to chew it slowly, so she need not be obliged to engage in conversation as her thoughts and worries churned on. If Meggie had spoken truly — and why would she lie?

— and little Charles had no further family, then how would she ever explain the true nature of his birth to Mother? To Catherine? To Lord and Lady Carmichael?

The fork slipped from her fingers, echoing with a loud clatter on the china plate.

Mother's head swiveled up, her eyes, not completely without concern, watching Julia curiously.

Julia forced her facial movements to approximate a look of nonchalance, as she picked up her fork and resumed eating.

Dear God, what a tangle of deception she had woven with her lie. What would they all say when they learned the truth? She could only hope they would be as understanding — well, perhaps *understanding* was the wrong word, *forgiving* perhaps might suit better — as Jon and Thomas had proved.

She thought back to that moment when Thomas had plucked Charlie from her arms, and then caressed him with a tenderness she had not expected to see. Another reason her feelings remained conflicted. Sometimes she barely recognized the man she'd married.

The servants returned to clear the remnants of dishes, but even after they left Mother still refused to leave. Julia glanced at her, waiting.

"I wonder if they have arrived yet."

"Jon's letter suggested that they should have arrived by now."

Jon's business affairs had necessitated his venturing north, to Manchester at least, and he had agreed to take Thomas for part of the way on his journey to Scotland.

She had begged Thomas not to leave: "You have only just returned! I want us to be together."

"I want that, too," he had whispered. "But until certain matters are resolved, I fear that will prove an impossibility."

"Because Mother will not have you in the house?"

He sighed. "I must speak with McKinley about the missing money."

"I don't care about the money! I just want to be with you. Please stay," she'd begged.

"But I must find out what happened."

"Why? I'm sure Mother and Jon will be happy to release my dowry. Well, Jon might be —"

"No. I do not want to be dependent on such a thing."

"But why not?"

"Because I am your husband, and *I* want to provide for my wife as I ought, and not let her depend on her family."

"Oh, but —"

"And if I am absent for a little while longer, then that gives your mother time to grow reconciled to how things are." He had swiftly kissed her. "Believe me, I would not go if I did not feel such a thing necessary, and I certainly will return as quickly as can be."

"Promise?"

"I promise."

She wanted to believe him — she ached to believe him — but the past haunted the present with memories of his broken word. Coupled with this was the knowledge that it was, in part, her fault that he was returning north again. Guilt nudged her. Perhaps she *had* been a trifle hasty in leaving with matters unresolved. Perhaps she should have tried a little harder to find out from Meggie if she had relatives she could turn to. It fell now to her poor husband to finalize the arrangements she should have settled. Such guilt, mingling with fears and trepidation, had contributed to her nearly refusing to kiss him, but she had overcome her hesitancy and touched her lips to his in a manner he found unsatisfactory, judging from his whispered plea for more. But more she could not do with her mother watching them so avidly. The wild and shameless creature from two weeks ago had shrunk

244

back into timidity, and she had forgotten how to be brave.

Her mother cleared her throat, returning Julia's thoughts back to the present. "Perhaps tomorrow we should see how Catherine is getting on."

Julia murmured agreement, pleased that her mother had thawed enough to once more engage in trivial musings about their friends and her various social acquaintances, many of whom Julia no longer remembered, nor — she suspected from some of Mother's comments — cared to renew an acquaintance with. Their conversation had been filled with gossip about the latest news: the anniversary of the death of poor Princess Charlotte and her stillborn son. Julia's eyes pricked, her heart going out again to the widower. Poor man. Never to know his child. Never to hold his beloved wife again. How desperately devastating for them all.

"Julia? Are you quite well?"

"Yes, Mother." Her mother's narrowed eyes seemed to demand further explanation. "I was thinking about poor Prince Leopold."

"Ah, yes. A sad tragedy."

As her mother began a discourse on the terrible trial this had proved for the English monarchy, Julia nodded and tried to appear

245

interested, but soon the welter of dark emotions led her thoughts to return hundreds of miles away. Thank God Thomas was still alive, that he still loved her.

Now all she could do was wait.

And hope.

And pray that Thomas would find the answers he needed — and not the ones she feared.

The mail coach bumped along the pothole-ridden North Road on Thomas's return to Edinburgh. He clenched his teeth as the carriage dipped alarmingly to one side. A cracked whip signaled a desperate lurch forward, and they were freed to continue again. Outside, the stark hills and barren landscape dusted in snow made him decidedly thankful he was inside for this particular trip north, and not atop in the cheaper seats as his pecuniary difficulties had previously demanded.

The long drive had provided much fuel for thought, fuel for reminiscing. Jon's change of heart seemed truly remarkable. His offer to accompany Thomas for the first half of his journey, generosity in paying for the second half, and recommendation of a good solicitor, had reminded Thomas of when they had first met, five years ago, when circumstances had knit their souls almost like brothers.

The icy landscape faded, the coughs and sniffles of the other passengers receded, replaced by memories of a warm sun and air redolent with exotic spices.

He'd first met Jon in India, when the upright, serious gentleman with frank manners and keen eyes had stood out among the weak and dissolute, those emaciated by disease or sickened by greed. Jonathan Carlew had been different — honest, tall, and strong — his blond height making him a good head taller than the natives and even most Englishmen. His thoughtfulness stood out also, among a group of men whose dissipated and debauched natures had led many to seek comfort in whatever they may. Thomas himself was not averse to finding strength from a bottle, his bouts at boxing, or gaming — a man needed some form of distraction from the heat and the mounting death toll from dysentery, diphtheria, and typhoid. He had kept lucky, never succumbing to more than just a mild dose, not forced to endure the lingering ravages of the tropical diseases that blighted so many.

They'd met in Poona, when Carlew was instructed to go to the military station to retrieve a document for the Company. Carlew had seemed the archetypal clerk the East India Company preferred to employ, carrying out the orders of a superior, usually a family member or someone with title and rank. Thomas had never had either; he had to work his way up from the bottom, earning his rank the hard way through discipline and diligence. He'd certainly never expected favors from anyone.

When the request was made for a military escort for a viscount to see a mine near Ratnagiri, Thomas had been unsurprised to learn the task had been assigned to him. Most things deemed a waste of time by his superior officers fell on his shoulders. Colonel Fallbright had made no secret of his displeasure that Thomas's recent promotion, a reward for dealing with a mutiny in Calcutta, had also led to secondment to the Poona garrison. There had been whispers Fallbright sought political advancement, and resented those he deemed less worthy as he sought to ingratiate himself with those of greater power.

It had proved a pleasant change to accompany Carlew and the viscount, Lord Carmichael, one of Carlew's university friends — the likes of whom Thomas had never before met. The viscount — Harry to his friends — had proved affable and easy-going, ready for a laugh as well as for a round or ten of cards, a man as much a favorite with the ladies as Thomas tended to be. Indeed, in many ways Carmichael seemed as unlikely a friend for Carlew as he himself must appear. But the trio had bonded over shared wry humor, a willingness to enjoy and not merely endure India's vast treasure trove of new experiences, and an event he'd felt sure would forge a bond to last a lifetime.

Thomas had led the small caravan of men on horseback to an area whose hills with black bandings had fascinated the viscount. Such things had made more sense when Carlew revealed the Company's interest in finding minerals that may be of use in manufactories. Thomas hadn't minded. He was simply glad to be freed from the regimen that governed his days at the barracks, and glad to be with convivial company, and had done his best to appear friendly, not like those English soldiers whose goal seemed to be to strike fear and intimidation.

Carmichael learned what he wanted, and partway on their return they had come across a group of villagers, children who could not have been more than eight or ten years of age. They'd been struck by Carlew's height and fairness, and had laughed and giggled and pointed at them all. Carmichael had been all charm and joviality, and Thomas himself had felt an easing in his spirit for the first time in a long time. For once he did not need to worry about responsibility, he could just relax and enjoy.

It was while they were resting under the shade of an impressively large mango tree, imbibing the beverages Carmichael had thoughtfully brought along, that it happened. A thunder pounding the earth, a crashing through the trees, it had taken him some moments to understand, although the village children seemed to know exactly what it presaged.

"Haathi! Haathi!" they'd called.

An elephant. And from his understanding of a smattering of Indian phrases, the startled exclamations of the locals suggested it was "the wild one," an elephant known to have terrorized the village before, and destroyed a village not five miles from here. And from their anxious postures, and the way two village elders propped an ancient firearm towards the beast, he knew that it was not something they had any wish to repeat.

Thomas drew out his musket, brought along for emergencies. Yelled for his com-

250

panions to retreat. Then he could see the great gray beast crashing through the trees, and, detecting a note of terror in his heart, he raised his Brown Bess and fired.

The creature hadn't stopped. As the children's screams intensified, he reloaded his weapon, prayed a desperate prayer, and shot again. The elephant buckled at the knees, even as its momentum carried it forward. In a moment as profound as it was strange, the giant beast had seemed to know he was the cause for its injury. Its eyes flashing, locking on his, it desperately tried to surge on. Heart in his mouth, he frantically reloaded and pulled the trigger, aiming between its eyes. With a great roar of pain, the gray beast finally crumpled to the ground, dust puffing up as it collapsed not ten yards away. The earth trembled like his knees.

When Carlew had finally spoken, it was with a fervent "Thank God!" and in subsequent moments Thomas had an overwhelming sense of God's protection. He'd always prided himself on his speed at reloading, but to do so that quickly had to have been a miracle.

A few seconds later, he grew conscious of cheering children, of parents clasping their hands together in gratitude, of Carmichael's vocal appreciation. His chest had glowed with their praise as he tasted the rare experience of being someone others esteemed. He might not have money, or a title, or connections, but he had some skills deemed worthwhile at least.

The experience had appeared to impress Fallbright, too. He seemed to regard Thomas in a different light after that, perhaps because Carlew and Carmichael had made sure the Company knew of Thomas's heroics, and Fallbright was loath to appear lacking in appropriate attentions. Fallbright certainly had not been lacking, inviting Thomas to his inner circle of officers whom he had, until now, looked on with neither envy nor dismay. It was during this time he'd come to know Major Joseph McKinley, who, like Thomas, worked in a unit alongside those controlled by the East India Company, something that usually invited a degree of disdain from those British-trained soldiers. But Thomas had worked hard to ensure the natives were accorded a level of respect, and had prided himself on treating others as his father had so rigidly proclaimed from the pulpit: doing unto others as he would have them do to him.

It wasn't always possible. Indeed, he and

McKinley had once experienced an incident that had severely tested what little sense of honor Thomas knew himself to possess.

Fallbright had requested them to attend a private meeting with himself and the Resident of Poona, Montstuart Elphinstone. Elphinstone's fellow Scot, McKinley, had quickly ingratiated himself, and it was only after several glasses of whiskey that he finally learned their mission.

Elphinstone, caught between representing British interests and those of Indian rights, had sought to end the bloodshed between raiding parties by a group called the Pindari, a guerrilla-type group of marauding native horsemen, made up of dispossessed villagers and disgruntled former soldiers, who sought to bring terror and torture to villages in an attempt to provide for themselves. Fallbright had endorsed both McKinley and Thomas to track these men and preserve Poona from attack "by whatever means necessary."

Thomas had raised his brows, yet had remained quiet. A soldier was bound as much by the code of honor as he was by rules and regulations. Officers might use their private judgment as to obeying orders, but would need strong evidence to disobey illegal orders, as was outlined in the Articles of War.

The next two months had proved a trying time, as he and McKinley tracked those responsible for atrocities worse than anything a rampaging *haathi* might create. He had been forced to flog two soldiers who had killed a Pindari chief and then cut off his hands, in the gruesome ancient punishment for thieves.

He'd heard later that McKinley had approved the barbaric punishment, but he'd never believed it. As personal circumstances by that stage had demanded his return home, his decision to resign his commission and return to England had put such matters far from his mind, until he had, most fortuitously, encountered McKinley one day last year at the Black Harp in Edinburgh.

"I thought you were from Dunbartonshire," Thomas had said, shaking his hand.

"And I thought you were from much farther south than that," McKinley had countered with a smile, their Indian experiences relived over several drams and shared laughter, laughter that seemed so far away now.

Thomas frowned, the action seeming to cause the middle-aged lady sitting opposite to startle and look away. What had caused

McKinley to lie to him? Had the fog of his post-escape exhaustion caused Thomas to somehow misunderstand?

He drew in a breath, glancing at the pocket-watch he'd been touched to see Julia had salvaged from the mess of their Edinburgh life. He would get answers. One way or another. To both this mystery with McKinley, and that which surrounded the relatives of Julia's claimed child.

CHAPTER SEVENTEEN

"And Julia, how are you feeling these days?"

Julia smiled at Catherine, hiding her surprise at her sister-in-law's perspicacity. "Quite well, thank you." Well, she would be if she didn't feel a degree of nausea all the time. She must have caught a form of the cold that seemed to be stalking so many Londoners, the chilly mid-November temperatures conducive to racking coughs and the casting up of one's accounts. But she would not admit to such things, else Mother might insist she stay at home, and the past few days had dragged so slowly she felt like she might scream if she did not escape the house.

"And have you heard from my son?" Mother asked. "He does not write as often as he used to."

Catherine blushed, but met Mother's gaze evenly. "A letter arrived from Jon this morning. His dealings with the manufactories in

Manchester seem to have gone well, and he plans to visit Lord Carmichael's family in the next few days, then return for Christmas."

"I'm sure Henry will appreciate Jon's visit," Julia said. "It must be such a difficult time for them all."

Catherine nodded. "I am glad that Henry and Serena were able to return when they did. Serena's recent letter suggested it might only be a matter of days until Lord Bevington . . . is no more."

Julia dropped her gaze. Was she feeling overly defensive, or did that sound like Catherine blamed her for their delay in returning north?

When next she ventured to look up, the warmth lighting Catherine's eyes soothed away some of the sting. No, perhaps this illness was making her a trifle sensitive. She should not be so quick to believe that everyone was against her.

"That poor family," Mother said with a sigh. "I cannot imagine what it must be to lose your husband in such a sad way."

Cynical laughter spurted, forcing Julia to swallow her chuckles with an effort, an effort rendered all the more challenging as she met the amusement in Catherine's eyes. No, Mother had never lost any of her three husbands to lingering illness and malaise of the mind. Instead, while the sudden death of Julia's father had proved a great shock and had indeed induced great sadness, from the way Mother had always talked, the demise of her first and third husbands had been met with something Julia suspected was rather more like relief.

Her cough to hide her amusement triggered a wretched wrenching from within. She pressed fingers to her mouth and willed the nausea away.

"Julia? Are you quite well?"

"Forgive me. I feel a little out of sorts." She drew in a deep breath. Attempted a smile. "There. I'm better." To turn attention away from herself, she said to Catherine, "It must be strange to consider your sister will one day be a countess."

"Julia!" Mother said in agonized tones. "One should not speak in such a vulgar manner."

"I can hardly think it vulgar to acknowledge what must be. Henry is the heir to his father, and as Serena is his wife it is only natural —"

"Thank you, Julia. I am well aware of the rules of primogeniture."

Catherine said, in a manner not unamused, "I suspect Serena will always care more for her paints than for those responsibilities attached to a grand title." Her brow clouded. "I'm sure both she and Henry believed they would have more time before the assumption of such duties would be theirs. But she is not the first young lady I've known who has stepped into a social sphere they had not always known."

"You refer to Lady Hawkesbury?"

"I do. And although Lavinia has confessed that at times she finds certain social mores a trifle challenging, I don't believe for a second her husband regrets asking her to be his wife, even if she can be a little unorthodox in some of her ways."

Like taking an interest in the development of parish schools, and writing letters that were published in *The Times* purporting the same. Julia had seen such things printed in the newspapers. It was certainly not the conduct of most countesses.

"I suppose in light of writing letters to newspapers Serena's painting can be considered quite tame."

Catherine bit her lip, and exchanged a considered look with Mother.

Julia frowned. What did they know? What did she not?

"I forget sometimes that you were not privy to all that happened earlier this year,"

Catherine said. "Serena's painting of Henry caused something of a scandal at the Royal Academy exhibition."

"She had her painting exhibited at the Royal Academy? How wonderful!"

"It was a great honor." Again, that hesitation.

"And it was a most marvelous picture," Mother concurred. "Henry looked like he could step from the canvas he seemed so real."

Julia's mind whirred. "But that would mean she painted him *before* they were married."

"Yes. You can see now perhaps that such a thing was not met with universal approbation, especially among those of ill-nature and low minds. But I can assure you there was no hint of impropriety. Serena only ever painted him in this very house, and always in the company of others, so there was no basis for speculation. But I'm afraid some people will always rejoice in evil gossip at the expense of the innocent."

"Of course." Somehow the news of the fair Serena's scandal made Julia's own trials seem a little less dramatic, although she was sure that running away to Gretna Green to be married would always label her as one quite beyond the pale. "It is sad that people seem to prefer to focus more on impropriety than on someone's meritorious deeds."

"Impropriety." Mother sniffed, and sent another look to the ceiling. "When I think of all that I did for you, young lady, the fact that you could have married into nobility, just like Serena and Catherine did, and instead, you squandered your future by settling for a fellow —" She drew in a ragged breath. "But no. I refuse to talk about him. Even if he is a scapegrace —"

"Lady Harkness!" Catherine's voice came louder than Julia had ever heard before. She chased it with a smile. "Forgive me, but I cannot help but think such musings are better left unsaid. I'm of the opinion that it would be in everyone's best interests if we were to offer our support, not our censure, so that Julia and Thomas may know there will always be an open door for them with us. Surely we would not wish for them to feel as though they must flee, simply because we persist in wallowing in what cannot be changed, rather than focusing on the joy of their reunion. I'm persuaded you would not want them to feel as though your dislike must force their departure."

"But I do not dislike Julia," Mother complained.

Well, that was something at least.

"But can you not see that your continued criticisms concerning Thomas puts Julia in a very difficult position?" Catherine persisted. "How can she be expected to feel your love if all she hears is your disdain for the man she has chosen as her husband?"

Mother looked at her daughter-in-law with an expression that mingled guilt and surprise.

"I am sorry, but I truly think such things must be said." Then Catherine added, in a softer voice, "I have known what it is to hold onto bitterness and resentment; it is not something I wish for anyone I care about to dwell with. Unforgiveness is a poison that shrivels the heart. It means a person cannot truly live in the present as they're always thinking about the past."

Julia studied her unexpectedly passionate sister-in-law as the words rang around her heart, echoing with truth. How many times had she felt exactly that when she allowed anger and resentment to reside within, at the expense of joy and hope? Was this the reason Catherine so often seemed at peace?

Catherine drew in a breath, exhaled, smiled. "Now, I wonder if you had seen little Elizabeth's newest talent. I will have the nurse collect her so you can see just how clever she is."

Julia breathed a sigh of relief as Mother, now happily distracted, directed her full attention to Catherine. Julia shot her sister-in-law a look of heartfelt appreciation, which was met with a quick smile.

Perhaps in Catherine she had truly found an ally at last.

Edinburgh

Tracking the Pindari had proved child's play compared to this. Thomas stared at the mound of earth, which the kirk session clerk had assured was the final resting place for one Margaret McConnell and her husband, Charles. Investigation had elicited nothing more. No relatives. Nobody from either family who had attended either burial. It was all so very sad, so very hopeless, so very final.

The sight fueled determination that he would not permit the estrangements of the past to remain so. That on his return south he might even pay a visit to his father, and see if he could swallow his insults, and perhaps forgive the man for his misdeeds against his family. Poor Meggie's demise and complete lack of wider relations had also loosened the lump within his chest that had been there ever since Julia had first admitted the child was not his own. Know-

263

ing that little Charlie was in fact nobody's — save, perhaps, Julia's — he felt a measure of hope that one day, when he finally untangled this knot of responsibility and obligation, little Charles might regard them as his parents. A future filled with assurance and hope, a family such as he had never known. But that could not happen until he found McKinley, reclaimed his money, and found a house where he and Julia could live.

An hour later he was back at the dingy flat, exchanging words with Henderson, which swiftly put him in possession of the few remaining articles he cared about. Another chat with Becky, to clarify what exactly she recalled about Julia's report of McKinley's visit, and then he was back at the Black Harp, exchanging greetings with the publican, perusing the crowd as he waited for a head to appear.

There. McKinley strode through the room as if he owned the building, his smiles and shallow charm just as Thomas recalled. He moved into the man's line of sight, pleased at the look of shock McKinley gave as he recognized him, a look he quickly masked. "Hale! Well, I did not expect to see you again so soon. I thought you had returned to London."

"Really?" Why had he thought that? Had

264

he been watching him? Thomas fought to keep his expression neutral. "I would not think my movements warranted much interest."

McKinley laughed, a grating sound. "Your movements usually don't. But when a fellow officer comes in looking a little worse for wear — you don't mind me saying such things, do you? — then I cannot help but take an interest in his welfare."

"I appreciate your interest," Thomas said, with heavy irony. "I gather that was your ten pounds I found in my coat pocket?"

Another burst of guttural — guilt-laden? — laughter. "Oh, just a small token."

"Was it? Or was it something of the fifty I gave you to give to my wife?"

McKinley's eyes flashed. "I thought I had cleared up this misapprehension of yours last time. I gave her the money —"

"You did not."

McKinley drew himself up. "I assure you I did so."

Thomas sensed that the bandying of words would not stop for some time, so sought another method of attack. "Tell me, have you ever heard from anyone from our India days? For instance, Colonel Fallbright?"

The flicker in his eyes, the slight slackening of his mouth, gave evidence to something quite different from his muttered denial.

Thomas's mind spun furiously. What did Fallbright and McKinley have against him? Was such a leap in conclusions a leap too far? Or was there something very sinister at work here? Unease rippled through his gut.

"That is strange," Thomas eventually said. "I was speaking to him not more than a fortnight ago."

"Were you?" McKinley looked around, signaling a man to draw near.

"Mr. McKinley, is this man bothering you?" The man, possessing a sallow complexion and a wide girth, eyed Thomas like he might a rabid stoat.

"I believe this man is just leaving."

"No," Thomas said, leaning back in his chair. "This man is not. Not until he is given the remaining forty pounds he is owed." He watched McKinley's face carefully, but when the man adopted a similar pose of hauteur, felt a disconcerting niggle that perhaps the direct approach had been overly direct.

"Then I'm afraid you are doomed for disappointment. I cannot give what is not yours."

"What is not mine? You are a liar, sir!"

266

McKinley's eyes narrowed, as he said softly, "Are you certain of that?"

That sense of internal alarm grew more clamorous. "Can you deny I gave you money for Julia?"

"I deny nothing." He lifted his hands in a sign of complaisance.

"Except that."

McKinley looked up at the man still watching them, a frown upon his swarthy face. "Bucknell, do I seem the type of man to want to bring division between a man and his wife?"

"No indeed, sir."

"You must allow that I find such accusations . . . challenging, to say the least." His attention returned to Thomas. "I cannot give you what you ask —"

"Will not, you mean."

"*Can*not," McKinley corrected in that too-soft voice, so at odds with his hard countenance, "but I may find it in my heart to make you a small loan, say, in the vicinity of another ten pounds."

His chest grew hot as magma. He flexed his fingers. Counted to ten. Then said in his own soft voice, "I will not be silenced by your bribes."

The hand extending money to him withdrew. "I do not understand why you feel so strongly about this, Major Hale," McKinley complained. "Bucknell, here, can see I am only trying to help —"

"You are trying something, all right, but it certainly isn't help. What *is* your scheme, I wonder?"

"Me? I have no 'scheme' as you so delicately put it. I like to consider myself as a fair, generous-minded individual, but I'm afraid your accusations are sorely trying my patience."

"As your denials are trying mine."

Thomas eyed him, but the smug look in the other man's eyes was like a shield, not permitting the smallest chink of doubt. Yet Thomas *knew* he was hiding something. Or was he starting to lose his mind? He *had* given McKinley the money. Hadn't he?

As if conscious of Thomas's doubts, a queer smile stole across the other man's face. "I feel it only fair to tell you, Hale, that I do not like to be accused of being a liar."

"I am not the only one who knows you did not give Julia what you said you did."

"No?" An eyebrow lifted. "You interest me."

Should he say something about Becky's information? Perhaps he should keep her name out of things. He sensed McKinley might take exception to another person's contradiction of his claims, poor widow though she may be.

McKinley leaned forward. "Forgive me, I am a busy man. Is there anything else you wish to say?"

It was like talking to a brick wall. The desperation intensified. Should he challenge the man to a fight? Search his pockets for cash? What should he do?

He plunged his hands into his breeches pocket, found the card inscribed with the name of the solicitor Jon had recommended. Purpose firmed. An answer. "If you still refuse to pay, then you force me to seek legal restitution."

"Over a matter of forty pounds? Come man, don't be absurd."

"Do you consider honor absurd?" McKinley's eyes flickered. A hit. "It was fifty pounds," Thomas said, continuing to watch him carefully. "I thought you said the other ten was a gift."

"What you think and what is true appear to be two very different things," McKinley said with a yawn. "Now, excuse me, but I have many pressing matters to attend to." He gestured to the man standing behind him. "Bucknell will escort you out."

Thomas wrenched his arm away. "This is

269

a public establishment. I need no escort, sir."

He pushed to his feet, hating the feeling of being summarily dismissed, yet unable to think what else might be done. Nothing he said seemed to make a whit of difference. He could only hope this Mr. Osgood fellow might have a solution.

He picked his way through the crowd, unhappily aware that many of them were following his progress with intent speculation, and reached the outside, and the choke of smoke-fogged street. He glanced at the card again, noting the address before returning it to its hiding place deep in his pocket. He would just have to hope that Mr. Osgood was not averse to an evening visitor.

The streets turned and twisted, a ropelike snarl of back alleys and lanes, as he wended his way across Auld Town to where the address proclaimed Mr. Osgood's premises in the New.

A scuffle sounded behind him. He glanced back. No one.

The uneasy feeling returned, doubling, redoubling. Perhaps he would have been wiser to have sourced a hackney, but these steep streets ill lent themselves to such things, and he could scarce afford it anyway. His pace increased.

"Oy, Hale."

Thomas paused, turned. The man Bucknell stood there, leering. "Yes?"

"McKinley felt sorry for you. He wanted to make sure you got what you was owed."

A knot loosed in his chest. He'd relented, after all? "I am glad he has seen sense and —"

The flash of knife surprised him, forcing him to block with his arm, even as he tried to twist away. The blade pierced his coat sleeve, elicited a gasp as the steel met skin, ripped into his flesh. Thomas fisted a punch to the man's abdomen, satisfied as the action caused Bucknell's grip on the knife to release, and Thomas kicked it across the laneway. Breathing hard, he watched the man gasp for air. Thomas pulled a handkerchief from his pocket and pressed it against his wound. "Fighting dirty, is he?"

Bucknell looked up, the pain contorting his face changing to a smirk. "You could say that."

Just then, fire crashed through Thomas's head from behind, and he slumped to the ground in an agony of stunned pain.

CHAPTER EIGHTEEN

Julia watched as Catherine departed the sitting room to greet her newly arrived guest.

"Dearest Catherine!"

The voices in the hall continued, Catherine's low voice underscoring the higher tones of Lavinia, Countess of Hawkesbury. From the conversation at dinner last week, Julia knew Catherine had been looking forward to seeing her friend again.

Julia looked back down at her sad attempt at stitchery. She would never master the patience required for such fine detail, patience her sister-in-law possessed in abundance.

She had welcomed Catherine's invitation to visit this afternoon — really, these opportunities to escape the icy stillness of Portman Square were something of a godsend — but now felt a mix of trepidation and anticipation. If Julia was to ever make her reentrance into society, it might as well

272

be with people she sensed would regard her with more consideration than contempt. And that had been her experience with the ebullient countess back in Gloucestershire two years ago. But time could change things. She hoped Lavinia's kindness would be in evidence again today.

The door reopened, and Lady Hawkesbury entered, her face lighting as she saw Julia.

"Oh, my dear Julia!"

Seconds later she was ensconced in a hug so warm, filled with such acceptance, tears started to her eyes.

"Dear Julia." Lavinia pulled back, eyes searching her. "How truly wonderful to see you."

"I . . . I hope you don't mind my being here. Catherine said you would not." Julia shot her sister-in-law a small smile.

"Mind? How could I mind such a wondrous thing? You have been in my prayers these many months, and I confess it seems almost miraculous to see you again, looking so fresh and lovely."

Julia forced a smile. Flutters of unease in her midsection certainly did not lend themselves to thinking herself in such a generous way. " 'Tis kind of you to say so."

"Not kind. Merely the truth." Lavinia

turned to Catherine. "Jon and your mother must be so pleased to have you returned!"

"They are delighted."

"And your husband? Where is he?" Lavinia asked, her attention returning to Julia, without the flicker of an eyelash to suggest anything other than polite enquiry.

"My husband has recently returned to conclude some business matters in Scotland."

"By all that is wonderful, so has mine! Well, not returned exactly. Nicholas is merely visiting his solicitor. Apparently, he has a cousin whose idea of estate management does not precisely accord with Nicholas's intentions, and he feels it best to deal with such matters in a manner less confrontational, shall we say, than that which might more naturally be his bent."

A chuckle escaped. "He sounds not unlike Thomas in that way."

Lavinia peered at her. "Well, I should imagine they might possess similar qualities. They were both majors in His Majesty's army, were they not?"

"My husband served in India."

"And did some good work there, so my husband tells me."

Surprise curled warmth within. How rare it was to hear her Thomas praised.

Lavinia smiled, a gesture so full of sincerity and friendliness Julia felt the shackles surrounding her heart loosen a fraction more. "And may I be so bold as to ask when you expect Major Hale's return?"

"I am hopeful it is within the next week. It depends on the success of his mission." Like whether he learned more about little Charlie's family. Her sagging spirits were surprised at Lavinia's laughter.

"Oh, your husband talks like that, too, does he? I declare, sometimes it seems that Nicholas will never forget his army days and fully settle down to married life, and fatherhood, and all that that entails."

The door opened, admitting a footman carrying a tray of tea things. Catherine quietly directed him to place it in the corner, then began to pour.

Lavinia took a sip of tea, complimented Catherine on its superior quality — "but that can hardly be wondered at, seeing as your husband has such superior connections!" — then glanced at Julia again, her head tilted. "I suppose you must have become used to enjoying such things when you were growing up. I imagine the Carlew family never lacked for those products India is renowned for. Tea, and cotton, and silks." She sighed. "Sometimes I wonder at myself, being interested in the frivolous things my Aunt Patience would never have approved. But I cannot apologize for preferring my tea to be delicious rather than stale."

Julia smiled and murmured something of her agreement.

"I knew you were sensible. Now, Julia — I hope you don't mind if I call you Julia?"

"Of course not."

"I do not know if you remember that we have a little girl. Grace is a sweet thing, nearly two years of age now. She and young Elizabeth will soon be playmates."

"And there is another little person to become a playmate," Catherine said with a smile at Julia.

"We . . ." Julia swallowed. Had Jon told his wife the truth about little Charles? It did not seem so. Conscious two pairs of eyes were studying her, she finished with a rush, ". . . have a little boy. His name is Charles." There. There was no word of lie in that, was there? Little Charles was in her — their — possession, after all. At least for the moment.

"Oh! How wonderful! Well, my congratulations to you both." Lavinia turned to Catherine, and said with a knowing look, "I wonder how long it will be until Elizabeth might have a sibling?"

Catherine blushed, but said calmly, "And as soon as I saw you, I wondered the same about your little Grace."

Lavinia chuckled. "Oh, your powers of discernment are indeed marvelous as ever, dear friend. Yes" — her eyes lit like stars — "we have reason to hope for another addition in the next few months." She peeked at Julia. "All the more reason for Lord Hawkesbury to conclude his time in Scotland so he can return in plenty of time before the babe's arrival."

"Congratulations," Julia murmured, fighting the pang of envy. How wonderful it must be to be so secure in their marriage that she could speak so confidently.

"Thank you!" She beamed, accepting a small pastry from the plate Catherine offered, adding, "And thank *you*. I find I'm terribly hungry these days, which can make my manners a trifle unseemly at times."

Catherine denied this with a smile, and offered the plate to Julia.

Her stomach protested. "Thank you, no."

Lavinia turned to Catherine. "And how long do you think your interesting condition might last for?"

"Until early summer, perhaps. But we have not told anyone in the family, not even dear Julia." She shot Julia a look tinged with apology. "And I do not quite know how to share such things with Serena and Henry, especially at this time."

"Oh, yes, I heard Lord Bevington is extremely unwell," said Lavinia, her features soft with sympathy. "He has been in our prayers also."

Lavinia seemed to spend a great deal of time praying for people, Julia mused. Her gaze shifted and she caught a different look in Catherine's eye, as if that wasn't what she'd meant to imply, before her face blanked to smoothness. The Earl of Bevington's illness was not why Catherine was reluctant to share news of her pregnancy with her sister. Half-spoken words, recollections of Lord Carmichael's anxiety about his wife's reaction to little Charles whirled through her mind, settling into certainty. No wonder Catherine had said nothing. Serena herself had spoken of her fears that she was unable to have children.

By the time her attention returned to the other ladies, their conversation had moved on to other elements associated with their mutual "interesting" conditions.

"Yes, this time I feel so much better than I did when I was carrying Grace." Lavinia glanced at Julia. "Forgive me for being so indelicate, but it's wonderful to have some-

278

one who understands such intimate matters. Don't you agree?"

What could she say? Julia could only nod.

"I have heard it said that the sicker one is the healthier the child will be," Lavinia continued in a conspiratorial tone, "and that one's pregnancies differ according to whether one is carrying a boy or a girl." She touched her midsection. "I am hopeful that my different experience this time means Nicholas might finally have his son."

She shared a look with Catherine heavy with meaning, before glancing back at Julia, the corners of her mouth tipping up. "Forgive me if you find this question too bold, but I'm interested in finding out if other ladies suffered more with carrying boys than with girls. Did you suffer overly when you were pregnant with Charles?"

"I, er . . ." Julia swallowed.

"Forgive me. I should not ask such a thing."

"No, no," Julia moved to assure her. She frowned, trying to remember just how Meggie had described her experience. "There were . . . symptoms of nausea, I recall."

"Oh, yes! And such tiredness! I felt completely drained . . ." Lavinia's voice faded.

Catherine murmured, "I craved quite

strange foods. And had headaches. And felt . . . a little sore and tender . . ." She glanced at Julia. "You were fortunate if you did not experience much in the way of these."

"I . . . did not," she said, wincing internally at her honesty.

As the others continued their somewhat surprisingly candid descriptions, Julia blinked. Why, the symptoms they described might well be describing how she had been feeling these past days. The scent of egg from the plate wafted before her, causing a familiar clenching from inside that mingled with a new lightheadedness. She gasped.

"Julia? What is it?"

She shook her head, placed a hand to her mouth, and willed the nausea away, even as the previous conversation washed through her consciousness, gaining new meaning.

Oh, dear God!

Could she truly be in an interesting condition also?

The scent of decaying fish and brine assailed his senses, stirring him to wakefulness. Thomas blinked, but his vision remained blurred. All remained indistinct, all remained dim. He tried to move, but couldn't. Pressure bound him. A staying hand.

A vague murmur of voices stole into his awareness, deep tones, higher tones, something in a Scottish brogue. A seagull's caw. The slap of sea.

He felt a hand touch his scalp, and he closed his eyes against the sheer roar of pain, muttered an oath. But words refused to form. His tongue felt engorged, his nerves splintering into a thousand tiny pinpricks. He turned his head, smelled the scent of something pungent, something damp, something that smelled half dead. His stomach protested and he jerked his head to retch. Almost vomited again at the enormous pain swelling within.

"Och, the poor wee laddie."

A spark of humor pushed past his wretchedness. He'd never been accused of being "wee" these past two dozen years.

He forced his eyes to open, saw something striped, like an apron, a basket woven of sticks like willow, the bare feet and rolled up trouser legs of a small boy.

A guttural sound came, then he felt himself being lifted, felt an arm around his shoulders, a small hand pat down his coat and pockets.

Thomas tried to protest, but only heard

the guttural sound again, and realized it must have come from himself.

The voices overhead and behind him continued in their strange and unfamiliar tongue. His brain could not follow, and he gave it up, closing his eyes against the harsh insistent light.

Sleep beckoned, unearthly stillness, even as a tiny whisper begged him to remain, to pray. *God!* He felt his spirit cry. *Help me.*

A gabble of heavily accented brogue assailed his ears, words he could have no hope of understanding. He exhaled, and succumbed to the darkness again.

Chapter Nineteen

Rain pattered against the bedroom window, tapping certainty into her soul. Days had passed and she could not avoid the truth any longer. She would have to see the doctor.

Julia released a shaky breath. But she could not! Seeing a doctor would mean a doctor must see her — and see parts of her nobody but Thomas had seen in an age — and then the doctor would know she had never birthed a child. She frowned. He *would* be able to tell that, wouldn't he? And if he learned the truth, then Mother would also, and then there would be such a to-do about little Charles that she could not bear to think —

"Oh, good, you are awake." Mother walked into the bedchamber, without a knock to preface her entry. Really, Julia thought, the sooner she and Thomas could live somewhere else, the better. "I was beginning to wonder if we might ever see you again."

"Here I am," Julia said, offering a pitiful attempt at a smile.

"I am sorry you have not felt well these past days. I have on several occasions tried to see if you would like a doctor to visit, but each time you have been asleep."

Well, Julia's lips grew heavy with guilt, she'd *pretended* to be asleep. For how could she agree to be examined when it would confirm what she suspected? How could she disappoint her mother, when her mother's feelings towards little Charles vacillated according to the pitch of his cries? Some days she seemed to barely tolerate him, while others she seemed charmed by his full-cheeked smile. What would Mother say when she learned Thomas's visit weeks ago had resulted in another "consequence"?

"I do hope you're feeling a little better now."

"A little," she hedged.

"Good. For I have Dr. Fairburn down-stairs, waiting to see you. No, there is no need to look like that. He's very well-known, all my friends declare him to be the best. He possesses the bedside manner of a prince!"

Julia swallowed a hysteria-laden giggle.

Judging from the exploits of certain members of the royal family, she certainly hoped this doctor did not wish to emulate them!

Mother looked at her oddly, shrugged, then called for a servant to send the doctor up.

Julia eyed her mother with no small degree of trepidation. Would she insist on staying? What could she do to make her leave?

"Now, please do not worry. I will be here with you. As I said, he's come highly recommended — ah, doctor, thank you for agreeing to see my daughter Julia."

"Miss," he offered Julia a bow, before casting a look at her mother, as if requesting permission.

Somehow that look fired grit within. "I am Mrs. Hale," she said loudly.

His gaze returned to her. "Oh! Forgive me. I did not realize. I assumed —"

"I imagine assumptions could prove fatal in your line of work."

Dr. Fairburn blinked. The crease in his forehead deepened. He glanced at her mother, as if unsure what to do.

"Please ignore my daughter's attempt at levity. She has been unwell these past days and I'm afraid that has put her out of spirits."

He inclined his head, then turned to Julia.

"You have not been well?"

Perhaps she could answer with half-truths, as now seemed to be her way. "No, I have not."

He took a moment to ask her symptoms, to which she gave vague answers, resulting in his frown. "And have you done anything out of the ordinary, perhaps been someplace unusual? Do you have any idea as to what might have caused this?"

She had *some* idea . . .

"Perhaps you have eaten something that did not agree with you?"

Well, that was certainly true. In the past week meat of all varieties had definitely not agreed with her. "Perhaps," she allowed.

"And have you experienced other symptoms of ill-health?"

"She has been very tired," Mother offered from her corner.

"Hmm." The doctor frowned, then moved closer to the bed. "Perhaps if you might permit me to look at your throat, Miss — forgive me — Mrs. Hale."

Julia nodded, following his instructions as he extracted a silver instrument from his bag and asked her to open her mouth. Perhaps she could pretend to be suffering the effects of a cold, then he might leave —

"Hmm. Well, the good news is I see nothing of redness, nothing to suggest a putrid throat." He offered a thin smile. "It's good to know what you have is most likely not catching."

Another spurt of hysteria had to be smothered in a cough. No, it was likely not catching.

He frowned. "Have you had that cough for long?"

"A little while," she murmured.

"Please permit me to listen to your lungs. Now, lean forward, like so . . ."

He placed a cool metal instrument at her back, then pressed his ear against it, so her mirror informed her. He listened for a moment, then instructed her to pull her shift down. "I hear nothing to suggest any inflammation. Would it be too much trouble to ask if I may listen to your chest?"

"I think I would prefer that you did not."

"Very well." He frowned, angling his head to one side as he considered her. He glanced back at her mother. "Lady Harkness, would you be so good as to permit me a few moments alone with your daughter?"

The hairs rose on Julia's neck. No. Why would he wish to speak with her alone except . . . ?

Her mother acquiesced. When the door had closed, the doctor eyed her gravely.

287

"Mrs. Hale?"

"Y-yes?"

"May I ask a few questions of a more personal nature?"

She nodded.

"I am sorry if you find such things distasteful, but I must have all the facts if I am to assist you. Can you recall the last time of your menses?"

She licked suddenly dry lips. "I believe it was a few weeks ago."

"How many weeks? It is best to be as precise as possible."

"I . . . I'm afraid I cannot exactly recall."

He nodded. Scribbled something in his little notebook. Glanced up again. "And can I be so bold as to enquire whether you have had intimate relations with your husband recently?"

"Sir!"

"It is necessary to rule out all possible scenarios."

What could she answer? What should she say?

"Mrs. Hale?"

The words pierced her guard, prickling heat at the back of her eyes. "Yes?"

"I'm sorry, would you mind answering the question, please?"

Yes, she did mind! She didn't want to

288

answer. Oh, what should she say?

She licked her lips again. "H-how recently?"

He shrugged. "Have you been intimate with your husband in the last few weeks?"

"M-my husband is away in Scotland at the moment."

"Oh, I see." He frowned, wrote something in his notebook before glancing up again, his gaze impenetrable. "And he was last here when?"

"Several weeks ago."

His brow cleared. "And were you intimate with him then? I ask simply because I wish to know if you might be in the family way."

"And —" Julia gulped. "And if I were, would you be obliged to speak of this to anyone?"

"I see. So you were intimate."

She was starting to hate that word! "Yes," she whispered.

"Then as my patient, I would be bound to speak of this only to those whom it concerns."

Julia shook her head. "I do not want my mother —"

"She will hear nothing of it from me." He looked kindly at her. "But you do know such a thing will not be able to remain hidden forever?"

She nodded, made an attempt to listen as he issued instructions, and made another attempt to smile as he offered quiet congratulations.

But all the while her mind was ticking, ticking, ticking, with what reason she would give for her illness to her mother, and what her husband would say when he finally returned.

When next he awoke, it was to awareness that the scent of brine had disappeared, that he lay in a cot-like bed, and could hear English being spoken in cool tones. He forced his eyelids to unfasten, caught a glimpse of a man, two men, neither of whom seemed familiar.

"Ah, the patient awakes."

Thomas willed his vision to focus, to not waver. Who . . . ?

The other, shorter man, pushed back into his vision. "Sir? My name is Osgood. You had one of my cards of business on your person."

Had he? Well, if the man said so. Thomas nodded. Lightning ripped through his skull.

"Please don't move." The man — Osgood? — drew near, his graying hair gleaming in the candlelight. "You have been quite badly injured, and the doctor says — ah, here he is now."

The second man returned into view. Now his vision was clearing Thomas observed he was in a cream-papered room. A smell, like alcohol, but no alcohol he ever wished to sip, had replaced most of the sea scent from before.

The new stranger, the doctor, murmured something to the other before approaching Thomas, a heavy frown punctuating his brow. "Do you know your name?"

His mind held a foggy kind of heaviness that permitted no quick answer. He strained to think. His name? Something to do with the weather? Rayne? Yes, that was his name. He tried to utter acquiescence but his throat did not cooperate.

"Please, do not distress yourself." He continued speaking, his words a garble of accented English Thomas could barely follow.

"You were attacked, sir. Which is why you are now here at the infirmary."

What? That did not make sense.

"He is perhaps confused."

"It would seem so," the doctor muttered, a heavy frown causing his eyebrows to jut out alarmingly. "I'm afraid you will need to spend quite some time here before your body mends sufficiently."

Again, Thomas tried to speak. Again, he failed.

"Please, try to rest." The doctor's brows plunged and he turned to the older man and said in a lowered voice, "I cannae like what has happened to him. I'm wary about advertising his placement here in case whoever is responsible attempts to complete what they began."

Mr. Osgood sighed heavily. "I think that wise, and I assure you that I will do all in my power to ascertain how he came to be carrying my card. Perhaps then we can learn who he is."

"I suspect he is an Englishman, that much seems clear from his mutterings at night, and from the cut of his clothes. And with that tan I wonder if he has spent time abroad, somewhere hot." The doctor wiped his hands upon a towel. "I confess I cannae like the scars on his back, almost like he's been whipped or tortured once upon a time. But he does not quite hold the aspect of a convict."

"Poor lad."

"Indeed. He has experienced terrible things. We can only hope his memory returns soon."

"And pray that the good Lord above heals

his body, and brings his attackers to justice."

"Aye. And until then, I think it best to keep both him and his location quiet." The doctor shook his head. "Such ferocity I have nae seen since the war."

Osgood nodded. "I will return to Newhaven again, and see if anyone remembers anything from three nights ago. And I'll have a word with the night watchman. Perhaps he can help us in some way."

Thomas listened, helpless, unable to speak, his body throbbing with pain that only sleep could ease. And so, with his soul desperately clinging to the hope that the solicitor's prayers would be answered, he closed his eyes and slept.

CHAPTER TWENTY

The trees flashing above them lifted twist-ing branches to the pale blue sky. Recent storms had played havoc with the park, lit-tering the ground with broken twigs and leaves. On this, the first fine day in what felt like months but was probably only a week, Julia had allowed herself to be coaxed outside to join Catherine on a drive through Hyde Park. Truth be told, she had not required much coaxing, Mother's over-anxiousness in past days proving as stifling as ever, and Julia's nausea becoming in-creasingly challenging to hide. Charles was in good hands with Crabbit back at the town house, or so the nursemaid had in-sisted. She hoped so, anyway. She loved the little boy, but not his clingy need for her, nor the cries that wormed inside, stirring guilt and unease. To be elsewhere, outside, smelling the freshness in the brisk breeze, was wonderful. She drank in another breath.

"There," Catherine said, with a sideways glance at Julia. "That is what I wished to see. It's been too long since roses have appeared in those cheeks."

There was a good reason for that, Julia thought, but didn't say. She offered a wobbly smile in lieu of reply.

"Poor thing. You have not been terribly well of late, have you?" Catherine said, as the driver continued their course past the Serpentine. "I am sorry for it. I can imagine being cooped up at home must prove a little dreary at times."

Rather, all the time. "I am not used to feeling this way," she allowed.

The horses began a slow turn. In the distance a horseman on a brown hack drew nearer.

Julia peeked across. Blinked. "Why, it's Mr. Amherst."

"Who?"

"Mr. Amherst," she murmured in an undertone, as he caught sight of her and instantly pulled up beside the carriage.

"Why, Mrs. Hale! Good afternoon."

Julia greeted him, a corner of her heart lifting at the respectful regard which filled his eyes. "Good afternoon, Mr. Amherst. May I present my sister-in-law, Lady Winthrop."

As he and Catherine exchanged greetings, Julia eyed him surreptitiously. Would he make any more remarks on her appearance today? It was strange how much she had savored his comments from before. Or perhaps not so strange, for it had been a long while since anyone had complimented her looks, after all.

"I *am* pleased to see you again." His smile seemed ingenuous. "Tell me, how have you been faring in these recent days? It appears the weather has not played havoc with your health."

She murmured something of her obligation, conscious of Catherine's wide-eyed look, before quickly enquiring as to Miss Hatherleigh's whereabouts.

"Oh, Caro. Well, she has returned to Somerset with her family, although I expect they shall return when the Season begins. Tell me, do you have plans to be here for the Season, Mrs. Hale?"

"My plans are not yet certain, Mr. Amherst."

"We await news of her husband's return," Catherine said in a cool tone quite unlike her.

"Well, I cannot imagine that he would wish to delay returning a second longer than he has to," he responded gallantly. "I wonder, Mrs. Hale, if I might be so bold as to request an opportunity to visit you while I am in London. I have found there are not as many people in town as I had thought, and I confess that some days are quite lonesome."

Well she knew that feeling. "Of course, I do not mind." She gave her mother's direction.

He thanked her, inclined his head to Catherine, smiled his winning smile at Julia, and rode away. Leaving her to face Catherine's scrutiny.

"What?"

"I cannot understand."

"What can you not understand?"

Catherine shook her head. "I thought you were missing your husband. I did not expect to see you engage in a flirtation with another man."

Her cheeks heated. "I was not flirting."

"No? Merely giving him permission to call upon you?"

"At my mother's house." Julia summoned up a laugh. "Really, Catherine, there is nothing to be worried about. He is friendly, that is all."

"I don't know if that truly *is* all," Catherine countered. "But if you say so."

Why, when people said that, did it always

sound like they did not trust you? But there seemed little sense in protesting her innocence; Catherine would believe what she believed. Her lips twisted. As if Mr. Amherst could be interested anyway. Not when she was a wife, and caring for little Charles, and about to be —

She lifted a hand to her mouth, willing the nausea away. Forced a smile at Catherine's concern. Waved away her enquiry as to what was wrong as another carriage pulled into view.

Catherine instructed the driver to take an alternative route, and soon they had veered from the main drive to one that crossed closer to the Serpentine, whose banks overflowed from recent rain.

They traveled on for some moments in silence, as Julia wondered what she could say to change the mood induced by the earlier topic of conversation. "You . . . you seem a little different from what I remember from before."

"Do I? Well, time has a way of changing people, I suppose."

"I did not expect to see you confront Mother as you did the other day."

Catherine's brow puckered, cleared. "Oh, you mean about her comments regarding Thomas? Well, I cannot imagine you find it easy to have to listen to such criticism all the time. It must be very hard to not let yourself be swayed into . . . a hardened heart against your husband."

Julia swallowed.

"And having experienced the freedom that comes with choosing to forgive, I can only recommend such an action to others. And I'm afraid poor Lady Harkness seems to be allowing herself to be entangled by animosity's power, which is never a good thing."

"You said allow?"

"Yes. I believe we give feelings permission to live in our hearts by whether we choose to think upon such things or not. The more we think about certain matters the greater impact they effect, until they can tend to obsess us. Have you ever experienced this?"

Like when she had lived at home and obsessed over being elsewhere, until she snatched at the first chance to leave — by running away with Thomas? Guilt bade her say, "Yes."

"I have, too. In fact, when I was in Bath, I needed my Aunt Drusilla to remind me I had a choice at my disposal."

"Was . . . was that in relation to Jon?"

Catherine gave a wry smile. "I had loved your brother for a very long time, and it was . . . very challenging to see his affections engaged by another. I certainly struggled with anger and resentment for quite some time."

"And how did you change?"

"God used Aunt Drusilla to help me see that unforgiveness binds, but forgiving others sets us free. It actually does us more good because our heart is not so cluttered with poisonous thoughts against others. So, I had to ask God to help me, to forgive me, in order to forgive others. I still do. I certainly do not mean to imply that I am never angry or resentful, simply that I am learning to not let such emotion possess me."

Was this why Catherine seemed so different, seemed to own a peace Julia had never known?

"It reminds me of a story Jesus told, about a servant who had done wrong and amassed great debts for his master. He confessed, and the master forgave him. But when a fellow servant confessed of a small debt against this first servant, he had him thrown into prison, forgetting that he had been shown mercy for a much greater sum." Catherine smiled. "If I remember the many sins for which God has forgiven me, how can I then hold such things against another?"

300

Julia's heart twisted. She was only too good at holding on to offenses.

"This is why I am concerned for your mother, and wish her to release these emotions so she does not have to bear their weight unnecessarily. It is far better to trust God with our future."

Again, Julia felt a touch of conviction. Trust God with her future?

"I wonder," Catherine said, with a tilt to her head that gave her the look of a brown robin, "do you think your mother would be conducive to a stay in the country?"

"Mother much prefers London," Julia began.

"Oh, no, I meant *you* staying in the country." She smiled. "I don't mind being in London when Jon is here, but he's away on business — I believe these storms have made traveling somewhat difficult up north — and I would much prefer to be home in Gloucestershire where one can truly relax, rather than wondering who might take it upon themselves to visit."

Julia chuckled. How many times had she felt exactly that? On more than one occasion she had been trapped in the library or the drawing room while Mother's many society callers engaged her in too-long conversations, or worse, spied Julia, and then spent the next minutes trying to engage her in social inanities, all the while eyeing her with deep looks of speculation. To escape such things . . . "Sounds like bliss."

Catherine's dark eyes lit. "Well, then, perhaps we should speak to her. I can phrase things in a way that she may think such a plan of greater benefit for me than you, if you think that wise."

"*Very* wise," Julia agreed. "Perhaps if she was also made aware of the benefits of not having a small crying child in near vicinity she will be more likely to agree."

"I remember those days," Catherine said sympathetically. "It is not easy, is it?"

"No." Julia offered a small smile, but Catherine's gaze, soft with compassion, urged her to look elsewhere, lest the tears prick anew. Really, she was being so emotional these days.

Her gaze traveled over the parkland, past the sheet of gray-metal water, to the red-bricked Kensington Palace beyond and the huge stone gates that marked the entry to the park. While all this was very pretty, and certainly nicer than the dreariness she associated with Edinburgh, it would be nice to live where trepidation did not loom with every passing carriage as she wondered whom she might meet. Jon's estate in Gloucestershire might be someplace she'd once decried as dull, but now anywhere seemed preferable to where she was.

"Have you heard from Thomas recently?"

Another heart pang. "No, not recently." Not at all. Had he forgotten that he said he would write? It had been over two weeks; surely he should have written something by now.

"Oh, I'm sure he will write soon. I imagine these awful floods have made communication difficult also. After all, if one cannot get through on the mail coach . . ."

"Of course," Julia murmured. Perhaps that was it. Perhaps she need not worry *all* the time. Really, she was growing almost as tiresome as Catherine's mother, someone whom Mother had whispered had long-earned the crown of Queen Worrywart, and who certainly did not go out of her way to encourage peace —

Her musings were cut short by the advance of another carriage.

"Oh dear."

"What is it?"

"Lord Snowstrem." Catherine sighed. "I really would have preferred not to have met him."

This seemed so out of character for the

sweet and mild Catherine that Julia couldn't help but ask why.

"He is something of a gossip. Poor Serena and Henry learned earlier this year about the unfortunate consequences of his tongue. I would request the driver to take an alternative route, but it is a narrow road, and the ground is so muddied that such a thing would make it too obvious we hoped to avoid him."

Within half a minute their carriage was drawing to one side of the path, as another drew nearer, a carriage containing a rather bulbous individual, with eyes every bit as sharp and penetrating as Julia had ever encountered. She shivered.

The opposite carriage slowed to a standstill. "Ah, dear Lady Winthrop. 'Tis a wonderful thing to encounter a pair of ladies willing to venture outside in such adverse conditions."

"It is a little blustery still. Which is why I think it best to not linger —"

"Oh, but before you go, you simply must introduce me to your charming companion."

Julia felt, rather than heard, Catherine's sigh. "Of course. Lord Snowstrem, may I present Mrs. Hale."

Julia nodded.

"Mrs. Hale." He offered her a nod, then a look of speculation. "Now, where have I heard that name before?"

Julia refused to answer; Catherine said, with an air of desperation, "Forgive me, Lord Snowstrem, but I really must insist —"

"You're not married to that soldier fellow, are you?" His eyes widened. "Not the little runaway? But of course! I see it now. You are Carlew — I mean, Lord Winthrop's sister."

As Lord Snowstrem continued talking, eyeing Julia with avid curiosity, looking all the time as if he'd like to clap his hands with glee, Catherine leaned forward to murmur something to the carriage driver. The carriage moved forward with a jerk.

"Goodbye, my lord," Catherine said.

He ignored her, eyes fixed on Julia. "But I heard Major Hale was dead."

She gasped, covering her mouth with her gloved hand.

"What?" His thick lips pulled back in a leering smile. "Never tell me I am the bearer of bad news!"

The carriage moved away, his face — his gleeful face — replaced with Catherine's look of concern. "Oh, my dear! You cannot believe such a thing." She placed a hand on

Julia's arm. "Please, do not even consider it. Buffy Snorestream is known to like to cause trouble, even to the extent of presenting lies as fact."

The panic swirling within settled on the absurd name. "Buffy Snorestream?"

"Oh, forgive me. I should not have said that. I have heard Henry describe him thus, due to his propensity for long-windedness. But truly, forget him."

"But he said Thomas was dead!"

"Well, how would he know that? Let us think about this calmly. If we have received no correspondence from Scotland, then how can one expect someone not even in our circles to have news related to your husband? Truly, I think it best not to concern yourself with him."

"But why would he say that if it were not true?"

"Because he has no great liking for us, you or me." Catherine's dark eyes flashed. "He is the type of man to stir up trouble and dissent, and in doing so does the devil's work. No, the best thing to do is to ignore him. Please —" She gently squeezed Julia's arm. "Please do not trouble yourself with him. I'm sure he was referring to when the major was missing for that great period. There is no reason to suspect otherwise. If

306

something had recently happened to Thomas, you would be the first to be informed."

"But these storms — you said before we have heard no news because the storms have cut road access. What if something has happened and we just don't know about it yet?"

"Then how would Lord Snowstrem have heard? I beg you not to worry over this."

That was easy for Catherine to say, Julia thought, drawing in a deep breath. But if Thomas were truly gone — she hated to use the word *dead* — what would that mean? The familiar ball of helplessness seemed to suddenly triple in size. Her lungs were full, she was struggling to breathe.

"Julia?"

She waved off Catherine's concern, focusing on her breathing. In. Out. In. Out —

The carriage veered, the shifting momentum causing her insides to spasm. She gasped.

"Julia? What is it?"

"Nothing," she murmured, pressing her fingers to her mouth. Oh, how wretched she felt.

Catherine frowned. "That is not nothing. You are unwell. We shall return immediately." She gave orders to the driver; the carriage picked up pace.

The brush of chilled breeze against her face brought a modicum of relief, but still the unsettling feelings continued.

"I am so sorry. I wish we had not met Lord Snowstrem. We shall return soon, and then you may feel better."

"Returning will not fix this," Julia muttered.

"But you are pale, and — forgive me — appear to be nauseous. I thought today's outing might prove of some benefit from the past weeks —" Her eyes widened. "Julia!"

Julia closed her eyes. She could not look into honest eyes when she did not want to admit the truth to the question she could see forming. Catherine would tell Jon, who would tell Mother, who would —

"Are you — ? Can it be?" Catherine whispered urgently.

Julia shook her head. Swallowed the sour taste in her mouth.

"Oh."

The voice of disappointment begged the truth to be spoken aloud. She pressed her lips together even more firmly, and opened her eyes to catch sight of a man who appeared to be watching them intently.

She frowned. Who was that?

Probably she was mistaken, and he was

merely looking somewhere beyond. She turned for one more glance. Ice stole up her spine. The man still watched them keenly.

She turned to Catherine, and said urgently, "Can you see a man by the great oak over there? Is he still watching us?"

"Why, yes."

Julia turned to look once more, but he had gone. She shivered. The unknown observer coupled with the unnerving meetings with Mr. Amherst and Lord Snowstrem firmed her purpose. The sooner she could convince Mother of the merits of removing from London to the country the better.

Chapter Twenty-One

"You are a thankless son! A wound to my soul, a blight on our existence!"

Thomas said nothing.

The curse continued. "The Scriptures say that if a man has a stubborn and rebellious son who does not obey his father and mother, who will not listen to them when they discipline him, that his father shall take him to the elders and he shall be stoned to death. God hates sinners! The evil among us must be purged! Is this what you wish?"

"Charles, please!"

His father ignored Thomas's mother, and continued to shake his fist. "Do you know what it is like to have members of the vestry question my judgments, simply because my son is a profligate and a drunkard, and refuses to obey my decrees? Answer me!"

Thomas lifted his chin. "I am sorry that my actions have brought embarrassment —"

"Not mere embarrassment! Your actions

310

have called the very nature of my ministry into question! How dare you describe yourself as an unbeliever?"

"I dare because it is true. I do not believe in the god you do."

His father's palm connected with Thomas's cheek, causing his teeth to rattle, and his mother to again cry out in protest.

Thomas stifled the part that wanted to whimper like a child, instead holding himself tall, looking his father in the eye, in the way he knew his father loathed. How dare his son become a man? How dare Thomas wish for a life nothing like Father had known?

"You cannot stand there and tell me you wish to leave! What will the parishioners say?"

He gritted his teeth. Father cared more for his congregation than his only son. It had always been this way. He and his mother and sister had always run a very distant second to whatever the Reverend Charles Hale felt his church needed. Thank whatever gods might be that Jane had married and escaped their father's influence last year. Since then, she had urged Thomas to finally speak his mind about his wishes for his future — wishes that ran very contrary to their father's plans.

"Well? What have you got to say for yourself?"

Thomas swallowed, but said firmly, "You are right." Placate the old man.

"What? You will give up these foolish notions?"

"I should not stand here and tell you I wish to leave."

His father seemed to slump into the hearty sigh. "I knew you would see sense —"

"I should not have told you I wished to leave," Thomas continued, eyeing his father steadily, "rather, I should have said that I *am* leaving."

"But, but —"

"I am sorry, Mother," he said, turning to her, "but I cannot stay."

Her eyes brimmed with tears as she nodded. Oh, well she understood his reasons for leaving.

"Where will you live? Do not think you will ever be welcomed into this house again!"

"I have not felt welcomed in it for years." He took a step back, out of the way of his father's fist, before quickly turning, gripping his father's arm as hard as he could. "I am not your whipping boy anymore."

"I will pray that God will smite you for

your sin!"

"This is how you treat your flesh and blood? And this represents the oh-so-merciful god you want me to believe in?"

"Blasphemer! Wastrel! Drunkard!"

The words fell around him like bullets.

"You will never amount to anything! I wash my hands of you."

Deep sorrow twisted past his anger. Thomas firmed his lips, lips that wanted to tremble when he saw his mother's piteous tears. He had tried. God — if He existed — must have seen that Thomas had stayed longer than he'd wanted to provide some measure of comfort for his mother. But lately the accusations had grown worse, the threats more real. And the militia were moving on tomorrow, so his chance was never or now. He stepped closer, hugged his mother firmly, caught her scent of lavender, and muttered a goodbye against her hair.

"I'm so sorry," she murmured against his chest.

"As am I. I will write," he promised.

"You can write, but she will never read it," his father said, arms crossed, face hard. "As of now, I have no son."

"Goodbye, Father." Thomas collected his sack of meager belongings and, with a last apologetic look at his mother, walked through the front door and out into the darkness.

Pain rippled through him. Sorrow. Regrets. Perhaps he should not have succumbed to cards and liquor, but escape at night seemed the only way to cope with his father's rages. How could his father ask him to believe the way he did, when those beliefs had shaped him into a man Thomas — and his mother and sister — feared? What kind of god demanded such things? How could he believe in such things?

From somewhere very far away, he heard a rumbling sound, a voice that stole past his memories and begged him to awaken from this slumber.

". . . know this man, I believe?"

"Ah, yes," a deeper voice, an English voice, said. "Yes, I believe I do."

Thomas pushed open his eyes, to encounter a man whose features caused the faintest stir of recognition. He frowned, struggling to remember. Who . . . ?

The man drew closer, his dark hair glinting in the candlelight. "Good afternoon, Major Hale."

Hale, or Rayne? His head was foggy, his confusion real. He opened his mouth to speak, but could only emit a sound more croak than voice. His mouth was so, so dry.

"Now, don't try to strain yourself, sir," the doctor said. He helped Thomas to a glass of water, blessed water that slid coolness down his throat and sharpened reason to his brain.

He mumbled his obligation, and turned to the darker-haired gentleman. Who?

"He does seem to recognize you, m'lord."

"I am pleased. One never likes to think that one might be utterly forgettable."

"I'm sure that is not something you would have much experience with, Lord Hawkesbury," the doctor said in a dry tone.

"H-hawkesbury?" Thomas rasped.

A small smile crossed the other man's face. "I am gratified you remember."

"What . . . ?"

"What am I doing here?" Lord Hawkesbury asked. "Well, I had a meeting with Mr. Osgood — he has responsibility for arranging matters for me here in Scotland — and through the course of conversation learned about a mysterious Englishman who had been washed up at Newhaven's port. Naturally, I could not remain idly by, not when Osgood mentioned that this man had his card upon him, yet had never met him in his life." A smile glinted. "You can imagine my surprise to discover the man to be one who has dined at my house."

315

Dined . . . ? Oh, now he recalled. Staying with Jon at Winthrop. Visiting the Earl of Hawkesbury's house in Gloucestershire. Traces of his father's long ago words twisted his lips. He might not have amounted to much, but he had at least dined at an earl's house.

"You remember?"

Thomas nodded, sending a dull spear of pain down his spine.

"Now, Mr. Hale —"

"It is *Major* Hale, I believe," said the earl.

"Major Hale," the doctor continued, "please forgive me but I must ask . . ."

What followed were a litany of questions about Thomas's limbs, his eyesight, his movement, even the scars upon his back. Lord Hawkesbury quietly withdrew, leaving the doctor to his examination.

When he had finished his mild interrogation, and Thomas had complied with all his prodding and poking, the doctor sighed. "I'm afraid I dinnae have good news for you."

Thomas watched him, conscious of a tightening of breath, a new hammering in his veins. What could have the doctor looking so dour?

"I cannae like the swelling on your spine. It gives me great worry that your mobility

316

will be affected."

"What?"

"I fear you may have some degree of trouble with walking again."

Coldness swept his skin. No.

Lord Hawkesbury moved into view, his expression grim. This time he was accompanied by the older man Thomas vaguely recognized from the last time he was conscious.

Politeness bade him to exchange greetings, while desperation bade him to curl into a ball. What would he do? What could he do?

"It would seem whoever inflicted this upon you was doing their best to ensure you would not live to report such things," the earl said, his brow lowered. "I hope you know we shall do all we can to ensure you return to health as quickly as possible."

Thomas lowered his gaze to hide the sudden burn at the back of his eyes. He swallowed. Nodded. Winced. "I appreciate your help."

But how could he help? If the doctor was right and Thomas might not walk properly again, what on earth could the earl do to help? Fear slashed his chest. How on earth could he ever seek to provide for Julia if he could not walk? He drew in an unsteady breath. Forced himself to meet the concerned expressions of the other men, willed his features to not betray his distress.

"You can be sure we shall also do all in our power to find the perpetrators of this crime. That is why I thought it best to include Mr. Osgood once more, seeing as he has local knowledge that might prove helpful." Lord Hawkesbury added with a frown, "Hale, have you *any* recollection of what happened? Anything at all?"

Thomas pushed his brows together, straining to remember, but the whirl of worries stole every wisp of memory, the fear inside a heavy mist that shrouded all.

"My lord, I do not wish for him to worsen," the doctor protested.

"And I have no wish for the scoundrel who did this to get away with near murder." Hawkesbury leaned close. "Do you have any idea who might have done this?"

Thomas closed his eyes, in a vain effort to think clearly. But still the fog refused him. What had he been doing? Where? *Dear God, help me!* The fog lifted a corner, revealed a figure, released a name.

"Bucknell," he rasped.

"Bucknell." A frown crossed his forehead. "I shall make enquiries."

"Now, sir, I really must insist —"

"McKin . . ."

"What was that?" The earl leaned closer still. "McKin . . . ?"

"Ley," Thomas finally managed to utter, before the effort pushed him back against the pillows.

"McKinley? No, don't try to answer. Just blink once if that's correct."

Thomas obeyed.

Lord Hawkesbury's brow lowered further. "McKinley. Now that *is* a name I have heard. How very interesting."

"My lord, please."

Hawkesbury gave an impatient nod. "Of course. Well, Hale, I want you to do your best to rest while I make enquiry. Rest and pray. Such wickedness shall not prevail."

He murmured something further to the doctor and Mr. Osgood before executing a bow and exiting. Mr. Osgood now approached the bed, the wrinkle in his brow suggesting questions still remained. "Forgive me, sir, but I am most curious how you ended up with one of my cards."

Thomas forced himself to utter, "Carlew" before relapsing once again.

The small man's brows pushed together then cleared. "Ah, you mean Lord Winthrop. He is a friend of yours I gather?"

Another blink. Well, perhaps he was again.

"I'll take that as a yes. Very interesting. Yes, well that makes sense. I am known to specialize in matters concerning Englishmen and their dealings with Scottish lands and business interests. Thank you. I shan't prevail upon you a moment more, but you can be sure I will send word to Lord Winthrop immediately, although I suspect it might take a while to go through, what with these rains and all. My best wishes for a full and speedy recovery. Good day to you."

Upon his departure, the doctor spoke something soothing, his lyrical tones causing Thomas's eyes to close, to feign sleep, as he tried to assemble scattered thoughts into some sense of order. So much did not make sense, so much filled him with unease. But at least he was here, knew a sense of protection, could feel an easing in his soul at the recognition of the other men's concern. It had been so long since he had not had to fight for what was his, for what he needed, he barely recognized this feeling as relief.

The last time he felt this way had been that morning in Kirkcudbright, when he'd woken to discover Julia beside him, their marriage still undetected. He had watched her, marveling at her innocent beauty, marveling that she had plighted her troth to him, that she could see past all the external to the man he wished to be. With her, he had felt less need to pretend.

As he fixed his thoughts on her, gradually, steadily, the other worries faded. And he found himself following Hawkesbury's advice and praying to the God he'd not believed in, the One who had still protected him, that He would heal his broken body, and be with Julia, and give her comfort, hope, and peace.

CHAPTER TWENTY-TWO

The sounds of London traffic stole through the drawing room window, only increasing the agitation inside her heart. Mother — still unaware of the cause of Julia's illness — had listened with all the appearance of amenability to Catherine's request for Julia to come stay with her, before insisting that Julia stay until she felt more the thing. Catherine, quietly gracious as ever, had conceded, only to be drawn from town to visit her sister in Derbyshire, whose father-in-law had finally succumbed to illness and passed away.

With Catherine's absence, every day seemed to only increase the pressure within. Worries about Thomas, young Charles, her mother, her pregnancy, her future wove a nest of restless fears, making her snappish as she itched to leave. Some days she felt as though she might explode from the tension, that lightning might spark from her fingertips. She longed to escape, but apart from Catherine's offer she had no other place to stay. And until she renewed said invitation — and Julia had a strong suspicion that even if Catherine were not distracted by her sister's grief she would be too polite to do so anytime soon — then Julia would need to stay.

Wondering. Hoping. Fearing.

Was Thomas alive? Had he sorted out the tangled mess? Oh, why hadn't she heard from him? News had come through from Derbyshire days ago; surely *something* should have come from Edinburgh by now. Oh, why wasn't Jon here to help? Before her departure, Catherine had promised to mention Lord Snowstrem's comments about Thomas's death to Jon when they reunited at Lord Carmichael's family estate, but until then, Julia had to keep the secret locked within her heart. Unable to speak of it to anyone, not even Mother. For she knew what her mother would say, none of it good.

Catherine's words about trust stole through her mind; she dismissed them. Trusting God seemed so passive, like she had given up and decided to let the universe steer her course. She had spent too many years fighting for what she wanted to give up now. Although — her lips twisted — being stuck in Mother's house was definitely *not* what she desired.

A hawker's call passed through the window, teasing her restlessness. She felt trapped, imprisoned by circumstances, by her choices, by the decisions of others. The drawing room seemed too small today, the walls too close, the atmosphere leaden like the still-gray skies outside. Today she could understand why Jon preferred the mellow warmth of Winthrop Manor.

For a moment she imagined what her ideal house would be like. She used to imagine a London town house, but the gossip and speculation so evident in Mama's cronies had put that idea to rest. They would need to live somewhere where small children could play freely, but she did not think Thomas would like a grand estate; he had come from far less wealthy stock than she. When she had once asked about his family, he'd murmured something about a father in Norfolk, but she sensed from his restraint that there was some degree of estrangement.

She wondered where his father lived . . .

The front door's heavy knocker sounded. She ignored it, but William's answer, heard through the opened door, made her pay attention.

324

"You mean Miss Julia?"

She frowned. Wasn't he supposed to deny entry to her callers, especially when Mother was out? She pushed to her feet, peered through the curtained side window that gave a narrow glimpse of the front steps. The slender fair-haired man was one she did not recognize.

". . . bring a message concerning the major."

He did? Her heart thumped. Oh, she *knew* he could not have forgotten her!

Another low exchange of murmurs, but she ignored it and hurried through the hall and said to William, "Thank you. I shall speak with Mr. . . . ?" She raised her brows.

The pock-scarred man offered a quick smile, his eyes not quite meeting hers.

She could not account for the ripple down her spine. But what did it matter? She would have news from Thomas at long last. "Mr. . . . ?"

"Lieutenant Harrow, at your service, ma'am." He offered an awkward bow.

"Well? What is it about Major Hale? Where is he?"

He cleared his throat. "As to where he is precisely I cannot say, but —"

"I thought you had come from him."

"I regret I have not had that recent plea-

325

sure. But I was with him, when we were in Spain."

Her breath caught. "You were in prison with him?"

"And helped him escape."

"Oh! You have my deepest gratitude! Thank you so much for all you did." She smiled. "He did not say too much about the conditions there, and I gather it was not an easy time."

"No."

"Please," she gestured inside. "Won't you come in and have something to eat? Something to drink? It is the least I can do for the man who has done so much for my husband."

"Well, I would not say no to a glass of something, if you are sure that it is not too much trouble."

"Oh, I am sure. Please, come in."

Within minutes he was seated in the drawing room, enjoying a glass of wine, while she peppered him with questions about his time, and hoped Mother's errands would keep her away from home for just a little while longer. Lieutenant Harrow was not exactly a mine of information, but the little that he did share helped her understand afresh just how awful conditions had been for poor Thomas.

Eventually, when he had downed the second glass of wine, and the few things he had shared had been repeated several times, she felt it prudent to remind him of his initial purpose. "Forgive me, you said you had a message from my husband?"

He coughed. "Well, not a message precisely —"

Her heart fell.

"I was interested in learning if your husband has . . . er, is in receipt of payment for services rendered."

"Oh! Do you refer to Spain?"

He nodded.

"Well, that I could not say. I'm afraid you would need to speak with him."

His eyes flashed. "You mean he has not?"

She drew back, startled at his aggression. "I mean I do not know, and you will need to speak with him."

He muttered something under his breath that did not sound entirely complimentary to her husband's leadership skills. ". . . leaves me no choice."

Julia eyed the bell rope, wondering if she should summon a servant. "Is that all?"

A flush suffused his freckled cheeks. He cleared his throat, eyeing her in a manner not wholly pleasant. "Not quite all, ma'am. I do have some more information concerning him."

"Oh. I thought you said you didn't know where he was."

"And that remains the case." By now the flush overspreading his countenance had reached the roots of his blond hair. "No, this information pertains more to his time in Spain."

"But I don't understand. Have you not just told me about what happened?"

"Not quite everything, Mrs. Hale."

"Well, please don't keep me in suspense."

"Very well." He coughed again, as if nervous. "I regret to be the bearer of disturbing news, especially to such a respectable young lady as yourself, but I must inform you of an incident that your husband was involved in."

She waited, twisting her fingers together to stop the tremors. Why did people always say they hated to share bad news when their countenance suggested anything but? She forced her posture to straighten, to adopt a pose of which her military husband might be proud. "What incident?"

"Your husband, Mrs. Hale, was involved in a liaison with a Spanish whore, who became pregnant with his child."

She stared at him, the words falling around her, like stars dropping from heaven.

His words did not make sense. She could not understand. "I beg your pardon?"

"When we were in Spain, Major Hale got a Spanish whore pregnant. I'm sorry to tell you your husband is an adulterer."

Her heart caught on that word. "No," she whispered. "No, you must be mistaken." Or lying. Catherine had said Lord Snowstrem lied. This man had to be of similar ilk. She shook her head. "No."

"I regret that I am quite certain of it. Magdelena even screamed that Major Hale was the father of her baby when we were trying to flee."

Magdelena. Hatred ripped through her soul at that name. How dare she? How dare *he*? But something softer begged her not to believe —

"I knew it." Mother's voice came from the door. Julia forced herself to look. Mother's face was glacial. "I always knew him to be the sort to play you false." She eyed the lieutenant like she might a sewer rat. "Well? Is that it? You've obviously accomplished what you came here for. I think it best you now leave."

The world had shrunk down to one question: Had Thomas truly done such a thing? Tears filling her eyes, Julia barely noticed as he murmured excuses and left.

"No, Mama, I cannot believe —"

"So you keep saying."

"He *cannot* have done such a thing. The lieutenant must be mistaken —"

"Why is it that everyone else must be mistaken when you refuse to see the truth? Why did you think I did not want you to know the man? He is a rake, has always been a rake, will always be a rake. He is a depraved man, stained with sin."

"No, no." Julia shook her head, willing the past few minutes to be undone. "I refuse —"

"Refuse all you like, my girl, but it won't change facts. You should never have trusted him, should never have married him —"

"What is the point in saying such things? It is done; we are married; it cannot be undone."

"Can it not?" Mother said, a militant sparkle in her eyes. "I will speak with our solicitors again. Perhaps now you will consider finally severing this connection once and for all."

"Surely you don't mean — ?"

"Yes, I'm afraid I do. I think it's high time you sought a divorce."

She plunged her head in her hands, as gasping breaths shuddered from her body. He could not have done such a thing. Could he? He would not. Would he? The tears she had so vainly tried to suppress slipped through her fingers to stain her gown, as her mother's words stole inside her soul. And for the first time, she could find nothing in her heart to disagree.

The Great North Road
Nottinghamshire

"Not long now," Hawkesbury said with a sympathetic look.

Thomas nodded his obligation then gritted his teeth, the carriage's interminable rocking had set his teeth on edge two days ago. But he could not complain; Hawkesbury's generous offer to return with him to England was one he could not afford to ignore.

He could neither afford it, nor, truth be told, could he manage without the assistance of a strong back to bear his inability to stand. Hawkesbury's largesse and continued kindness had again made him wonder about just why the earl was being so generous towards him.

He'd once broached the question, but all Hawkesbury would say was that as a Christian he would not let the husband of Winthrop's sister rot in Scotland while he had it in his power to do something. "Good Samaritans need not only come from Samaria."

And it seemed that the earl had other motives to ensure Thomas's removal from Scotland, something Thomas was left to speculate as he overheard the whispers between the solicitor and Lord Hawkesbury. It seemed the McKinley investigation had failed to produce any further leads, and despite Thomas's ill-health, both Mr. Osgood and the earl had felt it best that Thomas be removed before McKinley could learn of his survival and make another attempt on his life.

"I will escort you back to London," the earl had promised, "but I feel it best if it was put about that you were dead."

"But Julia —"

"If these men are as dangerous as I believe, then your wife is far better off believing you are dead for the moment. You would not wish her to encounter them, would you?"

The thought sent ice into his veins. "No."

Lord Hawkesbury offered a smile. "Please know her safety is in my prayers."

"Needs to be," he managed.

"And yours, too?" This was said with a raised brow.

"Yes." Even if he doubted God paid his

pathetic prayers much heed.

God forbid anything terrible happen to her.

He thought back to his arrival in Edinburgh, when he had first sent a letter to Julia. Had that even made it through? The trip south had revealed just how bad the roads were, and it would not surprise him if his letters had not been received as yet. But still this urgency to return to Julia ate at him. Would she have misinterpreted his latest nonappearance? *God, have mercy . . .*

The journey south had been punctuated by halts, frustratingly delayed by rain showers, as the hired coachman made easy stages and lengthy stops to ensure the horses were kept from being wearied too quickly. In its favor, such mild traveling meant his injuries had less reason to worsen, and despite the varying quality of the inns they stayed in, by the time of their midafternoon arrival each day, his weariness was such that he was more than happy to bed down shortly after their evening meal, and enjoyed a dreamless, if not precisely comfortable, sleep.

But he couldn't help wishing that he could somehow get to Julia faster.

"Ah. It seems we are coming into Newark," said the earl, peering outside.

The coachman, who had made no secret

of his interest in his passengers, slowed the horses and shouted through the opened window, "We be at Newark, m'lord!"

Thomas's lips curved in amusement.

"I don't mind telling you, Hale, that I shall be very glad to get out and stretch my legs. I cannot imagine how uncomfortable you must be finding this experience."

"I've had worse," Thomas managed. Like the whippings he'd received during their imprisonment in Spain.

"Hmm. Well, I am hopeful that we might find a decent enough meal in this establishment."

Within a minute, they had pulled into a coaching yard and were surrounded by a number of ostlers. The earl helped Thomas inside to a table in the taproom and bespoke two rooms and two meals before disappearing to take care of some matter of business. Presently Thomas was joined in the taproom by the talkative coachman.

"And how be your leg, sir?"

"It remains attached."

"Well, and I am right glad to hear you say so. I did try me best to avoid the rough parts of the road, but I'm afraid it weren't as smooth as one would wish, and what with the road washed clear away between Doncaster and Bawtry, I'm afraid I was forced to take a somewhat more circuitous route than I would normally take. I hope his lordship weren't too displeased with the little delay."

Thomas swallowed a smile along with his wine. The "little" delay had added an extra four hours to their journey, so Lord Hawkesbury had muttered, before adding that at least each hour brought them nearer their destination. He now said something to this effect, which was met with a nod.

"Yes, his lordship said as much when he paid me." Mr. Glossop took a long sip of his ale. "Well, and I don't mind saying this here establishment appears much better than I first feared. I had me doubts, but it seems his lordship knows as good a spot as any. Me, I much prefer Stamford. Sure, and there be a couple of nice turns in that street which makes a less experienced man suffer, but it does have the George, which I don't mind telling you I think is the best little coaching inn on the North Road, even if it does boast a gallows sign at its entry. D'you know why they do that?"

Thomas admitted to his ignorance.

"No? Well, I understand they have the gallows to welcome the honest traveler, and warn the highwayman." Mr. Glossop nodded sagely. "I don't mind telling you I think there should be more of that kind of deterrent on our main roads. These highwaymen — well, thank the good Lord above that there be less of them now than there used to be. The stories my da used to tell me! But never mind that. I was telling you about the George, weren't I? Did you know it was Lord Burghley who first established it? That's why his coat of arms is above the main door. And its cocking pit was considered the finest in the world. Not that I hold with cocking; seems a waste of a good bird if you ask me."

Mr. Glossop continued sharing his opinions freely, a state perhaps not wholly unconnected to the amount of alcohol he imbibed. While Thomas sipped his liquid refreshment, Mr. Glossop continued offering his views concerning comparison of the current establishment with that of the George, remarking upon its cleanliness, the apparent experience of the ostlers, and expressing his mistrust that young Hale would enjoy as comfortable sleep as he had in recent nights.

After his hasty consumption of a mutton pie he pronounced tolerable, and a pint of ale he said was flat, Mr. Glossop hefted to his feet. "Well, and I do hope your leg improves soon, sir. And I must say it's been a pleasure to have driven you here. Well, all the best, young Hale."

With the departure of his voluble companion, Thomas was freed to glance around the room. Its wood paneled walls and low ceiling seemed synonymous with every other inn he'd stayed in during the past week, Lord Hawkesbury's generosity stretching to inns of high quality, regardless of whatever the coachman might say. Where Lord Hawkesbury had disappeared to must remain a mystery, as Thomas had neither physical strength nor finances to find out otherwise. He could only hope the reason would become apparent before long.

Another half hour passed before such reason became clear. Hawkesbury reentered the room, with profuse apologies for his delay, and hopes that Thomas had begun his meal without waiting for him. But it was not his apologies that captured Thomas's attention; rather, it was the man who stood behind him, a man he knew only too well, though he had not spoken to him for nearly two years. A man, like Lord Hawkesbury, whose position in life would always remain far above him, whose position in life was such that Thomas would never have even met him were it not for the leavening effect of a certain Jonathan Carlew in his life.

337

He tried to push to his feet, but the pain shooting up his spine made him slump back in his chair with a gasp, which drew the other men forward with protests that he should not move.

"Lord Carmichael," he finally managed, as he shook the black-garbed man's hand.

His friend's face twisted. "It's Bevington now, I'm afraid."

Meaning his father had died, and Harry had succeeded to the earldom. "I am very sorry. Forgive me."

"Why?" A spark of the old mischief twinkled in the hazel-green eyes. "You had nothing to do with my father's death, did you?"

"Of course not. I meant —"

"I know what you meant, Hale." Lord Carmichael — no, Bevington — pulled up a chair and sat beside the earl. "So, what is this I hear about you being nearly killed in Scotland?"

CHAPTER TWENTY-THREE

Betrayal.

She had never realized just how powerful that word was, just how poignant that word could be, until the last two days. Yesterday she had kept to her room, searching for a way to approximate her usual demeanor, unable to find one. Today she had managed to go downstairs in an effort to avoid the questions that circled her bedchamber, questions that the memories of his presence only stirred.

How could he have loved her, if he had betrayed his vows by being with another? How could he have looked at her so hungrily, if that truly were the case? How could she not have known, or even suspected? Or had she suspected, in his great long absence, that he might not be faithful?

Catherine's words about forgiveness were laughable. What did she know? Jon would certainly never have betrayed trust as

Thomas had. Her eyes pricked. Thankfully the tears delayed. She had cried so much since learning the news that surely none could still remain. She still felt so fragile, like she might shatter at any moment. She cared for Charles mechanically, but Crabbit seemed to sense her detached state, and had requested Julia to "leave the young scallywag to me, Miss, whilst you have a rest." So she now sat in the drawing room, pretending to read, which at least held ability to distract her from the nausea, and the sickness in her soul.

The door knocker struck. Julia braced. What would she say to Thomas when he appeared? *If* he appeared. Maybe he would not wish to have anything more to do with her. Maybe he had been looking for another excuse to leave, once he'd had his fun —

A cleared voice came at the door. "Excuse me, Miss," the footman said, "but there is a gentleman to see you. A Mr. Amherst."

"Who — ? Oh." Perhaps he would prove effective distraction from her ruminations. "Please send him in."

"Very well, Miss," the footman said, his expression one of curiosity.

She lifted her chin, arranged her skirts, arranged her features into something she hoped looked like she had not spent much of last night in tears.

"Ah, Mr. Amherst, how good to see you."

He bowed, picked up her hand, and pressed it lightly to his lips. "I hope you will forgive the intrusion, but you did promise I could call should I find myself in the area, and lo and behold, what should happen but I found myself in the area."

She gestured to a seat, turned to William who remained at the door. "Please inform Cook that we shall have tea." She turned to Mr. Amherst. "We shall, shan't we?"

"Indubitably." He released her hand, and sank into the seat beside her. "My dear Mrs. Hale, I have been hoping to speak with you again. I so enjoyed our little tête-à-tête the other day."

What little tête-à-tête? Oh, that time in the park. So much had happened since, it now seemed very long ago. Conscious he was looking at her, she fumbled for a reply. What was the correct response? "I'm glad?"

"I'm glad that you are glad, for I would hate to think my presence unwelcome."

She smiled to hide the fact that his presence was becoming increasingly just what he had feared, as his conversation moved briskly on to chatter about the weather, the Prince Regent, and other news of the natural and social worlds.

Partway through his chatter, the tea was brought in, and Julia was able to distract herself by pouring and then sipping, glad his conversation skills were such that they restricted her to only having to answer with the occasional yes or no. But after a while, the soul-numbing tiredness made his words swim. Inviting him to partake of tea was yet another sad idea. "Really?"

"Indeed." He paused, his eyes wandering over her face. "Forgive me," he said in a low voice, "but have I come at a bad time?"

"I . . . I confess I have not felt terribly well lately."

"Oh, I am sorry to hear you say so. Perhaps it is best if I leave."

Politeness bade her to insist he stay, but he shook his head firmly, and pushed to his feet. "I will not. I think it best if you perhaps get some rest, and I shall endeavor to visit when you are feeling more the thing."

His solicitude brought tears to her eyes. "Thank you, you are very kind."

"My best wishes for your recovery." He bowed, and exited, and was gone.

Within a minute, Mother walked into the room. "I did not know you were expecting company. Who was that?" She moved to the window, pulling aside the drape. "A young gentleman caller?"

"That was Mr. Amherst."

"And who is Mr. Amherst?"

"A . . . a neighbor of Lord and Lady Aynsley."

"Lord and Lady Aynsley? The viscount from Somerset?"

"I believe so."

"Well! And what were you doing with him?"

A blush heated her cheeks. "Nothing! We were only talking. He is simply a gentleman friend."

"Hmm." Mother eyed her carefully. "Well, if there is nothing, then I fail to understand the significance of that blush."

"I . . . I am rather hot, that is all. This room," she waved her fingers, fanlike, "feels rather overheated."

"I notice no change." Another piercing look. "Well, I suppose a little flirtation cannot hurt. Not when you will be free to do so soon enough."

"Mother!"

Further discussion was interrupted by yet another knock at the door. William's enquiry to the visitor was met with a murmured low-pitched male voice. Mother looked at Julia but she could only shake her head.

"A Mr. Macleary to see you, Miss."

"Macleary?" Julia frowned. "I know no

one by that name."

"Shall I stay?" her mother asked, in a tone that suggested she'd be loath to leave.

"If you like," Julia said with a shrug. Nobody could say anything worse than what had already been said.

The mustachioed man was ushered in, and Julia was struck by the appearance of his sunburned face, a coppery tan that suggested he, like Thomas, had spent much time on the Subcontinent. She peered at him. He looked not unlike someone she had once met, but who precisely, the recesses of her mind would not release.

He looked at her. "Mrs. Hale?"

Julia nodded. "Mr. Macleary, I believe?"

He offered a small bow. "Forgive me for my intrusion, but I thought it best not to delay." His voice held traces of a Scottish accent. "I bring word concerning your husband."

Her heart flickered despite herself. Conscious her mother was watching carefully, Julia bade her expression to smoothness. "Do you, indeed?"

"Aye. And I am extremely sorry to be the one who tells you this, but —"

"I'm afraid we have already heard, sir."

"Already heard?" His brow knit. "I did

not think news traveled that fast from Scotland."

"From Scotland?"

"Aye. I came as fast as I could, as soon as I heard. I was a great friend of your husband's, you see, Mrs. Hale."

She swallowed. "Was?"

He inclined his head, his face adopting a look of sorrow. "Aye, I'm afraid it is my solemn duty to inform you of your husband's demise."

What? Her heart stilled.

"I beg your pardon?" Mother asked.

"I regret to say that Major Thomas Hale met with an accident in Edinburgh and, I'm terribly sorry to have to tell you this, is believed to have drowned."

Her breath caught. "No," she whispered, as her heart gave a painful throb. No! He could not be dead. She sucked in a deep breath, willing her features to neutrality, as Mother continued.

"You said *believed* to have drowned. Is there some question?"

"Oh, no question at all," he said. "Forgive me for the confusion. No, it was confirmed, and in the newspapers."

No. No, no! *Oh, dear God!* So Buffy Snorestream had been right; Catherine had been wrong. The all-too-ready tears started to

345

her eyes. How wretched was she? Why did her heart — her poor battered, bruised heart — wrench like she still cared? Why did she wish to flee to her room and release the tears pressing behind her eyes? Thomas had been unfaithful to her. Hadn't he? Reality still seemed too hard to credit. Was this some nightmarish dream?

"Mr. Macleary, I have no wish to doubt the veracity of your word," Mother said, "but you must understand that as you are a stranger to us, it is only natural to perhaps wonder as to why you felt it necessary to impart such information to us. In fact, I cannot help but wonder how you were able to ascertain my daughter's whereabouts."

"I . . . I got to know the major when we served in India together. He mentioned you, Mrs. Hale, when we met again in Edinburgh recently. I felt it my duty to report to you what had happened, so you were not left wondering about him."

Bitterness shafted her chest. Wondering about him. That was all her husband was good for.

"That was very good of you, sir," Mother finally said.

His mouth twisted in something resembling a smile. "Again, I am sorry that my news is not what you had hoped."

Julia glanced at her mother, but surprisingly, upon receiving the news she had surely hoped for, Mother appeared more grim than glad.

As for herself . . . she could feel no spark of gladness that justice had been served to her philandering husband. Instead, her soul seemed weighted with a heaviness unlike anything she'd known. Thomas was dead. Dead! The word was so final, Mr. Macleary seemed so certain. And yet . . . and yet . . .

Something about his words twirled uncertainty. Was it shock-induced denial, or something else? "You said newspapers."

He paused in the act of standing. "I beg your pardon, Mrs. Hale?"

"Excuse me, sir, but you said his death was reported in the newspapers." Julia gazed at him with blurring eyes. "Did you bring one?"

He patted his coat pocket. "Forgive me, but it appears to have been misplaced." He eyed her with compassion. "I am sorry for your loss, Mrs. Hale."

Why could she not believe him? What else had he said? "Mr. Macleary, you . . . you said the news was not what we had hoped."

"Well, yes."

She shook her head. "How could you know what we had hoped?"

He paused. "I beg your pardon? I do not understand. I imagine you were uncertain as to his whereabouts, seeing as he had been in Scotland for some weeks."

"How did you know that?"

Another pause. A flicker in his eyes fueled further doubts.

"The newspapers reported that the, ahem, body, had been in the water for some time." He hurried past their gasps to add, "I'm sorry to distress you both."

But for all his expressed sorrow, not much lived in his eyes. "Where did you say you served with him?"

"In India, ma'am."

"But where?"

"Oh, in a little place on the West coast near Bombay."

"Was it at Poona?"

He blinked. "Aye, it was. I really must be going now."

Julia rose unsteadily. "I never heard Thomas mention your name."

"Well, we were not precisely in the same vicinity all the time."

"And where did you say you met him in Edinburgh?"

"Oh, here and there."

She stared narrowly at his wide, thick-lipped face. "I feel like I have seen you somewhere before."

He gave a small laugh. "I'm always being told that. Must have one of those faces. Now, if you'll excuse me?"

"It was good of you to come, sir," Mother said, before escorting him to the door.

He paused with a slight bow. "Please accept my condolences."

Julia barely acknowledged his departure, as for the second time in three days she struggled to make sense of the world. How could Thomas have died?

Her breath snagged, the action triggering tears.

"Oh, my darling girl," her mother said, rushing to her side and wrapping an arm around her shoulders. "He is not worth your tears."

She knew that, but could not seem to stop them anyway.

"There, there." She offered more ineffectual patting. "I cannot own that I am somewhat relieved we shall not have to seek a divorce after all. Such a lot of muckraking that would have entailed. No, don't cry, Julia. Please. I know that I have not always spoken well of him, but believe me when I say that I am sorry for your sake that he is gone."

Gone. Gone! Pain wracked her chest. Had

her heart snapped in two? How would she survive? What would happen to her now? To Charles? *Dear God!* What would happen to her child?

Her sobs escaped in a series of chest-wrenching pains. "Oh, no."

"What is it?"

Julia wiped ineffectually at her eyes, her cheeks. "He will never know now."

"Never know what?"

"That he is . . . was," she swallowed, "going to be a father."

"Julia! Do you mean to tell me you are expecting?"

She closed her eyes, unwilling to see the censure in her mother's eyes, and nodded.

"Oh, my darling girl!" She was clasped in her mother's arms. "Please do not fear. I will protect you."

Another sob escaped, triggering a fresh avalanche of emotion. How could Mother ever expect to protect Julia from the bleakness of her future?

Nottinghamshire

"You cannot be serious."

Thomas had finished retelling his story for what felt like the umpteenth time, conscious that the new Earl of Bevington's gaze had barely shifted from his face. Next

350

to him, Lord Hawkesbury's brow wrinkled as if he was puzzling out what to do. And seated beside him sat Jonathan, Lord Winthrop, his grave countenance wearing the familiar frown he had come to associate with Julia's brother. His arrival at the inn was the reason for the repeated story.

"I'm afraid he is serious," Lord Hawkesbury finally spoke. "And what's more, from what Hale tells me, it seems to have some connection to what occurred in Spain."

"You mean you were truly tortured?"

Thomas met Jon's gaze. "Yes."

"If you don't believe him, I'm sure the scars on his back would be enough to prove his claims," Lord Hawkesbury interposed. "The doctor at the infirmary in Edinburgh was most perturbed. I cannot imagine Hale put them there willingly."

"But who would want to do that to you?" Harry said, his face flushed with anger. "Such a man must be a monstrous kind of animal!"

Relief seeped through his chest. Finally, he was being believed.

"You say this man McKinley is the only connection between the two incidents," said Jon, the inflection at the end of his words giving a hint of a question, which instantly gave rise to defensiveness within. Did his brother-in-law not believe him?

"I would not be at all surprised to learn that this Fallbright character is someone who has been less than honorable in his dealings. There has been word in the London clubs . . ." Lord Hawkesbury fell silent.

The private room filled with the swirl of speculation and seething anger. Just what had been said in the clubs? But he refused to press the earl to give gossip a helping hand.

"I cannot believe the man refused to pay what you were owed," said Jon. "I imagine you were not the only one he refused to pay."

Thomas listed the other men involved, finishing with Smith, "Who, as it happens, lives not too far away in Leicestershire."

"I think we should make our business to see him at once, and get his side of things."

"I think it more prudent if we send a man of law who can be shown to have no vested interest in supporting Hale's claims," Hawkesbury corrected gently.

"You think this will go to court?" Harry asked.

"I would hope not, but I believe it wise to cover every contingency." Hawkesbury leaned back in his chair, glanced at Thomas. "For some time now I have been made aware of certain, shall we say, shortcomings in various elements of the War Office. Such things have given rise to speculation that some of the decisions have been more about political maneuvering and point scoring, rather than about what might perhaps be in the nation's best interests. As matters would have it, on account of my military and political experience, I have recently been given the charge to discover some of the truth of these dealings. And I don't mind telling you that what I have learned so far makes me very ready to believe the implications of McKinley and Fallbright being involved in something underhand."

"But for what purpose?"

"That is indeed the question." Hawkesbury steepled his fingers. "Hale, I understand you served with them both in India. Do you recall anything that occurred during that time that might now be considered suspicious?"

Thomas mentioned something of his concerns about the Pindari episode.

"Yes, but I don't see how McKinley's approval of such an evil action could be relevant to these recent events," Jon said, his brow wrinkled.

What was the answer? Thomas closed his eyes. Wisps of memory slowly taunted.

"Unless McKinley was acting under Fall-bright's orders," Hawkesbury said slowly. "But why?"

"Because," Thomas's eyes snapped open, "Fallbright wanted to be considered for the role of governor, and thought heavy-handed tactics might be the display of force he needed to ensure such a thing was possible."

Hawkesbury sat forward, his eyes glittering. "Have you any proof?"

Thomas shook his head. "There was always talk about his aspirations, but nobody took them terribly seriously."

"But still, there might be letters or journals that reveal something of his ambition. I wonder . . ."

Thomas watched Lord Hawkesbury sink into a brown study, tapping his thumbs together.

"And you believe Fallbright wants Thomas dead," Jon said.

"That I do," the earl said thoughtfully. "I am nearly certain he had no intention of seeing you again after the Spanish debacle. I'm sure your return was a most unwelcome surprise, hence his need to engage in certain physical measures after your visit."

"I never truly understood what the objective was for that particular mission," Thomas admitted.

"Did you attend the briefing alone, or with others who can vouch for what was said?"

Thomas thought back. It had been nearly a year ago. "I believe Lieutenant Benson was there also."

"And is he someone you can trust to speak the truth?"

Thomas's lip curled. "Provided his hand is greased appropriately with coin, then yes."

"Money was the object for you to take that job?" Jon asked quietly.

"Of course." Thomas met his eyes. "I had no desire to leave my wife, I assure you."

Jon studied him a long moment, before saying, "I am sorry that circumstances have led to such consequences. Perhaps if I had not been so quick to judge then none of this would have happened."

Thomas savored the apology, but said in an undertone, "It is my own fault for not seeking or waiting for your blessing." He managed a smile. "Not that I had any real hope of receiving it."

"Perhaps not. But I am well aware of my sister's impatience and headstrong ways, which would have made many a man act in such a way. But never mind that. Let us agree to let the past remain in the past, and look to what can be done about the future."

Jon's handshake at once swept away the

shadows and solidified inner resolve. Thomas would live with honor, would do his utmost to live up to his brother-in-law's approval. "I do appreciate your belief in me," he muttered.

"I have faith in God that He would use you for His purpose."

Thomas nodded. After his experience in Edinburgh, he too felt like he was part of something bigger than mere circumstances, almost like God *was* using him for His plans.

"I still do not understand how McKinley got involved," Harry complained.

"It would seem that was perhaps bad luck —"

"Or perhaps deep stratagem." Hawkesbury sat up, looking at him. "Do you recall when you first met McKinley in Edinburgh?"

"It must have been . . . within the first three months of our moving there."

"And how did you meet?"

"It was in a taproom, not unlike this." Thomas gestured to the surroundings. "Munro called out my name and before I knew it, McKinley had spotted me and we got to talking."

"I don't understand," Jon muttered. "How he could find you when my enquiry agents obviously could not."

"Because Rayne was a nickname he gave me when we were in India," Thomas said slowly. "And the Black Harp was not exactly unknown to former military men, so if he suspected I might be there —"

"Which he might, given the notice sent to the newspapers about your marriage," Jon said.

"Then it seems there is every likelihood that Fallbright was waiting for an opportunity to gather you back into the fold, so to speak, and sent McKinley north to discover your location." Hawkesbury's mouth was grim. "I bet the idea of working for Fallbright originated from McKinley."

"Yes, now I think on it, I believe he did first mention it." Thomas groaned, placing his head in his hands. "What a fool I am to have been so misled."

"It is difficult when we want to trust those we think we know."

Was this another dig? "I am sorry my actions have proved less than trustworthy."

"Please, do not think on such things anymore," Jon murmured.

Thomas nodded. When would he stop taking things so personally? But forgiveness seemed so hard to receive, so hard to extend to himself.

"I wonder, do you believe they think Hale is still dead?"

"We can only hope so. Everything was done to keep things quiet." Hawkesbury glanced at Thomas, his eyes sober. "I think it best that your death remains as reported in the newspapers. I did not want to tell you, but a newspaper article from Edinburgh has a report of a missing woman from the same address of where you lived. A Rebecca Girvan? It seems she has been murdered."

"Good heavens, no!"

"It seems too coincidental to be otherwise. I think it is their way of ensuring anyone to whom you may have spoken is silenced, permanently. Whether they suspect you are alive or not, it seems they wish to hurt you as much as possible."

Thomas stared at Jon, fear clutching his chest. "What will this mean for Julia?"

CHAPTER TWENTY-FOUR

Days passed, one week, two, melding into a kind of blank nothing. The Advent season, usually her favorite time of year, this year held no loveliness. She could not abide the sight of decorated evergreens, she could not stand to hear choristers sing. How dare people sing when her heart was broken? How could life go on as normal when everything she thought she'd known had been ripped away? How could Catherine have ever suggested Julia trust God with her future when it seemed she existed in a whirlpool of uncertainty, the only known things being her need to wear black, little Charles's constant demands for attention, and her own troubling nausea. Wonderful signs of the season, indeed.

She looked up from her book as the door opened.

"Ah, Miss Julia, Mr. Amherst is here to see you."

Her heart lifted a notch. In the trials of recent weeks, Mr. Amherst's attentions had not been completely unwelcome. Mother no longer felt it necessary to chaperone, and truth be told, Mr. Amherst himself never gave her reason to suspect he looked at her with anything beyond friendship in mind. Besides, what man would seek to be more than friends with a newly grieving widow, especially once her condition became obvious? She suppressed thoughts of her mother's situation, who, faced with that very same scenario, had married Harold Carlew when she was but a recent widow herself, thus leading to the gossip over many years concerning Jon's true parentage.

"Mrs. Hale." Mr. Amherst bowed. "How do I find you today? I was hoping with today's milder weather I might persuade you to a visit out of doors."

And be seen by the matrons of society, who would sneer at her the way they had at Mother? No, thank you. "I'm afraid that while a visit would be very pleasant, it might not yet be wise to undertake."

"I understand."

He smiled at her in a way that made her think he truly did understand. Really, she thought, looking at him, it was amazing how he could be so charming and understanding but she never felt anything but sisterly affection for him. He was like another Henry Carmichael in that way. But he never excited her senses or made her breath catch the way Thomas did. The way Thomas *had,* she reminded herself.

Conscious he was talking again, she did her best to pay attention, to disentangle what was being said. ". . . drive to Hyde Park in my phaeton."

"Oh, but —"

"You need not trouble yourself about being observed. There are few ladies of society still remaining in London, and we can always raise the hood if necessary."

She nibbled the inside of her bottom lip. Perhaps it would be good to escape the confines of the house, and the day *was* unseasonably mild. Who knew how long it might be until she could do such things again? And if she could venture out unseen . . .

"Please, my dear, you cannot have allowed for my concern about the loss of roses in your cheeks. You seem very pale, indeed."

After a few more minutes of his smooth talking, she allowed herself to be persuaded, and, having informed her mother of her movements, she soon found herself in a phaeton, dressed in her warmest pelisse and

361

black veil, enjoying the crisp morning air.

"You are not cold?"

She pulled the silk shawl closer around her throat. "No."

The scents of winter lifted to meet her: smoke and burning leaves, and that of the cows that grazed on St. James's Park. But despite the questionable virtue of this last scent, being outside did have a cleansing effect on her soul.

They cleared the gate and the horses moved into a trot. Julia huddled into the cushions, glad for the protection of the raised leather hood, cautious of receiving attention, although she knew the black garb would mark her identity, should anyone care to peer closely.

As Mr. Amherst took care to point out the park's features, her heart lifted a fraction more. "The weather has proved most agreeable," she admitted.

"Which makes the day all the more agreeable because we can share it together."

Her heart stuttered at his words. Surely he wasn't implying anything more to their friendship? Perhaps she best let him know the current state of her feelings. "Mr. Amherst, I hope you know how much I appreciate your thoughtfulness in taking me for these drives."

"It is my pleasure indeed."

"I . . . I did not think I would find pleasure in things again."

"It is my hope that you find pleasure in a great many things, and I would be honored should you . . ."

His voice trailed off, and she followed his gaze to where a man was watching them. "What is it?"

"Nothing, I'm sure."

Still, a shiver brushed her skin. "Why would he be watching us?"

"Perhaps he is envious that I have such a fair companion."

But she could not think it so. She peered at the man as they drew nearer, narrowing her eyes as he seemed to notice her scrutiny and turned away. He looked a little like . . . "that man from before," she murmured.

"I beg your pardon?"

"Nothing."

But if it was Mr. Macleary, why was he here? Did he have anything else to say?

"Stop the carriage." She placed a hand on Mr. Amherst's arm. "Please stop!"

He slowed the horses to a walk. "What is it?"

"That man. I want to speak to that man back there."

"Do you know him?"

"I believe so, yes."

He eyed her with an expression bordering on doubt, but obeyed nonetheless. Minutes later, they were back near the grove of trees, and she was scanning the park to catch sight of him, to no avail.

"Where could he have gone?"

"It certainly seems strange that he has just disappeared."

Another shudder ran through her body. "It does not seem right that he should spy on us when we do not know where he is."

"I believe that is generally considered to be in the nature of spying —"

BANG!

There was a mild oath, a loud groan, then before she knew what was happening the reins slackened and the horses were running away. Julia's horrified glance at Mr. Amherst saw him lolling in his seat, blood staining his shoulder, his grasp on the reins now useless. The horses were frantic, Mr. Amherst ineffectual, and they were running straight towards the pond.

"Mr. Amherst! Mr. Amherst!"

He muttered something, his eyes glassy.

She reached across his lap and tugged at the reins, screaming at the horses to stop. The momentum pulled her to her feet and she leaned back in a desperate effort to not be dragged forward and crushed beneath the flying hooves. Her arms burned and tears were falling from her eyes when she felt the horses finally slow. From her peripheral vision, she saw a man racing towards them — not the spying man from before; this one was dressed in the breeches and leather jerkin of a cowherd.

"Miss! Miss!" he called, running to the horses' heads and grabbing valiantly at the bridles. The horses whinnied their displeasure, but slowed to a standstill, leaving her breathless, panting, as she sank into her seat and turned to examine her companion. She gasped.

His blood spattered the back of the leather-bound seat — and her sleeve. "Mr. Amherst!"

He groaned something, his head falling onto her shoulder then her lap.

"Oh, dear God!"

"He's been shot!" the cowherd said, wide-eyed. "We best get you out from there, miss, and get him down from there, too."

By now several other park visitors had made their eager way to the phaeton, and soon she was surrounded by so many exclamations of wonder and horror and "good gracious!" that she could barely think. But something bade her to ignore her first inclination to run away, bade her to stay and continue to press her gloved hand against his wound, even as she felt the sticky blood ooze between her fingers.

"Miss, I saw what you did back there! Awful brave, you was!" the cowherd said, admiration in his eyes when she briefly glanced at him. "A real heroine!"

She released a shaky breath, and raised her voice above the hubbub to demand someone fetch an officer of the law, her mind galloping as the horses had but moments earlier. Who could have done such a thing? Why? Or was it in some way connected to Thomas's mysterious disappearance and death?

Before long a park keeper had run towards them, followed not long after by an officer of the law, whose demanding questions so similar to her own thoughts soon had her begging for the respite of home. Back at Portman Square, Mother's shock was swiftly replaced by concern, as Julia was interrogated before finally being released, with promises a magistrate would need to visit her the following day.

But the questions refused to release her, and she shivered under the bedclothes, her heart raw with panic-laced memories, and fears that the nightmare of her situation had just taken another turn for the worse.

Hawkesbury House, Lincolnshire

If his father could only see him now. Thomas shifted awkwardly against the cushioned back of the sofa, but though pain rippled through his body he permitted himself a small smile. Who would have thought he would be ensconced in an earl's principal estate, being treated like a king? Certainly his father never would have anticipated anything of the sort. But Thomas's generous benefactor had refused to see him depart, insisting that he stay for a few days respite from their journey. "For my protection as well as yours. You have no conception of the degree of trouble I face with my wife due to my absence. Lavinia will pity you and I have hopes that might extend to her feeling a drop of mercy for me."

The earl's trouble had been grossly exaggerated, the warmth and affection with which Lady Hawkesbury greeted her husband as apparent as her concern for Thomas. Indeed, seeing the earl with his wife and daughter ignited hope that Thomas might one day somehow obtain but a quarter of such happiness with Julia and little Charles.

The quiet of the drawing room was punctuated by the earl's sudden exclamation. "Oh!"

"What is it?"

"It is — oh, here, read it." The earl thrust the newspaper at him. "The third column, second page."

Thomas scanned the page. "You mean about the shooting?"

"Yes."

He read the small print:

It is reported that a shooting occurred in Hyde Park on Monday afternoon. The Honorable Edward Amherst, second son of the Earl of Rovingham, Somerset, was seriously injured whilst in the company of Mrs. Hale, the recently widowed daughter of Lady Harkness. Investigations have yet to produce any leads. Witnesses to the event which occurred on Monday afternoon are encouraged to speak with the Chief Magistrate at their earliest convenience.

Thomas muttered an oath not dissimilar to the one already heard, as a welter of emotions consumed him. Who the blazes was this Amherst fellow? Why was Julia with him? Thank God she hadn't been injured! He was even conscious of a grim satisfaction at the retribution that saw the man so quick to take Thomas's place had been struck down, before feeling a twist of remorse for thinking such things.

He lowered the paper to encounter the concerned gaze of the Earl of Hawkesbury. "Do you think they are after her now?"

"Perhaps they were aware you had met briefly, and now consider her a liability."

"I should go —"

"No." Hawkesbury shook his head. "You must remain here, like we agreed. If they believe you to be dead then your appearance would only complicate matters."

"But we should send word. Julia must be worried out of her mind!" But — a niggling thought whispered — would she? Did not her driving out with another man suggest she did not care?

"Winthrop will know what to do. He shall arrive in London tomorrow at the latest. And Bevington has also promised his assistance."

And the help of his friends was appreciated, was necessary for their plan to work, but . . . "God help us," Thomas groaned. "God knows what Fallbright and his men will do next."

"Exactly." He met the glint in Hawkesbury's eye. "God knows exactly what will happen next. And as for your other prayer — for prayer it was, was it not? — God *will* help us."

Doubts assailed him. How could the earl hold that promise as true? "But you have seen what they are capable of."

"And I've also seen what God can do. Please, do not let your heart be troubled. Trust in God. In fact, let us commit this situation to Him once more."

Thomas followed the other man's lead and closed his eyes as Lord Hawkesbury prayed in low, confident tones, "Thank You, Heavenly Father, that You love us, and that You work in all situations for our good. We ask for Your protection for Julia and Thomas and all those connected to them. Thank You for bringing those evildoers to justice. Thank You for giving us wisdom to know what steps to take. Guide us, lead us, and protect us I pray, in the name of Your Son, Jesus Christ. Amen."

Thomas echoed the amen, his spirits lifting a tad. Maybe God might still be ignoring him, but surely He would listen to this man who really seemed to believe?

The room settled with a kind of peace. From outside came the sound of a small child's laughter. Guilt twisted within.

"My lord, I . . . I know my situation has

interrupted your time with your family. I . . . am sorry for it."

"I am not sorry for the opportunity to assist you, my friend," the earl said. "Please do not tease yourself with that notion any longer."

"But —"

"Neither do me the disservice of doubting my words. My wife and I seek opportunities to serve our God and bring what form of blessing to others that we can. My concerns and use of time are therefore not my own; they are to be used for God's service, and according to His timing."

"I know this has inconvenienced you."

"Ah, but those things that may seem inconvenient in the immediate I have learned can often prove to be more about my obedience to God's purposes, and perhaps seeing His plans outworked in a scheme far broader than what I had imagined and envisaged."

Like the dismantling of injustice.

"So, while we may feel like little cogs in the grand scheme of things, rest assured God can use even small cogs to achieve His purposes."

Thomas managed a small smile. "Even the smallest cog?"

"Our Savior used even the doubting

Thomas."

The words lit a corner of hope in his heart. God knew Thomas was utterly sin-stained, and had so little to offer. Was He truly willing to accept what little Thomas had?

Chapter Twenty-Five

"Oh, my dearest!"

Catherine's arms around her felt so soothing after the past few days of interrogation; first from Mother, then from the magistrate who had arrived on the doorstep yesterday morning. The shooting had absorbed their time and energies. Mr. Amherst had wakened from his comatose state unable to remember anything, so it fell on Julia to offer what she could to help the investigation. That experience had left her drained, and the morning calls from the curious and the kindhearted had left her wanting nothing more than to hide in her bedchamber until the visit to Gloucestershire could be arranged, a visit Mother had said would take place as soon as the magistrate gave permission to leave.

"And even if he does not, I feel it best we leave within the next day or so. I cannot like how so many of those I once considered my friends have come to ogle, as if we are nothing better than exhibits at a museum. Do they not know we have feelings? No, we must leave, and the sooner the better."

Catherine and Jon's visit was indeed welcome, even though Jon's eyes held a question she was reluctant to answer.

"You cannot know how sorry I was to be in Derbyshire when this all happened," said Catherine, breaking into Julia's memories. "I cannot imagine what it must have been like to learn of Thomas's death. My dear, I am so terribly sorry I was not here to help comfort you."

Thomas's death. She glanced at the black crepe gown she wore. His death still felt unreal.

"Julia?"

She peeked up to encounter the warmth in Catherine's eyes. "I beg your pardon?"

"I was just wondering what plans you have regarding funeral arrangements."

"I . . ." She lifted a hand to her head. Glanced at her brother.

He nodded, his gaze shaded with something she could not decipher. "I will endeavor to undertake such matters as necessary."

His words did not seem to hold much sense, but she nodded anyway, murmured a thank you.

"And you are well? I cannot imagine what it must have been like to be forced to undergo such a terrifying experience."

"I am as well as I can be."

Her arms still ached, the muscles feeling near wrenched from her body from the dreadful incident; the bloodied gown she had been wearing was now thrown away. She had no desire to see that ever again.

"And poor Mr. Amherst! It would seem he was most unfortunate."

Mother began a homily on exactly how unfortunate was poor Julia's new friend, her words, encouraged by Catherine's soft murmurs of interest, expounding upon his goodness in taking pity on poor Julia, and contrasting his qualities with a certain someone who would not be named.

"Indeed, he sounds a very paragon." Jon's expression, his tone, held an inscrutable, ironic quality. Julia frowned at him, and was unsurprised when he soon requested a private word with her, which his wife acceded to readily, while Mother took a few moments to conjecture his motives before eventually conceding he would not give satisfaction, and exiting the room.

The mantelpiece clock ticked ominously. Julia eyed her brother. He seemed unsure as to how to proceed, his brow furrowed, his mouth downturned.

"What is it, Jon?"

"I cannot like this." His lips pursed. "Who is this Amherst fellow?"

She felt her defenses rise. "He is a friend."

"Yes, but where did you meet him?"

"I met him at Lord Carmichael's — I mean, Lord Bevington's — town house, when I was staying there. He was accompanying one of Serena's friends, Miss Caroline Hatherleigh. He is a neighbor of theirs."

"Yes, but what was he doing accompanying *you*?"

"I told you. He is a friend."

"I cannot like it. It seems too convenient . . ." His voice trailed away, yet his gaze remained speculative.

"What is convenient? The fact I had a friend who wished to provide some measure of distraction when I first learned that Thomas was dead?"

"Putting aside the fact that I have doubts as to whether or not a man and a woman can ever be friends without one side or the other wishing for more, I *cannot* like the fact that you were encouraging the attentions of another man. Can you not see what that must appear like to other people?"

"He is my friend."

"Not in the eyes of others."

"Then *others* are mistaken — and possessing minds of a degenerate nature!"

"But you are supposed to be in mourning, are you not? Forgive me, but you do not give that impression."

"But I am!" She fought to calm herself, to not let the interview revert to those previous encounters when she had always felt like the child fighting the older brother's protective censure. "I *am* very sad. You do not know —" what it's like to feel torn between grief and pain at Thomas's betrayal. "You cannot know what it is like to have lost . . ." trust in someone. She swallowed a sob.

"You are right," Jon said, his tone gentle. "I do not know your pain."

"No, you cannot!" She wiped her cheeks. "But neither do I want to hide in my bedchamber, crying for the rest of my days."

"I understand it has scarcely been two weeks since you learned of his death. Surely you must be aware that most ladies would not be receiving the notice of other men in that time."

Indignation sparked. "Most women, perhaps. But not our *mother.*"

He flinched, and drew back. "I do not think that is a helpful comparison."

377

"No? But it is a true one." Mother, who had married another man only weeks after Jon's father had died. "Besides, I had no one else to turn to. *You* weren't in town."

"And for that I am very sorry."

His expression supported the sentiment, taking the wind from her anger, forcing her gaze to her clasped hands. The truth of Thomas's betrayal she could not speak of, would not speak of. Such shame would never pass her lips. She could well imagine her mother holding no such compunction.

"It is just . . ."

She peeked up. "Just what?"

He seemed to reconsider his words, as he shook his head again. "I am curious about how you discovered Hale's death."

She shrugged. "We had a visitor, a Mr. Macleary, who —"

"Macleary, did you say? Not McKinley?"

"Macleary, he said his name was. He had a Scottish accent."

"Can you describe him?"

She thought back. "He was much shorter than you, so about medium height, and stocky," she added. "Dark haired. A moustache. I cannot remember what color eyes he had. Oh, but he did have a tan, because I remember thinking at the time he looked a bit like Thomas when he first returned

378

from India. Remember?"

Thomas, who had looked *so* handsome in his military garb. Her heart panged. Another memory triggered, releasing a gasp.

"What is it?"

"I just remembered! I thought at the time that he reminded me of someone, but I could not think who. He *was* the same man who came and visited me in Edinburgh, and told me Thomas had left for Spain. I did not recall it at the time, for he was not dressed in military clothes, and back then he had no moustache, and I am sure he said his name was McKinley."

"Who? The man who visited you in Edinburgh?"

"Yes." She frowned. "It was so long ago, I cannot be certain."

"Julia, please try. It is very important."

"Why?"

He groaned. "Why must you question me all the time?"

"Because I am your sister."

A smile ghosted his face. "Please. We need to know. Was this man who came to call the same as the one who visited you in Edinburgh?"

"I believe so. Yes, I am nearly certain."

He exhaled, sat back in his chair. Silence filled the room as his forehead creased. "Julia, there is something else I must tell you."

"Yes?"

"I'm afraid that man was not honest with you, neither recently, nor in the past."

"Well, I know he wasn't in the past. Thomas said he'd given this McKinley man money to give me, which McKinley then denied. That is, if Thomas was telling the truth."

Jon nodded. "He was."

"How do you know? I cannot know what to believe about him anymore."

"Then believe this — you are a married woman."

"I am not. Thomas is dead. There was a notice in the newspaper —"

"I'm sorry to tell you — or perhaps not sorry, as the case may be — but that notice was false."

"What do you mean? I don't understand."

"Thomas is not dead."

She blinked. "No."

"Yes." He moved nearer, grasped her hands. "Thomas is alive."

"No. The man said —"

"He lied. You must believe me. I spoke with Thomas but two days ago."

"You cannot be serious. Why are you saying this?" She pulled her hands away. "Why would you want to make me believe such things?"

"Forgive me, but there was no other way."

She gestured to the door. "But Catherine was expressing her condolences. Why would she —"

"She does not know."

"Then why . . . ?" Her head was spinning. Who could she trust? What was real anymore? "Is he really alive? Truly?"

He held her hands firmly and looked deep into her eyes, the way he had years ago when he'd informed her that her father had died. "Yes."

Her breath caught. "Then what — ?"

"I — we — didn't want —"

"Who is this 'we'?"

"Thomas, Henry, Lord Hawkesbury, and myself."

"What has Lord Hawkesbury got to do with this?"

"It was he who first learned of Thomas's injuries."

"Macleary told me it was an accident, that Thomas had drowned."

"That is near the truth. Thomas was severely beaten and left for dead in the harbor."

She gasped. "No! Where is he? I must go to him!"

"Please, let me finish." He repossessed

himself of her hands. "When he was found, he was taken to an infirmary, where he spent some days unconscious while the doctor wondered if he would ever waken."

Her eyes filled with tears. "Where *is* he?"

"He is safe. It would seem his attackers believed him dead, which is a belief we wanted to perpetuate, in order to discover who would wish that on him."

"But who would do such a thing?"

He paused, and then said, "When Hawkesbury learned of his condition, he sent missives which finally reached me in Manchester. Hawkesbury wanted to get Thomas away as he felt it was no longer safe. He believes McKinley has a vendetta against Thomas that is somehow connected to their time in India. This may be why this so-called Macleary fellow came to see you. Can you remember Thomas ever talking about McKinley, or a man called Fallbright?"

"No, we barely spoke when he was here." At the sardonic gleam in her brother's eye her cheeks heated, and she hurried on. "Wait, did you not say Thomas was now safe? Could you not ask him?"

He sighed. "I'm afraid his injuries are so severe that his memory has been somewhat affected."

His pause prompted her to say, "And?"

Jon gently squeezed her hands. "There's some question of whether he will be able to walk properly again."

Her mouth fell open. "No. Oh, no! Where *is* he?" Tears burned and leaked from her eyes. "I need to see him, and he would want to see me."

"He is safe, and is desperate for you to be safe also." His hands moved to her upper arms. "Please, believe me, Julia. We all want you to be safe."

"But —"

"No, we really do," he said.

His smile smoothed away a mite of her tension. "But what am I to do?"

"I will speak to Mother, and we will expedite arrangements so that you can remove to the country as soon as possible. We want you and Charles and Mother to be safe."

"You think they might hurt us?"

"It would appear they have already tried."

Her breath stilled. "And they got poor Mr. Amherst instead."

"Forget him. He is not your concern."

"But —"

"No, Julia. He made his choices in pursuing friendship with a married lady, and I cannot allow you to be concerned with his affairs anymore. You must instead focus on what is your concern, your husband."

"My husband," she echoed. Her heart twisted, and she peeked up. "Does he know about . . ."

"Mr. Amherst?"

She nodded.

"I would think by now he would. The shooting was mentioned in the papers."

What must Thomas think of her, allowing the attentions of another man so soon after news of his death? Oh, how shameful was she? She swallowed a sob. "I thought Thomas was dead."

"Do not condemn yourself in that regard. He is not precisely blameless."

"I know."

"What do you know?"

"I know about the woman in Spain."

"What woman in Spain?" he said sharply.

"When Lieutenant Harrow visited . . ." She realized by Jon's puzzled frown that he did not know. Her breath caught. She could not tell him. She shook her head. "It does not matter. Thomas is not blameless, and neither am I." For she had not exactly discouraged Mr. Amherst's attentions, had she?

Jon's frown had plunged even deeper, and she hastened to steer his thoughts back to their previous track. "So, you want us to leave London?"

He nodded. "I want you to be somewhere where they will not be able to find you." His face creased in a brief smile. "I could not bear it if something happened to you."

The tenderness in his expression hugged warmth around her heart. "I am sorry I have been such a burden to you these past years."

"I am, too."

She gave a choke of laughter, relief easing across her chest at the humor glinting in his eye. "So, when will you tell Catherine and Mother?"

"I won't. Not until everything is finally sorted."

"But they believe him dead."

"And hopefully everyone else will also. But I did not think it fair to allow you to continue to believe such a thing. But you will need to do your best to continue in the mode of a grieving widow. We would not want your actions giving rise to anything that might draw suspicion."

"Of course."

He made a few more suggestions, and then went to find his wife, and to encourage their mother to make their departure from London even sooner than she had arranged.

Leaving Julia alone in the drawing room, filled with a mix of renewed hope mingled with underlying dread.

Chapter Twenty-Six

"Gentlemen, please excuse me," the Countess of Hawkesbury said, "I find I am not feeling quite the thing."

Thomas pushed to shaky feet as the countess murmured to her husband, before offering him a wan smile. "Major Hale, please sit. I might be counting on you to do your best to distract my husband from worrying about me, but I would not have you do so at the expense of your health."

He glanced at the earl, whose frowning attention remained claimed by his wife, and slid gratefully back into his dining chair at her gesture to sit.

"You are sure you are well?" Lord Hawkesbury asked.

"I will be, once I rest." She stroked his shoulder. "Please do not worry, Nicholas. Now you can resume your conversation about matters I know you would prefer to discuss." And with a further smile for her husband, and a murmured good night for Thomas, she departed.

The earl's brow remained knit a moment longer, as he resumed his seat and glanced at Thomas again. "Lavinia has something of a resolute nature."

"A wife of resolution is a blessing," Thomas said, thinking of his own. Would Julia resolve to stay with him, after all that had happened? Conscious the earl still wore a frown, he said, "Lady Hawkesbury has been all consideration."

"Yes." Lord Hawkesbury shook his head as if clearing away concern, and said, "And knowing her as I do it probably is best we follow her advice, lest I find myself in trouble later."

"Heaven forbid," Thomas murmured.

A smile tweaked the earl's lips, before his mien took on a more serious aspect. "It would seem that young Smith is prepared to confirm your testimony. My investigator is preparing a written statement as we speak, and I am hopeful that this, along with what those in Scotland have offered, will persuade those in authority to listen to our cause."

"That is good news."

"Matters seem to be progressing, at least." Hawkesbury took a sip of wine and eyed him over the rim of the glass. "Is there any word from Winthrop? He has not returned?"

"Not as yet." He forced down his apprehension, his great desire to flee the strictures of these walls and find his Julia and ensure her safety once more. But frustration only fueled foolishness, and he would not do anything to jeopardize her safety, or compromise Hawkesbury's investigation.

"I'm sure he will let us know as soon as he can." Hawkesbury's smile glinted. "I'm equally certain that his news could not have been imparted to a more grateful recipient."

"It would help ease her mind," Thomas acknowledged. At least, he hoped it would. He could not help but feel hurt that she would so quickly turn to another man for solace. Who *was* this Amherst person, anyway? So far, Harry's enquiries had turned up nothing to indicate that he was anything but a neighbor of the Aynsleys, the younger son of an earl. Is that why she had turned to him, for his noble connections? But what if, somehow, he was in the employ of Fallbright . . .

Dear God, have mercy.

"And how are you feeling today?" Hawkesbury asked, his forehead wrinkling.

Thomas gingerly shifted his right knee.

Bit back a curse at the pain. "Things appear to be improving." Marginally improving, but something was better than nothing.

"Hmm. I may have to see if we can get a doctor to examine you. There might be some exercises that can help."

"Any help would be welcome," Thomas said. "Although I feel like I have used up everyone's generous acts of service already."

"Nonsense. You should know by now that you are merely a pawn in my game, another reason for me to more fully investigate matters and hopefully see the Foreign Office finally cleared of the corruption I fear exists within its walls."

"You make yourself sound like an arch manipulator, my lord."

"I prefer the term tactician."

Thomas released a chuckle. "Of course."

Hawkesbury took on a pleased look. "I am glad to see you finally smile. I know matters are somewhat desperate, but I tend to find a measure of humor helps leaven the pain."

"I agree."

They continued with their meal, the conversation shifting to other things: political doings, the dissent of workers in the north.

The tablecloth had been removed when

the door opened, and a footman announced the arrival of Lord Winthrop.

Hawkesbury instructed a plate be prepared for him, and within the minute, Julia's brother strode in, his weariness evident in face and posture.

"Any news?"

"They are safe."

Thomas exhaled. "And Julia?"

"Seems to have suffered no adverse effects from that episode in the park."

"Thank goodness," Thomas said, heart easing a mite.

"Thank God," Hawkesbury said. "And the Amherst man?"

"I visited him as well. He denies having any knowledge of Fallbright and McKinley, and for my part, I am inclined to believe him. It appears that he is truly who Harry says he was: a friend of the Aynsleys."

Another internal sigh of relief. But while it was good to know Amherst was not part of his attackers' game, and their plan was not filled with extremely deep subterfuge as he had feared, he still couldn't help the doubt that asked why Julia had been spending time with the man.

He forced his thoughts to the present, to what still begged to be done. "So, what now?"

"I intend on visiting Fallbright in London, and I'm hopeful that he will release some information about you."

"And I suppose I stay here again?"

"You cannot afford to be seen, my friend. Now, if you'll excuse me, I must go check on my wife." The earl pushed to his feet, made his bow, and departed, leaving him with Jon.

That man now studied Thomas with a lowered brow.

His skin prickled with apprehension. Why did Jon look so grave? "What is it?"

"I don't know. Why don't you tell me?"

"Julia is well, isn't she?"

The gaze grew hard, arctic. "My mother had something interesting to say."

Thomas blinked at the abrupt change of subject. "Did she?"

"Yes. She said Julia had been more than a little nauseous of late."

"Oh. Poor thing." Regret gnawed at him. If only he had been there to comfort her —

"You seem to be a trifle oblivious as to what this might mean. Perhaps I should make myself clearer. But I cannot decide if I should or not — whether this is any of my business, or if it is something that you should speak of with your *wife.*"

This last was said with an edge Thomas

had not heard since that initial encounter upon his return from Spain. "Perhaps it is best if I speak with her."

"Yes, I should think there are a number of things you might wish to discuss with her."

The hard gaze sent a chill up his spine. "What are you implying?"

"My sister mentioned she had recently received another visitor. A Lieutenant Harrow —"

"Harrow? Why, he's the best of chaps."

Jon's brows rose. "Apparently this 'best of chaps' spoke of a Spanish woman you were . . . friendly with."

Dear God, no. How could *Harrow* of all people speak of Thomas's shame?

"Yes," Jon continued, his gaze narrowed and formidable. "In talking later with my mother I was given to understand that my sister's husband was less than faithful to her while he was in Spain." He leaned forward in a sudden savage movement. "Can you deny this?"

Thomas swallowed, forcing himself to meet the censure in his friend's eyes. "I cannot."

Jon swore, something which Thomas had never heard him do. "If you were not already injured, I would ensure you received a beating at least as good as what you got up north. How could you betray Julia like that?"

He forced his gaze not to waver, forced the words out, "I have no excuses."

"No excuses? You just happened to forget your marriage vows and took another woman?"

"It wasn't like that."

"No? Then how was it? Not that I really care to know. All I care about is my sister's well-being, and I don't mind telling you I think she would be happier in the long term if you truly were dead as everyone supposes!"

The words lashed inside. Jon was right. Thomas was wrong, all wrong for Julia. Hadn't his actions always proved it?

Jon's eyes were like granite. "I have promised my help to Julia and Hawkesbury, which I will fulfill. As for you —" He muttered something under his breath. "I cannot abide the thought that my actions will benefit you in any way, but know that I will do all I can to keep her away from you when this is all finally sorted."

Thomas examined the remains of Jon's meal on the table. "You were right."

"About what?"

He lifted his gaze. "That this is something I should discuss with my wife."

Jon uttered an expression of disgust and walked out.

Thomas exhaled, sank his head into his hands. Pain heavier than that lacing his body settled in his soul. He could not blame his — former — friend for his words. He could not blame him for his future action. He could only blame himself for his choices, his misdeeds, his sins. The words rang in his head with recriminations.

He was at fault. He was to blame. Julia would be better off without him. Everyone would be better off if he no longer existed. He was a failure. A sinner. An adulterer.

He'd be better off dead.

The words circled the room, encircling his heart, birds of prey seeking to devour.

The knife remained upon the plate. He eyed it, wondering . . .

"There you are." Hawkesbury returned to the room. "I thought I heard raised voices, and caught Winthrop as he was exiting."

So now his one advocate knew his sin.

"He said nothing, save that he needed to leave immediately." Hawkesbury frowned. "Did something happen?"

"I have . . . done something to upset him."

"You? You haven't left here in days."

"It happened before, in Spain."

"I don't understand."

Thomas's gaze lowered to the emptied wineglass, and, half relieved at finally sharing his burden, half despising himself for speaking of something that concerned Julia that he still had not had the chance to speak with her about, he told him.

He finished and awaited the condemnation.

But the earl said nothing.

When he finally braved to look up, Lord Hawkesbury's face was a picture of concern. "Well?"

The earl shook his head. "You do not need to tell me of your remorse. It is written all over you."

"I wish I was dead, that Julia could be freed from being married to such a burden."

"You cannot mean that."

"I can. I do!"

Silence.

"You can have no idea what it is like to live with regret, to wish the past changed."

A beat. "You do not know my past."

"You have not betrayed your wife!"

"But regret is something I am all too familiar with." Hawkesbury gave a wry smile. "What soldier does not wear some measure of guilt?"

Perhaps. But this felt so much more weighty, so much more critical, than anything he'd faced before. "Jon knows; he detests me. He's determined not to promote my cause with Julia anymore."

"That is understandable. He is a loyal brother."

"He will always despise me."

"Perhaps. Perhaps not."

Thomas kneaded his brow with his fingers, wishing he could press away his heart pain.

He was a failure. A sinner. An adulterer. What had his father said? Thomas was a wastrel, a blasphemer, a drunkard. A blight on their existence. He'd surely proved a blight on Julia's existence. He shoved his face into his hands and groaned.

Silence filled the room, despair drowning his heart. Would a merciful God allow him to die?

The earl cleared his throat. "In addition to a loyal brother's natural indignation, you might make allowances for the fact that he is not familiar with conditions during a war, especially those that pertain to imprisonment and torture."

"No. He will never forgive me." He shook his head. "Julia will never . . ." His eyes burned. He shuddered out a breath. If only he might show her how much he regretted the past, how much he still loved her.

Loved her.

How could the depths of regret reveal the extent of his love for Julia? He knew now, in a way he never had before, just how precious she was. More than just her beauty, he now had new appreciation for a myriad of other qualities: her strength, her compassion, her spirit, all proved in her willingness to care for poor Meggie's child, and her long and desperate flight from Edinburgh to London. What other woman would have done such a thing?

Then there was her loyalty, which had looked past the months of his absence, had believed him in the teeth of opposition, had wanted him near when he'd fought to clear his name. Would her loyalty, would her love ever extend to the depths of forgiveness demanded by this betrayal of her trust? Could it?

He groaned again. "Dear God, have mercy."

"Major Hale."

Thomas shuddered out a breath, pried opened his eyes.

The earl's gaze was grave. "I do not condone such actions, but I do know that God's mercy is far wider and deeper than we realize it to be."

"He can never forgive me."

"Why? Do you believe your sins to be

398

greater than what God can forgive?"

"Well, yes — no. Perhaps."

"It may surprise you to know just how many people have thought themselves too sinful for God to ever forgive them."

"But I *am* sinful." His father's words sang in his ears. He was a wastrel. A drunkard. A blight —

"As are we all. The Bible says no man is perfect, not one. Sins of pride and deceit and envy cast a shadow on our souls just as murder."

Thomas snorted. "No, they don't."

"No? You are like God now, are you? Able to hold the measure of sin and grace in your hands and determine what is sin enough? How wonderful it must be to be you."

His sarcasm prompted Thomas's muttered, "Of course I don't think that."

"Are you sure? Exactly how bad does sin need to be before it is considered sin?"

Thomas looked away. How bad *did* sin need to be before it was considered sin?

His father had certainly thought some deeds worse than others, branding Thomas's sins as wicked in the extreme. And that was before these latest had plunged Thomas into further depths of depravity. And didn't God hate sinners?

But if what the earl said was true, that

God considered every sin equally a shadow, whether it be a lie or adultery, then nobody could consider themselves righteous. Not even Thomas's own father.

"My friend, we are all in need of God's forgiveness. And no matter how much we might delude ourselves into thinking we are sinless, we have all done things we know are wrong."

"Some of us more than others."

"Some actions will have consequences far more readily known than others may, but it does not change the fact that we have all done wrong. Nor does it change the fact that God still holds out His olive branch to us, in hope that we will find the peace that is only found through Jesus Christ."

"But —"

"There are no buts, my friend. Even the worst sinner in the world can find forgiveness and reconciliation with God through Jesus." He smiled. "Ask me how I know."

Thomas swallowed. "My father believes God hates sinners."

"The Bible says that 'God commendeth his love toward us, in that, while we were yet sinners, Christ died for us.' " The earl eyed him intently. "God loves you, Thomas."

"He cannot," he muttered.

"Are you God? How can you know what

He thinks about you?"

"My father was a harsh, tyrannical man, yet had the nerve to preach on Sundays about a merciful God. Merciful? I could not see it."

"Was your father always right?"

"No."

"Can you not instead believe what the Bible says? Surely you, a minister's son, know what the sixteenth verse in the third chapter of John's gospel says?"

Long ago memories stirred.

" 'For God so loved the world, that he gave his only begotten Son, that whosoever believeth in him should not perish, but have everlasting life.' God loved the world, His love for us, *before* we acknowledged our sin, prompted his sending of Jesus to be the propitiation for our sins." The earl's eyes softened. "God is not a tyrant, Thomas. God is love. He did not send Jesus to condemn the world, but to save the world through Him. One simply needs to believe."

"I want to believe such a thing is possible, but I cannot think it is that easy."

"It is not easy, in the sense that believing such a thing is not always simple. But it is easy in that God does not require anything from you other than your belief in Him and what Jesus has done." The earl smiled. "And

401

are you not tired of trying to do things your way? I know I was."

Oh, yes, he was tired. So tired. But really, did God truly want this broken mess of a man? "You really think God loves us?"

"Yes."

"But I'll never be good enough —"

"And you don't need to be. Jesus Christ, the only perfect man who ever lived, is good enough for you, for me, for all of us. That's why He took our sins upon Himself and became the sacrifice God needed to restore relationship between us and Him."

What a different point of view to that of his own earthly father, whose demands for perfection had led to Thomas's running away all those years ago. "I don't need to be good enough?"

"The Bible clearly states that all have sinned and fall short of the glory of God. But it also says that the gift of God is eternal life through Jesus Christ our Lord. God doesn't demand perfection from His children; He knows we are frail. But He does stand with His arm stretched towards us, asking us to trust Him with our lives." Another smile glinted. "And surely trusting Him has got to be better than whatever efforts we attempt."

That was certainly true. Thomas's efforts

at righteousness were as foul as that filthy Spanish cell he longed to forget.

"God loves you, Thomas Hale."

Tears pricked; he blinked them away.

"His Word is true."

Something sown years ago whispered that this was indeed so.

"God wants you to trust Him. With your life, with your eternity, with your future, and with Julia."

His spirit tugged. Yes, he wanted to believe. Something within him *longed* to believe.

"The Bible says that if we confess our sins He is faithful to forgive us our sins and to cleanse us from all unrighteousness. You want to be clean, don't you?"

"Yes," he said in a broken whisper. The thought of being clean, of not having any stain or blemish caused another heart tug.

"Then ask God to forgive you, and ask Him to be your Lord and Savior, ask Him to guide you into His plans for your life."

His eyes closed, he was aware of how strange he must look, but did not care. He sensed the earl would not judge. *Heavenly Father, I am sorry, please forgive and save me.* He shuddered out a breath. *Show Your mercy, guide and lead me. And please, please protect Julia.*

For a moment, nothing seemed to be any different, save for a dimming of the welter of confusion, a slight easing of the pressure in his heart. And then . . .

And then he sensed a slow unfurling of warmth, of something deep, deep within. Love, more profound than anything his parents had offered, purer than anything Julia had shown. Love. Real love. Something strong, something that made him feel assured, secure, like he wasn't floating driftless in this world, but was anchored deep in life's purpose. He breathed it in, felt peace lodge. Yes, God loved him.

Alongside this assurance, he felt somehow cleaner, lighter, like the stains of sin had been washed completely from his soul. The mottled slate of sin was wiped as if new. This felt nothing like what his earthly father had said; he did not feel fear so much as humbled awe, that the God who created the universe could deign to care about one poor lost soul. He inhaled again, exhaled shakily. Smiled.

When next he looked up it was to see the earl looking at him, a small smile lighting his features. "It feels good, does it not?"

"Very good."

"I would recommend you find yourself a Bible — in fact, I'll give you mine."

"Oh, but —"

"No, I will get another. I sense that you will need to take this time to discover more about who Jesus Christ is, and what our Savior has done for you."

"Our Savior." Thomas's smile felt like the first one in years. It seemed so strange that he now shared something in common with this aristocrat. "Thank you, Lord Hawkesbury."

"Ah, don't thank me. I'm nothing but one of the vessels God chooses to use at times."

Another moment passed, then the earl continued. "While you were getting matters sorted between yourself and God, I was reminded of something. I do not know if you were aware that when you were in Edinburgh in your barely conscious state you were heard to mutter various things."

He talked in his sleep? Fire crept up his neck. "I — no. Forgive me, I did not —"

"The doctor mentioned that on a number of occasions you mentioned the name Magdelena, but always in a state of panic. It would seem that if she were the woman Winthrop refers to, that she is hardly a creature to arouse your wife's jealousy, and rather might provoke her compassion."

His understanding threatened to unman him. Thomas rested a hand over his eyes. "I cannot even be sure exactly as to what happened. I was half-crazed. We were near starved, my men were dying, getting shot. You cannot know how desperate we all felt."

The earl regarded him with something akin to sympathy in his expression.

"I thought perhaps . . ." Thomas shook his head. "It was stupid I know, but at the time it seemed the only way we could escape, the only way for the nightmare to be over. She promised it would be so." He groaned. "I thought myself a fool to believe her, but in the end she *did* help us flee." He glanced up, wishing he did not sound so defensive.

The earl gave a small smile. "It can be very easy to cast judgment when one has not undergone such a trial. I think we always like to imagine that we would do better than what we might actually do, given the reality of our circumstances."

Again, the earl's compassion wrung emotion from within, making it hard to speak. He cleared his throat. "She . . . she said she was pregnant."

An intake of breath. "Ah. That is unfortunate." Another long moment passed before the earl spoke again. "Who else knows?"

Thomas shrugged. "Harrow — apparently he's the one who told Julia. Though I still cannot believe it of him. I would have far more readily believed it of Benson."

"This man Benson, is he the one you attended Fallbright's office with?"

"When we were given our orders, yes."

"And you believe he does not like you?"

"Not much, no."

"Hmm." The earl's brow puckered. "You are sure it was this Harrow man and not Benson who spoke to Julia?"

"That is what Jon said."

"I wonder . . . would either of them wish to further discredit you?"

"I don't know." Thomas finally glanced up. "Why?"

"I wonder if such allegations of your infidelity," at the word Thomas winced, "would hurt our campaign."

Were Thomas's marital woes now to be fodder for Hawkesbury's campaign against Fallbright? "I could not bear for Julia to be shamed any further."

"I have no desire for that, either. It just means that we should be a little circumspect in our actions."

"I beg your pardon?"

"These men, Benson and Harrow. Have you any idea of their direction?" The earl's smile glinted. "I think it best we find them before any more damage can be done."

"You mean — ?"

"I mean it would be best if we found them, and secured against any further damaging allegations. And it might be best to learn more about this Magdalena person. Would you not agree?"

"Yes, but I cannot think such things will matter to Julia."

"They may not. But while there is life, there is hope for forgiveness and understanding. And we do have life, do we not?"

Thomas dragged in a deep breath that seemed to draw up from his toes. "Yes."

While he lived, he would hope. God — his heavenly Father, his Savior Jesus Christ — would somehow have to anchor his soul.

CHAPTER TWENTY-SEVEN

Chatteris, Cambridgeshire

"But Jonathan, I do not understand the urgency," Mother complained. "Why did you insist on us leaving in the middle of the night?"

Julia exchanged a look with Jon but said nothing.

"And why did you insist we come here to this glorified farmhouse, instead of your manor in Gloucestershire? Such a place is hardly where I envisaged spending my Christmas."

Catherine said something soothing, allowing Julia a moment's respite.

Well she knew, or at least suspected, why Jon had been so insistent. She shivered, and clutched little Charles closer to her chest. Poor Mr. Amherst had very nearly been killed, and Jon's anxiety to remove her and Mother from London had been because he was concerned for her safety. But truly, who would want to hurt her?

Crabbit drew near and offered to take the sleeping boy. Julia pressed a kiss to his brow and released him to her care. The darkness seemed to rush in more deeply.

"Well, I am for bed. Today has been quite long enough," said Catherine, casting a look at Jon that didn't fail to communicate her thoughts on the subject. "Good night."

"Quite long enough indeed," grumbled Mother. "Really, Jonathan, you have been acting in a most peculiar way, coming then going then coming again, dragging us from our beds —"

"Now, Mother —"

"Well, I'll grant you did not exactly drag us from our beds. But it is most inconvenient to be forced to leave one's home and come to this, this . . . place." She looked around the room with an expression of distaste. The drawing room held little of the elegancies with which Mother preferred to surround herself, instead consisting of plain, bare walls and unremarkable, rather less-than-comfortable furnishings. She sniffed. "How long do you expect us to stay here?"

"As long as is necessary," he answered, with the patience of a saint.

"And pray, how long shall that be?"

"As long as is necessary," he said, lips

410

tweaked in a small smile.

Mother gave a reluctant chuckle, lifted her cheek for him to kiss, then following Catherine's lead, made her way up the stairs, with loud exclamations about her anticipation of the discomfort of the bedchambers, and exhortations that Julia not stay up too late either.

Jon's usual gravity, eased for a moment by Mother's nonsense, returned as he glanced at Julia again. "You do understand why such measures were necessary, don't you?"

"You are worried about us."

"Lord Hawkesbury felt it best you were removed someplace you could not be traced."

"This place belongs to him?"

"Yes." He studied her with another deep, long look.

"What is it?"

He shook his head. "I should not, perhaps, interfere in matters that do not directly concern me —"

"Yet your saying so suggests you will nonetheless," Julia murmured.

"It concerns your marriage."

She sighed. "Really? Have we not discussed your antipathy to Thomas long enough? What more is left to say?"

"We have not discussed this," he said

411

grimly. A muscle ticked in his jaw.

Her heart clenched. Somehow she knew what he was going to say, and she had no desire to speak about such things with her brother. Not now. Not ever. "Really, I'm very tired," she said, feigning a yawn.

"I can imagine you would be." His eyes softened for a moment. "These past few weeks have not been easy for you."

"No, they have not. Which is why I would really prefer to go to bed." She summoned up a smile in an attempt to leaven the mood. "Not all of us are used to staying up through the night to conclude important business matters."

His lips flattened as he acknowledged her comment. "I understand your weariness, but there is something I really think we must speak about before you retire."

Another heart pang. "Really, Jon, I would prefer we do not —"

"I know this is hard for you, but we must discuss what you plan to do once this is over."

She bit her lip. She would not say it.

"Julia, I'm asking plainly, do you want to remain married to an adulterer?"

A gasp escaped. "You have no right to say such things!"

"As your brother, and someone who loves

you very much, and as the executor of your estate I have every right to consider what might be in your best interests. And I cannot see how remaining married to such a man can possibly be beneficial to anyone."

"Jon, you do not know what you are talking about."

"I most certainly do." His eyes flashed with arctic fire. "I had a very interesting talk with your husband before I returned to London, and he admitted certain . . . aspects of his character that were not at all what I want for my little sister to endure."

Her chest heated. "You had no right! I need to have that conversation with him, not you. He is *my* husband, after all."

"But every time you see him you seem to forget all your good intentions — and forget yourself as well."

"I do not!"

"I am sorry, Julia, but that is how it seems to others."

"How dare you judge me!"

"I dare because I care about you, and I would rather say something and risk your anger than stand by and watch you tumble into yet more pain."

She drew in a shaky breath, willed her voice to not waver. "I appreciate your solicitude, but I have no wish to speak of this with you anymore until I have spoken with him."

"But he is an adulterer!"

The word scratched against her desire for a semblance of self-control. "You do not know that —"

"He admitted as much himself, Julia."

Breath caught, wrenching a sob from deep within. "Perhaps there was a mistake."

He gave a short laugh. "How can there be a mistake? No, he is wicked, and I cannot bear for you to have anything more to do with him. Hale has nothing to offer you, nothing! No money, no means of supporting you, no faith, no honor, even. I would much prefer you to part with him and we do what we can to dissolve the marriage once and for all."

"But —"

"No, Julia. Enough is enough. You would do far better to be rid of him. And I will help you. If you decide to part with him then I can speak with the other trustees and ensure your settlements are released once and for all. Your father certainly wanted you to be living in style, not a hovel, and you would definitely have enough funds to enable you to choose whatever house you preferred. Something appropriate for you and Charles. I am sure you would prefer to

414

be out from Mother's apron strings, would you not?"

"Well, yes . . ."

"I can help you with that. I can help you with everything. But I cannot help you if you are determined to stay attached to that man."

She swallowed and looked away. While the idea of her own — nice — place held no small amount of merit, was parting from her husband too high a price to pay?

"I cannot believe you even need to consider this. He has betrayed you, Julia. Do you forget that? He betrayed your marriage vows. Why do you still hesitate?"

"I . . . I don't know." But she did, the memory of Catherine's words about forgiveness like a promise drifting on the wind.

"Please, let me help you. I can ensure he never speaks to you again."

But she had to speak with him! She had to tell him about the life she was carrying, even if she dreaded hearing about his extramarital activities. She *had* to tell him. Didn't she?

"Julia, I love you, and I cannot stand to see him make you miserable anymore."

"I know." She shook her head. "But until I speak with him, I cannot give you an answer."

He let out an audible breath, disappointment writ large upon his face. "But you will after you do so?"

"I will," she said wearily.

"Good."

"Can I go to bed now?"

"Of course. I'm sorry to have kept you from your rest." He gave a small smile. "But not sorry for the chance to speak so honestly to you."

She moved to go, but he clasped her in his arms, and she closed her eyes, the weariness that had her almost swaying on her feet finally releasing into tears against his chest. What a coil she had created for herself, what a dilemma she now faced. Should she tell Thomas about his child? Should she leave her broken husband and certain poverty and regain the riches that were her birthright?

Jon continued to hold her, and she soaked in the comfort of his strong embrace, drawing in a shuddery breath as the whirling questions firmed down to two.

Did she still love Thomas?

The second challenge stemmed from this first question's answer.

Could she ever find it in her heart to forgive him?

■ ■ ■ ■

Whitehall, London

"Well, it ain't every day I gets paid to sit and wait while the gentry do what gentry does. I s'pose I'm being paid well, even if I just be keeping my horses still. But I can't help thinking this 'ere be a trifle smoky, guv'nor."

Thomas leaned back against the squabs, wishing the hackney cab driver wasn't quite so prescient in his observations. He supposed it was not usual for a hackney to be asked to wait outside the offices of the Secretary of State for War and the Colonies while an earl visited inside, but neither had they wanted to lose the chance of learning more about the truth of Fallbright's and McKinley's dealings. And even though he felt uncomfortable — this conveyance hardly held the comfort level of the curricle awaiting Lord Hawkesbury's exit — Thomas was glad to finally be a part of things, instead of feeling cast aside while the others had their sport.

He peered out the window, scanning the pedestrians, unable to recognize any familiar faces, as the last few days rolled through his mind. His initial moment of euphoria at knowing he was forgiven by God had not abated, had instead become a deep certainty, the more he read the verses Lord Hawkesbury had recommended. It fueled the promise of hope, that the God who had forgiven Thomas so much might extend His loving mercy to somehow work this situation out for their good. For Julia's good. For Charles.

His prayers for them had scarcely ceased these past days. Prayers for their safety, for their health, for Julia's peace of mind, for her trust. Sometimes it seemed he could glimpse a corner of their future, when they would be happy, when he would be as Charles's father, a provider, a husband loved by his wife. He scarcely dared pray she might forgive him, yet in the light of God's mercy something whispered he pray this, too. So, he prayed that God might touch her with His grace and mercy, and help her extend that grace to him, too. Such mercy and grace that he found in the Bible readings suggested by the earl fueled hope for today, hope for his future.

Such hope had only grown with this morning's news sourced by Hawkesbury's groom, a curmudgeonly Scot named McHendricks, who had visited the London lodgings of Harrow and Benson upon the earl's orders. The visit made it plain that Benson had lied and used Harrow's name, in an apparent effort to gain some form of remuneration, and hurt Thomas by making him question his friendships. From what McHendricks had said, it seemed Benson had been refused admittance to Fallbright, and desperation had bade him seek payment in a more roundabout method. Upon learning of Benson's deception, Harrow had been horrified, and thus reiterated his support for Thomas, evidenced in a short note which promised "all he could do." But Harrow's desire to give Benson his just deserts had been speedily answered by Thomas in the negative, such need for revenge quashed by Thomas's recent experience of divine forgiveness which bolstered grace and hope.

This heartening result had only added to Thomas's relief at Hawkesbury's other schemes of late, his stratagem worthy of a man who had served under the Duke of Wellington. Jon had withdrawn Charles, Julia, and their mother to a safe locale in Cambridgeshire, thus removing them from any danger. Harry's recent return to London — ostensibly to deal with various legalities following his father's death — would ensure that the house in Portman Square could be watched. Hawkesbury himself was this very moment confronting Fallbright regarding Thomas and McKinley. Should that confrontation prove to rattle the colonel's equanimity, Thomas's role was to follow Fallbright, a plan of his own devising, now that he was aware of just how devious his former commanding officer had proved.

He breathed in and then exhaled, filling the minutes with further prayers. For Julia. Their marriage. For Charles. For their protection. For the earl. For justice.

Hawkesbury's tall, caped figure came striding down the steps before he paused, tapped his curly brimmed beaver twice — the signal — then moved to his waiting curricle. He spoke to his groom, McHendricks, whose brusque manner and look of decided dissatisfaction underlay a sense of very real affection, evident earlier in his gruff approbation of the earl's plan.

They set off, and within a minute, Thomas saw a figure slink to a hackney ahead of him and speak urgently to the driver. By now the earl's curricle was slowing, turning at the corner, before pausing ever so briefly as McHendricks stepped down and moved to a shaded shopfront.

The earl's shadow had by this stage convinced the hackney to follow the curricle, leaving Thomas to wait for Fallbright to make his move. Sure enough, the toad-like figure soon waddled down the steps, casting a look in either direction, which made Thomas draw back into the dimness of the interior, and hope fervently that the hackney's exterior shabbiness would not draw Fallbright's desire to hire such a conveyance.

"How much?" came the voice outside.

His pulse accelerated. *Dear God, don't let him peer inside.*

"I'm sorry, sir. This vehicle is already hired."

"Really?"

At the sound of annoyance, Thomas lumbered to the forward seat, stretching his legs across the seat where he had just been sitting, and slouched, face averted from the window.

"I see no one — oh, I beg your pardon, sir." The voice faded, the sound of footsteps suggested he had moved away.

Thomas exhaled, but it was only when he heard the cab driver mutter, "He's gone now, sir," that he moved back to his previous position.

"Has he found a cab?" Thomas asked.

"Yes."

"Follow him."

"Right you 'ave it, then."

Within seconds they were moving, were approaching the corner where McHendricks had departed the earl's curricle only minutes earlier. Thomas unlatched the door, opened it, and the groom — proving far sprightlier than his age would suggest — scrambled inside, much to the vocal disgust of the driver.

"Never mind that," Thomas called. "Just don't lose him." He turned to Hawkesbury's groom. "Did his lordship say anything?"

"He said to tell you that Fallbright appeared quite shocked at the allegations, that he denied everything, but his lordship suspected he was more unnerved than he wanted to appear."

Thomas nodded. "And where is his lordship going now?"

McHendricks gave a rasp of laughter. "He plans on leading any pursuer on a very extensive trail through what he called the 'better parts of London,' as much to give any tail an education as to tire him out, so he said. The horses be very fresh, and will be right to go for hours."

Thomas's grin faded. "He was being tailed."

"Aye, by a nasty-looking fellow in a gray coat. I memorized his face, and know what to look out for."

"Good."

"I don't mind telling you, sir, that I do not like this business."

"No. We can but pray that things resolve quickly without any injury."

They relapsed into silence as the hackney continued its winding progression. Then it slowed, and finally came to a halt.

"He's getting out, sir," the hackney driver called.

Thomas peered out the window, spied the bowed window of White's Gentlemen's Club. Muttered an oath under his breath.

McHendricks frowned. "I don't think his lordship imagined Fallbright would come to such a place."

"No. It certainly won't work to have you follow him in there." Thomas thought quickly. "I think you should take the cab and get reinforcements." He gave instruction. "I will have to go in."

"You, sir?" McHendricks looked at him doubtfully.

"I have been a guest in the past. I hope the doorman remembers."

"Very good, sir."

"Oy!" called the cab driver. "You planning on getting out anytime soon? I've got places to be."

"Exactly so," Thomas said, climbing gingerly down the steps, balancing with his cane. "You will need to go to this address as quickly as you can. It is a matter of some urgency." He dug into his breeches pocket, gave the man a more than sufficient coin. "There is another one for you if you can return within the half hour."

"Very good, sir."

Thomas nodded to McHendricks and limped towards the steps. He wished now that he had taken more pains with his attire, but he had certainly had no expectation of being in such an establishment today. He could only hope that he could persuade the doorman to help him.

Drawing himself up, he moved to the steps. Nodded to the burly man on duty. "Good afternoon."

The doorman blinked. "Major Hale? I thought — we heard that you had died, sir."

"News of my demise has proved rather premature."

"Indeed, sir."

He stepped closer, averting his face as a trio of gentlemen exited the establishment. "I have need of your help."

"Of course, sir."

"You may remember my friends Lord

Winthrop and Lord Carmichael that was
—"

"The new Earl of Bevington, that's right,
I recall."

"Yes, well, I find myself a little early in my
meeting with Lord Bevington . . ." Thomas
paused.

"Well, we don't normally permit entry
without a member, but seeing as you're not
dead, after all."

"Thank you. You are a prince among
men."

"If you say so, sir."

"I do. And I would be most obliged if you
were to forget that I am not dead."

"Sir?"

Thomas gave a thin smile. "It seems some
would prefer the accounts of my death to
be factual, and I am hopeful to accord them
the pleasure of that belief for as long as possible."

"Very good, sir." The man drew open the
door, gestured to the member's register. "I
believe you will find the name Smith to be
quite a popular one."

"Thank you. Oh, and one more thing. The
gentleman who entered before?"

"Colonel Fallbright?"

"Yes. I wonder if you know with whom he
meets. I did not figure him to be a member

of White's."

"Ah, well that I can tell you. He *is* a member, but he visits infrequently. I believe he was to meet a military person."

"Thank you." Thomas nodded, and gingerly maneuvered his way inside.

The marbled hall gave way to a reading room, beyond which was a dining area and several private rooms, with the gaming facilities farther on. He hoped Fallbright would not have ventured that far; he lacked funds, and doubted he could keep his identity — and lack of death — quiet for much longer. *Merciful Father, keep me from recognition . . .*

"Well, Hale!"

He turned, caught sight of an old acquaintance, a General Whitby, with whom he had served in Calcutta. So much for God answering his prayers. "Hello, sir."

"I read that you were dead!" Whitby frowned. "I'm glad to see you're not, but you do not appear to be at all the thing, my dear fellow. What has happened to you, and whatever was that notice doing in *The Times*?"

"A sad piece of misinformation."

"Indeed!" The general began what threatened to be a long exposition on the falsehoods printed in the papers, prompting

Thomas to interrupt.

"Sir, I need your help."

"Certainly. What can I do?"

He gestured to a small alcove, and said in a hushed voice, "Colonel Fallbright —"

The general made a noise of disgust. "Can't stand the man. Pompous little popinjay, and all the more so since he got that confounded promotion. What about him?"

"I am not a member, but I need to know with whom he is meeting."

The general nodded, murmured for him to wait, then strode into the reading room, exclaiming loudly about his missing eyeglasses. Within a minute he had returned, and murmured about a rather tanned, mustachioed, Scottish-sounding fellow. "Why do you want to know?"

"That death notice you read? I believe it was they who tried to make it true."

"No! You don't say." Whitby stroked his chin. "Well, I'm not about to lose one of my best men to the likes of a toad-eater like him! Come, let's see what we can learn. Follow me."

Sincerely hoping that the general would not feel the need to advertise his presence, Thomas followed him, head lowered, to a high-backed sofa positioned behind where

Fallbright sat. Thomas snatched up a news-paper, and pretended to read, while the low-voiced conversation continued behind them.

". . . think he is! Had the nerve to threaten me with parliamentary inquiry . . ."

"We need to deal with him also," came a voice, unmistakably McKinley's.

Thomas's breath suspended. He sank lower in his chair.

The whispers continued, and he listened avidly to their complaints. It seemed they still had not learned that Thomas had survived, which made his current position all the more precarious. He heard further details about what Fallbright wished to do about Hawkesbury, but the threats sounded idle.

The conversation moved to other things, leaving Thomas wondering how to extricate himself, when a familiar face appeared in the doorway.

Harry spied him, and gestured for him to come close, but before he could move another voice said, "Well, Bevington, I certainly did not expect to see *you* here."

A somewhat corpulent figure strode into view, one Thomas recognized from his time playing cards in many a saloon. Thomas froze. The conversation behind him had ceased, as had every other conversation in the room, what faces Thomas could see all turned expectantly to the two standing at the door. Lord Ashbolt's dislike of Harry was well-known.

Harry sighed. "Alas, it seems I was born to forever disappoint certain people."

"What do you do here? I thought you'd be tucked away in Derbyshire trying to sort that sorry mess."

"Your condolences on my father's recent passing humble me with the depth of their sincerity, my lord."

Ashbolt flushed, muttered something, to which Harry responded with a sweet smile. "You are right, I have been plagued with a number of sad events of late." He pushed into the room, addressing the assembly at large. "Forgive me, gentlemen, I know it is not at all the done thing, but I cannot abide being mocked while my grief is still so raw. I'm sure you can all understand."

This speech caused the other man to quickly disappear, while Harry searched the room. "Why, General Whitby, how are you?"

What was he doing? Did he not remember the plan? Thomas gestured for Harry to move away, but after one half smile in his direction, Harry refused to acknowledge him.

"I'm sure you must also be lamenting the

loss of our dear friend."

The general harrumphed and agreed, saying, with a sideways glance at Thomas who quickly resumed his newspaper screen, "There are many of us who feel that way." Then, as if taken by surprise, he said, "Why, here is Colonel Fallbright!" He stood, moving away to stand near the center table, thus drawing attention away from Thomas's position on the sofa. "Well, Colonel, I'm sure *you* would have learned about the recent death of one of my most highly decorated soldiers."

Thomas froze. This definitely was not how the plan was supposed to proceed.

"Ah, I'm afraid I cannot be certain of whom you mean."

"Major Hale, of course. Did you not see his death notice in the papers?"

Thomas shifted lower in his seat, hitched the paper higher.

"I . . . er . . ."

"I would have imagined you would know," Harry said sweetly. "I understood he worked for you."

What? Harry, no.

"I'm afraid your lordship must be mistaken —"

"Oh, no, there's no mistake," Harry continued. "He told me so himself."

"I beg your pardon?"

"Colonel, you surprise me. Did you not know he was in your employ? Mind you, he also told me something very interesting about a little trip to the Continent, for which he and several others did not receive the recompense they were due."

Behind Thomas's seat, Fallbright made a gobbling kind of noise.

"I wonder, did he ever mention that to you? No? Hmm, again, that strikes me as strange, seeing as he told me he had mentioned it to you."

"Is this so?" the general said, his voice now harder. "I cannot like to hear my men being treated in such a shabby fashion."

"Then you probably won't like to know that poor Hale was set upon not ten minutes after leaving Fallbright's chambers. A coincidence? I wonder."

There was the sound of a chair pushing back, then Thomas heard Fallbright say something about scurrilous accusations, libelous allegations, and promises to sue for character defamation.

Harry laughed. "It's only defamation if it is *not* true."

"You cannot say such things!" McKinley said.

"You'd be surprised at just what I can

say," Lord Bevington continued. "But there is no need to wonder at the veracity of my claims."

Oh, no.

"Why don't you instead ask the man himself?"

Dear God, no. Thomas lowered the newspaper, silently imploring Harry to cease.

His friend only smiled. "Yes, gentlemen," Harry continued, "I stand before you today in the presence of a true and living miracle! It is not every day that a man can be said to have returned from the dead, but today, in this very place, it can be said to have happened. And you are all witnesses."

"What do you mean?"

"I mean . . ."

"Major Hale?" Ashbolt's voice came from the door.

Thomas looked to the door, then looked at where Fallbright and McKinley stood open-mouthed, staring at him. He heard the room fill with soft mutters of disbelief, the odd curse.

"You're supposed — I thought —"

"I was dead?" Thomas pushed to his feet, wavering slightly until he steadied himself by grasping the back of a chair. "I understand you hoped that would be the case."

"Well, no! Of course not," Fallbright

432

blustered. "Why would you think such a thing?"

"Because you did not want everyone knowing about what happened in Poona all those years ago."

"What's this?" the general said, looking between them.

"I can well understand why you would be keen to silence those who knew," Thomas continued. "But it seems your methods are not as effective as you might have hoped."

"Hale, you do not seem well, you are not talking sense. It seems you have misunderstood some things. Perhaps if we were to discuss things in a more private location —"

"So you can attack him again?" Harry asked sardonically.

"Of course not!"

"Once — I beg your pardon — twice now, was enough, was it?"

"Sir, I really must take exception to such remarks!"

"Well, of course you would," Harry murmured, with a glance at Thomas. "What do you say, Major?"

"I would ask," Thomas said loudly, with a glance around the room, "whether I misunderstood you, Fallbright, when you agreed with your companion just now that Lord

433

Hawkesbury should be 'dealt with also.' "

The murmurs around the room took on a new intensity as Fallbright protested. "You lie!"

"No, I heard you also," said the general. "What did you mean by such a thing?"

"I . . . er —"

"It would seem that you were making threats against a peer of the realm."

Various other peers of the realm leaned forward, now also wearing scowls.

"I did not!"

"Then perhaps," came a lazy drawl from the doorway, "you can explain why I was followed this afternoon after I left your office."

The room took a collective gasp as Lord Hawkesbury strode into the room. He nodded to various gentlemen, gave Thomas a small smile, before his gaze hardened on Fallbright and McKinley. "It may interest you to know, gentlemen, that upon my return home I was in receipt of a letter, a letter from my solicitor in Edinburgh. The contents itself proved interesting, all the more so when I learned from my groom that one of the men it mentioned had immediately left my interview with him to come here."

Fallbright's face paled.

"This was despite the colonel saying he was tied up in government business all afternoon, and could not spare me a moment longer. It left me with the distinct impression of being fobbed off."

Thomas glanced around the room, unsurprised by the engrossed faces.

"I don't know about you, but I hate to be fobbed off, although such seems to be some people's way. Now, would you like to know what my letter from Edinburgh contains?" He gave Fallbright and McKinley a hard stare. "No? Somehow that does not surprise me. Well, I think for the sake of those in the room who have no wish to see their fellow club members mysteriously disappear that I best share from it anyway. It seems that after my brief sojourn in that fair city, during which I was so fortuitous as to make the acquaintance of our Scottish friend here, that a young boy recalled seeing a certain man named Bucknell following Major Hale down an alley, this man having been seen speaking with McKinley not an hour earlier."

"You believe a small boy?" McKinley sneered.

"Yes. I do. And it seems the chief magistrate does also. And he has taken the testimony of a retired sea captain who recalls

435

seeing the same man dumping a suspicious load in Newhaven harbor, only an hour or so after the boy spied Bucknell with the major here. Now it does not take a genius to join certain points of interest and reach a particular conclusion."

"I will sue you for libel," said McKinley, white around the jaw.

"And I will see that you are tried for attempted murder," said the earl, looking as fierce as Thomas could recall seeing him. "Arrest him!"

But before the earl's raised voice could bring in the burly doorman, McKinley was rushing through the room. Thomas tried to trip him with his cane, but although McKinley stumbled, he soon righted himself and escaped through the door.

"Forget him," Hawkesbury said. "My men outside will give chase. I think there might be a few people more interested in having a chat with the colonel there. Perhaps he might be able to explain what he was doing with such a villain."

Harry cleared his throat. "A chat isn't the only thing one might wish to happen with the colonel."

Hawkesbury's smile glinted, but he said, "I think it best to respectfully request the colonel to attend the office of Lord Bathurst with me. I am sure he would like to understand why one of his men has been engaged in activities that reek of corruption. Perhaps, General, as you were witness to a particular conversation concerning a threat against me, you might be willing to attend as well? Major Hale, I'm sure you would also have some interesting things to contribute." He glanced around the room again. "My apologies, gentlemen, for interrupting your afternoon in such dramatic fashion. I'm sure you understand my desire to see an innocent man spared."

There was a chorus of approbation, and Thomas was struck by the number of people who seemed genuinely pleased for him. It seemed that Fallbright was an unpopular figure, his exit from the room being treated with the ultimate of put-downs, as man after man turned their back on him as he was escorted past. By contrast, Thomas's flight to the border seemed to have been forgotten, as his limped passage to the door was accompanied by many of the gentlemen members who shook his hand or murmured encouragement.

When he attained the entrance, the doorman was waiting for him, his widened eyes and doffed cap telling Thomas he had certainly risen in his standing at least.

"Ah, Major," said Hawkesbury, from beside his curricle. "I hope you will not find it too challenging to continue with proceedings for a little while longer. I do not wish for today to place too much of a strain upon you, but I'm sure you are as keen as me to see matters resolved as quickly as possible."

His mind flashed back to an offer made several months ago. "I know of some others who might be willing to testify about this man's corruption."

"Excellent! Who are they?"

Thomas reminded him about Harrow and Smith.

"Of course." Hawkesbury assisted him into the curricle, and they followed the hackney which contained the general and Harry, who were keeping careful watch on the vehicle's other occupant, Colonel Fallbright.

"Things did not go quite as we planned," Hawkesbury said, snapping the reins gently. "It appears McKinley evaded capture, but I have every confidence he will be found soon. But as Fallbright is our main suspect, I think we have done well. I confess that I was a little perturbed to receive McHendricks's summons to White's, but really, such a public dressing down could not have been more perfectly placed than at the club where England's peers are guaranteed to talk."

Thomas chuckled. "And there I was, praying that God would keep me from being recognized."

"God answers our prayers in the way He sees fit, which is far better than what we ask or imagine. Tell me, how did the general get involved?"

Thomas explained, to the earl's low whistle.

"I was not aware that you knew him, but how wonderful that he was there at that precise moment."

"One could almost say providential," Thomas murmured.

"One could," said the earl with a laugh, before giving Thomas a sideways look. "And if God can do miracles with this situation, what is to say He will not provide another of a more personal nature?"

Thomas swallowed, nodded. God help him trust that His love would extend that far, too.

CHAPTER TWENTY-EIGHT

Cambridgeshire
Two days later

". . . and that is what happened."

Julia released breath that seemed to have been held for years. "And this Fallbright person is behind bars?"

"He is awaiting trial, but it would appear that imprisonment is a certainty," Jon continued.

"And Thomas is safe?"

Jon shrugged.

Her heart clenched. Somehow, his dismissive action hurt her like a pressed bruise.

"And Lord Hawkesbury?"

"He plans to drive over here in the next day or so." He seemed to hesitate, studying her, his frown creasing perceptibly.

"What is it, Jon?"

"Forgive me, but have you made any decisions about your future?"

"I told you, until I speak with Thomas I

can promise nothing."

He shook his head. "Just don't let him deceive you."

Her heart caught. "Is he coming, too?"

"I believe so."

"Oh." She turned away, so her brother would not see the trepidation his words provoked. Yes, she longed to see Thomas, but what would he say? What should she say? After so many weeks apart it seemed almost like they would meet for the first time. Only this time there was so much uncertainty, things to explain, things to confess . . .

Like a baby.

She placed a hand to her mouth, and moved to a seat.

"Julia? Are you well? I hope this news isn't too much of a shock."

"It . . . it is a little startling, that is true, but I am glad for everyone's sake that matters seem to be resolved."

"I think we have a lot to thank Lord Hawkesbury for. There is talk in town that he will be given some new role in the Cabinet."

"Really?"

"Apparently Lord Bathurst says he is just the man we need, someone of principle and action, who is not afraid of hard work or of taking responsibility to see a matter brought to its right conclusion."

"Well, that is good, I suppose. I wonder how Lavinia feels about such things?"

"I believe she will be more than a match for the challenge. Hawkesbury chose well."

The implication being that she had not.

Julia nodded, looking away through the door to where Crabbit was pushing little Charles in a baby carriage. Jon's comments suggested that Thomas had been something of a hero — not that Jon would ever admit to such a thing. And despite his very obvious flaws, she couldn't help but wonder: was she someone for whom it could be said that Thomas had chosen well in a wife?

She was not heroic. She was not very clever with people or with conversation. In fact, the only thing she was good at was holding on to hope that she and Thomas could somehow see this marriage work out for good. Even if everyone around them seemed to wish otherwise.

Afternoon sunshine drifted across fields white with snow. Outside was all slow calmness. Inside impatience writhed. Her brother's words from yesterday had commenced a slow torment. How long now? Would Thomas come? What would she say?

Gradually she became aware of a cry coming from the room next door. Julia forced herself to wait a moment, but when the cries did not cease, she tapped on the door and entered.

Crabbit looked exhausted. "Oh, Miss Julia. I'm afraid Master Charles seems a trifle fractious. I didn't mean to disturb you."

"It is no bother," she said, plucking him from the nursemaid's arms. Attending to the child would provide distraction from her fears. "I'll take him downstairs with me."

"Oh, thank you, miss. You are very good." She frowned. "If you are sure he's not too heavy?"

"I will manage," Julia assured her.

She took him down to the small drawing room, the effort such that she needed to take a seat. "You are not so very little anymore, are you?"

Charles gurgled at her, the sweetness of his dimpled smile drawing her own.

Or perhaps it was just the fact that her lap seemed a tiny bit smaller than it used to be. She did not like to think just how big she could get, not when it was still early days, and she had been busy casting up her accounts each morning. But apart from Mother, nobody else seemed to know, although she wondered if Crabbit suspected, judging from her comment earlier.

"Charlie, my little love. About to enjoy your first Christmas." She cuddled him close, thinking of the gaily wrapped gifts abandoned in their sudden flight from London. Catherine had promised the day after tomorrow would still be special, but how could it be, when so much remained uncertain?

"Oh, Charlie." He reached out to touch her face with his fingers, his dark eyes serious. Her heart panged. Poor Meggie. How sad she had not lived to see her child grow. "What are we going to do with you?"

But what to do with him had become a question that refused to leave. She could only hope and pray that Thomas would understand what she had done, and be willing to raise him as their own. That was, if he could ever admit his sin, and she could ever forgive him.

She lifted Charles to her shoulder, caressed the coppery curls, and kissed his plump little cheek.

"That is a charming sight."

Julia glanced at the door, her pulse increasing to a rapid tattoo. "Thomas!"

"Hello, Jewel."

Her heart caught as he limped toward her. *Limped.* Like an old man. Like an old broken man. "Oh, my goodness! I cannot believe — oh, how dreadful!"

His lips twisted wryly. "Is it that bad to see me?"

Breath caught on a sob as she placed little Charles on the rug and rushed to Thomas, wrapping him in her arms. For a moment, he seemed to teeter, then his arms encircled her. She closed her eyes, breathing in the old familiar scent of him, feeling his arms wrap tighter, his lips in her hair. Oh, how sweet it was to be reunited at last! How wonderful to know he was safe, even if, in that earlier glimpse he seemed almost frail. But still, he was here, his heart thumping reassuringly against her ear.

"Darling Julia, how I've missed you."

"And I, you."

His arms released, he edged back, as his eyes — dark, soulful, yet somehow brighter than she remembered — drank her in. "I love you so much."

Her heart missed a beat. His words held a measure of reassurance, something she had not heard before, something that made her believe his love had somehow deepened these past weeks.

And he tilted her head back, and leaned closer until his lips slowly, determinedly, possessed hers. Leaving her senses reeling, her thoughts scattered, her heart pounding. He held her like she was treasured, like she was precious, like she was everything he'd ever wanted, the only woman —

But wait.

She pulled away with a gasp. He had held another in his arms, had kissed another woman, had been *intimate* with someone else. She wrenched from his arms, and took several steps back, her chest heaving as she fought to find breath. "No. No."

His eyes shadowed, disappointment lined his face, wariness filled his features. "Julia, please —"

"How could you?"

"Please let me explain."

"No." She shook her head. "I thought seeing you would fix everything, but it doesn't, it can't, it won't!"

"Julia —"

"I cannot help but picture you with someone else, kissing her . . ." Her heart wrenched. Moisture gathered in her eyes. "I trusted you."

His face seemed to suddenly age. "I'm so sorry. You will never know . . ."

The ragged note in his voice, the glistening of his eyes — was it tears? — momentarily checked her anger. Was he truly holding back tears? The poor man —

446

But no! She was the one sinned against, the one he had wronged. The resentment flared. "How could you do that to me? How can you say you love me when you did *that* with her?"

"It wasn't like that."

Her fingers clenched. "Then what *was* it like?"

"Julia, please, let us talk about this later —"

"How can I believe you? How can I believe anything you ever say?" Her voice was shaking. Blinking away the tears, she took two steps closer and hit his chest. "I *hate* what you did." Another whack. "I hate you!"

As the words echoed around the room he seemed to sag. For a moment she thought she saw his lips tremble. Then, in a broken whisper, he said, "Please forgive me."

The words pushed against her resentment, halting the invective that longed to flow. She eyed him. Who was this man? He seemed so broken, so different from what she remembered. She turned and picked up Charles, held him close, and finally dared to glance up.

The door opened, and Lord Hawkesbury swept into the room. "Ah, Major Hale, there you are, and with your lovely wife and son. Mrs. Hale, how are you?"

Julia blinked, working to get her bearings, as she dipped a flustered curtsy. "My lord! G-good afternoon."

"I'm sure it is a good afternoon, now your husband has returned."

Her smile grew strained as she murmured something noncommittal.

"I hope you'll forgive the interruption, heaven knows I've no inclination for being any kind of intrusion, but I cannot stay long, and I wanted to ensure you were appraised of all the facts."

"The facts?" she repeated.

"Yes. I wanted you to know that the prime minister considers your husband to have proved quite the hero."

"Lord Liverpool said that?"

"Indeed, he did, not a day ago."

"Oh!" She glanced at Thomas, who looked far from heroic with his downcast mien. Her heart wrenched again. She hardened herself, her gaze returning to the earl. "Thank you for coming to tell me."

"I wanted to ensure your husband arrived safely. He holds much courage, but I'm afraid I've rather wearied him in recent days, what with various interviews and matters concerning government and the like. To come here and have the opportunity to congratulate you on your husband's success was simply an additional benefit."

She nodded, yet confusion remained. Did he not know what her husband had done?

His expression gentled. "I know he has been looking forward to seeing you again. The doctor believes his determination to protect you a key factor in his recovery. It seems he loves you very much."

Her throat filled; she could say nothing.

"In fact, I have it on good authority he has been dreaming about seeing you again."

She was surprised at the need to blink away the sudden tears. "H-how can you know that, my lord?"

"As you likely know already, he mutters in his sleep." He grinned. "When your husband was in the infirmary his midnight prattle became a source of much fascination among the nursing staff in Edinburgh."

"Really?" She eyed Thomas as his cheeks reddened.

"I am reliably informed that yours was the name that brought great comfort," the earl continued.

"My lord —" Thomas interposed.

"You should tell your wife *all* that I told you about such things. I believe you will find that truth will set you both free." The earl smiled. "Now, I must away and return to my own hearth. If I leave now I should make home tonight. I know Lavinia will wish to add her good wishes to mine as to your continued healing and good health."

As Thomas shook his hand and murmured of his tremendous obligation, Julia's heart continued its wrestle. How could this honorable man hold Thomas in esteem? It did not seem right, or fair. Didn't he know what Thomas had done?

"Good day to you, Mrs. Hale." He bowed to her curtsy. "I hope and pray your reunion will be all that Thomas has dreamed it may be, and that God will guide and bless you both in your marriage."

"Thank you, sir."

"And Hale, if I can be of service, you need only ask. Again, good day, and my best wishes for the season."

He exited, leaving her to stare wide-eyed at Thomas. "Does he know anything about your indiscretion?"

Fatigue washed across his face. "He knows, Julia."

"And still he can say such things?"

Thomas closed his eyes, and for a moment she thought he was going to crumple. She took a step toward him, then hesitated.

"Julia —" He opened his eyes, eyes darkened by disillusionment. "I love you, but I understand you might not believe that right

450

now. Please, I know we need to talk, but at this moment I am so weary I doubt anything I say will make sense."

Remorse crossed her heart. Indeed, he seemed near exhaustion.

"I know your brother resents me being here, and I am quite prepared to endure his and your mother's hostility, but right now, all I want to do is go to sleep."

Compassion chased her earlier resentment. "Of course. I will see that a bedchamber —"

"You would not consider — ? No, of course not."

She swallowed. "I . . . I cannot think about . . . such things yet."

Wryness twisted his lips. "I can assure you I have no thought of such things, either." His eyes closed, and again he seemed close to collapse before he jerked himself upright again. "Anywhere will do."

The disillusionment shading his eyes stole beneath her defenses, inducing her to say, "You can stay with me."

Again, she saw something glisten in his eyes, causing another heart twinge, as he rasped, "Thank you."

Moments later, she was giving instructions to the servants who took him upstairs to bathe and go to sleep, and she braced

451

herself for her mother's and brother's re-actions. Sure enough, they were horrified at her permitting Thomas to stay with her tonight.

Jon shook his head. "It is exactly as I knew it would be. You are a prisoner to that man's charm."

No, she was a prisoner to compassion.

But she did not know just how deep she had plumbed the wells of her compassion until later that night, when she escaped after the evening meal and went to her room and found Thomas asleep in her bed. He had not been wrong; he was so deep in slumber that he did not stir when she finally braved sliding into bed beside him.

Flickering candlelight showed that his nightshirt had twisted and tangled, some-thing sure to disturb his rest later. She stretched out a hand to smooth it down, then stopped. She had not seen that scar before. Nor that one . . .

Heart swelling her throat, she carefully lifted free the back of his garment, then gasped. His back was hatched with scars, whip lashes some of them, ones she had not noticed on their too-brief reunion two months ago. *Oh, dear God!* Why had she not noticed? These were not new; the welts had healed. He must have had them before, must have received them in Spain, but he'd said nothing. He'd said nothing . . . but neither had she noticed.

Shame washed through her. She should have realized something of his injury, but had been so busy feasting on his face. She gently traced a finger over the red ridges, her eyes filling with tears. Who could have done this? Was it punishment for his indiscretion? Or — her mouth dried — had that been something rather more punishment than pleasure also? Is that what the earl had meant, and why he did not treat Thomas with the measure Jon did? Had Jon — and she — judged too harshly?

As she wrestled with these new thoughts, she noticed a dull bruise, pale purple, crescent shaped, extending from his lower back to one hip. Tears slipped down her cheeks as she remembered the way he had limped, the way he had stood oddly, as if he was afraid to move in case he fell. Was this what he had been recovering from in the Edinburgh infirmary?

He suddenly shivered, jerking away. "Get away from me. Get away!"

She drew back, hurt cramping within.

But . . . his eyes remained closed. Was this a dream?

He shuddered, and she could feel the tension emanating from him, yet still she remained unsure. Perhaps she should find another bedchamber —

"Magdalena."

She froze, the hatred caused by that name rekindling.

"Get away!"

Was it *Magdalena* he begged to go away? Oh, what had happened to him in that Spanish cell?

Gradually his shivers eased, his body resuming the posture of sleep. She lay there, watching him, wondering, questioning, doubting. Was Thomas innocent of his former cellmate's claims?

And yet — indignation flared — Thomas had acknowledged he was not completely innocent, that he had done something he bitterly regretted. Surely that meant he knew what he'd done was wrong.

The stripes on his back reproached her. The heat of anger abated, subsiding into something like sorrow, as memories of what had been said in recent days flashed through her mind. Comments about his courage, about his desperate will to live thwarting those who had done their best to kill him. His determination to see her, to protect her, because he loved her. His brokenness when he finally did see her. His brokenness because he'd nearly died. Again.

Her Thomas. Her *poor* Thomas. *Her* poor Thomas.

She pressed the softest kiss against his shoulder.

He stirred, and murmured something she did not hear. She leaned closer, ears straining to catch his broken whisper.

"Jewel."

Her heart caught. The earl was right; he did whisper her name.

"Jewel, please . . ." A ragged breath. "Forgive me."

Her eyes filled afresh. She could not hold bitterness against him. He was a broken man, a shadow of himself. Whatever he had undergone had the power to reach him in slumber.

"Jewel, I . . ."

"Shhh." She stroked his hair, like she would little Charles — softly, tenderly, as if the action could bring comfort.

His whisper came again. "I . . . love . . ."

Her breath halted, her nerves tensing as she waited for his next word.

". . . you."

Heart wrung, tears seeping across her skin, she folded her arms around him, and snuggled against his back. And determined she would keep his nightmares at bay.

CHAPTER TWENTY-NINE

Somehow, the dreams that filled his night had eventuated into reality. Julia — Jewel of his heart — holding him in a way he'd scarcely hoped possible. When he'd woken, and seen her pale arm clasped around his torso, it had taken a moment before he realized this was no dream. That the light shafting through the bedchamber was real. That his wife had not only shared her bed but shared her arms. That this Christmas Eve morning had begun with so much promise. Hope lit his heart. Did this mean she would forgive him?

He'd lain there, reveling in the sound of her soft breathing as a thousand prayers of thankfulness filled his soul. *Thank You, God, for Your protection. Thank You, God, for Your mercy. Thank You, God, for Julia. Thank You, God, for all You've done.*

When he'd finally sensed her stirring he'd tensed, waiting for her horrified reaction as she realized what she'd done. It hadn't come. Instead, he heard her good morning, felt her lips brush his shoulder, then the bed dip as she got out, and moved to change.

He rolled onto his back, ignoring the spasms, and watched as she moved to the window, where the sun caught the gold in her hair. His heart clenched. She was so fair, so lovely.

"Good morning."

Julia glanced back over her shoulder, the curve of her cheek illuminated in the light. She smiled. "It seems so strange to see you there."

"Thank you for letting me."

She shrugged, the light fading from her face. His spirits sagged. How carefully he must learn to tread, to not let the past dominate the present, to encourage his wife to love, not rancor.

"Are you hungry?" she finally asked. "I could have some breakfast sent up."

Was such solicitude so he could avoid seeing Jon and her mother, or so they could avoid seeing him? "Is that what you think best?"

She pursed her lips, studying him, then shook her head. "I think it's time they faced the fact that you are here, and we . . ."

His pulse quickened. "And we . . . ?" *Lord, have mercy.*

"I . . ." She shook her head. "I don't know what we are."

Disappointment crashed against his ribs, causing a physical ache. But love demanded he tread softly, not demand or seek his own way. "We are . . . whatever you wish us to be," he finally dared.

Her chin wobbled, and she turned away, but not before he caught the trembling lips and sparkle of tears.

His heart wrenched, but he refused to press for clarification. He would be patient, and endeavor to show her that her trust in him was not misplaced.

Breaking his fast had rarely felt so challenging. Julia's mother had given an audible sniff when he entered the dining parlor for luncheon — they were too late for breakfast, it seemed — before treating him as nonexistent. Julia's brother had eyed him narrowly, but at least had the grace to fling the occasional remark in his direction; perhaps Lord Hawkesbury had had a word in his ear about Thomas's new faith. Catherine was, as ever, gracious, wishing him the joy of the season with a look that spoke of her sincerity. As for Julia, she seemed to treat him with a mix of pique and shy concern, a mix that deepened his longing for the chance to finally explain things, as desperate hope battled the lash of doubts.

"It was good to see Hawkesbury yesterday," Jon said.

Thomas glanced up from his plate. Judging from Julia's brother's mien, that remark had been addressed to him. He swallowed his mouthful of salmon, and murmured, "He has been most obliging."

"I should think he has!" snapped Lady Harkness, finally deigning to look at him. "I could scarcely believe my ears when I heard he had personally escorted you from the north."

Thomas inclined his head, not daring to say anything that might further incur her wrath.

She muttered something, and he caught the words "ungrateful wretch." The words tore at the thin strands of forgiveness he'd felt God had laced across his shame, but though his cheeks burned, he held his tongue. *Lord, have mercy . . .*

"Mother," Jon said. "I do not know if you were apprised fully of the situation yesterday when Lord Hawkesbury visited. He did have, er" — he glanced quickly at Thomas before his attention returned to his mother

459

— "some rather illuminating things to say."

A corner of hope lit within.

"It would seem that Hale is in line for some sort of commendation from the prime minister."

He was?

"Congratulations," said Catherine in her quiet way.

"You appear surprised, Hale. Did you not know of it?"

"These past few days have been a blur," he said cautiously. "I find I cannot remember all that has been said."

Lady Harkness gave another disapproving sniff.

"That, coupled with some other, rather more important news, has given food for thought."

"More important news?" Lady Harkness said. "I should think any man should be satisfied with a commendation from the prime minister."

"But this news is of far greater significance," Jon continued, turning back to Thomas. "In fact, it can be said to have eternal significance. Is this not correct?"

The anger shading his eyes had gone; instead, Thomas thought he saw something approaching approval. Well, not approval, perhaps; more like acquiescence, like he had been forced to concede to a heavenly authority that demanded forgiveness.

"I . . . I have much to learn," Thomas admitted.

"We all do," said Jon. "I find I am constantly learning just how much I do not know."

"What are you talking about?" demanded Lady Harkness, looking between them.

Jon offered Thomas a half smile, one seemingly tinged with apology, before turning to his mother. "Do you remember in those first days when we thought Julia lost to us, how you said you found comfort by reading the Scriptures?"

What?

She looked a little nonplussed. "Well, perhaps I did . . ."

"Lord Hawkesbury reminded me yesterday how we should not underestimate the power of God to transform lives. And I . . ." He glanced at Catherine. "I was challenged also."

"About?" Julia finally spoke.

Thomas watched her face, as her brother said in his deep tones, "About remembering how much I have been forgiven, and how that should lead me to treat others."

Her blue eyes widened, and she slowly turned to face Thomas.

"Hale," Jon continued, "I cannot help but be glad for the good news I have learned."

He managed to smile past his surprise, to offer a quiet thank you. God was merciful indeed if Julia's brother was extending forgiveness.

"Thomas?" Julia wore a slight frown.

"Mother, Catherine, if you have both finished your meals, I believe we must discuss some of the preparations for tomorrow, then get ready for tonight's services."

"Oh, we should also —" Julia began, looking at Thomas.

"I believe God will overlook your nonattendance, if you find yourself occupied otherwise."

With this decidedly less than subtle diversion, Jon herded a reluctant Lady Harkness and a smiling Catherine away, leaving Julia to face Thomas across the table.

"What was all that about?" she asked.

"I . . . I have some things to tell you."

Her eyes shadowed. His heart twisted. *Lord, have mercy.*

The drawing room was quiet, the soothing blues and cream a hopeful reflection of his soul. Or at least what he hoped the outcome would be. He'd taken heart at Julia's compliance, her willingness to sit beside him, his legs suddenly unsteady when earlier he'd tried to stand, before realizing his confessions would take a physical toll and he'd need to be seated.

His prayers had barely ceased: that Julia would have understanding, that she would forgive him, that those words of hate she had spoken yesterday would remain forever in the past. His heart hurt at the memory, before he reminded himself to let such things go. Love held no wrongs.

Julia opened her mouth then closed it, sweetly unsure. This was a new Julia; the boldness he had once known her for seemingly far away.

"What is it?"

"What" — she gestured to the direction of the dining room — "what was that back there, with you and Jon?"

Lord, have mercy. He said slowly, "I believe he was referring to a conversation I'd had with Lord Hawkesbury, that Hawkesbury must have shared."

Her brows rose, her look one of expectancy.

"I . . ." Where to begin? "I cannot remember if I ever told you much about my father."

His look of enquiry only drew forth a shake of her head and a murmured, "Only that he wanted nothing to do with you."

463

"He was a church minister, one who believed in a vengeful God who hated sinners." He offered a small smile. "Therefore, it must have seemed only right that he hated me."

She made a small noise of protest.

"I'm afraid that it is so. His tolerance was never very high, and my desire to accord to his will was always rather low. I suppose he was somewhat justified in thinking me rebellious and wild."

Her hand placed on his arm engendered strength, the compassion in her eyes giving hope she might understand.

"For a long time I resisted any thought of God — why would I want anything to do with someone who hated me? — but after Edinburgh . . ."

"After Edinburgh?" she prompted gently.

"When I . . . when I met Lord Hawkesbury, and was brought to realize God's mercy in keeping me alive again, I . . . was brought to see that perhaps God might not be so harsh and unforgiving as I had believed, that in fact He was quite the opposite."

He swallowed. *Lord, help her see.*

"I know how much of a disappointment I have proved to you, and that so many things have not happened as you might have liked.

464

You have no idea of the depths of my regret." Honesty demanded utterance. "There . . . there have been times when I wished I'd never met you, so I could have saved you from this pain."

Her eyes filled, she looked down, biting her lip.

The rawness sweeping his soul balled hard within his chest. "I know that I have sinned against you, and against God. I have scarcely had the chance to speak with you, but have had many hours alone to think, to speak with God. And I have asked for His forgiveness, and have sensed that He, in His great mercy, has given it."

He could sense the slight stiffening, though her hand remained.

"Not because I deserve it, but because of His great grace. I deserve nothing, I know."

His throat cinched, his eyes watered, as his renewed consciousness of the great largesse of God's grace towards him burned within. He was a sinner, but God had rescued him, pulled him from the mire of his many poor choices, and set his feet upon a Rock, a Rock to whom he would cling, regardless of the outcome with his wife today.

"And Lord Hawkesbury?"

"Encouraged me to seek forgiveness from

God, and was there when I finally did so. I cannot tell you what peace I have found in knowing such a thing."

He dared glance at her. She was looking at her lap, her expression unreadable.

"I know I have no right to ask, but part of me still dares to hope: Julia, will you somehow find it in your heart to forgive me?"

CHAPTER THIRTY

Forgiveness.

It felt as though all her life had led to this one moment, this one word. The wrestle inside had not abated, had only grown more fierce. She could hold on to this resentment, this bitterness that Catherine had long ago said would poison her heart, or she could do as Thomas requested and forgive.

But forgive what, she still did not know. Did she even need to know? Or was that another thing she should just leave in the past, as Catherine had suggested? She did not want to live in the past, but neither did she want this specter looming over them, shadowing their future. If they even had a future, that was. Oh, what should she do?

"I understand," Thomas said. "I've asked too much, too soon. Believe me, I have no wish to cause you pain, but neither do I wish to continue living with what needs to be spoken. If we do not speak of it, it becomes something that will fester between us, that will bring irritation between us, and eventually infect our lives with bitterness."

Bitterness. "Like poison."

"Exactly so." His eyes were sorrowful. "Words can never tell you of the depths of my regret, but I am so sorry, more sorry than you can ever know."

And he was. She could read it in his eyes. His disillusionment, his agony, the hurt that seemed to weigh his soul like it did hers. She had a choice: to turn away, or to listen. To speak with anger, or hold her peace. To trust her instincts, or trust God.

She swallowed. Thomas seemed to have found some measure of peace by committing himself to God. Catherine had. Lavinia, the earl. Jon, too. *God, do You care about me, too?*

Something within her seemed to cry *yes.*

Her eyes burned; her throat clogged. *What do I do?*

Trust Me, that same voice whispered.

She drew in a deep breath. Very well, she would do things God's way. "Tell me."

With a look filled with gratitude, he began to speak of his time in Spain, his words according much with what his cellmate had said, with some notable differences. Thomas spoke of the jailer's daughter with loathing

468

— something she'd expected, as no doubt he'd want to reassure her — but the sickness in his face, the way he'd had to pause every so often as though he wanted to retch, these she had not expected.

Had his actions been ones more about survival than betrayal?

If so, who was she to add to his obvious pain by deliberately holding on to pride, instead of offering love, offering forgiveness, as she sensed she ought? *God, what do I do?*

Catherine's words from weeks ago stole into memory. Bitterness bound; forgiveness freed. The story of the unforgiving servant, forgiven much but unwilling to forgive. Was she like that servant? How much had she sinned? She wasn't perfect by any means. She pushed her head into her hands, the choice looming before her. What should she do?

She somehow knew.

Swallowing the giant ball of emotion lodged in her throat, she finally dared utter the prayer she knew needed to be prayed.

God, forgive me. Help me to forgive him. I don't really want to, but I know I need to. Please help me.

A litany of sins flashed through her mind: her pride, her lies, her selfishness, her resentment.

Heavenly Father, I'm so sorry. She swallowed. *How can I judge him when I'm a sinner, too?*

Her chest grew tight. She dragged in a deep breath.

God, forgive me. Please help me to forgive him, to love Thomas as I ought. Moisture burned in her eyes. *I don't know what to say except help me to trust You with all of this, with all our future. Lead me — lead us — into Your plans.*

The rush of tears surprised her as much as the breathlessness, which preceded the sweetest sensation stealing across her heart, something which felt a lot like . . .

Peace.

"Julia?" Thomas's arm was around her. "Julia, please don't cry. I'm so sorry —"

"No —"

"Sweetheart, please." A note of desperation filled his voice. "I never meant to cause further pain."

He drew her close, the gush of emotion dampening his shirt, until finally her shuddery breaths allowed speech.

"No, Thomas, it's not you." She lifted a tear-drenched face, saw the concern writ in his eyes. She exhaled. "I'm sorry I have held this against you, when it's obvious I did not know all. I was angry and hurt, and allowed

470

you to feel that —"

"It was deserved."

"No, you did not deserve that. I have always been too headstrong, and followed my feelings rather than what is right." She managed a broken smile. "And my feelings are all too susceptible to circumstances."

"As are everyone's." His face shadowed. "But I assure you, as far as Spain went, I had no feelings about her —"

"Oh, I know! I believe you."

"You do?" His eyes lit with hope.

"I heard you last night, when you talked in your sleep, you were begging her to stay away." He winced. "And I knew you had no thought of her, not the way you think of . . ." Her cheeks heated.

"Not the way I think of you. I could *never* think of anyone like I do you, Jewel of my heart. You were the promise that kept me alive back in Spain, up in Edinburgh. When I despaired, I thought of you, I remembered us, and wished to see you, to be here, like this, holding you, feeling like you loved me —"

"I *do* love you. I'm so sorry for saying what I did yesterday. I was wrong. Please forgive me."

"It's forgiven."

She clasped his hands, well, one of them,

they were so much bigger than hers. "I love you, Thomas."

"Really? Even despite . . . everything?"

"Really." She gave a smile of reassurance. "Truly."

Then his face was against hers, his arms around her, his lips pressed to hers. He whispered of his thankfulness, of his joy, of his love, of her beauty.

She chuckled. Love was truly blind if he thought her reddened eyes and nose were beautiful.

"My dearest, I'm sorry I did not believe you about little Charles."

What? Oh. "It must have been strange, I know. To suddenly see me with a little child you must have known could not be yours."

"You were right; Meggie had no further relatives I could find. So we will raise him, as our child, as she wished." He hugged her close. "My kindhearted, courageous wife."

Except — she stiffened — not so courageous. *God forgive me.* She had to tell him about his child. She opened her mouth to speak —

"Here you are!"

Mother. Julia stifled the groan as her parent advanced into the room. She caught Thomas's amusement as he gently disengaged his arms from around her, but grasped her hand, intertwining her fingers with his.

"Well? What have you to say for yourself?"

"Mother, please —"

"No. I want to know what he's been saying —" She stopped, peered closer at Julia. "He's made you cry! Well, that's it. I demand —"

"No, Mother. Thomas has not made me cry."

"He has in the past!"

Julia felt him stiffen. "But not today." She squeezed his hand for reassurance, and eyed her mother. "God made me cry today."

Her mother blinked. "God?"

"Well, not God so much as . . . as my recognition of my need for Him, and for God's forgiveness." The wonder of such grace rushed through her again, and it was another moment before she could speak. "I have held on to such things that have made me bitter, and caused me pain, and led me to make choices that hurt others for far too long." She swallowed. "I'm sorry that some of those choices have hurt you."

"Oh! Well . . ." Mother glanced at Thomas, her features sharpening again.

"But I am *not* sorry for marrying Thomas, and the sooner you realize that, the better."

"But he betrayed you!"

"And Julia has forgiven me, Lady Harkness. I hope that one day you will, too."

She shook her head, her gaze fixing on Julia. "Tell me this isn't true."

"It is. I love him. He has my forgiveness, just as I have God's."

"You . . . you believe?" Thomas said, recapturing her attention.

"Yes." She smiled, as that peace once more filled her heart.

Joy suffused his features, and he kissed her hand with fervor. "I'm so glad."

"I am, too." With God's help, perhaps their frayed marriage might have a chance to heal. Especially if . . .

She turned back to her mother, eyeing them both narrowly. "Life is too short for estrangement, would you not agree?"

Her mother flushed before muttering something in the affirmative.

"If you do not show your support and cease from making accusations against my husband, then I'm afraid I will have to take what measures I must to preserve the happiness of myself, my husband, and our children."

"Our children?" Thomas echoed, puzzlement in his eyes.

"Oh, so she hasn't told you?"

"Mother." Julia pushed to her feet. "I need

to speak with Thomas. Alone."

"Apparently you do!" And with a swish of skirts, Mother exited, in high dudgeon.

Julia released a shaky breath.

"Julia?"

She turned. "Oh, Thomas, I should have told you. I was going to, then . . ." She shrugged helplessly.

"Told me what?"

"Charles will not be our only child."

He smiled. "You cannot know how much that thought gives me hope." He pulled her down beside him, wrapped his arms around her, and leaned his cheek against her hair. "Are you saying you would like to try for an addition?"

A chuckle escaped. "I would like to try, yes, but there is no need to try, if you take my meaning."

"Never tell me you have another friend who wishes you to adopt her child?"

"No." She placed a hand on her abdomen. "I'm saying that you will be a father."

He stared at her. "You are expecting?"

She nodded.

"How?"

Heat scampered up her neck, across her cheeks. "The usual way."

"But when?"

"That night you returned to London."

"I will truly be a father?"

"Yes." She sighed, snuggling close. "Is that not truly wonderful?"

Truly wonderful. And truly humbling. And a little daunting.

But he *would* be a good father, someone who not only would teach their children right from wrong but would demonstrate that with grace and love. And if — when — he failed, relying on a merciful God's forgiveness would help, as would trusting in His guidance for their future. *Lord, have mercy.*

The remainder of the afternoon passed in a kind of dream: Julia snuggled in his arms, Charles sleepily blowing bubbles as he glanced between them. They had talked, and prayed, and talked some more, until his heart felt as though it might burst. How merciful was God to allow such mercy to flow to him? Never had he expected these amazing revelations of love, shown through the offering of forgiveness and the promised gift of a child. Never had he expected God to answer his prayers for his wife quite so quickly. Such undeserved gifts were so very humbling, making him prone to a degree of weakness in his emotions to match that of his legs, feelings he sought to hide, conscious Lady Harkness already viewed him somewhat askance.

For the first time in what seemed like forever he felt himself relax, as the peace infusing the room filled his heart. He glanced at the coppery curls of Charles, sleeping between them, gold lashes fanning the chubby cheeks, thumb stuck in his mouth. His heart tugged. Warmth filled his chest. Protectiveness surged within. So this is what it felt like to be a father. He couldn't wait until his and Julia's child was born.

"I might return this sleepy boy to his room," Julia said, as she moved to get up.

"Here, let me." He gathered the sleeping Charles in his arms, before remembering he was barely in a condition to walk, let alone carry another, baby though he might be. Still, he gritted his teeth against the pain as he struggled to get upright, he would prove himself —

"Thank you, but you should rest," Julia said, neatly scooping Charles away. "I'd prefer you to save your energies for later."

"Later?"

"Later," she said with a wink that made his heart beat faster.

She carried Charles through the doors, and he slumped back against the cushions. In the absence of others he need finally not pretend to be stronger than he was, that the past days — or was it years? — of subterfuge and scurry had not taken their toll. It was really over. He closed his eyes. It *was* really over, wasn't it? McKinley was yet to be discovered, and certain matters pertaining to their future — like the matter of a house — still remained to be resolved, but even in these things he felt a kind of certainty that God would somehow provide.

"Ah."

His eyelids snapped open. Jon. Wearing an expression that could almost be called sympathetic. He pushed himself upright.

"No, don't bother," Jon said, gesturing him to relax as he claimed a seat opposite. "I imagine you must be quite exhausted."

"Yes." Thomas eyed him. Despite Jon's earlier words at the dining table, he still remained uncertain as to what Julia's brother really thought of him. He cleared his throat. "I hope you know how much I appreciate your forbearance in allowing me to stay."

Jon's eyes narrowed. After a moment he said, "You are not being sarcastic."

"I know you do not like me and probably still wish me at the devil, so I really do appreciate you looking past your antipathy at this time."

Jon sighed. Shook his head.

Thomas's chest tightened. He wasn't going to do such things?

"I see now that I . . . I have not exactly behaved in a manner that was warranted."

After a moment of surprise, Thomas said, "Oh, I'm pretty sure it was."

A corner of Jon's mouth lifted. "Regardless, I want you to know that I am sorry for the hard words I have spoken, and for my unChristlike attitude that has brought division between us in recent years."

"I do not blame you. How can I?" His lips twisted wryly. "If Julia were my sister I would have done everything in my power to stop a rogue like me from absconding with her."

"But you are not a rogue anymore, are you?"

"I . . ." A rush of emotion clamped his throat, surprising him into the need to blink away heated moisture. "I am trying to live a different way now, trying to trust God with my future."

"Trying is all any of us can do."

"Julia and I both have a lot to learn about doing things God's way, but I sense His leading."

"Wait — are you telling me Julia believes?"

Thomas nodded. "This afternoon. It

seems God has been challenging her, too."

Jon's eyes grew shiny. He swallowed, ducked his head, and drew in a long breath before exhaling slowly. "I . . . I thought my methods might have scared her from seeking truth, and to think it was you who helped her realize —" He broke off, cleared his throat, before adding gruffly, "Thank you, Hale."

Thomas savored his friend's acknowledgment, before saying, "I think Catherine sowed more seeds than I did. She is a good woman."

"Yes." Jon eyed him a moment longer, then reached out his hand. "Welcome to the family, Thomas Hale."

Stupid weak emotion forced him to clamp down on an unsteady lip as he shook his friend's hand. "Thank you."

Jon exhaled heavily, then eased back against the sofa. "Well! This Christmas certainly has given us some wonderful surprises."

"That it has," Thomas said, still dazed by his friend's acceptance.

"I know such a place," Jon gestured to their surrounds, "is not exactly what my wife and mother envisaged as our locale for this season, but —"

" 'Tis better for everyone's protection,"

480

Thomas finished. "We shall have to pray that this sad business with McKinley is resolved soon."

"Indeed we shall. I cannot like thinking my family is in danger, no matter how many men Hawkesbury has employed to guard the place."

"McKinley is a weaselly cur, but I assure you, I would rather die than let him hurt anyone in my family."

Jon smiled. "I know."

The remainder of the evening and the following Christmas morn passed as something beyond his dreams, the message at the Christmas Eve service and that of this morning touching his heart anew, humbling him with God's grace, and the undeserved favor he received from his wife, Jon, and Catherine.

Throughout the midday meal of roasted goose and sweetmeats, and the exchange of gifts that Jon had somehow forwarded on from London, Thomas had been aware of their efforts to include him, to make him feel part of a family the likes of which he'd never known. He had struggled at times with the fact he had nothing to offer — his lips twisted wryly, such seemed to be his way — but they had proved gracious as ever,

481

Catherine even going so far as to slip him a wrapped parcel with whispered instructions to give it to Julia when the time drew near. Such thoughtfulness had proved a gift in itself, as Julia had exclaimed over the silk gloves and given him a kiss that held nothing of shame, conducted as it was in front of her family, and not stolen as one had been before under the mistletoe that graced the hall.

Now, Lady Harkness having followed Jon and Catherine's lead and retiring to her room, he and Julia had the drawing room to themselves, and could relax once more. Outside, snow padded softly against the window. Inside, the fireplace crackled with welcome warmth.

He wrapped an arm around her. "Have you enjoyed today, Jewel?"

Julia burrowed deeper into the space between his neck and chin, before placing the lightest of kisses on his neck. "It has been practically perfect."

"Practically?"

"I am thankful my brother seems to have warmed towards you. His recent manner gives me hope. Now, if only my mother can see reason."

Another battle he would face, remembering the grace of God, remembering God said he was forgiven, even as he faced the opposition of others. He prayed a prayer for strength, for compassion to lace his words. "I cannot blame her. Letting go of hurts held for so long is very hard." He tugged her closer. "But you have enjoyed today?"

"I have enjoyed time with you all, and the food, and my gifts, but you know, there is only one thing that I want," she whispered.

"Really? What is that?" Anything. He'd give her anything.

"I want us to be a family again. Somewhere without my mother's or brother's interference, somewhere like when we first were in Scotland, and felt so happy and free. Somewhere we can just be, without others watching, where we can talk without ears listening. I wish we had our own house somewhere."

Anything except that. His spirits plunged, his mind racing as he struggled to think of ways he could provide the one thing he knew she had always dreamed of. But as always, nothing came to mind. *Heavenly Father . . . ?*

A thought pricked. No. That would be the last option. She would not wish to — *he* had no desire to. Such a thing would be so difficult, anyway. He sighed. But how many more options were left open to him?

"You know, I have always wondered . . ."

"Always wondered about what?" he murmured against her hair.

"I've always wondered where you grew up."

He froze. Had she read his mind?

Dear God, help me. Would the battles from his past ever cease?

CHAPTER THIRTY-ONE

Boxing Day arrived, a day normally set aside for the giving of boxed goods to the neighboring poor, a day when the feasting and celebrations of Christmas might culminate in a local ball. But here, in this unfamiliar part of the country, guarded as they were, they knew none of their neighbors, much less any of the poor, though the provisions brought from London had a sufficiency with which they could well afford to be generous.

Still, Julia thought, there could be worse ways of spending time than with one's family, with this new joy in her heart, a peace that underlay her thoughts and reminded her to trust God instead of worry. She glanced across the drawing room at her husband, still so frail and bruised, but the haggard look from three days ago had quite gone. Perhaps its disappearance was due to Jon's acceptance, their reversion back to the genial tease of former days as welcome to Julia and Catherine as it puzzled Julia's mother.

This long-awaited improvement in relationships was so very pleasing, and helped combat the slight strain of unease she still sensed.

"How much longer do you think Hawkesbury intends to keep us locked up as prisoners?"

"We're hardly prisoners, Mother," Julia murmured.

"I'm sure Lord Hawkesbury's intention is to keep us safe until other matters are sorted."

"Hmph. Well, we would not be in this mess if it wasn't for —" She cast Thomas an angry glare that would have quailed a lesser man. But — Julia noted with satisfaction — she had not married a lesser man, as evidenced by the fact that Thomas did not acknowledge the slight, his gaze remaining focused on little Charles.

Her heart warmed anew. How wonderful it was to see him hold Charles, to see the equally dark gazes lock on each other as they engaged in something like silly baby babble, conducted in a low voice on Thomas's side at least. How excellent a father he would be. Last night they had spoken more about the future, about his need to see his father and do what he could to bring a painful past to a healed resolution. About their need for a house of their own she had not pressed Thomas further, conscious that he would wish to provide rather than depend on the funds she felt sure Jon would now release to them. How could this resolve? What would he do for finances? The worries rose. She drew in a silent breath and exhaled. She would have to trust God for their future.

"Well, all this sitting around is making me tired. Would anyone care for a game of cards?" Mother rose. "I shall see if this place affords such things. Catherine? Julia? Would you care to join me?"

Apparently Catherine did care to join her, and Julia bowed to their looks of entreaty — not a little persuaded by Charles beginning to fuss as well. "Of course." With an apologetic smile for her husband, she collected Charles, who immediately calmed, and joined the other ladies and young Elizabeth in the little parlor beyond the dining room, leaving the two men to quietly converse.

"Really, I never thought I would see the day when a man would stoop to holding his child in that manner," Mother complained.

Julia bit back her initial response, dragging in a breath to calm her voice to sweetness. "How would you prefer Thomas to hold Charles?"

"I just think it most undignified, and unnecessary, when we have Crabbit whose job it is to do so."

"I think it shows a wonderful degree of affection," said Catherine.

"As do I," Julia said. "Love and affection should never be demeaned, as they can be all too hard to find in this world."

"Well, I suppose such things are preferable to violence, after all," Mother conceded.

"Very true," Julia agreed, smiling at her sister-in-law.

And they began their game of cards in a new spirit of accord.

The new spirit of accord between Jon and himself continued to both amaze and humble Thomas. Even Lady Harkness seemed to be slowly thawing towards him; something that must truly be accounted another miracle of God.

"I hope McKinley can be found soon," Jon said, the ease in his features melding into a frown. "I can't help but feel a little anxious that there has been nothing communicated yet about his whereabouts. And while Hawkesbury is very good to have us stay here, I cannot like to think how too many more days of being housebound will affect everyone's spirits."

Thomas nodded. He didn't like it either. But giving voice to those concerns seemed only to give voice to doubts, and he wanted to trust God not his instincts.

"But enough of those matters." Jon smiled. "Have you given any more thought to the future?"

"I . . . I intend to visit my father in Norfolk as soon as we are freed from here."

"Your father?"

"Yes. I am hopeful he will be amenable to seeing reason." And amenable to forgiveness.

"He is sure to be charmed by your growing family."

Thomas forced a smile. He was certain Father had never been charmed by anyone or anything in his life, much less anything of Thomas's doing. But the way matters had been left long ago, he could not be truly certain about anything regarding his father.

"I know you will do what is right and good for Julia. I will hold you to it." But Jon's smile told him such accountability would not come at the price of earlier suspicion.

"Thank you. I am —" Movement outside the window distracted him. "What — ?"

Jon frowned. "Did you see something?" He got up, peered outside. "There is nothing now."

"I might have been mistaken," Thomas admitted. "It would not be the first time."

"It was probably a bird, or perhaps one of Hawkesbury's men."

Thomas nodded. He pushed awkwardly to his feet. Thank God he would soon not need these wretched sticks. "Shall we find the ladies?"

"I'm sure they'd appreciate our company," Jon said with a smile.

He led the way to the dining room, where he'd assumed they'd be. "Julia?"

No answer.

"Julia? Where are you?"

Nothing. Not even a muffled cry from Charles.

He limped into the parlor, and the sticks fell from his grasp.

McKinley stood there, with a knife held at Julia's throat.

Julia saw the way Thomas whitened, his look of horror, the way his still frail body seemed to buckle. Saw Jon move suddenly. Felt the prick of steel against her throat.

"No, Jon!"

Thomas stayed Jon with an arm, his coffee-colored eyes on her, eyes that held a promise that he would do all in his power to save her. "McKinley, please, leave them out of it. Release the ladies, and the children. You know it is me you want."

"Of course it is you! It's always been you. You with your cursed principles, and good fortune, and inexplicable luck. Did you think I wouldn't find you?" The arm hugging Julia tightened. "You and Hawkesbury are such fools, thinking I wouldn't know to follow him." The knife jerked towards Jon.

"You followed me?" Jon said, in a voice that sounded far away.

McKinley muttered something about Jon's intelligence, something further about tracking Jon's servants. "Then waited, like in Poona days, until Hawkesbury's men could be knocked out." He laughed. "No one is coming to help you. You're out of luck now."

"I don't believe in luck." Thomas shook his head. His gaze flicked to Julia before returning to McKinley. "I will do whatever you want. Please, leave Julia alone."

"Then come here."

Horror filled her as Thomas stepped closer, a willing sacrifice. "Don't do it,

491

Thomas!" She had to do something to save him. Thomas was still too weak; he could never last in a fight.

Behind her she heard the whimpers from the children, Catherine's soft pleas, Mother's outraged gasp.

"Killing someone won't solve anything," Jon called.

"But it will make me feel better."

"Not when you're hanging on a hangman's noose!" Julia struggled to remove his arm. His grip remained as iron. "Thomas, please."

"Julia, I would rather die than see you hurt." He smiled sadly at her. "I love you more than life. I always have. I always will —"

"Thomas, no!"

She felt the moment McKinley's grip loosed, saw the flash of steel as his arm swung at Thomas, and she twisted free and elbowed him in the chest.

He released an *oof* of pain, and stumbled back, clutching at her, but Thomas grasped her arm, jerking her to safety behind him.

"Leave her." Thomas turned slightly, drawing McKinley's attention as he staggered upright, his eyes fixed on Thomas, thus enabling Jon to steal past and hurry Catherine, Mother, and the children from

492

the room. "Leave them. They have nothing to do with this."

McKinley slashed again with the knife, forcing Thomas to lurch backward, nearly stepping on Julia as he did so.

"Julia, you need to get out," he muttered.

"But —"

"Please!" he said, eyes still locked with the intruder, who sliced the air again as they slowly circled the room in a treacherous dance. "Just go."

Perhaps there was a time to obey her husband, but it wasn't now. From the slight tremble in his legs and voice it was evident he was fast losing strength. She snatched up Thomas's wooden walking sticks, passing him one. "Here!"

He grabbed it, eyes trained on his prey.

"You come at me with a stick?" McKinley swore before hurtling forward, knife poised for attack, and dragging Julia to his side.

She screamed, then clamped her lips together, holding in the fear. She could not frighten Charles or the others anymore than they already were. The foul stench of stale sweat and desperation reeked from the man's body. He wrapped a thick arm around her neck, pinning her to himself. She could not move, she could barely breathe.

Jon edged back into view, his face holding

493

fear she had never seen him wear before.

"Stay away!" McKinley panted past her ear, and then drew the knife closer. "I will hurt her."

The knife was drawing nearer, nearer. She tried pushing his wrist away, but he was too strong, too strong!

Thomas inched closer, stick leveled, his gaze fixed on Julia.

The arm pinioned around her neck tightened. Air constricted. Black dots swam before her eyes. "Thomas!" she gasped.

In a move startling in both its abruptness and ferocity, Thomas raised the stick and smashed McKinley's shoulder. A cry like a wounded animal ripped from the man beside her, his clutch around her eased, and the knife clattered to the flagstones in front of the fireplace. Then they were falling, falling . . .

Until they crashed onto the cold hard floor.

The next minutes were filled with chaos and sensations both horrific and tender.

Pain ricocheting through her head from where she'd slammed into the floor.

The feeling like she might suffocate as she lay beneath McKinley's smothering weight.

Thomas's cry of "Julia!" before he dragged her free.

A glimpse of Jon's white face as he rushed to tackle McKinley while demanding to know if she was unharmed.

Her husband's "Oh, thank God!" as he wrapped his arms around her.

The sight of one of Hawkesbury's men running in, joining Jon to bind then drag a bloodied, cursing McKinley from the room.

Her mother's screech of "Julia!" before Catherine's soothing tones drew her away.

Thomas's thundering pulse as she nestled against his heart.

She held him close, he held her closer. "My dearest Jewel." Thomas's voice was shaky. "Are you hurt?"

"No, no." She shuddered.

"The baby?"

Dear God . . . "Oh, no!"

"Come." He gently led her from the room to the drawing room and a sofa, his solicitude, his tender touch curling warmth inside. "You need some tea."

"No. I just need you to hold me."

He thumbed away her tears, pressed his lips tenderly to her forehead, then held her for a long, long time.

CHAPTER THIRTY-TWO

Norfolk

The house they now stood before might appear unprepossessing to some, but for her it looked like the cottage of her dreams. Not too large nor small, the square fronted red brick house possessed three levels of windows, from the large-paned glass windows either side of the central door to those tucked up in what must be the servants' quarters beneath the eaves. A sweet-looking house, with rose vines growing across the doorway, and a stone-walled garden filled with old varieties of plants, and a lovely outlook to the sea. A house big enough for the child she held, and the one her daily nausea promised, nestled still safely within.

Julia adjusted Charles, weighty in her arms, and glanced at Thomas.

"Baby Charlie, do you think you can make your Papa smile?"

His gurgle of assent drew a small smile

from Thomas, whose stern countenance had barely changed since he had gruffly agreed to visiting the town of his boyhood, Caister-on-Sea. Such a place did not seem to equate with what he nor his sister had said, the memories she sensed he had no wish to revisit. But in recent weeks she had seen something new in her husband, a willingness to face problems, to accept consequences, demonstrated in the aftermath of McKinley's attack, now finally settled after the evidence of Lord Hawkesbury, Jon, and Thomas saw the former soldier imprisoned. Thomas's commitment had also been evident in his interviews with her mother and brother when the couple had explained their need to leave the London town house and settle elsewhere. Mother's gratitude for Thomas's actions meant that what would once have secured her hostility now resulted in her cautious approbation. Yet traces of her former manner remained in the questions about their future, the careless comments that left Julia in tears and him with flushed face. Yet through the stilted conversations she had come to see and appreciate anew Thomas's strength and resolve. He might still be weak in body, but his spirit seemed more mature than she recalled.

Perhaps that was fostered by his new faith.

Instead of getting angry he had been gentle, returning a soft answer, and then retreated, allowing Mother's irritability to finally dissipate. Such gentleness she now recognized as a quality of strength, which only served to make Julia love him all the more.

Even Jon seemed to have recognized the changed man in his former friend, a status which seemed to have altered once more, given the frank conversations they'd had prior to Jon and Catherine's return to Gloucestershire. Their conversations had left Thomas feeling happier, more settled, which only helped to ease her heart, too. Reconciliation seemed the order of things, as their journey from London had involved a brief stop to visit Thomas's sister, Jane, a happily married mother of three, who had given her brother one glance before clasping him to her ample bosom, amid tears of joy.

Their reunion had been all too short, their reminiscences bringing Thomas's boyhood to life, whilst fueling some level of concern for the future. Had Julia been wrong to push for a close to this estrangement? She could only offer prayers that things might be sorted at last.

Thomas glanced at her, ruffled Charlie's auburn curls, then knocked on the great wooden door. "I cannot promise a favorable outcome."

"At least you will finally know."

There came a scuffling sound from within, then the sound of locks being withdrawn, before a wizened face appeared. "Yes?"

Julia stared. The man looked most unlike what she had imagined, and held no trace of Thomas in his features.

Thomas coughed. "Who are you?"

"I take exception to a stranger knocking at my door and asking such a bold-faced question." The small man scowled at them. "Who are *you*?"

"*Your* door?" Thomas's voice held an edge. She heard him take an audible breath. Saw him adopt a conciliatory expression. "Forgive me. I am Thomas Hale. Charles Hale is my —"

"Father! Well! I'll be." The man lifted a hand to stroke his chin. "The black sheep of the family returns at last."

Julia placed a hand on Thomas's arm, felt the corded muscles relax.

"Well, you won't mind me saying that you don't look much like him, do you?"

"We were never accounted as being terribly similar, that is true. And you are?"

"I be Josiah Peachtree," he announced, thumbs in his braces, as if that name alone should provide clue enough.

"Mr. Peachtree," Julia interposed, "is Mr. Hale at home?"

"No."

"Oh." She sensed Thomas starting to withdraw, and she clasped his arm tighter. "Could you please tell us when he might be expected to return?"

"That I can't do."

She blinked. "I beg your pardon?"

"I can't be saying what will never happen."

"What do you mean?" A terrible thought struck, eliciting a gasp. "Is he — ?"

He chuckled. "No need to be looking like that, young lady. He's alive still, but after that last bout of apoplexy, hasn't been right in the head."

She noticed a muscle contract at the side of Thomas's mouth, and hastened to say, "Could you tell us where we might find him?"

He gave them direction to a local hospice, for which she thanked him, as Thomas remained silent. She moved to go when Thomas stayed her, turning to Mr. Peachtree. "And can you tell us why you are living here?"

"Oh, I don't live here. I just come in once

a week to check everything is as it should be."

"Then the house is vacant."

"Aye, that be so." His lips twitched into something approaching a smile. "Which is such a shame really, as it boasts such a nice view of the sea."

Within a short amount of time they had met his father, and Julia understood why Thomas had avoided coming home all these years. The Reverend Charles Hale might be somewhat senile, and his paralysis evoked pity, but his manner of address was everything she knew would rankle Thomas's soul. She completely understood now why her husband had avoided church attendance for so many years.

"You! I know you," Caister's former reverend said to his son. "The death of your mother, the plague on our existence all these years."

Thomas seemed to sag, before straightening. "I am sorry you still think so, Father."

"And I be sorry, too. To think —"

"I would like to ask for your forgiveness," Thomas continued quietly.

His father's eyes bulged. "My what?"

"Your forgiveness. I am sorry for my actions that led to estrangement between us."

501

"Oh! Right, well, I don't know . . . I . . ." He seemed to draw himself up. "I cannot forgive where God cannot. God hates sinners, you remember!"

"God hates sin," Thomas gently corrected. "It may interest you to know that I have sought God's forgiveness, and have made my peace with Him."

"Really?"

Thomas's head bowed in acquiescence.

The visit did not last much longer, a coughing fit wracking his father, and leading the doctor to insist that they leave. They left, but not without obtaining permission to visit again the next day.

That night, in the privacy of their bedchamber at Caister's small inn, Julia tried to be encouraging. "He does at least acknowledge you as his son. That is something at least."

Thomas nodded. "He remains as contrary as ever. I thought, I'd hoped, that saying something of my belief might help restore matters a little more than it seemed to."

"You cannot know what is in his heart. Perhaps God is even working in him now." She drew him close. "Only God knows the extent of a man — or woman's — regrets."

Her words fueled his anxiety. He didn't

want to doubt, but sometimes he couldn't help but wonder over whether she referred to her own regrets — with him.

"Is there something you regret, Julia?"

"You mean for the past two years to be undone?"

Pain filled his chest. She did not want to be with him?

She sighed, her head drooping into his neck. "Please don't misunderstand, I'm still glad we got married, but I wish we had done things differently, that we hadn't all this tension with my family, that we could have done things so they approved."

"I suspect Jon would never have approved. I think his love for his sister was greater than any affection he had for his friend. Which is how it ought to be. If someone precious was taken from me, then I would do everything in my power to restore her to me." He drew her nearer.

"Which is the right answer," she said, reaching up to kiss his jaw in the precise spot that elicited heat within.

"Ah, Jewel, please do not tease . . ."

"Who says I am teasing?" Her grin faded, a frown knit her brow. "Do you regret seeing your father?"

"No. You were right, it had to be done." It would just be good to have their future sorted. But love required patience, something he'd have to remember these upcoming days.

The next day they returned to the hospice, where Thomas was drawn aside by the doctor who shared more about his father's condition. It seemed he'd experienced some form of apoplectic fit, which, combined with underlying issues pertaining to dropsy, suggested he might not have long to live. "So, it be a good thing you finally returned home."

But the question of his home remained obscure. When he broached the idea of staying in the house, Father had grown quite agitated so that Thomas was inclined to drop further discussion. Except for Julia, he would have. She seemed to have taken Father's measure, eyeing him as he spoke on the house now.

"A fine old place. Needs a good caretaker, which is why I nabbed Peachtree."

"Oh!" she said, eyes wide. "You think him a good caretaker?"

Father scowled. "What do you mean by that?"

"Only that he is not there very often. Apparently, he visits only once a week."

"What? How do you know this?"

"He told us when we went to visit you there," Thomas said.

"Fools. I've been here for months now."

Thomas drew in a deep breath. Patience. He would have to remember patience.

"It is certainly a pretty-looking house, I suppose," Julia continued, "but, I don't know . . ."

"What? You don't think you'd want to live there?"

"It seems a *little* small. And perhaps it might be damp."

"Damp? What would you know? Who be you to make such bold claims?"

Had his father forgotten yesterday's visit when Thomas had introduced Julia?

She subtly waved off Thomas's concern. "I am Julia, Thomas's wife."

"Well! I did not know he was married."

"It was a sudden thing," she said, smiling at Thomas. He grinned, despite himself.

"And who be your family?"

"My family name is Carlew. My brother and mother live in London."

"You can rest assured that *that* smelly place ain't as nice as here. I ain't been to London above twice in my life, and I've no desire to go back." This moment of lucidity was followed by a gleaming, narrowed look. "Have you ever lived by the sea, miss?"

"No."

"So, you have no idea if a house would be damp, do you?"

"Well, I suppose not, but . . ."

"Then you should live there and see. I would not have that Peachtree fellow thinking he has one over me . . ."

Epilogue

London
April 1819

Candlelight glittered across the ballroom filled with the proud and the titled. Thomas nodded to his new colleagues and moved to the balcony, grasping the balustrade firmly. He felt his exhaustion keenly, but would not admit to any tiredness for all the world. Julia was here, finally in the echelon of society that she deserved, and he refused to give cause for her to feel the need to steal away. So he watched the dancers twirling below, glad his injured status gave excuse to not participate, although he entertained hopes of yet obtaining a waltz with his wife.

What a wondrous day today had been. What a wondrous few months he had lived. His heart was full, his life with Julia and young Charles like an impossible dream. He felt almost deliriously happy, his nightmares near forgotten.

507

Who would have thought he could find happiness in the house of his youth? But he had, his home fast filling with new memories. Julia's smiles. Young Charles's laughter. So many good things. He was an expectant father. He had reconciled — of sorts — with his own father, and reunited with his sister and her increasing family. He'd never known just how agreeable the notion of family could be. And most of all he was growing in relationship with his heavenly Father, and learning something of the extraordinary grace that covered his shame.

Nothing could be sweeter.

Last week's news from Hawkesbury had only compounded such joy. Magdalena had lied; there was no baby. Hawkesbury's investigator had learned she had fled to a neighboring village and recently married a shipwright's eldest son. She was not Thomas's responsibility anymore. Breath released, in a sigh that seemed to come from his toes.

"That is the look of gladness if ever I saw one."

Thomas acknowledged Jon's words with a handshake and a smile. "I am enjoying the evening."

"It is well deserved. Now I hesitate to speculate whether you stand here because you feel drawn to matters of work or away

508

from laboring in another field."

"Your hesitation to speculate on such matters does you credit."

Jon laughed. "I am pleased to see Mother seems a great deal warmer to you today."

Understatement indeed. "Julia made her sentiments very plain."

"I admit to feeling no small measure of gladness at the return of her spirit. For too long she seemed but a shadow of herself."

Thomas said carefully, "I think she is learning when such spirit is necessary, and when, perhaps, it is not."

"Your influence?" Jon said with a raised brow.

"God's influence. She — we — have been spending much time in learning more about God's character and His ways."

Jon's face relaxed into warmth. "I cannot ever thank you enough for helping my sister find salvation. And to see how under your spiritual stewardship Julia is growing in her faith."

Pleasure unfurled across his chest like a banner. How good to hear approbation from Jon. He knew he was loved by God, but sometimes it felt necessary to hear words of approval from men, too. Good men, whose words he valued, like Jon and Lord Hawkesbury. And . . .

"Harry? Have you spoken with him lately? How are he and Lady Bevington?"

"The last time I saw Harry he seemed to be in high altitudes — no, not drunk, just ridiculously happy. It seems his good wife will need to take a break from her paintings in several months, in order to attend to matters that have more direct impact on the future of the earldom."

"She is increasing?"

"Yes."

Thomas smiled. "Well, that is good news."

"You have no idea how good. Now, tell me, do you plan to stand here all night or will you come downstairs with me? I promise you I shall not allow my mother to eat you."

"Julia has already made me that same promise, you may be interested to hear. But I assure you, I am merely conserving my energies."

"I was sure it must be so. I did not think a man brave enough to face a charging elephant would lose courage at facing his wife's mother."

They shared grins, and once again Thomas thanked God for the change wrought in his friend. For truly he and Jon were friends again.

Jon nodded and departed, leaving Thomas

once more to his perusal of the dancers. As he observed, he listened to the chatter of those around him, many of whom had already congratulated him on the day's chief news, his new appointment, and some of whom had congratulated him several times already.

"There he is!"

He tensed, then forced himself to relax as his mother-in-law drew near. Perhaps one day he might be able to enjoy, not merely endure, her company. Julia, trailing in her mother's wake, smiled sympathetically at him.

"Oh, my dear Major — I mean, Lieutenant Colonel Hale! Oh, how proud we all are of you." Lady Harkness patted his arm. "A commendation from Lord Liverpool, *and* an invitation from the Prince Regent. I never . . ."

As her mother stumbled to a conversational pause, Julia met his glance, amusement in her eyes. "It is good to see Thomas rewarded for his endeavors."

"Indeed, it is," Lady Harkness said fervently, as if she'd never expressed a doubt about him. Since that horrid day in Cambridgeshire, she'd slowly come to regard Thomas in the light of a hero, which made him by turns pleased yet uncomfortable, as he certainly did not see himself in that way at all. But she'd grown so insistent that his actions had saved Julia — "so heroic, as if walking to your death!" — that neither of them had wanted to admit that, but for Julia's quick thinking, the outcome might have been very different.

"Ah! The man himself. Congratulations, Lieutenant Colonel, on your new posting and new address." Lord Hawkesbury shook Thomas's hand. "I am more pleased than you can ever know."

"I thank you again, sir, for all you have done."

Hawkesbury held up a hand. "All your own merits, Hale. And I cannot think such a role could be in better hands." The role being Fallbright's old position at the Foreign Office, but with new responsibilities. "Lord Bathurst seems most impressed."

Something the Secretary of State for War and Colonies had said earlier to Thomas, during the ceremony at Whitehall. He smiled. "I am pleased this means that my men will finally see recompense."

"It is important to have men you can trust."

"Indeed." Thomas cleared his throat. "I trust the young viscount is well?"

Hawkesbury grinned. "Very well. Lavinia

512

says he behaves just like his father, and my mother is inclined to agree, which is a thing so rare it is most wonderful to see." He leaned closer, and said in a conspiratorial tone, "It is a blessing, is it not, when a mother finally approves their child's marriage partner?"

"I believe it *will* be," he said.

"I believe it already is," Hawkesbury said, a smile glinting in his eye before he clapped Thomas on the shoulder and moved away.

"Now, are you free, oh heroic one?" Julia smiled. "I have committed the most appalling social solecism by refusing to dance with everyone who asked, simply because I insist on dancing with my husband. But he's proved such a popular man that I've barely had a chance to see him."

"My humblest apologies," he said. "Had I known my wife wished to dance I would have told the Duke of Sussex that I had far more pressing matters to attend than listening to him." He offered his arm, and they moved slowly down the stairs towards the musicians. "I trust this will be a waltz?"

"Your trust will not be misplaced," she said, smiling up at him in that way that caught his heart. Her gown of pale blue highlighted her eyes; her hair dressed high in a style that made her seem regal. The only sign she was a matron was the swelling of her stomach, and the confidence she wore brighter than a crown.

It was like their first meeting: she, looking so fair and lovely; he, wondering how someone of his origins had stumbled into such a place. But this time, honor preceded him, and with his heavenly Father's assurance ringing through his soul, he felt no shame, even though he knew himself to be the subject of some speculation from the wagging tongues behind fluttering fans.

The music struck up, and he swung Julia onto the dance floor, holding her as close as propriety allowed. She smiled up at him. "How are you feeling?"

"How I always feel when you're in my arms: like I've found home." He smiled as she sighed, her smile sweetening. "And how are you feeling, Mrs. Hale?"

"So much better than those first few months. I thank God for so many things every day, and not having that nausea is one."

"I'm glad."

And he was. God had worked things out so much better than he could have asked or imagined. Tonight had even provided opportunity for him to meet Mr. Amherst, Julia's one-time admirer, and that meeting had laid to rest any concerns Thomas might once have felt. Upon meeting them, and Thomas offering his appreciation for his valiance in protecting Julia on that day in Hyde Park, Mr. Amherst had flushed, and mumbled of his obligation for the major's — no, the lieutenant colonel's — forbearance in such a matter, before stumbling away to find his partner, one of the Aynsley girls, or so Julia said.

"He could barely look at you!" Julia had whispered.

"Am I so very frightening?"

"No, but in that coat and neckcloth you do appear rather awe-inspiring and grand."

His lips curled to one corner. "Are you flattering me?"

"I don't think I need to, do I?"

Thomas laughed. "Are you calling me proud?"

"Never. Although I do admit to feeling rather proud of my brave and clever husband, especially as he is the handsomest man in the room."

But he — holding her now, a *little* closer than society's matrons might approve — had no thought of his appearance, no thought of anything save how blessed he was to hold his wife amid the esteem of society and her family's approbation.

515

"You seem happy, Lieutenant Colonel."

"I am happy," he said, smiling deep into her eyes. "And you?"

"There is nowhere else I'd rather be when I'm with you."

Gossips be hanged — he kissed his Jewel, right in the middle of the dance floor.

She laughed. "How scandalous you are, sir!"

" 'Twould be scandalous not to, in my way of thinking."

"I like your way of thinking," she said, smiling mischievously at him. "I love you, Thomas."

"And I love you, Jewel of my heart."

And he held her, and led her, and twirled her, all the time hoping this dance would never end.

Their dance of love, that had taken so many turns in the wrong direction, had proved instead to have always been of their heavenly Father's creation.

AUTHOR'S NOTE

Eloping to Gretna Green carried a massive social stigma during Regency times, yet hundreds of couples did so. But what happened afterwards? Could a runaway marriage be redeemed?

I wanted to explore some of the possible consequences of such an action, so readers may find this book is perhaps a little more real, a little more raw, than some of my others. I hope, though, that you have still managed to enjoy the story, and gain a measure of hope that whatever situation you face, or people you may despair over, God's grace is at work to bring all people to Himself.

For part of my research into Regency elopements, I used Peter Hutchinson's fabulous resource *Chronicles of Gretna Green*. Interestingly, a number of those who eloped did manage to obtain positions of influence, such as government office — there is hope for everyone!

For my research into the British Indian Army, I used a number of online resources, including *The Political History of India, from 1784–1823* by Sir John Malcolm, which gave access to political events of the time as well as a suggestion of the style and address of contemporaries. I'd also like to acknowledge my friend Seema Khan for her first-hand knowledge of conditions in the Poona region, and her willingness to share this with me.

While the characters in this book are purely fictional, I have used a few known names from British parliament, including Lord Liverpool, Lord Goulburn, and Lord Bathurst, who did indeed hold the positions mentioned in this story.

I want to thank my publisher, Kregel Publications, for allowing this unusual love story to be incorporated into my Regency Brides series. We live in a disposable society, where it's all too easy to give up on people or on institutions such as marriage, and to be led by feelings rather than vows uttered before God. I hope and pray that my readers will be encouraged to find strength and hope in God and His grace, and in the promise of hope found in the Bible, epitomized in the life and sacrificial death and resurrection of Jesus Christ.

May all who are lost come home.

For behind-the-book details and the readers discussion guide, and to sign up for Carolyn's newsletter, please visit www .carolynmillerauthor.com.

If you have enjoyed reading this or any of the other books in the Regency Brides series, please consider leaving a review at Amazon, Goodreads, and/or your place of purchase.

ACKNOWLEDGMENTS

Thank You, God, for giving this gift of creativity, and the amazing opportunity to express it. Thank You for patiently loving us, and offering us grace and hope through Jesus Christ.

Thank you, Joshua, for your love and encouragement. I appreciate you, and all the support you give in so many ways. I love you!

Thank you, Caitlin, Jackson, Asher, and Tim — I love you, I'm so proud of you, and I'm grateful you understand why I spend so much time in imaginary worlds.

To my family, church family, and friends, whose support, encouragement, and prayers I value and have needed — thank you. Big thanks to Roslyn and Jacqueline for patiently reading through so many of my manuscripts, and for offering suggestions to make my stories sing.

Thank you, Tamela Hancock Murray, my

agent, for helping this little Australian negotiate the big, wide American market.

Thank you to the authors and bloggers who have endorsed, encouraged, and opened doors along the way: you are a blessing! Thanks to my Aussie writer friends — I appreciate you.

To the Ladies of Influence — your support and encouragement are gold! Thank you to everyone who helps share the love!

To the fabulous team at Kregel: thank you for believing in me, and for making *The Making of Mrs. Hale* shine.

Finally, thank you to my readers. I treasure your kind messages of support and lovely reviews. I hope you enjoyed Julia's story.

God bless you.

ABOUT THE AUTHOR

Award-winning author **Carolyn Miller** lives in the beautiful Southern Highlands of New South Wales, Australia. She is married, with four gorgeous children, who all love to read (and write!). A longtime lover of Regency romance, Carolyn's novels have won a number of Romance Writers of American (RWA) and American Christian Fiction Writers (ACFW) contests as well as the Australian Omega Christian Writers Award. She is a member of American Christian Fiction Writers and Australian Christian Writers. Her favourite authors are classics like Jane Austen (of course!), Georgette Heyer, and Agatha Christie, but she also enjoys contemporary authors like Susan May Warren and Becky Wade. Her stories are fun and witty, yet also deal with real issues, such as dealing with forgiveness, the nature of really loving versus 'true love', and other challenges we all face at different times. Her books include: *Regency Brides: A Legacy of Grace, The Elusive Miss Ellison, The Captivating Lady Charlotte,* and *The Dishonorable Miss DeLancey.*

The employees of Thorndike Press hope you have enjoyed this Large Print book. All our Thorndike, Wheeler, and Kennebec Large Print titles are designed for easy reading, and all our books are made to last. Other Thorndike Press Large Print books are available at your library, through selected bookstores, or directly from us.

For information about titles, please call:
  (800) 223-1244

or visit our website at:
  gale.com/thorndike

To share your comments, please write:
  Publisher
  Thorndike Press
  10 Water St., Suite 310
  Waterville, ME 04901